THE
PLACE

THE
PLACE

A Novel by

A. R. Saunders

XULON PRESS

Xulon Press
2301 Lucien Way #415
Maitland, FL 32751
407.339.4217
www.xulonpress.com

Unless otherwise indicated, Scripture quotations taken from the
English Standard Version (ESV). Copyright © 2001 by Crossway, a
publishing ministry of Good News Publishers. Used by permission.
All rights reserved.

Printed in the United States of America.

Paperback ISBN-13: 978-1-6312-9520-1
eBook ISBN-13: 978-1-6312-9521-8

CHAPTER ONE

W e have been living here for ten years. I have decided to document our journey in case we are eventually found incoherent, or dead. With no record of this unexpected twist of fate that has fallen upon us, it would be irresponsible of me if it were not documented for others to understand. I am forced to hand write this due to my laptop's keyboard beginning to fail, and analogue is fast becoming the best option.

Should my parents still be alive, along with my sister, I would want them to know exactly what had happened, particularly from a spiritual stand-point, given their earnest desire for me in that arena.

Our prime focus on a daily basis in this place is to stay alive. When that is your reality, with limited resources, and the weight of an uncertain future, you rethink your reason for doing things for the sake of your life and the lives of your family.

As I unpack the details of our difficult journey, a journey that has painfully revealed, who we really are, my description might be considered by some, as graphic. This is probably partly due to my medical background. The horrific events that led to our arrival offers little option but to tell it as it happened. I have taken this course for reader clarification, if not also therapy for myself. This autobiography will be an accurate description of the events as I saw them.

Some may think our standards questionable but, this is who we are, and this, is what we are doing here. We are staying alive, *whilst tracking a unique walk with God. I ask you not to judge the morality of our life, but try to put yourself in our position. One's own cultural origin is quickly questioned as relevant in this place. We are confident however, that we are clear before God. It is He who we stand before and it is He to whom we will give an account. Therefore, when it's all said and done, we are simply part of His family, living in The Place, that He calls home …for us.*

CHAPTER TWO

———— ∽ ————

T he air was thick with cigarette smoke, in the dim light of the
US Joint Chiefs of Staff board room. The decision had just
been made to drop the Atomic bomb on Hiroshima.

In the previous year of 1944, the grim-faced generals under
the command of the president of the United States of America,
had decided that the recently captured islands in the Marianas in
the central Pacific should have strategic airfields built on certain
small islands to support long range strategic bombing operations
against the Japanese as stand by airstrips.

It was given the code name, Bravo. To support this strategy, a
massive construction project was finished on the island of Tinian,
a previous Japanese airfield, in mid-August 1944. A part of this
project was to upgrade and lengthen the runway. It was renamed
West Field. The base became operationally ready in the early
spring of 1945. The 58th Bombardment Wing was assigned there
and initiated strategic bombardment operations directly against
the islands of Japan.

Bravo was put in place to support the endeavour of the
eventual nuclear offensive. This would be activated should the
Japanese refuse to surrender. It was considered essential, should
the primary bases of the B29 bomber squadrons be destroyed by
the enemy with a strongly suspected new weapon in the making
by the Japanese. Smaller nuclear weapons would be made operational using smaller bomber aircraft such as the B-17. These aircraft were to be specially fitted with longer range fuel tanks. They

were to be a lighter aircraft with up to date weaponry, pressurised fuselage and modified bomb bay to cater for the different payload.

Small uninhabited islands in the Marianas area would be sought out to facilitate the requirements and small airbases would be built for the new B17 bombers. These bases would be manned by small crews. Prior to leaving the mainland of the USA, the aircraft would be dismantled into primary pieces and shipped to their assigned bases.

The aircraft engineers would assemble the aircraft once they were freighted to the assigned island base. It was a simple matter of attaching wings to fuselage and engines to mounts and the process would take a week at best, per aircraft.

Each Island was assigned a code name and to it assigned aircraft which also carried a code name. In the top-secret circles of the military, one of those islands was known as *The Place*. One of its' assigned B17 aircraft was named *On Eagles Wings*. The island was an oblong shaped land mass that jutted out of the Pacific, south west of the Palau group of islands. It was approximately five miles long and two miles wide at its thickest point and stretching across an East West direction. This beautiful uncharted island possessed a three hundred- foot volcanic plug, that crowned its position central to the island.

Halfway up the igneous monolith of this landmass facing due west, a cave was discovered that overlooked a small bay, skirted with a white beach of fine sand. This area was protected by a reef close by and stretched further out to encircle the island. A well protected bay and a smaller lagoon area were also carefully carved at its point of creation, offering beautiful coral formations in both sanctuaries. The cave in the igneous outcrop was a major asset as it was considered by the engineers to be a possible place for the storage of excess ammunition which would arrive with crew. The cavern was well hidden by a reasonable growth of bushes and palm trees across the entire western face of the volcanic plug.

The project was undertaken by the *Seabees*, the US Naval Construction troops. These men were especially recruited construction workers from the United States of America. The *Seabees* moved from island to island.

Their goal was to advance step by step in a northerly direction to Tokyo.

The project commenced on time, however due to extreme weather conditions, its deadline for completion began to lag behind and soon it was realised that the island code named *The Place* would not be operational within the allotted timeframe.

In addition, further delays were experienced due to the time required to blast a way through the reef to create a suitable channel to transport earth moving equipment. Once cleared, the bulldozers were given first passage and went straight to work making a rough road to the designated site for the airbase. To navigate their way to this area, they cleared a path along the flat area that shouldered the beaches edge. The scar was deep and intrusive, as the metallic bullies tore their way through this beautiful virgin garden of Eden island. In conjunction with the moving of great amounts of tropical volcanic soil, engineers were quick to begin construction of a hanger large enough to cater to the aircraft's maintenance needs. In addition to this, other buildings were constructed such as small quarters for the crew and a large fuel hut was erected at the furthest point away from the hanger. In this area were housed many forty four-gallon drums of aviation gasoline and a fully loaded fuel truck also carrying the same fuel. The runway was constructed with the material dredged up from the channel project.

There was a delay in the scheduled delivery time for the allotted aircraft and only one was available. This was shipped and finally, the first Boeing B17 was transported to the islands' new facility. This was assembled within a week. All engines and systems were checked and found serviceable and signed off accordingly to then await the crew to check its airworthiness.

Once the project was completed and signed off, the fully fuelled *On Eagles Wings* was locked in its' new home waiting for the remaining aircraft. All the engineers were transferred back to their waiting vessel anchored off-shore, leaving this new base to wait for a crew that would never arrive.

By the time *The Place* was ready for occupation, the bombing offensive on Japan, carried out by the B-29 bombers was well under way. The Boeing B-29 Super fortress was considered by many, as the weapon that won the war in the Pacific.

This aircraft was designed to carry large bomb loads over very long distances. These characteristics made it possible to perform this strategic offensive that many believe brought Japan to its knees.

The B-29s launched their famous low-level incendiary missions over Japanese cities. In the first raid over Tokyo, it was recorded that two hundred and ninety-nine B-29s carried out one of the most destructive bombing raids when they levelled many square miles of the city with firebombs. Japan still refused to surrender.

Then the flight that has gone down in history: That flight departed from Tinian on August 6th, 1945 when *Enola Gay,* under the command of Colonel Paul W. Tibbets, dropped the Atomic bomb on Hiroshima. Three days later, another B-29, the *Bockscar,* dropped its nuclear payload on Nagasaki and with that the Pacific war came to an end. Japan conceded to defeat and surrendered.

All temporary air bases were written off which included the island, code-named *The Place*.

Not a soul stepped foot on the island after it was readied for battle, positioned in that isolated part of the pacific from all major shipping routes, the aircraft sat in its' lonely surroundings, waiting for her assigned crew.

CHAPTER THREE

———— ❧ ————

My father was, or still is a Baptist pastor. My mother was an early childhood educator and had retired a year before I took a break from medicine. I had been working in a large hospital in Brisbane, the capital of Queensland, Australia, for over six years. The work offered good money, but the hours were often long and at times the conditions were less than favourable.

The only time I had to myself was when I would hire a Cessna 172 and get above the stresses of life. I achieved my private pilots' licence just before I had completed high school and later went on to achieve my commercial licence. The long semester breaks from university over the Christmas holidays proved an ideal time to study the commercial theory and do some training. Within eighteen months I had my commercial licence in hand. I had no intention of using it professionally. I just wanted to be a better pilot. In addition to this, later I went on further and achieved my light aircraft mechanical engineer's licence. All this offered something else to think about other than medicine.

In that six, almost seven -year period I had achieved specialization in emergency medicine. However, it all began to catch up with me and I finally decided to take a break from medicine due to what I considered to be a potentially dangerous situation. Because of my schedule, particularly over those last three years it was difficult to keep my aviation licences current.

During that time working long hours, experiencing sleep deprivation and little time off, a potential misdiagnosis was waiting *to happen. This almost took place early one morning, when a patient lied to me about certain drugs they were taking. There were checks I should have undertaken but didn't, due to a perfectly timed distraction in the form of an emergency that I was presented with during that cold wet morning. That patient who was in fact on illegal drugs would have died without a doubt had the nurse administered the treatment that I had prescribed.*

The shock was too much to bear. I remember I took a coffee break and shortly after I began to shake considerably at the reality of the moment. I realised that I was on the verge of something serious, maybe even a break down. I needed to reconsider my whole life. So, I stepped aside from this vocation, if only for a short period of time to recoup and regroup.

I had saved a lot of money in those six years, as I was living at home, paying a meagre board and lodging and always working. I had no time for a girlfriend, therefore marriage was a pointless thought and with the exception of some associates at the aero club in Brisbane, no real friends to speak of, so therefore no need to spend a lot of money.

I had made some wise investments that literally trippled my money over a period of six years. I cashed it all in and I deposited it in the bank where I received some reasonable returns as a result of a fixed investment. I wonder what has become of all the money today.

My 'leaving medicine' was met with an unsavoury reaction from my mother who was looking forward to having a doctor in the family for a long time. To say that I was the source of great pride for her was an understatement. My father on the other hand reacted far more modestly. He was a wise man, very balanced and possessed a broad world view. He took me aside, and said if I needed to leave my medical work to deal with things, he was happy with that but he asked me not to abandon my faith. I didn't have the heart to tell him that, along with my medical career, my faith was also on the rocks.

After finalizing my employment, I found myself at home with my parents, feeling lost, depressed and defeated. Whilst I possessed a profound love for them, I realized that I had never discovered who I was whilst living with these great people. Some would say that that is rather selfish, and they may be right, but it seemed to me at the time that I had spent most of my life studying. When others were out celebrating life, and having a good time I was in sacrificing my life and getting good grades.

I was thirty- one years of age at the time of my career departure, and what had I done with my life, besides make a lot of money, help save lives and nearly kill one person. On one particular Saturday afternoon, my father asked me to come to church. Given that I hadn't attended for some time, due to my schedule, I agreed to come. I could sense his pleasure at my response even though he didn't show it. I could also sense his concern for my spiritual status or lack thereof.

I had questioned a number of issues regarding the western church. I really had no problems with God, his will for man, nor His great commission however I hardly had a healthy relationship with Him at the time. My concerns were more with denominational leadership. I was a full-on bible believing Christian as a teenager but found a very different philosophy awaiting me at university. In my senior year at high school I made a decision that I was going to be a missionary doctor working somewhere in tropical Asia. This came about as a result of a mission trip to the Philippines. However, by the time I finished my tertiary education which included a devastating romantic relationship, I began to question much of my Christian faith or possibly I was questioning myself in the faith. However, I still couldn't deny the existence of God and the relevance of the Christian doctrine, but I detested how the western church, generally speaking, was displaying it, or not displaying it, which was more the point. To this day I still don't know why I accepted his invitation. Given my grievances within the faith, I walked into this new church that morning with a little fear and trepidation.

It didn't take long before I realized that there was a special speaker preaching. This guest and his wife were missionaries in some pacific island group in Micronesia. He was a doctor. Feeling set up, I decided I would sit through the entire presentation with an open mind. I couldn't tell you what mission he represented but I will never forget his sermon.

The doctor and his wife spoke together first, sharing the work that they were doing with folk on a group of Islands using a medical ship. They were based on some main island that was well civilised, but would spend a lot of time on this ship travelling around these small islands. It seemed that the locals in these communities didn't wear much clothing, and had no exposure to dental and medical facilities other than what was given them from this mission. The local women were topless and the chiefs of the islands expected all westerners who visited their island home to dress in the same manner as the locals.

This proved an interesting concept for the western women. The doctors' wife shared that they weren't there to change the culture but to bless the people. The mission wanted to honour the people and their culture and that's why they chose to obey the chief's wishes and dress accordingly.

She explained that initially the locals would make rings of flowers, which she would wear around her neck and would sit across her chest, which was quite acceptable in that culture. She went on to share how difficult it was for her at first but after a while she said she had gotten used to it and now thinks nothing of it. Then she finally admitted that if it were just she, her husband, their two daughters and young son, she wouldn't bother with the flowers.

The reaction around the church was interesting too say the least. I had never heard such an attitude before from missionaries. Frankly, I was rather impressed. After university, I couldn't give you a good word regarding missionary endeavours, there outcomes, and particularly as far as culture was concerned.

I was also interested to hear that this couple would bring their three small children with them and chose to home school them. They explained that when on the islands, their children would be like the local children. She shared how well their kids integrated into the village life. She explained with a great deal of humour, how difficult it was to keep clothes on the children and offered some examples. The missionary told her tail very well and with beautiful authenticity With that, the congregation burst out with a raw of laughter.

Shortly after this presentation the doctor returned to the pulpit and began to preach. Given this couples' credibility, I listened. His dissertation was simple. However, every point of his message was dipped with effect. Every word was cutting through to the congregation.

There wasn't a sound in the auditorium.

I had always enjoyed a good speaker, particularly when the presentation was structured well, and it really didn't matter if it were secular or theological. He based his presentation on the final days of John the Baptist. This great prophet found himself incarcerated in Herod's prison. For those who know God, the missionary claimed, we have every right to ask God for anything and He will answer. The answer could be 'yes', 'no' or 'wait'. The interesting thing was that John was the cousin of Jesus and Johns' cousin didn't help him. John did nothing wrong. In fact, the reason why John was in jail was because he told the truth. The missionary went on to explain that John couldn't see past the four walls that imprisoned him and because of his limited vision he began to doubt Jesus. He couldn't see what God was doing outside.

He continued by saying that the Most-High God had a much bigger picture and His plans for us were good but sometimes it didn't seem as though it was good. I saw the connection. Toward the end of the speakers message he looked around at the congregation and said ... 'you may be going through something really tough, a break down, maybe, where you couldn't go on any further, well don't beat yourself up'. It's not your fault. Just let God take you through the journey that you are on. He has allowed this to happen for a very good reason.

He looked around and stopped, then, looking straight at me he said, 'you've done the right thing now trust God through this journey of yours. His provision for you will be great!

Just trust Him right now…. do it!!' He paused, whilst maintaining his gaze at me. I felt a little uncomfortable. Then he said his God-given direction for me, 'Maybe you should get your passport current and leave the country. Go and see what God is doing beyond your four walls. Those walls are keeping you imprisoned. Break free! It is written … 'If Christ sets you free you shall be free indeed'.

I was welded to my seat. The Creator spoke directly to me in person. I was in shock. I have absolutely no idea what this man said after that. After the service, I heard people commenting on the things he said after the 'passport' thing, but for me I remember nothing beyond … 'get your passport current and leave the country … Break free!'

Monday morning offered an early awakening but, the first thing that welcomed me was 'get your passport current and leave the country … Break Free!'. The more I thought about it the more I warmed to the idea. Why not? Why not leave the country? 'Take a vacation.' I thought of where I could go and the more I pondered on the possibilities the more I became confused. How long … a month, six months, a year, two years? 'What would I do, missionary work'? On that matter, I remember laughing to myself at such an absurd thought. There's no way I'll be running around half naked. Though, the thought of working with that missionary couple, was appealing.

I made myself some brewed coffee and opened the daily newspaper. The smell of fresh print accosted my nostrils with new vigour.

It was a new day, but everything seemed especially brand new. I felt brand new. I began my visual grazing across the pages to the sound of crisp rustling as I separated page one from page two.

Most of the news was bad ... Political problems, national economic statistics, global economic news, murders, terrorist attacks, floods, an Australian soldier killed overseas. Then on page four, I saw a quarter page advertisement in full colour advertising a five-star tropical cruse. It headlined, BREAK FREE!

I was once again welded to my seat. I went on to read, 'Break free from the stresses of your life. Relax in Five Star comfort and let us take you around the beautiful islands of Palau, on the 'Pacific Fair.' Ten thousand dollars for three weeks which included a five-star air-conditioned room with bathroom, all meals, drinks, economy air fares included, five-star hotel accommodation in Palau and a maximum of twenty guests allowed on the ship.

This was a super yacht and it looked just magnificent. A great idea, I thought.

'Get your passport current and leave the country ... Break free?'

'You bet I am out of here.' I whispered into the cool of the early morning.

By midmorning I had rung the number advertised in the paper. There was one position left on the ship. The trip was due to leave the former capital Koror within a week. I made my way to the travel agent by lunchtime and paid for the trip in full. I had never done such an impulsive thing before and it felt good.

The flight to Koror, the former capital city of Palau was to fly from Brisbane to Manila then to Guam and then on to Koror where we would stay in the Palau Pacific resort for two nights before embarking the Pacific Fair.

The week leading up to my departure flew past quickly. I had attended to essential things such as vaccinations, stocking up on various medications, updating passport, buying some clothing more appropriate to tropical climates and packing.

On the day of my departure, I intended to take a taxi to the airport but my father insisted on taking me. My mother then decided that she was coming, and my sister Lynn arrived home just as we were leaving. She decided she would accompany us as well.

I reinforced my gratitude to all in the car that it was great that the family see me off but it wasn't as if I was going away for good. They all told me to pipe down, after which a merry time was had by all during the thirty-minute trek to the Brisbane international airport.

On the way to the airport I remember Lynn asking me what I intended to do after I return from my vacation. I suggested that I had no plans at that stage. I quickly backtracked and reminded my family that I needed some 'me' time to get a handle on life again, to which my father offered full support to my future plans. I waited for a religious wrap up from him, but he offered nothing. I could sense a note of concern in his tones, which bothered me. A slither of fear pieced my heart. I'll never forget that day.

CHAPTER FOUR

⟨~⟩

Doctor Langley put down his pen, closed his eyes and rubbed his hands over his face. He looked up and drank in his surroundings as he sat in the outer section of the summer dwelling. The entrance offered plenty of natural light by which to write and was a welcome cool relief from the humid conditions. Through the trees growing twenty feet or so in front of their abode, a beautiful view of the turquoise blue lagoon was on offer every day and a cool breeze was enjoyed most afternoons. Further inside, it was a different story.

No longer beautifully filtered light, but rather, blackness was one's constant companion. Fortunately, they had heavy-duty portable sola lanterns, which were carried in every night. There was a system of solar panels anchored some thirty feet to the left of the caves entrance. They were fixed firmly against the rock facing north. These five panels, controller, twelve-volt inverter and battery system were taken from the stranded vessel. It was crudely assembled by the doctor, but had continued to be faithfully functional over the years. This equipment played an important role in their daily life. They were quite comfortable, given the limited resources at hand and the young family had plenty of room to move in this island cavern.

Their rocky retreat was found halfway up the only hill on their island. This outcrop was of volcanic origin. The walls of the cave were solid rock and the inner section of the cave had a glassy substance covering all the walls. This was of considerable advantage at night as the light from the sola lanterns splashed their brilliance in all directions around the rooms. Paul and his wife had explored the cavern when they first arrived on this uncharted atoll and deemed this as very suitable for protection against the tropical elements. The main area of their cavern travelled some fifty feet into the three hundred-foot high igneous plug. Their summer home then split into three additional chambers. Each chamber was of equal size, and large enough to be used as bedrooms. One of the rooms was set aside for storage.

They were a valuable asset during the typhoon season. Paul had skilfully devised a way of closing off the entrance of the cave using the cabin doors from the yacht. They were particularly an asset when the typhoons were in the area.

Comfortable furniture taken from the stranded super yacht was placed fashionably throughout their home. Over the last five years, they had been using their subterranean mansion more often than not. This was mainly due to the unsettled weather patterns and also the ship was beginning to be breeding ground for mould, particularly during the wet season. Another reason was one of safety. The couple were always on the lookout and their home was very difficult to be seen from the bay, due to the trees growing in front of the small entrance.

Paul's thoughts were quickly interrupted by excited squeals of an eight-year old girl.

The sound of her bare feet on the moist tropical earth could be heard from the entrance of their rocky dwelling.

'Daddy, Daddy,' heralded the small voice.

The child's father quickly arose from the source of his focus, walked out to the entrance of the cave and looked down. The brown form of his daughter could be clearly seen running up the winding path to the castaways' home. She was very nimble and could run like the wind.

'What's up?'

'Mommy has found really big oysters and she wants you to bring the yellow bucket.'

'Is that so ... where?'

'Just down from the yacht at those rocks,' she replied.

'OK, I'll be right down.'

Paul walked into the storage room, fumbled around in its blackness and took hold of one of their prize possessions. *It's hard to believe how one's values had changed living in this land.* He thought. A bucket was of more value there on their island than a bucket full of gold.

The availability of seafood on the island was more than he could wish for, but he would pay a thousand dollars to be able to feed his family just one meal of prime filet steak with French fries and a full side salad. The fruit and vegetables that they were able to cultivate were a blessing, but how he missed some of the food back home. He thought of all the facilities back in Brisbane. To be able to go down to the supermarket and buy anything he wished from a wide variety of products was now a wonder.

He pondered on that for a moment, as he made his way down to where his daughter had decided to wait. The idea of all that choice, he thought, now seemed obscene.

He made his way down the damp tropical path to the patient young messenger. In many ways, he was happier living in the middle of the Pacific with his little family. His children were safe from all that materialism, and from other dangers such as, drugs, pornography, the sexually transmitted diseases, now at epidemic proportions and the monstrous peer group pressure that had destroyed many young lives. As a doctor, he had seen graphic examples of the lives of teenagers being ruined and, in some cases their very lives snuffed out as a result of poor choices. These young people had begun mixing with the wrong crowd and the result ... was disaster. He had seen many parents enslaved to their careers, as they worshipped the effects of the dollar and the result was to the detriment of their children. Here, his family was safe.

'We have really lost the art of communication with our families,' he said softly to himself, as he continued his journey to his daughter.

'Husbands and wives have lost the art of loving each other because they are too busy, too stressed, too interested in the opinions of others and their children aren't being nurtured with the love that they need,' the Doctor said, suddenly realising he was talking out loud.

He had caught himself doing this frequently of late and proceeded to keep his pondering in his head. The years of isolation and segregation from any male fellowship was beginning to have an effect.

The Doctor was surrounded by females. Even the family pet was female. To be able to sit down and discuss cases with his medical piers would now be more than wonderful. He missed medicine desperately.

The doctor had felt for many years that the men had lost their way as husbands, fathers, and leaders in the family. When asked, once by a male patient, what was the best thing he could do for his children, Paul answered, *Love their mother*. The answer was easily found by the example he was given from his own father.

Yet, given all the unsavoury things at home in Australia, he realised how he took for granted all the blessings given to him then.

The blessings, however, became a type of distraction from the real reason for living. Now, it seemed that the creator had stripped him of all these distractions ... but that was then, this is now. Paul began to reflect on all the things he thought nothing of in the past, such as the food, the conveniences, electricity, bottled water, coffee, vegemite. Oh, how he missed Vegemite.

Just to be able to boil water at the flick of a switch would now be held in awe. After living ten years on this island he knew that back in Australia, *the Lucky Country* as it was known, people had no need of God, but here, in their isolated home, Paul and his family relied on God every day. Things had certainly changed.

Within minutes he found his daughter waiting patiently for him and together they walked hand in hand to where a great feast was to be found. Navigating through the cool rain forest, Paul listened to his eldest daughters' excited description of the oysters when they were met by his very wet, and rather bare five-year old daughter, Tiffany. Behind the excited minor, struggled an aging pet hen, flapping her wings in a desperate measure to duplicate velocity required to journey up the hill with the young child. Tiffany turned around seeking an update regarding the hen's position.

'Come on Chickadee, you are getting slow,' she said, scooping up the bird in her arms.

'Tiff,' Paul called, slightly annoyed.

'Hi Daddy.'

'What did I tell you about being in the sun in the middle of the day like that.'

'Daddy, we found oysters, really big ones,' she said, throwing herself into her fathers' arms with her chicken displaying a rather nervous look across its face at the possible collision pending. Using her favourite pet as a convenient distraction, Tiffany acted as though she hadn't heard her father's challenge.

'Yes, I know, Jess told me, but what about my question young lady?' he said, looking her straight in the eye. 'Will you put that chook down?'

'But Dad she's tired,' Tiffany said, rather relieved to consider a change of subject.

'That's because she's old,' the eldest daughter added.

'Yes, she is Dad. Mom said that we have to look after old people,' an insistent Tiffany demanded.

'Well there's no old people here,' their father said softly.

'Chickadee is old people, aren't you Chickadee?' His youngest rubbed her face up against her well- fed pet.

In an instant Tiffany lifted her head to face her father.

'Dad when will you get old?'

Before he could utter a syllable, Jessica offered the answer.

'Mom said that Dad will start getting old soon because he's a lot older than Mom.'

'Yeah, a lot, lot lot older. Mommy is pretty and you're not pretty and Mommy said that old people aren't pretty and so I think that you will get old, um maybe next year.... But that's OK cause Jess and I will love you anyway just like we love Chickadee, hey Chickadee?'

'What?' Paul suddenly sensed that his chosen topic was quickly being snatched away by his doting daughter's. 'No, I heard what Mom said, and she certainly didn't say that. What she said young lady was that men aren't pretty, whether they're young or old.'

'That's true Tiff,' Jessica confirmed.

'Thank you Jess. Well, anyway, let's forget about getting old and the chook. Let's get back to my original question. You know what happened last year when you got sun burn. Do you remember how sick you were?'

Tiffany nodded silently.

'I don't want you guys swimming in the middle of the day. It's too hot and I definitely don't want you guys swimming this time of the day ... with nothing on,' he said a little sternly.

'Well, what about Jess,' she replied.

'Yes, that goes for her too, but Jess isn't guilty of that today young lady,' her father replied.

Tiffany's bottom lip began to drop and, a little frown appeared from nowhere.

'Yes, she is,' she said, defensively with a slight quiver in her little voice.

'Tiff!' spat Jessica, as she directed a betrayed expression at her little sister.

'Well you were too,' Tiffany said, with the confidence of prosecution.

Tiffany threw her arms around her fathers' neck, burying her face against the man she loved. The family pet suddenly scurried out of the clutches of her minder and flapped to the safety of terra firma.

'Oh, for goodness sake girls,' he interjected quickly.

'This tropical sun can do some serious long-term damage to your skin,' he continued.

'Remember what I said? We can swim in the morning and late in the afternoon but certainly not in the middle of the day.'

Dad?' Jessica interrupted the oncoming lecture of skin cancer.

'Yes.'

'So is Mom.'

Paul looked at his eight-year old daughter feeling as though he was about to lose an important argument.

'So, is Mom what?'

'So is Mom swimming ...' she paused.

Paul just looked at his daughter.

'And?' he said.

'You know,' she continued ... 'like us.'

She finished the statement and waited for her father's reply.

Paul shook his head.

'The females in this family will be the death of me,' he said in defeat.

Tiffany, giggling, quickly raised her head. 'No, we won't, we love you,' she said, with a burst of delight as she quickly kissed her father on the cheek.

Jessica responded with a hug at Paul's side, to which he responded by scooping her up.

Now with these two in his arms, a bucket dangling from his hand and the family pet scurrying at his feet, he looked straight ahead.

'Oh, you lot are a bunch of rat bags.'

The result was more than favourable. Two sets of arms wrapped themselves around their father's neck in mutual response.

At this point he realised that he was carrying the most precious cargo a man could have … his children.

Paul started to think about his parents. *How they would love these two little urchins*, he sadly thought.

With that, he felt a sudden powerful desire to go home.

Minutes went buy and nothing was said and all parties were enjoying the purity of the moment. A small gust of wind eddied around them and the smell of the fresh salt air hit the senses. Tiffany looked over her shoulder. Seeing the rusting yacht beached high up on to the shore, she jumped out of her fathers' arms and raced to the spot where she had left her mother.

'Mommy, Mommy, get your clothes on Daddy's coming,' Tiffany yelled with great conviction.

A voice could be heard over the edge of the rock face from the water.

'Oh, I think Dad has seen it all before.'

'Well I'm just telling you Mom,' Tiffany said with conviction.

With that this little water baby jumped into the water to join her mother.

Paul smiled and walked a little faster, curious as to the size of their night's meal. By the time the man and his oldest daughter had reached the edge of the seven-foot rock face, the youngest of the family was already under the water with her goggles on, helping her mother pry the oysters from the rock beneath the surface.

Releasing Jess to the ground, he looked at her and said, 'So much for my lecture on skincare.'

'But Dad, it's not that hot today.'

Mm,' he huffed his stern reply.

As he looked over the edge into the crystal-clear water, he saw his five-year old daughter and thirty two-year old wife swimming in the liquid purity collecting oysters. Of late, he hadn't taken much notice when his wife swam in her natural state. Paul was struck by her rustic beauty. Her olive skin had caused her to become quite dark as a result of the suns effect over the ten years of living in this tropical paradise. The girls weren't as blessed, but still had better skin than their father and were quite tanned … all over.

At this point, Jessica tugged on her father's faded blue, long sleeved business shirt, that had certainly seen better days. He looked down at the small pathetic beckoning face.

'Daddy?' she said.

'Oh, go on, in you go,' her father replied, totally resigned.

She had dropped all covering in a flash and yelled back to him.

'Are you coming?' her slender form disappeared over the basalt ledge into the crystal tropical water.

'No, someone has got to show some sense around here.'

Before he knew it, she was busy helping her mother and sister collect their gift from God.

The bucket was finally called for and a generous load was carried back up to the cavern in the rock, in readiness for the evening meal. It was decided to walk the long way back to their dwelling, which took them along their white sandy beach, past the yacht and around near to their deep freshwater hole. Paul followed behind the most important people in his life, whilst carrying the bucket filled with the evening's meal and all the clothing belonging to the females in his life.

Claire and the girls began to run along the beach, closely followed by Chickadee, just as a sun shower dropped large heavy drops of rain, washing the saltwater from the bodies of on the only example of God's image on the island.

They soon steadied to a casual walk hand in hand, one daughter on each side of their mother. Claire began to sing and the girls joined her, adding some dance steps that the children had devised between themselves.

Paul watched his wife with the children some fifty yards ahead of him. The sight was a delight and the Doctor praised his God again at the blessing set before him.

On arrival at their home, the three quickly rinsed off any remaining salt and then dressed. The family's hen was fed and put in her cage for the night placed just inside the opening of the cave's entrance. Paul had acquired three empty, plastic forty-four gallon drums from the yacht and placed them outside the cavern to catch the rain.

With the amount of rain that fell in the area, the drums were always close to full.

It was two o'clock in the afternoon and after a lunch of fresh fruit, all settled down to a nap. The three females fell asleep quickly, but Paul decided to return to his task of recording the journey that had brought the couple to their appointed place of dwelling.

The Doctor looked down at the spiral note pad in front of him. He had begun something his wife had wanted him to do for some years. She had undertaken this task some time ago and had nearly completed it, but refused to let him read it until he had completed his. She proposed that they would swap journals. It was a difficult task for Paul. A lot had happened since their arrival. There were a lot of challenges for them both, but they were happy. He had struggled with this task for some time, but finally he had clarity to write.

However, he stilled battled with the reality of their experience at times. Would his writing be a stumbling –block to many? How could he explain the way they live? His high standards were constantly at battle with their reality in this place. He surrendered himself to what he felt he should write and trusted that people, should they ever read his lengthy article, would see Gods' context and blessing in their life. From the castaway's perspective, they both felt that they were blessed in a very special way. They had enough food. It came from the ocean, their garden, both hydroponic and naturally grown.

They also had an orchard, planted nearly ten years ago. Water was plentiful in this foreign land, as it rained regularly. Even in the dry season, it would rain heavily at least once a week.

They wanted for nothing. Sitting in his rocky retreat, he began to write again of their story of deliverance, of provision, of freedom, and … of salvation.

CHAPTER FIVE

———— ❧ ————

I t all began as we approached the airport. I suggested that my father, drop me off outside the departures area of the Brisbane international airport, but he insisted that he parked the car. My mother said that a coffee would be a good idea and therefore, it was settled.

I was rather surprised that I was able to check in immediately given that there was a delay of my flight due to weather. With this inconvenience in mind it meant that we had three hours to wait. This didn't affect my connecting flight in Manila as I was to have a six hour wait before my flight to Guam.

I was looking forward to spending time on my own, at the airport, but the alternative was in fact pleasant and we had an uplifting family time filled with laughter, reminiscing and general wholesome conversation. I recall at the time, that I couldn't help but feel very close to this wonderful group of people.

My father is a good man, full of wisdom, but so down to earth. He is a man's' man and he has a beautiful gift with people. He loves them, and all who met my father would often be taken by this man's genuine interest if not concern for them. However, the greatest love he possesses is a deep love for his God and his family and we were blessed because of it.

My father will be turning seventy years of age this year. Should he still be alive he would be retired I'm sure. My mother was always full of life. Should she still be alive she would be sixty-four *years old. I wonder what she would look like now. Her disposition was infectious and a delight to be around.*

Her gifting, besides that of encouragement, is with children. They seem to flock around her when she is in their presence. She is a faithful wife and a wonderful mother. My mother and father are a great team and have a beautiful love for each other. Whilst it was obvious that their love has not died for each other but grown deeper over the years, they are also each other's best friend. I had watched then over the years and had come to the conclusion that this relationship was very special, if not rare.

The latter had been a matter of much consternation for me personally, as I felt it impossible to find a partner with such character traits and this is one reason why I felt it better to dedicate my life to helping others in the area of medicine. I remember asking God to give me someone like her but shortly after, I began to question many things about the creator and my expectation began to wither away.

My sister Lynn is a lot like my mother but has that genuine concern for people like my father. Last time I saw her, she was single and had decided to dedicate herself to her studies.

She was working towards her PHD in education, specializing in early childhood. Unlike my mother, my sister had a wild side to her and would love to display it around Dad or myself, but I think she found Dad more fun. Our parents would remind us that Lynn was more like our great grandmother on our fathers' side. Apparently, our great grandmother would get up to some real mischief that would often unsettle our great grandfather who was such a gentleman. However, when our great grandfather wasn't around the fun would really begin.

Dad was often the target for Lynn and he would graciously entertain her nonsense. To say she was a fun-loving tease, was an under-statement.

After two hours around the coffee table at the airport with these wonderful folk, I decided that I should make my way to immigration. With that, goodbyes were made. I offered Dad money towards the parking but he refused, saying that I would probably need it if the flight was delayed any further. At that point, my sister wrapped her arms around me and whispered in my ear 'Be safe handsome, I am praying God gives you the best all the way over and a special trip all the way back. Come back with a wife.' She said. I remember at the time, I thought, 'what a dumb thing to say' and, looked at her mystified.

She promptly kissed me in the ear. I'll never forget that kiss. It felt disgusting. As she drew herself away, I saw the tears.

My mother also encompassed me with her arms, offering a far more civilised kiss while holding on for some time, but she said nothing, then let go quickly and turned away.

Looking at the women blowing their noses and drying eyes, my father slowly turned toward me, firmly shook my hand then hugged me. He looked me straight in the eye and said, 'Have a great time, relax, and I pray Gods journeying mercies for you mate.'

Lynn suddenly stepped forward and suggested that prayer was needed for me. Feeling awkward, I protested and said that I was only going for a few weeks. I remember looking at my sister and calling her a 'Ratbag', to which she suggested that I needed to shut my trap and prompted my father to pray. By this stage her argument was supported fully.

With that my father along with the others who loved me, gathered around closely and my father prayed. Oddly enough, I remember every word. He based his prayer on Psalm 91.

My father quoted the first verse: He who dwells in the secret place of the Most-High shall abide under the shadow of the Almighty. He prayed a few more things then he said: 'Father, because he will make you his dwelling place, you will be his refuge. Thankyou Father that no evil shall be allowed to befall him, no plague will come near him out of your will.'

I was pinned by my earthly father's words. I have never heard him pray like this before.

He went on to thank God that, when the time is right, the Lord would command His angels to protect me. Then my father said these words.

'Thank you, Lord, that on their hands, the angels will bear him up, as though on Eagles Wings.' He prayed for some time with the others in my family as they quietly offered their full support with a periodic 'amen' here and there. I'll never forget it ... NEVER ... even though it all seems such a long time ago.

To say the moment was deeply embarrassing at the time, was another understatement, but his prayer pierced my spirit to such an extent that I felt strangely pensive ... threatened if you will. It was a bittersweet feeling, but something happened. I knew I was covered but didn't understand what that really meant.

We said our goodbyes and I recall walking away then I turned around for some reason for one last look. I said to my sister, 'See ya in a few weeks Squirt.' A few weeks?

What a joke! My sister moved towards me and hugged me again and whispered, 'I won't stop praying till you're all home safely.'

That was so odd ... Will I ever see any of them again? I have no idea why I turned around. I'm so thankful I did ... so thankful. That is the last mental picture I have of my family.

I made my way down the escalator to immigration. With all my documentation ready, I cued behind a large crowd of travellers. The line was so positioned that we snaked our way parallel to the immigration booths. I was checking my paperwork and passport when I was attacked by a small backpack. As a result, I saw my passport with its immigration documents sliding across the floor to the next isle of travellers and the small carry on backpack at my feet. After my emotional departure with my family, this seemingly abusive gesture brought my senses into a spin.

Somewhat annoyed, I quickly retrieved my documentation off the floor, then I returned to find a most apologetic young lady who had endeavoured to take her pack off, swung it around, neglecting to consider the close proximity of others. As no harm was done, I explained that all was good and left it at that.

As the line began to make better headway as a result of more customs officers being placed on duty, I was overcome with an epiphany. The last time I left the country was when I went to the Philippines on a mission's trip. I was only eighteen at the time and had completed my second year at university.

The team was led by the youth pastor at our church, who was a missionary some years before with an international radio ministry. We stayed on the compound of the radio station in Manila and worked with The Valenzuela Christian Fellowship, a local church that was planted by our youth pastor and his associates in Manila. It seemed this is what he did when he wasn't broadcasting to Asia.

The team was broken up into groups. One was a medical group. I was assigned to this team.

That trip confirmed my calling into medicine.

I got through immigration without any fuss. As I placed my passport in my shirt pocket, I looked to see if my pen was safe, next to my travel documents. As I adjusted my writing apparatus, I saw that I had cut the top of my thumb on something. It wasn't a bad cut, more of a scratch, however, it needed attending to. I made my way to a newsagency, purchased a packet of band aides and covered the wound. I began looking for the gate to board the aircraft. It was gate thirty-one and I discovered its location was right down the end of the building. Checking the time of departure of my flight to Manilla, I noticed that I still had an hour before boarding. This would be a long trip and as I had my doubts about airline food, I decided to have something substantial to eat before boarding.

With that in mind I made an order of steak and a side salad at the Coffee Club, were I knew I could get two coffees for the price of one.

It wasn't long before I was tucking into a good meal and washing it down with an excellent half strength flat white coffee in a mug. It seemed only minutes and I had devoured the meal and was sitting back on my rather uncomfortable chair taking stock of the people around me. The transit area of this international airport was fascinating. All sorts of people, different nationalities were going about their business and all travelling somewhere.

I looked down at my watch to check the time but was distracted by my bandaged thumb. I suddenly realised that the wound was probably due to the collision with the young woman's small backpack, at the customs sections of the airport.

I looked back up and began gazing around at the masses when I made eye contact with a young lady, two tables away. I looked away quickly, a little embarrassed, not wanting her to think I was imposing. My curiosity however got the better of me, for I realised, after a little reflection, that she was looking at me. Given that my peripheral vision was excellent, I began to turn my head with the objective to give the impression of looking somewhere else, when in fact I was trying to gage if she was still looking at me. I felt stupid, vulnerable and a bit childish, but there was something good about all this. I was on my vacation. This was my first real break for many years. I felt suddenly exhilarated.

I maintained my gaze using my peripheral vision and discovered that she was still staring at me. I decided I would casually turn and make eye contact again but only for an instant, just to see what she would do. This time, she smiled, looked down at her carry bag, and picked it up. I realised that it was the very backpack that attacked me. She stood up and walked straight toward me. I was fixed to my seat.

CHAPTER SIX

———— ∼ ————

The sound of Pauls' pen could be clearly heard within the cavern as it scratched its way across the page, making a haphazard effort to stay between the pale bluelines.

His thoughts were moving faster than he could write, as he watched the written word pour out of the end of the ball point pen and onto the note paper, neatly placed before him on the desk.

His thoughts flashed back to that day.

She was standing at his table. Paul remembered their conversation clearly.

'Hi there.'

The young woman had an American accent and previously, at their brief meeting, the doctor hadn't taken much notice of her. It was her backpack that had his attention at the time.

'Hi.' The doctor said a little awkwardly.

'Did I do that damage?' she asked, pointing to his thumb.

'Um, well to be accurate, I think it might have been your bag,' he said, with a huge grin spreading on his face.

'Oh, I am so sorry,' she said, covering a faint smile with her left hand.

'Hey, it's fine, no harm done.'

'Well, hello I think I might have done a little,' she laughed, pointing to the collateral damage on his hand.

'Oh, well maybe just a little scratch.'

'I didn't sleep very well last night, and I can be a little awkward when I am tired. I hate to think what I am going to be like when I get to my destination. I have a long way to go.'

'Would you like to join me?' Paul said, not knowing what else to do, given that it seemed she wasn't making any move to leave.

'Oh, I don't want to intrude. I just saw your injury and felt really bad and just wanted to apologise.'

'Hey no, it's fine, as I said, just a scratch,' Paul watched her closely. She possessed an expressive face.

'Oh OK, so I didn't do any more damage. I am so glad,' she reinforced.

'Only other thing really damaged was my pride, but it doesn't hurt knocking that down a notch or two,' he said laughing.

She offered confirmation with a broad grin. Her smile was genuine and the Doctor couldn't help but recognise a strong, yet caring character.

'So, please join me,' Paul said, now a little more interested.

'Oh, thank you, but my flight is boarding,' she said. 'Lovely to have met you,' she started to walk away.

'Actually,' he blurted out the word.

The young woman abruptly turned around to face Paul again.

'I really don't think we have ... officially met,' he said laughing. 'Hi, my name is Paul Langley,' he said putting out his hand with full expectancy.

'Oh, I'm sorry, Claire, pleased to meet you Paul Langley,' she reached out to connect with his hand.

As they touched, he was taken by the softness of her hand and a strange desire to hold on a little longer overcame him.

'I really must go, sorry again, bye, lovely to meet you.' She released her hand from his insistent grip.

With that she moved quickly out of sight into the growing crowd. The doctor sat in his chair quite struck by what had just happened.

'How very odd,' he said softly, watching her disappear into the masses.

Paul returned to his observation of the travellers. Some minutes went by. There was sudden action in play. Passengers were moving along with a little more momentum.

The Doctor fixed his attention to one woman rushing her two boys and husband to their boarding gate.

'Did you hear a boarding call?' she snapped at her husband.

'I certainly did not.' He scowled. 'And the reason I didn't hear it, ... is because there wasn't any call,' he concluded.

'Is the aeroplane going to leave without us Mommy?' the younger of the two boys cried out in panic.

'No sweetheart, they will wait for us,' she said.

The husband looked sternly at his wife.

'If they don't, there will be hell to play,' he spat.

Paul hadn't heard any call. Others began to move also. Gathering their belongings and rushing to their given point for boarding. The Doctor casually gazed at the departures notice board, to check the current status of his flight. *FINAL CALL,* was displayed next to his flight number.

He shot up from his table almost knocking it over and with total dedication to his objective, began to run toward the end of the building where his flight was being boarded.

The doctor carefully wove his way around the travellers, passing the disgruntled family still complaining and with gate thirty -six in sight, he began to slow down his pace.

A commotion erupted some distance behind him. It was a strange sound. Satisfied that his path for potential human obstruction was clear ahead, he quickly turned to discover its source, but nothing could be seen to justify the disturbance. Returning to his primary visual path, he was met by a dark figure that offered no clearance and a sudden, solid collision proved to be the only possible outcome. Before Paul had any understanding of what had happened, he found himself on the floor looking up at an elderly aboriginal man. A thin, yet strong, welcoming dark brown hand offered assistance to the offended party.

Angered, though not prepared to display it, Paul humbled himself before this gentle indigenous person.

'I am so sorry. I didn't see you,' the Doctor said.

He was quickly returned to his vertical position by the stranger, who possessed unusual strength.

The old man nodded. His dark face was lined with age. Snow white shoulder length hair and an impressive beard framed the dial of this beaming character.

'I was running to catch my flight and I heard a noise. I turned to see where ... Did you hear that noise? It was the strangest sound. Anyway, I ...' Paul was cut off mid-sentence by the thick, accented words, that penetrated his soul.

'You will stand where the two tracks cross ... There, the *Fallen Ones* will try to spear you, but the *Ancient One* has sent us. We will fight for you and your tribe. The *Ancient One* will shield you and lead you to the narrow track, walk on that track. You will first rise up on the Big Waters. There, the *Mighty Ones* of the winds of all the lands will fight for you.

They will hold you and keep you from the Big waters. From the Watcher's mountain, they will blow you and your canoe to His place for you. There, He will hide you in His Rock. Later, when you learn to walk well on the Rock, then He will raise you up on 'Bunjl', the great eagle, who will take you home.' The old man's voice poured out his message with authority.

'Excuse me?' Paul's thoughts were spinning. He was beginning to feel that he had had just about enough of this holiday.

'I'm terribly sorry but, I have no idea what...' The Doctor was interrupted again.

'You will be hidden ... in the rock ...There, you and your tribe will find rest.'

The doctor had nothing to offer in response but, stood there staring at this peaceful face ... waiting.

The elder faintly smiled and directed Paul's attention to his immediate need, by pointing to the departure gate ahead. He confidently turned from the doctor and walked in the opposite direction. Paul watched, as this indigenous messenger mingled quickly with the crowd.

The sudden surge of urgency returned, and he spun on his heels to take flight towards his original objective. The doctor's thoughts were pounded by the old man's words.

After a few steps, he turned to take one more look at this parting messenger.

He scanned the crowd but, he wasn't to be seen. The indigenous man ... was gone.

Paul reached the departures counter where his boarding pass was to be processed.

The stewardess looked at his documents.

'Ah, Doctor Langley we were calling you over the intercom.'

'I am sorry but, I don't think it is working. In fact, you might get a complaint from a small family when they arrive. They are a little upset,' Paul said smiling.

'Where the departure boards operational?' she asked.

'Yes indeed.'

'Good, thank you and thank you for the heads up regarding that family,' she continued.

'Now, Doctor Langley, the reason for our need to contact you was to advise that you have been upgraded to business class. In fact, because your booking is a Global class booking you have been upgraded all the way to Palau,' the attendant continued looking very pleased for Paul.

'Wow,' he replied, 'Thank you so much.'

'You are most welcome doctor,' the young woman said, a little coyly as she handed him his boarding pass.

With new documents in hand, he made his way along the narrow tube leading to the waiting aircraft. His mind raced back to his collision with that old indigenous man. He reflected on his strange words.

'What was that all about?' he whispered to himself, shrugging his shoulders in defeat.

Once inside the aircraft, he walked up the isle looking for his new seat allocation.

'Here sir, let me.' A male flight attendant took Paul's backpack and quickly stowed in the tight-space available.

'Thank you very much,' the Doctor replied.

With carry luggage secured, he quickly took his seat and was busy fastening his seatbelt when a familiar voice gently announced its presence to his right ear.

'Well hello, I don't believe this.' The warm tones of a woman, moved from his head to his heart as he turned to the direction of her voice. Shocked, the Doctor stared into a plain face.

'Claire ... right?' he said confidently, with his broad smile revealing his perfect teeth.

'Paul Langley, right?' she returned, as though mocking him slightly.

Both felt a little awkward. They stared at each other, then suddenly, both began to laugh. An interruption was offered by way of a polite attendant with drinks on a tray.

'So, I take it you are from the States,' Paul said, accepting the juice, and placing it on his table.

'You think so?' she said. 'How can you tell?' she laughed, taking his lead by receiving the fruit cocktail. Claire took a sip and playfully waited for his response.

'You have a Bank of America pen in your jacket pocket,' he smiled a cheesy over exaggerated grin.

'Oh, so I do. Now that's a dead giveaway.' Laughter was shared freely between both of them again.

'But I must confess, I really don't know … um, where you are from,' she surrendered. 'I have been trying to work it out since I first spoke to you.'

'Really?'

'Maybe New Zealand?' she asked. Claire had taken him completely by surprise.

'You're joking, right?'

'Oh, so on that note can I assume that you're not from New Zealand?' she said concerned of any offence.

'Correct, I am certainly not a Kiwi,' he said politely, realising her sensitivity.

'British?' she said digging a deeper hole for herself.

'This is getting worse,' he said with a slight chuckle.

'Are you Australian?' she desperately blurted out.

'Yes, right the third time,' he said with a question across his face.

'Are you really?'

'Yes … why don't I sound like one,' he slowly questioned.

'Well frankly, um … no.' Her expression was painful.

Paul looked at her expressionless.

'Sorry…but you don't,' she said blushing.

'Oh, OK, but you definitely sound American.' He smiled, trying to calm the situation.

'Sorry,' she said looking away.

'Why?'

'Why sorry?' she asked.

He raised his eyebrows.

'Oh, well, we aren't that popular in the world these days, or haven't you noticed?'

'Well, I wouldn't worry about that … being popular? … hey, it's over-rated.'

The Doctor leant over towards Claire and looked her straight in the eye and said,

'It's who YOU are that really counts, you know, what's in the heart, not how popular you are.'

There was no response. Paul watched her face, suddenly concerned that he may have been out of line. Finally, with just the tip of her tongue parting her lips her mouth began to move to form a modest:

'Thank you.'

Then, there was nothing.

The Doctor pondered deeply. There was something in that *Thank you* that struck him. It was the way she said it. He thought further on the subject. His heart continued to warm to its' sound.

He had heard that before, but where? Then, he silently gasped a sudden rush of air.

His mother!

CHAPTER SEVEN

━━━━━━ ❧ ━━━━━━

An enormous explosion shocked Paul from his reminiscing. The shock waves rumbled around the island and through their rocky dwelling.

All three sleeping beauties woke with a startled look upon their faces. The two girls sat up rubbing the sleep from their eyes but Claire was alert, upright and looking to Paul for an explanation.

'Storm,' he said. 'Lightning … struck the mountain.'

'Oh, I hate it when it does that.' She looked to the children.

Within seconds of the rumbling making its way around the volcanic plug, torrential rain began to fall. An unseasonal thunderstorm had blessed their homeland. Claire and the girls raced outside with carefully rationed soap for washing. Such down pours could last for two sometimes three hours and rarely was the rain cold but as warm as the surroundings. Claire was in charge of the small piece of soap and washed the girl's hair that was recently cut short. The young ones were then allowed to stand in the welcomed down pour to rinse off. Their mother then addressed her needs in sound hygiene. Once all were satisfied with the job done they moved inside dried off and went about the rest of the day. Given the time, Claire began to prepare the evening meal. On the menu that night, would be oysters, and a crab that they caught the day before and kept alive in a container of saltwater with the lid firmly in place. This would be washed down with a choice of fresh rainwater with a hint of pineapple from some left-over juice from yesterday's lunch or coconut milk. Dessert would be cooked banana with shredded coconut and a tablespoon of sugar syrup. The syrup was made from a type of sugar cane that was growing wild on the island as were the bananas and the coconuts. Claire would crush the cane for the juice and boil it, bringing it to a sweet thick brown liquid.

She was hoping to have had chocolate, but the coco beans weren't ready for harvesting.

Claire had discovered the beans on the ship along with other items, soon after they were marooned and she experimented with a planting. The trial was quite successful, and they had twelve of the coco trees growing very well in the tropical volcanic soil.

The two girls eagerly helped their mother with the dinner preparations while Paul settled back to his writing assignment. Tiffany came over to her father to offer him the remnant of one of the bananas that wasn't required for evening meals' dessert. Paul was more than happy to comply.

'What ya doing Dad?' Tiffany asked.

Her accent was an interesting mix because of her Australian and American parents.

'Well I am doing some writing,' he said.

'Wow!' she said. Her face was filled with curiosity. Tiffany loved writing and would often get her parents to write down a sentence each that she would dictate. With that, she would study the different handwriting and try to copy their stile.

'What's it saying?' Her inquisitive mind was like a sponge. Without a doubt, Tiffany was the thinker of their two children.

'Well, it's the story of how I met your mother and how we got here,' he replied.

'OK.' she said thoughtfully. 'Can you read it to us when we go to bed tonight?'

Tiffany looked at her father with full expectancy.

'Maybe not tonight sweetheart,' Claire spoke warmly from the corner of the room.

'I haven't finished it yet Tiff,' Paul said, bending down and kissing his youngest on the forehead.

With that she was satisfied and moved back to the kitchen area and continued with her role in the dinner preparations.

The rain continued to beat its' fury down on the tropical ground. Paul got up and walked to the entrance of the cave. He looked around the corner to where the three forty-four gallon drums were placed. The rain was hammering its' heavy beads of water onto the waters' surface within the drums.

'Another half an hour of this type of rain and the three will be full,' he yelled back to his wife.

Having plenty of fresh drinking water was like having plenty of money in the bank. In this environment, they needed their water supply to be reliable, as it was very easy to dehydrate. They were very fortunate that there were plenty of coconut trees bearing good fruit. They even had the smaller coconut tree, which meant they could get the green fruit, which made for nutritious drinking. This milk introduced the electrolytes, which the body needed to keep a good balance on things. These trees only grew ten to twenty feet tall, which made obtaining the fruit much easier.

Good hygiene was imperative, as skin infections were easily acquired and all four would go swimming in the ocean almost every morning. A simple scratch on the skin could fester within hours and develop into a serious ulcer within twenty-four hours. If scratches were acquired, as they often were on offer, it became a ritual for the injured soldier to spend thirty minutes or so in the saltwater, then some honey, mashed Paw Paw and a covering. The honey was found on the boat. The large barrel of the substance was found at the back of the huge pantry in the galley, where they also found, oddly enough, a large cardboard box full of antibacterial soap. It was decided that the family would not eat any of the honey except on special occasions. It would be used for medicinal purposes. The soap was to be used sparingly for they had no idea how long it would be before they would be rescued, ... if ever.

The saltwater was a very good cleanser, but the fresh water was best for a quick wash before bed. The whole family agreed that the feeling of being clean for bedtime was the best feeling in the world. They would share a small bucket of water and wash the places of importance.

It was difficult for the young ones to come to grips with the consequences of such infections until they both experienced the problem and then their attitude changed.

The Doctor had found very adequate medical supplies on the yacht when they first arrived but he wouldn't use the antibiotics, until Claire contracted a bladder infection. It was a serious problem and she fell quite ill indeed. It took two courses of the drug to help her body fight this dreaded thing. The girls were frightened as a result of what they saw in their mother and listened from that time on when told to drink more water and to follow good hygiene practices as suggested by their father.

The lack of suitable clothing was becoming a problem. The tropical elements had proved to be quite destructive and the couple's clothes were either wearing out, or rotting.

Other than the curtains found in the VIP suite, their future for adequate wardrobe was looking grim. Any of the castaway's clothing blessed with elastic, proved unusable after a few years, due to the rubber perishing. This meant that underwear was gradually discarded for obvious reasons. Over the years, they had used all the clothing found on the yacht. With preservation in mind, it was decided that swimming in the ocean would be done naked, which wasn't a problem given their isolation. Claire made alterations where necessary to what clothing they had found on the yacht however, recently she had run out of cotton thread.

The woman of the island had begun considering the use of the leaves of the plant that looked a little like sugar cane, for possible future covering.

When the children were clothed, they were being dressed in all types of items, however, they were growing, and the ramifications were obvious. When practical, the family would wear sarongs made from various materials found on the yacht years before. Sometimes the children would wear very little, sometimes nothing, which was of concern for their father.

Claire wasn't as perplexed, as she felt that it would work out. She kept saying that *God would show them what to do* and in the meantime, she believed that the children should be left to enjoy their innocence. It was agreed that the curtains from the ship would be saved for the girls, when their need was greater in the future.

At times the doctor would experience mild panic attacks, when he considered all the things that could go wrong, but would then be reminded by Claire that *God was with them and when had He let them down*. Paul had to admit she was right. God had never let them down.

The young American wife was always a tower of strength, which was a far cry from what she was when they first arrived. Paul would often watch her in action on this deserted land and had come to the conclusion that she was born to live there and would never fit back in the western world. The children knew nothing else, so they were well balanced. They had each other to play with, confide in and they had their parents for love, nurturing, adult companionship, mentoring and role models.

Dinner was declared ready and the man stood up from his desk and walked over to the small table. He looked all in the face one at a time and said, 'Right then, who's going to thank God for dinner?'

'Me!' Jessica shot her hand straight into the air.

'But I wanted to,' Tiffany complained.

'You did last night,' Jessica defended her right of turn.

'OK Jess,' Paul said. 'away you go.'

The family bowed their head and Jessica began to pray.

'Dear God,' she said softly. 'It's been a great day.'

A little voice sitting at the table humbly interrupted.

'Except when Daddy got mad at us for swimming in the middle of the day,' Tiffany carefully added with a whisper as though confession was in order.

'Tiff,' Claire hushed her youngest.

'But he did Mommy,' she insisted.

'Shh,' Tiffany's mother tenderly reinforced.

'Continue Jess,' Paul's tones of authority won the moment.

'Thank you Lord for letting Mommy find the oysters and the crab.' Jess was interrupted again.

'God?' Tiff whispered, as though she was talking intimately in her creator's ear.

'It was Daddy who found the crab.'

Jessica ignored the small sideline prayer editor and continued.

'And the good time we had getting the oysters with Mommy,' she continued.

'Amen!' Tiffany exploded.

'Tiff, I haven't finished,' Jessica scolded her little sister.

'Oh sorry,' Tiffany said, in a whisper, shrugging her shoulders.

'And Lord?' Jessica concluded. 'One day, can I have a pink dress and Tiff and I want to see our grandparents, in Jesus name.'

'Amen!' Tiffany cried out as though impatience was getting the better of her.Claire looked across at Paul while the children began to help themselves. Out of sight of the children Paul simply raised his right eyebrow at his wife, as if to ask, *what was that all about*. Claire raised her shoulders surrendering to ignorance.

The two adults began retrieving order around the table and supervised the serving of the precious provision on the table.

Little was said that night except Tiffany's periodic muttering expressing her delight in crab meat. By the time their dessert was consumed movement shifted its direction to cleaning up and getting ready for bed. The sun was setting, which meant their cave was getting dark very quickly.

The sola lanterns were turned on and two were taken into the inner rooms. The one small L.E.D light that lit the general living area was switched on and the living chamber took on a new character. The light spread its softness for their early evening living. The dishes were washed, the remnants of the dinner not required was placed in a sealed bucket so as not to attract flies. This would be buried the next day.

The torrential rain was easing. A cool breeze had risen from the southeast and was pouring chilled air into their area including some fine rain still falling. It was decided that Paul would board up the entrance, which sheltered them from the elements. This did mean, however, that it could get a little warm inside later in the evening, but they all preferred to be a little warm then to get a chill early in the morning. One could undress for the warmth but it was a little more difficult to put on extra clothing due to the lack thereof. The only warm clothing owned were four hooded jackets, which fitted the adults well, but completely covered the children from head to toe.

All the beds had a thin blanket folded at the base of the beds and though rarely required, mosquito nets above supported by makeshift bedposts. The blankets, acquired from the shipwrecked yacht, would be a welcome covering if one awoke chilled early in the morning. The sheets and blankets were considered as acceptable fabric for future clothing, but after some discussion, it was decided that the bed linen was to be kept for that use only. A comfortable night's sleep was important for on- going health the doctor demanded. It was decided that if it came down to it, naked sleeping with sheets and blankets, would be better than not having bed covering at night.

However, until such time, Paul was not in favour of going to bed without some form of clothing on whilst they still had options, even though in the summer months it was easy to do. He insisted that all wear at least a *T-shirt*, while they had something to wear, to protect the chest area from the early morning chill. There were two very large *T-shirts* found on the boat and they acted like night shirts as they came down past Claire's knees and just lapped at the top of Pauls knees. The girls would wear adult shirts to bed, and both were quite happy with that. In addition to this common-sense strategy, the doctor in the house felt it wise for both he and his wife to dress as such due to the fact that often one or both of the children would climb into bed with the parents at different stages of the night. Paul and Claire were comfortable about such practise.When an unsettled night was had by one of the girls, Claire was the one who would get up and attend to the problem and often the upset child would be brought to the adult's bed to achieve a quick settle.

Paul looked up from his notes and saw the girls were making their way to the inner rooms. After checking the security of the front doors, he walked into the girl's area and was met with Claire talking to her precious offspring.

'Well …' Paul said, 'what's for the reading tonight?'

It was a family tradition to read to the girls before they went to sleep. Reading was a wonderful way, they found, not only to settle the children down from their generally adventurous day but to grow their relationship with their children.

'Can we have one of Moms' stories tonight?' Tiffany asked.

'Oh dear,' Claire explained, 'actually with all the excitement of the day, I hadn't really given any thought toward a story,' she said apologetically.

'OK,' Tiffany said. 'a Bible story then.'

'Okeydokey,' Paul acknowledged, 'and who do you want to read to you tonight?'

'It doesn't matter.' Tiffany said.

'Daddy? Can you read it to us tonight?' Jessica asked looking straight to her father.

'Of course, I will sweetheart,' Paul said. 'You don't mind Mom?' Looking to Claire.

'No problems,' she said. 'actually, I'd really like that too,' she confessed.

Paul took the old black bible that was taken from the ship many years previously and opened it at the beginning.

'Let's start at the beginning,' he said. 'we haven't done that for a while.'

He moved onto the bed as the females in his life made way to their hero.

Jessica was quick to claim the closest position to the most important man in her life.

Both Paul and Claire had noticed that Jessica was favouring her fathers' attention a lot more lately. He was careful to give her all the attention she needed given her stage of growth.

All four lay down on the bed with Jessica snuggling up to her Dad.

Paul accepted his daughters' need for closeness by wrapping one arm around her, which filled her with joy.

With the other arm, he steadied the old black book. During his medical career, he had seen the detrimental effects of fathers who couldn't reinforce what was required in their child's stage of growth. He was thankful that he was able to do the most important part a father could do and that is just to be there for them, to talk with them, accept them were they were in their development and to love their mother. Paul was a fulltime Dad.

He cleared his throat and began to read.

'In the beginning ...'

All were focused on the book. With Jessica tucked under her fathers' arm and Tiffany nestled against her mothers' chest, the words of the Book washed over their lives.

'It was the sixth day ... And God saw that it was very good.'

Paul looked at Claire. With her eyes, she beckoned him to look down at Tiffany. She was fast asleep.

Claire then motioned toward Jessica as though she was asking the conscious status of their eldest daughter. The man of the household looked and quickly choked a laugh. Jessica was also gone. He glanced down at Tiffany, across to his wife and then to his eldest daughter.

It was a beautiful picture. Carefully they laid out the girls on the bed, secured the mosquito net, even though there were no mosquitos to speak of on the island during that time of the year and quietly retreated. Hand in hand, they turned to look at that perfect picture of peace. Paul turned his wife to him and kissed her, then holding her closely he whispered, 'I love our kids so much and I their mother more than I ever thought it possible for a man to love a woman.'

Tears welled up in Claire's eyes. 'Oh, you sure know how to get this woman's attention mister,' she said then kissed him with full intent of greater things to come.

The moment was richly intimate. They were quickly being carried along with passion at the entrance of the girl's room when a little snicker was heard from the bed.

It was Tiffany.

They had no idea how long she was watching. The little intruder of this God given situation was softly told to go to sleep and they returned to their living area with smiles on their flushed faces.

Out of sight from their children, Claire eagerly reached up and threw her arms around her man. Instantly, a tearing sound ripped its way to the ears of both adults.

'Oh bother,' she looked down at the fabric under her arm.

'Oh no, there goes another shirt. You think you can fix it?' he asked with a sombre face.

'No thread left. Just have to wear it like this I guess.' She looked at her husband.

'The way everything is rotting on us.... I'll give us one year and ...' Claire cut him off.

'God will provide.'

'Sure.'

'This is timely.'

'Really? Why so?' Her husband's face was filled with interest.

'Well, just this morning I was reading in Matthew six ... Jesus says that we are not to be anxious about our life and he goes on and becomes specific ... like what we'll eat, drink ... about our body and what we'll clothe ourselves with ... he repeats himself later in the text on the subject of clothes and says why are you anxious about clothing? It really spoke to me Paul ... and here I am now with clothes rotting off me. Despite how it appears, I don't think we'll be running around naked ... I really don't. God will provide ... I really believe that.'

'I trust so, otherwise we'll have to start wearing those grass skirts you talked about.' He laughed.

'Ah, that won't be so bad. Maybe that's what He wants. Frankly it's the grass bras that I think is the really low point ... might pass on that,' she said adding further humour into the conversation.

'I guess that wouldn't worry you, would it?'

'As in no top?' she asked.

He nodded, studying her face for her response.

'No, but the thought of you wearing a grass skirt? ... I can't wait,' she said full of mischief.

Paul huffed a laugh, turned, walked to his notes, while mimicking a hula dancer and sat down.

'What are you doing?' Claire warmly asked

'Oh, I'm just going to go over what I have written. Need to get my mind off that grass skirt...scary.'

'Oh no you're not,' she whispered.

'I'm not what? The reading or the grass skirt?' he asked suddenly mimicking a hula dancer with his hands while now seated at his desk.

She didn't answer immediately but simply shook her head smiling.

'I need you to help me with something,' she said with an interesting look in her eyes.

'With what pray tell ... the grass skirt?' He chuckled.

'Come to bed and I'll show you,' she said beckoning him with her two index fingers.

'You know, I was actually disappointed that you couldn't tell us one of your stories,' he said making conversation.

'Were you now?' Claire said totally focused on her plan for the night with her husband.

'Or maybe I was disappointed that I couldn't hear the girls finish it for you,' he said moving toward her and those two index fingers.

'Well, we'll just have to overcome that disappointment for you, won't we?' she said, smiling from ear to ear. She reached out and gathered the hands of the man she loved and lead him to their room.

Claire was a high-spirited fun-loving woman, full of life and full of love. In the soft light of the sola lamp, the two came together and their spirits were joined that early evening ... the first night of the monsoon season.

CHAPTER EIGHT

~

P aul woke suddenly. Something was beckoning his attention. There was a knocking. It sounded as though someone was knocking on their front door.

Knock, knock, knock.

Pauls' heart began to beat faster. Fear surged through his veins, then panic kicked in.

He quietly navigated his way between the mosquito net and the beds' surface to finally free himself from their slumber cocoon. The solar lamps were still on as they were set to the lowest setting which allowed for a dim glow, just in case the girls needed to come in at any time of the night. The light in the general living area was also on. Normally, it was turned off but, due to the circumstances of the previous night's passion, Paul neglected its' status.

The battery bank placed in their caves' storeroom was blessed with considerable capacity, but he always tried to use as least as possible to conserve the batteries life. He knew, should their stay be long term, that there will be a time when the batteries will die and life at night will change.

Paul stood at the opening of his room dressed only in his oversized t-shirt and looked out to the living area and waited. It was still raining, and he felt a little cool. The cave was boarded up with the cabin doors from the yacht. It didn't take long before he heard the knocking again. He saw the problem.

The previous night he had neglected to insert the plank that secured the doors into their run that Paul had designed, and the wind was buffeting the caves wooden enclosure. He placed the plank into its place. The noise stopped instantly and so too his panic.

The Doctor was constantly watching out for intruders. Sitting down at the small desk he switched on the small twelve-volt light and looked over his notes.

Picking up the ballpoint pen, he began to write.

It was a little shocking to think that this person was not dissimilar to my mother in a number of ways and yet Claire was very different. However, there was vibrancy about her that I had never seen before in a young woman. I listened to her as she answered my questions.

She was from Kansas City Missouri USA and was quite the academic. Claire had skipped a couple of years in high school due to her academic abilities. As a result, she graduated from University of Kansas with a double master's degree in education and economics and a degree in I.T. Claire achieved all this by the age of nineteen, which I had to admit wasn't a bad effort. She secured a position with the Bank of America working in the IT department setting up in-house training for the Australian bank. After one year with BOA, she took two years off without pay to return to her studies and was offered an academic exchange with Australian National University in Canberra with the objective of completing a PHD in economics. Claire completed all this way ahead of time, despite the fact that she was forced to complete a couple of extra modules to satisfy the Australian academic standards.

When hearing this I looked at her, displaying a straight face and suggested that one of those modules must have been 'Queens English 101'

I'll never forget it.

The doctor put down his pen. He laughed to himself and reflected about that day such a long time ago.

'That would have been like starting all over again,' Paul said.

She continued to sit there still looking at him with a blank face.

'You must have done quite well, as your English isn't too bad for an American,' he blurted out.

Her face expressed disbelief.

'You are joking ... right?' she said wide eyed.

'Yeah,' the doctor said nodding, with a laugh surfacing.

'Oh you!!' The young woman exploded with laughter, punching him hard on his arm

'Ouch.' A surprised, somewhat pained expression overcame the doctor.

She saw the hurt she had caused again.

'Oh, I am so sorry, I forgot my place,' she said. 'I have big brothers and it was such a natural reaction,' Claire continued.

'Hey, no worries. Whatever floats your boat,' Paul smiled broadly. 'but, sounds a bit violent to me,' he joked.

'Oh, no, I hit them in a nice way,' she said. 'I only do that to the people in my life who I know and love.' Immediately, Claire's face turned very red.

The Doctor had no idea what to say to that. After a few seconds of silence, he brought the conversation back to her academic adventure in Canberra.

With a thankful escape from further embarrassment , she quickly took the opportunity to advise that it took her eighteen months of rather intense work to complete her PHD. She had been in constant communication with her superiors in Bank of American back in the States and was soon offered a position with the Westpac Bank based in Sydney.

The American bank had a working agreement with the Australian bank and Claire was working on a consultancy basis. The young American was on her way back to the states on banking business, but was intending to have some well-earned R&R before getting back to San Francisco. She had six weeks' time off owing to her, which consisted of three-week's vacation, then three weeks at with her parent's in Kansas City. She would spend six weeks in San Francisco on business, then back to Sydney.

She gave a detailed explanation of what her position with the bank entailed, but by that stage, Paul wasn't listening. He was watching … her. The doctor was taken by her mannerisms. He soaked in her character and listening to her accent. It was sweet. She was sweet. She was real, but in a rather strange way, she shone. Claire had very olive skin with a clear complexion. Paul studied her face for some time whilst she gave a detailed presentation of her work.

Claire's face was quite plane and yet, for Paul, there was something absolutely beautiful about her … something very appealing about her. The doctor was suddenly gripped.

She was the most beautiful woman he had ever met. He gasped. Claire stopped. Paul smiled desperate to hide his revelation.

'Keep going,' he softly prompted and with that she did.

Their time of deep association was interrupted by a pleasant voice.

'Excuse me, are you disembarking at Manila, or catching a connecting flight?' It was the flight attendant who stood before them with Philippine immigration papers in her hand.

'Connecting flight,' they both said in total synchronicity, as their eyes met, realising their chorus.

The flight attendant smiled and walked to the seats behind them to make her offer again.

Paul began to feel awkward, as Claire looked outside her window.

'Oh, my goodness,' she exclaimed. 'we have already taken off!'

The doctors' eyes dashed outside.

They had been so engrossed with each other, that they hadn't realised their aircraft taxing, and taking off.

Paul had an odd look on his face.

'Are you OK?' she asked curiously responding to his new facial expression.

'Yeah, fine. Can't believe that we missed the take-off.' He looked deeply a Claire momentarily. 'That's weird ... yes?'

Claire laughed quietly nodding her head, 'Yes, just a little,' she said pondering.

'How is that possible?'

'No idea.'

Another awkward event dominated as they stared at each other.

'Paul, if you don't mind, I have some work I need to get done and ...'

Her words were cut off by a relieved doctor. 'Hey, of course,' he said genuinely.

'Anyway, while you're doing that, I might get a little shut eye.'

'Now that's a good idea,' she said producing a small laptop from her large handbag.

Paul smiled and adjusted his First-Class business class seat. He then settled back, closed his eyes and thought. He had just experienced the most intense, yet wonderful time with the most

amazing woman he had ever met. His thoughts continued and he slowly drifted off to sleep.

'Paul?' The voice pieced his rest. A gentle touch on his right arm confirmed the need to return to the conscious world. The doctor opened his eyes.

'Paul, chow time,' Claire spoke softly.

'Chicken or beef sir?' The flight attendant posed the question to the wakening passenger.

'Wow. Ah ... beef please,' he said sitting up and adjusting his seat as the small table was being set up competently by the stewardess. An excellent wine was on offer and the doctor accepted. Claire asked for water.

'Wise choice,' he said softly.

'Do you drink?'

'Occasionally. But, I feel as though I have let you down,' he said, with a slight smile on his face.

'Oh no, not in the least,' she responded quickly. 'For some reason though you don't strike me as someone who drinks alcohol. Do you smoke?' she asked innocently.

'No!' the doctor said emphatically. Then shaking his head, he went on to explain his reason for such a quick comeback. The doctor explained that he had seen some sad consequences of the habit.

'Oh, listen to you. You remind me of my father. He is passionately against the habit and has been campaigning against smoking in public for quite some time now,' she said, with her eyes bright and excited. 'He has seen some awful consequences involving newborn babies,' she continued.

It seemed to the doctor, that he had regained his stamp of approval given his conviction, but was a little shocked at being compared as similar to her father.

A delicious meal, whilst seated in business class on a great airline, next to a very delightful young woman was more than Paul had bargained for.

After the meal and still feeling a little tired, he reclined his comfortable seat back again. Closing his eyes, he remembered his sisters' last words a few hours previously. *'Be safe handsome, I am praying God gives you the best all the way over and a special trip all the way back. Come back with a wife … I won't stop praying till you're all home safely.'*

'All? … Strange,' he thought, as he drifted off to sleep.

CHAPTER NINE

※

Paul took a break from his writing again. There was much to describe, much to share, much to put down on paper for the record, but his thoughts continued to focus of the young woman.

He had prayed to God a very special prayer when he was a teenager. He reflected deeply on the matter all those years ago. He asked his creator … for a wife.

Such a thought would never have entered his mind had it not been for his youth pastor. In fact, he was challenged to do so during a youth group meeting. The pastor had urged the young people that night to live Godly lives, to stand out, to be set apart for the creator which included keeping themselves for their life partner. The pastor suggested that God knew who would be the best choice for each one of them and that God already had the person in mind.

He said, *when God provides, it is very good. So why not give it over to God and let him be in charge of that important part of your life.* The youth leader then challenged them to ask God for a spouse and with that, they all got on their knees and silently made their request known to the Most-High God. The young pastor then closed in prayer. At the time, Paul felt a little self-conscious, if not rather odd about the event but, recognised the real need for God's perfect will in his life and certainly wanted the best from God. The pastor explained that they would be tested but, he said that if a person purposed in his or her heart to be true to God there was a blessing ahead. '*Wait,*' he said. '*Wait for what God will do.*

There is a WOW factor coming down the track for you. But you have to wait,' he concluded.

Seated in his business class setting, Paul recalled his request to the creator on that cold and windy night all those years ago and began to chuckle to himself. He asked for a wife who was a little like his mother, full of life, possessing a transparent character, and an excellent mother to their children.

She was to be very intelligent if not academic but she must have a sound practical side to her. This was important to Paul as after all his years of study in university circles, he had come to the conclusion that academics, whilst important, had their place but, hardly belonged in the practical arena.

Whoever this wonderful woman was, she needed to be a person who could understand him, his odd sense of humour and his other unique characteristics. Organizational skills, was one of those characteristics. He had problems with people who weren't organised and labelled their problem as *slovenliness*.

His list continued. He asked, that he would be a good listener, that he would have God's wisdom to be a good husband. She was also to be a beautiful looking woman … with a beautiful heart and blessed with a generous set of bosoms.

Sitting in their island dwelling, Paul exploded with laughter when he pondered upon his latter request. *How ridiculous*, he thought to himself. As quickly as his explosion manifested, he suppressed his comic relief with his hand pressed firmly to his mouth not wanting to wake the household so early.

Now settled, he returned to his reflections.

He remembered asking God that he and his wife were to have a soul mate relationship. He asked that they were to be deeply intimate, physically, emotionally and spiritually. He prayed that they would encourage each other in all aspects of their life including their personal relationship with the creator. His unique sense of humour was washed away by a sudden revelation. He was seized by the moment only to be followed by being overcome with emotion. God had answered this request, a request made by a nineteen-year old teenager so long ago and it was answered almost to the letter, even down to the very matters of her physical characteristics, with one exception. He was overwhelmed with gratitude and with joy.

A solitary tear flowed down the left side of his face and was chased by the chill of the air's morning freshness.

'Hey, what's so funny handsome?'

Paul turned to the direction of the voice.

The image of the subject at hand materialised out of the semi darkness with her hair in a tangle on the left side of her head. In a vain attempt to present herself to her audience, she began to run both hands through her hair only to have her left hand meet with the tangle which caused a twinge of pain. With focus improving on her subject, a look of surprise became the expression then.

Seeing the tear running down his face, she moved toward her life partner and her compassionate heart opened.

'Hey, Wow, what's with this tear gorgeous man?' she said kissing tenderly the tear streaked face.

Paul looked into the face full of love and compassion.

'Why so sad?' she said softly.

'Not sad, joyous.' Paul replied.

'Oh, sounds good,' she said waiting expectantly for an explanation.

Paul had never shared this story and proceeded with great detail to unravel each item with the love of his life. As he began revealing his secret, Claire, somewhat captivated slowly moved into him, sliding her form upon his lap and with her left arm around his neck laid her head on his shoulder and listened.

The doctor accurately recounted the event of years gone by, whilst Claire snuggled into her man, hanging onto every word.

'And that's it,' he said, winding up the recollection within a few minutes. 'I realised that the Lord had answered my prayer that I prayed all those years ago.' He positioned his face towards hers'.' I am so blessed,' he concluded.

Claire looked at him deeply but said nothing.

She broke the silence. 'Thank you for sharing that, I never knew that, but Um ...' She repositioned herself on his lap and sat up. 'You didn't get the ...' She pushed out her chest towards him.

He shook his head and said 'Perfect, just perfect.'

The woman slowly moved her arms around him, buried her face back into his neck and there she stayed.

This time was abruptly interrupted by the sound of a pair of little bear feet on the caves glassy stone floor.

Claire looked up to see a sleepy faced Jessica moving towards the two adults.

Confidently, the child included herself with the intimacy set before her. With her arms outstretched, she climbed up on her mothers' lap and hugged both parents. The three sat for some time together in silence. Finally, Tiffany moved out from her caverns' crevasse straight to the action. She straddled her sister and with considerable strength wrapped her arms around the three necks and drew them all in toward her.

This was one of God's unique little families and no one was to interfere with what the creator was doing.

The wet weather had been persistent all night and the combination of the rain and chill in the air called for the islands' population of four to remain inside. The enclosure across the caves entrance was kept intact and, the solar light was turned on, bathing the living area with a soft white light. It was decided that today would be kitchen day where a little baking would be done. Before a breakfast of fruit, the morning's ablutions were urgently attended to, but given that the rain had continued to fall, it was decided to remove all bed clothing and venture out in the rain in their natural state.

'Hey Claire, I'll stay behind to start the fire,' he said, opening the lid of their make-shift oven. 'but make sure you and the girls get a good soaping.'

'Yes, OK.' Claire agreed, as she walked into her room, calling out to her daughters to prepare for the outdoor shower from the heavens.

In no time at all, the three were ready to venture outside despite random flashes of lightening now out to sea. Claire, with soap in hand, asked the man of the household to release the door from its wedge and the small group of excited females ran into the weather with squeals of delight to attend to the necessities of life. After some time, the first to return was Jessica, who ran into the warmth of the cave and straight into the arms of her father with complaints of the rain being cold. With daughter wrapped around his torso, Paul took one of the towels hanging next to their island oven and vigorously dried the shivering girl. With the now damp cloth hung back on its hook, the child was told to quickly go into her room and get dressed. Then Claire was next to arrive, wiping some smalls leaves off her bare feet whilst calling to Tiffany to come inside. Paul handed his wife the second towel and with some authority beckoned his reluctant daughter to return.

'That girl,' Claire said, wiping the mornings blessing from her person and shaking her head at her husband.

'Mm, she reminds me of someone,' he said with his finger on his chin and eyes squinting as though pondering the possibilities then looking at Claire.

'Hey, don't look at me buster. It's got to be your side of the family,' Claire said, kissing him on the cheek then slapping her husband on his behind.

'Actually ...' he said, quickly turning to look back outside. 'I think your right. The older she's getting the more she reminds me of my sister.'

'Really?' Claire asked, stopping her drying and looking straight at her husband.

'You know, I really want to meet her one day, she sounds like fun.' She paused and looked at Paul 'And your Mom and Dad but especially your Mom, Paul.' A deep expression came over her.

The doctor studied his wife.

'Do you think we will ever get back home?' She waited for the answer.

'I don't know ... but God knows,' he said softly.

'Yes, He does,' she replied with assurance. 'but I ...'

A flurry of energy burst through the entrance of the cave.

'Hey Dad, that was so much fun. Mom chased me around the orchard, but she couldn't get me, because I am faster than Mom.' Tiffany said, proudly dancing around.

'Oh, did she.' Paul said looking at his wife. 'The orchard?' he mouthed the words to his wife.

Claire looked at her husband and shrugged her shoulders with a huge grin overcoming her face.

'All the way to the orchard?' he whispered.

'It was fun,' she whispered back.

'Did you actually remember the primary purpose for venturing out into this inclement weather?' the doctor said smiling.

'Of course,' Claire took her towel and placed it over the head of her daughter.

'Big mouth,' she whispered, as she began to dry off the youngest. Delightful giggles were heard from beneath the thick material. Clothes were quickly draped over clean skin and a breakfast of fruit was had by all.

It was time to cook, using their own flour made from the seeds of a grass that grew in copious amounts on the other side of the island. This made for a variety of dishes. It wasn't unlike oats but possessed a nuttier flavour and was easily ground to flour when allowed to dry in their makeshift oven. Cakes and biscuits would be made using this flour and over the last four years they had been able to introduce additional ingredients such as, almonds, peanuts, the Queensland nut or more globally known as the Macadamia nut. All these were planted by Paul and Claire as a result of their findings on the stranded yacht many years prior. Their oven consisted of an old forty-four-gallon drum with a bar-b-q grate wedged across its centre.

Coals were placed in the base of the drum beneath the grate. The drums lid was put in place and the cooking was satisfactory most of the time.

Coconuts had to be shredded, over ripened fruit would be turned into Island jam, by crushing the fruit, adding their sugar syrup, a little cooking then placed in a few jars compliments of the yacht's kitchen. Guava jam was the children's favourite. Mango jam ranked high with the adults, but when Guava and mango weren't in season, paw-paw jam blessed all.

Paul made the beds and tidied up the adults' room then proceeded back to his small desk where his notepad awaited him. He gazed across at his busy girls with their mother. He watched as they carefully followed Claire's' instructions, making their own suggestions and generally learning with great delight. The busy interaction was a sight to see, as all in the makeshift kitchen were busy being three wonderful females. The man of the house watched the happy group in action from his desk and admired Claire's gift with their children.

Paul moved his focus to the text before him and began to write. He watched the ink run once again from the end of the ball point pen to the page as a result of his will being commanded upon this writing apparatus. He stopped again looked up at the walls of his dwelling, reflected on his first flight with Claire, then he fixed his gaze on the task at hand and started to write for the second time.

CHAPTER TEN

———— ❧ ————

I was awakened by a considerable bump. I opened my eyes quickly and realized that turbulence was upon our flight. I also realized that Claire was still sleeping and had slipped across to my side of the seat. The turbulence had so moved her position that she was leaning firmly against me. She moved in closer, reacting to the disturbance around the aircraft but, didn't wake up. I felt it remarkable that someone could sleep through the event, but then remembered that she had said back in Brisbane, that she hadn't slept well the previous night.

Then, as though she knew me well, she moved closer up against my torso and with her right arm moving around my waist, snuggled in even closer still for some time into the flight. I sat there quite still, not wanting to spoil this gift.

I was in awe of this wonderful creature next to me. Everything about her ... even her scent was quite agreeable. As I continued my keen observation of this charming gift, I realised that my heart was pounding in my chest. Feeling somewhat vulnerable, I began to rationally consider all things and came to the conclusion that this was hardly a profitable situation. She was going back to the States and I was going to sail around some islands in the Pacific, so why get all stupid about a meeting with a lovely young woman that simply can't go anywhere.

The logic calmed me down, but the thought of saying goodbye offered little joy.

As I looked down to the side of her face, I felt a cold bead of 'something' travel down my right arm. I then noticed a bead of liquid running slowly down my appendage. With a little more investigation, I realized that she was sound asleep and as a result of the angle of her head against me, her mouth was slightly opened and a little saliva was running down the side of her chin. I laughed to myself but let her continue with my baptism, for fear of disturbing her and therefore, losing my close position to her.

Another considerable pocket of air lashed its atmospheric fury at our aircraft resulting in a concussive outburst which woke my companion with a jolt. She raised her head in bewilderment, slowly sitting up against me with her arm still around me. In a flash, she realised her position and sat upright being quick to remove her embracing arm from around my waist. She sat there looking at me in disbelief. I remember her awkward stare. I wanted to laugh but felt that might be in bad taste. I smiled and said, 'Hello sleepy head.'

She looked at my arm and winced as though trying to understand why my arm was wet. Then it seemed the penny had dropped and she quickly put her hand to her face. To her dismay she discovered why I was somewhat moist.

With a quick move, her wet face was attended to. I thought I detected a little anger, then, remorse and finally, her hands covered her face.

The doctor sat back in his chair reflecting on that flight. He smiled as he remembered how Claire was confronted with her human reality.

'Oh my, I am so sorry,' she said, 'how long was I asleep?' she asked.

'Oh, a while,' Paul replied confidently.

With her apologies streaming from her face, Claire quickly went into servant mode by taking a Kleenex tissue from her hand-bag and attended to the doctor's inconvenience. She was notably unsettled.

'I can't believe I did this, oh how embarrassing. I have never ever done such a thing to a perfect stranger.'

'Hey,' the doctor said laughing, as he reached out and gently held her arm to confirm his sincerity, 'it's all good, that's life, I am quite used to it.'

'Oh, sure you are,' she said, now displaying annoyance.

'No, no, be assured, I am certainly used to it. In fact, what you did, that's nothing.

I've had worst things deposited on my person,' he continued, followed by a reasonable chuckle.

Claire looked deeply at the traveller sitting next to her.

'Late one night I had a very drunk thirty-year old man projectile vomit all over me.'

Paul laughed heartily.

'Oh, that's gross,' she said politely with a distorted look appearing across her face.

'You can say that again. I was the talk of the staff for weeks after that.' The doctor's laughter persisted then he suddenly sensed that it may have annoyed his acquaintance seated next to him.

'And you really think that's funny?' She looked at him still in disbelief.

'Actually, at the time ... no, I didn't really think it was that funny at all, but the staff certainly did.' Paul stopped and reflected then broke the moments silence with laughter.

'The ratbags,' he continued.

'The what?' Claire said, now really confused. Her day, thus far, had been long and trying. Now, impatience was creeping in.

'Ratbags.'

'I am so sorry,' she said cautiously, putting away her tissues and tiding up around her.

'But I have no idea what you are talking about. First you are telling me that you enjoy someone throwing up all over you along with your friends or at least you found it funny or they did or something and then you call your friends or staff .... whatever... a bag of rats.

Who does that?' she said in a state of total confusion. Realising the need to soften the situation she laughed softly.

'Um, no, not a bag of rats,' the doctor replied, holding back his unique sense of humour to maintain credible posture.

'Rat bag ... quite different to a bag of rats,' he said, watching this poor American woman who was looking back at him trying to understand his Australian vernacular, with no apparent success.

'Rat Bags, bag of rats, whatever, I have no idea what you are talking about,' she finally said, shrugging her shoulders then releasing a painful expression across her face.

With that, Paul had no way of containing himself. He threw his head back in his chair and laughed so hard that he started coughing. After Paul contained himself, and wiping his tears away as a result of his sense of humour taking control, he then went on to explain, giving her the complete perspective. Claire smiled a little more hoping for clarity.

'So, you are a doctor?' she said, with a relieved look on her face.

'I certainly am Claire,' he said, feeling a very pleasant warm flush spreading throughout his body at the sight of her approval.

'I do apologise. You took me by surprise with all that ... Oh dear, I am so tired and I am so sorry. Please forgive me,' she said massaging her forehead. 'I'm sure you must think I'm pretty weird. I'm not really. I have had some real tall tales told me since I've been in Australia ... and of course I swallowed it all ... I must come across as real gullible. I'm sorry ... really I am.'

Paul laughed. 'It's all good. Sounds like you had a full emersion in the Aussie culture.' He pondered quickly.

Claire nodded her head slowly.

'You're a different breed ... your countrymen that is, but you are different again ... in a nice way ... oh. Not that Australians are ... oh dear I'm digging a hole here again, aren't I?'

'It's all good. If it's any consolation, if you receive that type attention by an Australian ... generally, it means that you are accepted.'

'One doesn't feel accepted at times,' she said, still embarrassed by her previous reactions.

'Well, most of the times one is ... and to be frank I can understand why ... I can see that you would be easy to have around ... easy to accept.' He smiled.

'Thank you.' Her face lit up.

'So ... you are a doctor. I find THAT ... amazing.' Claire stared straight ahead shaking her head slightly

'Can't see what's amazing about THAT,' he said authentically.

'No, it is amazing,' she insisted turning to looking him in the eye.

'Why?'

'My father is a doctor,' she said, still gazing into his face but this time with wonder.

'Really?' 'He's a paediatrician,' Claire announced with pride mounting.

The doctor shared his interest in the subject, then elaborated eloquently on his current specialisation, after which he proceeded to share some of the stories of the children he had helped come into the world during his time spent practicing in the hospital's emergency department.

Claire was a source of many questions. She asked about some of the other cases he had encountered over the years to which he gave enthusiastic answers.

The rest of the trip was spent in deep conversation. It was becoming increasingly obvious to Paul that they were well on their way to an interesting relationship, be it only for a short time. The seven-hour flight from Brisbane cemented their relationship.

The landing was a copy book effort on behalf of the pilot and before they knew it, they were being herded out of their security and thrust into the transit lounge awaiting the next flight.

The tropical humidity hit them both as they walked out of the aircraft, along with the distinct odour of diesel pollution as a result of millions of cars, badly tuned Jeepnies and busses that possessed the streets of this sprawling metropolis of Manilla, Philippines.

'What time is your flight due for take-off?' Claire warmly asked.

'Umm not sure,' he said, fumbling around his carry bag looking for the boarding information.

Claire smiled, as she looked at his pocket. Her eyes flashed back at the doctor, then pointed to his pocket.

'I think your documents are in your pocket,' she said giggling.

'They are?' He looked down.

'Yes sir-re bob. They sure are.' She giggled again.

'Oh yeah, so they are.'

At that point, she looked up at the departures screen noting that her flight was delayed for two hours.

'Oh, that's too bad,' Paul said, now looking up at the screen, but not making eye contact with her noted flight.

'So, when do you fly out?' she asked again.

'Oh, it's a few hours I think,' he said looking up at the departure screen to confirm his understanding.

'Hey, I might get a cup of coffee. Would you like to join me? she said, distracting his search from the departure's information towering above them.

'Sure.' he said, welcoming any excuse to spend more time with her.

They quickly walked over to a Donut shop. Paul remembered enjoying the donuts while last in Manilla all those years ago. They sat down to their purchase. Claire was amused that the doctor had ordered a half strength coffee.

'Why half strength?' Claire asked mystified.

'Well, I don't enjoy strong coffee.'

'No, strong and black,' she demanded playfully.

Finally, they agreed to disagree.

The time spent with Claire was so enjoyable that the Doctor hardly realised the time.

The magic of the moment was broken by a sudden outburst from Claire.

'What time was your flight.' she suddenly said almost panicked.

'Strike!' he said awaking from his coma of joy.

'I'll go and check … back in a tick,' the doctor said urgently.

Walking to the departures board he was accompanied by a strange sense of sadness that had come over him the instant he walked from their table. Expecting to see his flight indicating a boarding call, he focused on the digital display.

DELAYED.

What is it with these flights on this trip? he thought to himself.

The doctor returned to an expectant young woman and before he could share his good tidings, Claire blurted out her news.

'You know, I have been thinking while you were away,' she said with a strange look.

'Yes?'

'I hope you don't think me too imposing or forward.' Claire was struggling.

'Sure, no problem. What's up?'

'Well, I know this will sound a little odd, but I want to say it and be assured that I have never said such a thing before ... well at least to a person I hardly know.' She paused, thought for a few seconds then continued,

'Actually, I have never said such a thing to anyone,' she confessed.

Claire stopped and stared at her Australian acquaintance.

'Sure, go on,' he encouraged her as he sat down slowly.

'Well ...' she hesitated.

'Claire just say it. I don't think you can shock me.' The doctor laughed.

'Oh, all right ...well here it is...' She took a deep breath.

'I have so enjoyed my time with you,' she said awkwardly.

'I concur. It's been great,' Paul reaffirmed her in her struggle.

'Great,' she said.

'Right, Great ... Um, is that it? If so, that is hardly shocking,' he said laughing.

'I didn't say it would be shocking,' she said firmly.

'Well, I have really enjoyed my time with you also. You have been a real blessing.'

He said looking directly into her eyes.

'Yes, well um thank you, but what I mean to say is that, I mean, I have really loved you.' She stopped cold in her sentence.

'No No ... Oh my Goodness, I meant ...'

Paul couldn't help but laugh at her discomfort.

'What I meant to say was that I really loved talking with you, being with you. You are an amazing person. I am so thankful for my time with you. Thank you for being,' she hesitated, searching for the words. 'For being so ... YOU.'

He smiled politely. 'Well, ME is all I know how to be'.

'Well yes of course ... but I ... well ... I really am feeling so empty at the thought that you have to go and leave me in this state'. She laughed making light of her situation.

'Well, I'm sorry I have had this effect on you,' Paul said with a hit of humour in his voice. 'making you feel empty, that is,' he concluded.

'Oh no you haven't made me feel empty, it's just ...' she stopped again.

'You don't like traveling on your own, do you?' He interrupted her thoughts, noticing her insecurity for the first time and nailing her to the fact.

'Um, no, not really,' she smiled with her reply, relaxing back in her chair.

'That surprises me.'

'Really why?' she questioned abruptly.

'Well, you come across as someone who has got it together,' Paul stopped, realising that what he had just said could be taken the wrong way.

'I mean you are quite a lovely, confident, capable person Claire.'

She stared at the doctor, analysing all of his face.

'In some things, maybe, but I battle a sense of vulnerability at times when I travel, particularly international,' she said. 'It might be because of fatigue, I don't know … and I can be a little clumsy when I am tired, as you saw in Brisbane.' She stopped and looked at his hands. 'Oh, by the way, how's your thumb?' she asked softly.

Paul looked down on cue at the Band-Aid.

'Fine.'

'Oh, that's good. Yes … Now, where was I?' she asked even more awkwardly than before.

'Um something about being empty?'

'Oh yes. 'she said settling herself down.' I hope you don't find this offensive, but this is the first time that I have felt secure … when traveling that is. It's because of you. I'm certain of this. I'm really going to miss you … Is that weird?' she quickly added.

'No.'

'Good because you are the most interesting Aussie I have ever met,' she stopped and half laughed with misty eyes looking up at him. 'I hope I'm not being offensive … please tell me if I am.'

'No offence taken,' he said smiling.

The doctor looked into her blue eyes. The thought suddenly struck him that she had olive skin, brown hair and blue eyes.

'You don't have to worry about being on your own for a little while longer.'

'Why?'

'Because my flight is delayed,' he said, with a smile emerging. 'Go figure.'

'Shut up!' she said with great outburst.

He didn't answer, but quietly watched this intriguing woman set before him.

'Oh, I wish you could come with me,' she said surrendering to her emotions.

'I have had a strange feeling about this trip. Like a deep fear ... Weird.' Claire stared into his face.

'Really?'

'You know ... Oh this will sound strange I know but, I was praying you could come with me, how crazy is that?' she finally confessed. 'I know it sounds crazy, because it is crazy ... This is weird. What's wrong with me?' she laughed.

The doctor watched this woman before him.

'But I feel so safe when I'm with you ... why is that?' she said turning her head to one side as though needing a reprieve from his captivating face, if not just to think.

Paul looked at her. The question suddenly pounded in his heart.

'You were praying?' he asked slowly.

'Yes, indeed I was sir,' she said with newfound authority.

'Really?' His curiosity was growing.

'Well yes, and I make no apologies for that. In fact, I pray all the time,' she said, now with firm conviction. 'You have a problem with that?' she asked with soft tones.

'Oh no. Not at all,' he replied with slight hesitation, for fear that he was going to get a lecture.

'Good.' The young woman smiled.

'Well anyway,' Paul quickly changed the subject, 'regards my traveling with you, I don't think that I could afford to go all the way to the States with you,' he said with a stupid look on his face.

'And why not?' she said in mockery.

'Well after my baptism back on the last flight, going to the States with you might require a change of clothes and I don't have any with me.' He Laughed.

'Oh really,' she said, squinting her eyes at him.

'Well for your information, America is not my first port of call.' Claire reflected a snooty hi society character. 'I have other plans,' she concluded.

They returned to their playful antics.

'Oh, really?' He reflected her sentiment. 'And where might you be heading?'

'Guam,' she answered with her head held high, still playing her game.

There was silence between the two travellers.

'You're kidding, right?'

'Nope.'

'You are going to Guam?' he said mystified.

'Yep ... What? Don't you think I am up to it?' She laughed, tilting her head to one side.

He felt a shot of adrenalin surge throughout his body.

'Well yes, I certainly do think you are up to it and I also think that God has answered your prayer little lady'.

'My prayer?' she said now quite sedated.

'Yes, your prayer about ...'

'You're not going to Guam, are you?' Claire butted in wide eyed.

'That is exactly where I am going,' he explained with an expectation of a great reaction.

'Shut up! No way!' she squealed.

Paul suddenly felt he was dealing with a teenager. He was completely captivated by this person before him. What was it about this female and why was she speaking to him so deeply? He sat there thinking to himself. Why was she getting to him? What was it about her that seemed so familiar? The doctor felt he had known her for ever. Nothing made sense and she was an American. Paul had never been to America. He didn't know the culture. He didn't know her. So, what was it about this woman … this wonderful woman?

A calm demeanour came over her and she sat at their table now staring at her folded hands.

'Oh, my goodness,' she said softly. 'Thankyou Lord,' she said breaking to a whisper.

'What are you doing in Guam?' she asked with near pensive tones.

'Catching another flight,' he began to see where she was going with her questions and he joined her in this zone.

They were looking directly into each other's eyes.

'And you?' he asked.

She nodded and said quietly, 'another flight.'

He could feel himself being deeply drawn to her.

'Where to?'

She continued to look up into his eyes. 'Palau,' she said with hesitation.

'And you?' she said drinking in the moment.

The Doctor sat still, then broke his silence.

'Same,' he said softly.

There was more silence between the two, just two people staring at each other in a most comfortable situation.

'Claire?'

'Yes.'

'You wouldn't be going on a cruise, would you?'

'Yes,' her voice quivered.

He reached over to his carry on, unzipped its first compartment and pulled out the travel documents including a broacher of the Pacific Fair. Paul slid it across the table. Claire looked down for a short time, looked back into his eyes then gathered her documents in silence. She opened the top folder and revealed its contents to the doctor.

They sat there … more silence was shared between them amidst all the congestion of this international airport.

'Claire?'

'Yes?'

'What's happening here?' he asked with emotions running high.

Claire continued to fix her gaze upon him and finally just shook her head. The reality of their situation togethr seemed too deep for her to answer. They sat together in silence for some minutes.

Finally, Claire slowly opened her mouth and said 'Paul, I don't know what's happening, but I do know that nothing happens by mistake. There is a much higher purpose; a work is going on here. A work of the great architect of life and I am more than comfortable to rest in His unfolding's for me.'

The doctor's world stopped, and then he helplessly watched her next move.

She reached over and cupped his hands in hers and bringing them up to her lips, she unashamedly kissed them.

'Paul, forgive my forwardness but, I am speaking of the King of Kings and Lord of Lords, … the Lord Jesus Christ. Where are you with him?'

Where are you with Him? Those words pieced my heart.

I froze. I remember the time as though it were yesterday. She was a committed Christian and I was a runaway. I was laid bare before this person. I was found out. I had just lost any chance with this woman. My confidence before her had been washed away in an instant. I was disqualified.

Suddenly I realised a much deeper reality. I was laid bare before God. I was found out by him but, overwhelmed by His love. This wonderful person was running to me with open arms ... the Most-High God.

I had so many questions, but I had no reason to ask any more. My academic foundations, my objections and all their demands began to melt away. I had just seen the darling of heaven face to face in my heart. He had reached out to me through this simple question, 'Where are you with Him?' Where was I? I was off track, way off track. That's where I was. My God had just touched my life right there in the transit lounge of the city where I saw the dynamic of an amazing God so many years ago. Now He was, using His servant, an authentic American Christian woman in this sprawling, bustling metropolis of Manilla.

My heart melted and I surrendered. I recognised the beauty of Christ again but this time he was shining through this person before me, although I hadn't recognised Him in her. There it was, the fullness of my attraction to her. It was the perfect combination of Claire and Christ.

Claire reached out to hold my hands as she watched a single tear low freely down my face. I went on to explain my story. At certain points of my testimony, I had seen her joy as I poured my heart out and her thrill was obvious, particularly when I described my family.

She listened for quite some time, then after I went silent she said, 'I knew there was something safe, something familiar about you.'

With that there was an announcement that our flight was boarding. We gathered our belongings and walked leisurely to the boarding-dock. Not a word was spoken. I wanted to hold her hand again but dare not. There was too much emotion.

Things were moving too fast for my liking, yet I couldn't help but recognise the feeling of being at home with Claire.

We weren't able to rearrange our seating together and had to sit separated for the entire trip to Guam. This time gave us the opportunity to think and in my case to pray. We were both allocated isle seats and I was seated two rows in front of Claire.

The time went rather quickly. However, we were able to engage in conversation on one occasion as I invited her to go for a walk to the back of the Boeing 737. It was short lived however, as the 'Fasten Seat belts' light came on due to some serious turbulence. We both made it to our seats just in time before the worst of the rough passage came upon the flight.

The rest of our trip was rather uncomfortable due to our bouncing around the sky and by the time we landed most on board were glad to be back on Terra Firma.

We left the aircraft together. It was easy to discern that Claire was as much at home with me as I was with her. Our walk to the 'Arrivals / Departure board was again, in silence.

Our arrival into Guam was late due to the turbulence. We realised, that the flight to Palau was due to board in thirty minutes. As no meals were able to be served on our flight due to the rough weather, we looked for something quick and easy to eat. After only ten minutes of searching we surrendered to the fact that due to the time of day, little was on offer, therefore our hope for sustenance would have to be found on our next flight. With that, we decided to move to our boarding gate trusting that we might be able to get our seats changed, in order to be able to sit together. The counter was already manned with flight attendants and with that Claire began her negotiations.

However, when she addressed the subject, it seemed that our request from our previous flight was noted. Given that we were traveling with the same airline all the way from Australia, they had arranged it for this final leg of our journey. It seemed that Claire was the one who carried the weight of influence because of her VIP status due to her position with the Bank of America and her frequent business trips.

Once our new boarding passes were printed, we were offered entry on to the aircraft.

I felt a little awkward as all the other passengers who were waiting just stared at us, as we boarded first. Frankly I felt as though I had become a pork chop in a synagogue but Claire took it in her stride and competently displayed professional posture. Her delivery and this treatment suited her. I could see she knew how to handle herself in the corporate world and it was a joy to watch her in action.

We settled in well and by the time the other passengers were boarding we were already enjoying a pleasant fruit cocktail along with a tray of lightly salted mixed nuts.

Looking at my watch, I realised that I hadn't adjusted the time piece for local time and between the two of us we estimated that it had to be around twelve midnight Eastern Australian time. I looked at Claire and noted that she looked very tired.

I asked her did she think she could get some sleep on this final leg to which she thought it was unlikely. She said she always has problems sleeping sitting upright. I looked at her and said, 'If you're interested, I might be able to help you.'

She looked at me and said, 'Oh really, and what do you have in mind?'

I advised that when the time is right, I would let her know. I remember she squinted her eyes at me as if she was asking what I was up to, but it was obvious that I had her attention and she was enjoying my antics.

Dinner came as soon as we were flying straight and level. I had the beef and Claire had the chicken. No sooner had we finished our meal, the dishes were collected, blankets were offered and lights were turned off.

At this point Claire asked about my previous proposal, to which I placed a pillow on my lap and opened the blanket. I advised that given the wide seats, she would be able to lie down across the seat, tucking her legs up and placing her head upon the pillow on my lap.

She looked at me, hesitated, and then surrendered her tired head to the welcomed offer. I could feel Claire snuggle in against me. I then adjusted the soft woollen business class blanket around her with my right arm.

At that point, I realised that I had need to put my arm somewhere, so it was logical that it would have to be placed around her and that is what I did. There was no resistance at all from her. In fact, I distinctly remember her moving in closer to me.

She looked up at me and said, 'Thank you, I am so tired.' With that she placed her right hand on my right leg and it seemed she just passed out. I sat there in awe. There, sleeping soundly on my lap was the most wonderful woman I had ever met.

'What was going on?' I thought to myself with a laugh in my breath. I really had no idea what was going on but I knew it was good, in fact I knew it was very good and I knew it was from God. So much had happened since the prayer of my family at the Brisbane airport.

'Come back with a wife' was the demand in jest from my sister. Or was it … in jest? For some time, I just sat there and looked down at this gift sleeping on my lap.

Then suddenly a thunder of words came flooding into my heart with such a force that I felt dangerously weak. 'This is she who I have chosen for thee'.

My heart pounded in my chest. I was literally breathless and yet overwhelmed with joy and terrified at the same time. In the last ninety minutes the great God had turned my life around and now he had just revealed to me who would share my future until the day I die.

CHAPTER ELEVEN

D octor Paul Langley put down his pen. So much had happened all those years ago. He leant back in his chair, placed his hands behind his head and reflected. A series of flights to his vacation destination had changed his life. His thoughts went to the hotel in Palau. He was standing outside her room. He could see her face. He could hear her voice.

'Thank you,' she said with deep intent.

The Doctor pulled his head back a little and raised eyebrows though still facing her now with a fully developed surprised look on his face.

'For what?' he said softly.

'Just thank you,' she said gazing deeply into his eyes.

'You're welcome.' Paul had no idea what she was talking about and he chuckled softly.

'Doctor Langley, forgive me but I have wanted to do this the minute you shared your story with me back there in Manilla,' she said, reaching out and holding his face with both of her hands.

'You are a wonderful man,' she said.

Paul stood there overwhelmed by this rather delightfully forward American woman.

She dropped her hands from his face and quickly kissed him on his left cheek. The doctor's world stopped … again. This time he felt a little more embarrassed. He just stared at her for what seemed to be quite some time.

He took her hands in his them said, 'And you are a wonderful woman,' he said a little awkwardly. 'Goodnight'.

He turned to walk back to his room.

'Do you want to come in for a while?'

He turned to address the request.

'Um just to talk ... you know um ... Oh, nothing else,' she said, now realising how it could have been interpreted.

'No, we all need our rest. It's been a big trip.'

'Oh yes ... of course, sorry,' she said joining the ranks of the embarrassed.

'Don't be!'

'See you at breakfast.'

'OK, first one awake, rings the other ... you know, a wake-up-call,' she smiled.

'Looking forward to it.'

'OK. It's a date,' she said confidently.

'A date!' He replied with a wink.

Her face lit up with the most beautiful smile.

'Night,' she said opening her door, then turning to look back, made eye contact and smiled.

The door closed quickly behind her and he was left to navigate his way back to his room ... alone but feeling very much alive.

Back in his room, Paul took a quick shower. It was a welcome relief to clear his person of aircraft atmosphere that seemed to possess his person. After the brilliance of being peppered with thousands of tiny water bullets as a result of a setting that the doctor found on the showers' tap, he went to take the towel folded on the basin bench only to find that it was not a towel but rather a hand towel. The next minuite or so was taken up with a full search in all the draws only to find two towels that were tucked under the basin towards the back of the cabinet. With Paul's discovery now firmly wrapped around his middle, he decided to get the latest news before retireing for much needed rest. As he waited for the flat screen Sony television to warm up, he looked to the window only to realise that the curtains hadn't been drawn.

To his surprise there was the sun just beginning its prominance for the day. With all their travel, he had completely lost track of time. A smile blessed his face. He shook his head.

He laughed. The doctor looked at the clock at the side of the bed. It was six in the morning.

With that revelation, he picked up the phone and rang the reception desk to inquire as to what time breakfast would begin.

'Six thirty. Thank you.' he said looking at his watch.

He put down the receiver, paused, then, throwing caution to the wind, he rang Claire's room. There was no answer. He was just about to hang up when a rushed voice answered.

'Hello,' a husky and somewhat breathless person responded.

'Um Claire?' he said, suddenly suspecting that he may have rung the wrong number.

'Paul?'

'Yes. Have you checked the time?'

'No, why?'

'It's a bit after six AM.'

'No way!'

'Yep! Care for some breakfast? They're open at six-thirty.'

'Great idea. Give me fifteen minutes to take my shower. See you downstairs. OK?'

'I'll be at your door in fifteen to escort you down stairs mam.'

'Oh, OK. That's even better. Fifteen minutes. See you then. Bye.'

Claire put down the phone without waiting for his response. She remained seated. The young American woman smiled slowly reflecting on this Australian doctor. Suddenly time was of the esence, Claire stood up quickly, made her way to the bathroom, undressed and began her shower. She had never felt so happy.

Paul, neglecting to consider the timeframe given, was found knocking on Claire's door.

After a short delay the door of room *307* partially opened revealing a face only, followed by a giggle.

'Strike, are you still ...'' he said with a smile from ear to ear not wanting to finish the sentence.

'In the shower?.... yes. That was a quick fifteen minutes mister' she said with a broad grin over her face. 'More like five.'

'Really?' the doctor said looking a little mystified.

Claire laughed at this man standing before her.

'Anyway give me ten minutes ... max. In fact I'll meet you down stairs.'

'Down stairs in ten minuets?' he asked incredulously.

'Yes!' she said frankly.

'Oh Really?' he said in teasing disbelief.

'Oh so you don't think I can be ready in ten?

'Nope!'

Claire screwed up her face at Paul.

'In ten, good sir, in ten. Bye.'

With that she closed the door.

A look of delight posessed his face. The doctor walked to the lift, pressed the 'down button'and it opened immediately displaying its contents. A family of four along with copious amounts of luggage stood in his way.. As he squeezed in, he selected the *ground Floor* button, only to realise that he had entered a lift that was going up not down. It was headed for one of the penthouses. Once resigned to his inevitable increase in elevation, his sencses were suddenly accosted by this rather wealthy woman quietly complaining to her husband about their travel arrangements. This was accompanied by their two children who stood beside them complaining about their need to eat. The children were ten and seven years old respectively.

'I can't believe she forced me to wear this in public and then economy class for the entire trip. I feel abused,' the older girl said quietly to her younger sister.

The doctor held back a laugh and adiquately kept his emotions under control.

'Looks OK to me Trace,' the youngest in the family said as she maintained her gaze on the texting she was busily performing. Her phone was the high end model that Paul had considered purchasing some months previously but thought it difficult justifying due to the cost.

'Shut up you little grub,' hissed her older sister.

From his periffial view he watched for a reaction.

'Why don't you do the world a favour. Hold your breath and die,' she wisphered, continueing her gaze at her cell phone screen.

The doctor felt invisible.

It seemed the family hadn't even noticed his entrance or didn't care.

The parents were oblivious to their childrens attitude toward each other ... or didn't care.

'You know we hate economy class. I can't believe you let this happen. I was totally understanding when I found out that we couldn't use the corporate jet. I understood. Wasn't I understanding?' The wife whispered to her fatigued husband.

The man simply nodded in aggreement.

'Did I complain?' she wispered with a little more intent.

He shook his head

'No I didn't complain, but you know what Tracy is like. It was hard enough to get her to wear something reasonable in public but you weren't prepared to fight for our rights as VIP's and how much of that stupid airline do we own? Economy class? We are a large share holder Ronald and we are forced to fly Economy class. And now we are having to take our own luggage to our room. Why weren't they ready for us? Who organised our travel arrangements Ronald? It was that ditsy secretary wasn't it. She screwed up the Davenport's travel arrangements last year, remember? Actually, it doesn't matter who is responsible, you have to deal with it Ronald and Oh by the way, the penthouse better be up to standard. Oh ... yes and another thing, I didn't hear any mention of a butler and did I hear right? The chef doesn't start untill three this afternoon. So what do we do for meals in the meantime? Room service? I think not!! ' she said as her face became flushed with her eyes glaring.

'*I hope the hotel staff put the towels in the bathroom for their sake,*' the doctor thought to himself.

Paul suddendly felt all his senses kick in. He was about to explode with laughter but his sense of humour was quickly distracted when the angry woman of the house cut in again with her attack on this sad example of manhhod at the other side of the lift.

'This is a disaster and now you tell me ... now you have the audasity to tell us that we have to share the yacht with other people. My God Ronald,' the woman said now totally discusted.

'We own the dam thing,' she hissed.

Yacht? the doctor thought to himself. *Surely not,* he dismissed his thinking quickly.

'No, the company owns it, my dear.' the husband broke his silence slightly frustrated.

'Well we own the dam company Ronald and you are the founder, president of the thing, or have you forgotton that,' she spat her whisper to him.

'The board of directors all agreed this asset must now be profitable and I totally agree, which includes, I might add, the three aircraft. You need to understand my dear because of the global downturn we need to adjust. This is a good thing and if we can master this we stand to tripple if not quadrupal our worth in just a few years. Do you have any idea what that means to your life? Do you have any idea what you will be able to do? So master it we will. Your life is about to be completely different very soon,' he softly said maintaining his gaze directly ahead.

'Soon? I can't wait that long and it doesn't help with my humiliation. I am going to be humiliated in front of these.... PEOPLE!.. on OUR yacht, I just know it.

Who are they anyway? Do we know them? Do they have any social standing? This is just horrid Ronald, horrid,' she said and then remained silent all the way to the top of the building.

Paul could see where the girls had received their education.

The man of the house-hold said nothing. He looked straight ahead.

He looked exhausted. He looked defeated. He looked condemmed. All that obvious wealth, his position, his importance, his influence, a very beautiful wife, two attractive children and all, it seemed, rotten to the core, ruiened by selfishness, fueled by pure materialism in its capital form.

Paul watched this family pour out of the lift and walk to the door of their luxurious penthouse.

'If you can't find any towels, just look in the cupboard under the vanity basin,' the doctor called out.

The company of four all spun around and stared at the stranger, speechless, as though he had suddenly appeared. Paul pressed the ground floor button and waved goodbye.

Immediately the lift door slid closed and he was left to himself and his sence of humour.

After a quick burst of laughter, he reflected on the saddest people he had ever seen.

'What does it profit a man if he gains the whole world but loses his soul,' Paul whispered.

The journey to the ground floor wasn't interupted untill the third floor. The door opened and there stood Claire.

'Hey, are you ever a sight for sore eyes,' he said.

She looked at him as though what he said hadn't registered.

'Oh, Hello you,' she said lifting her watch up and showing him the time.

It was six twenty six.

'Six minutes, seven by the time we get down stairs with three minutes to spare' she said with a deep sense of satisfaction accompanied by that giggle of hers.

Her face beemed.

'I stand corrected,' he said enjoying her mindset.

'Indeed you do,' she replied smugly.

Claire's demenor changed.

'Um, how come your coming down and what did you say when I walked into the lift?' she said screwing her face up at Paul and tilting her head to one side with a frown appearing across her brow.

The Doctor laughed.

'Well last question first … I said that you were a sight for sore eyes.'

She looked at him surprised. 'Oh thank you and the answer to my first question?'

'Well, I have just been on a merry adventure … Not!' Paul said shaking his head and rolling his eyes.

She looked at him, paused, then smiled.

'You got into the lift that was going up instead of down, didn't you? she said giggleing and digging him again in his side with her finger. 'Didn't you?'

Paul stared at her, plesently shocked by her seeming firmilarity.

'That's a yes,' she declared.

'You did didn't you? You went up instead of down, didn't you? Yes you did … you did you did you did,' she said in a sing song manner almost dancing in sync with her near musical mockery of the bewildered doctor.

'Yes I did.'

She burst out laughing so hard that her eyes began to water.

'Oh this is precious. I can't believe it.'

'I fail to see what the big deal is,' he clamly demanded. A gentle smile rose over his face.

'Oh yes it is.' Claire paused again, looked to the floor then to her captivated audience.

'You're a doctor,' she began to laugh again.

'Excuse me, a rather sleep deprived, jet lagged doctor,' he defended.

'I can't believe it,' she said now calming down.

'Give a guy a break will ya,' Paul replied laughing.

'No no, you don't understand, my father, a doctor, does the same thing. He gets in a lift and doesn't check if its going up or down ... he just gets in. It drives my Mom to drink,' she said and started to giggle.

'Really.'

'Oh, she doesn't actually drink ... as in alcohol ... She ...' Claire was interrupted.

'Yeah, I get what you mean.'

The lift door suddenly opened. Groundfloor.

'Breakfast, my rather sleep deprived, jet lagged Doctor?'

'Sure, lead on good lady,' he said watching her as she promptly took the lead.

They walked towards the area where breakfast could be seen layed out on a series of tables neatly placed against a decoratively designed wall.

'So tell me all about your family. I am really interested,' Claire asked directly.

This sudden change of subject took the doctor by surprise.

'Well, OK. Um who do you want me to start with?' Paul asked.

'Your Mom,' she said softly looking up at him with an attentive face.

'OK, well, actualy may I start with the fact that you remind me a little of her,' he said settling in to the challenge given.

They arrived at the restaurant reception desk, booked in with their room numbers and were shown to their table even though they were a little early.

'Your mother?' she suddenly asked.

'What about her?' he replied.

'Do I really remind you of your mother?'

'Yep!'

They walked straight to the buffee setting and began to help themselves to an excellent sellection of cooked food.

'Mmm your mother?' she repeated.

'Yep,' he vollied back again.

' Good thing?' she said looking up at him conserned.

'No,' he said shaking his head, stoned faced, ' not good!'

Her expression sombred.

'Oh.' she said a little disappointed if not embarrassed.

'Very good.' Paul said smiling, raising his eyebrows.

Her eyes sparkled as she looked down at the table.

'Well, shall we eat, I'm so hungry. This was a good idea,' she said with face beaming again.

They sat down at their table. Claire bowed her head.

'Thank you Lord for this food and thankyou for the one who had the idea of breakfast.' She looked up at the doctor. Her deep blue eyes were looking into his very soul.

'Amen,' he said softly.

'Oh this is good,' she confirmed as she began to eat.

Their attention to breakfast was broken by a waitress offering freshly brewed coffee.

Paul watched as Claire's cup was poured first followed by his own. When it had reached the half full mark, he asked for the remainder to be filled with hot water. The waitress was quick to comply, to which he added full cream milk. Claire just shook her head.

'Why do you bother. Drink it the way it it surposed to be … strong and black,' she laughed.

'I like it half strength and white ... remember?.' he said defiantly.

'Oh yes of course.'

'Now' what about your family?' Claire said lifting her cup up to her lips and taking a sip of her strong black beverage.

'Well my father is a ... ' His words were cut off.

'Mm, can we start with your Mom. Lets leave your Dad til last. .. No offence!'

'None taken.'

'From what you have implied previously, your Mom, she sounds wonderful, if I do say so myself,' she said with that interesting little giggle that seemed so at home with her character.

The conversation over breakfast lasted for two hours. The doctor covered every thing he thought was relivent about his family and then answered a plethora of questions.

Finally claire was silent.

'A penny for your thoughts?'

'Mm probably not,' she said. 'I was talking to God,' Claire continued.

'Well that's a good thing.'

'Oh yes,' she slowly released.

'You know, I have to say that I feel I know your family quite well now and thank you by the way ... That was so interesting,' she seemed to drift away.

Her tones changed.

'Isn't that strange? I know this is a stretch ... I mean you need a relationship to get to know people, but this is special and I don't know why,' she said looking at this new man in her life. 'I don't mean to sound forward again but, I feel I know them ... you know, you are very descriptive when you talk Paul. You tell a story very well. That's a gift,' she continued.

' I would love you to meet them,' Paul said.

'You would?'

'Yes I would.'

'Paul, part of me wants to meet your family so much and another part of me says I have to wait,' she whispered staring down at her plate now servicing nothing but some bacon rhind and a discarded corner of toast surplus to requirements.

'Is that what your conversation with God was all about?

'Mm partly,' she said looking at him. 'Hey I'm sorry, getting too heavy, but I can't wait to meet them.'

'Um, by the way, if it helps, they would be more than happy to meet you. You would fit right in.'

'Really? How so?' she asked with intense interest.

'Well particularly with the women in the family'.

'And not your Dad?'

The Doctor laughed. 'Don't worry about Dad, he will see what I see.'

She smiled.

'OK good, but why the distinction between the two sexes?'

'Well ...' He poised himself as though he was about to expound a deep revelation.

'Well ... You are just as big a ratbag as they are. Particularly my sister.'

'I have to admit, she does sound like a lot of fun,' she replied.

The doctor glanced down at his watch.

'Hey, look at the time!'

'Wow! It's eight thirty. Sleep is in order I think,' Claire giggled softly as she stood up from the table.

The couple continued to talk about each others family as they made their way to the lift. Paul suggested that they walk up the stairs to the third floor for some exercise. Further conversation continued as they journied to Claire's room. She slid her plastic key card into the slot on her door, there was a click and with one simple movement Claire was half way in the door. She simply turned to this interesting man. 'You know, I think I'll sleep most of the day away,' he said as he suddenly yawned descretely.

'Wow, don't do that. That's just too catchy,' she smiled tenderly.

'Hey, what's say we meet for dinner say ... six thirty tonight?' he asked.

'Great! It's a date.'

'Is it?' Paul said softly his eyes were scanning her face waiting for that answer.

'Would you like it to be?'

'Yes ... yes I would,' he replied quickly. Paul noticed the softest look he had ever seen on a woman.

'Me too.'

'Well then Claire, would you do me the honour of accompany me tonight on our first date ... for dinner , I'll pick you up say six thirty?'

'Six thirty would be perfect,' she said standing on her tip toes looking into his eyes whilst holding on to the door for support.

'Then six thirty it is,' he confirmed and with that they parted.

Paul walked to his room feeling the strangest joy. His thoughts were running wild in his head. This was going too fast for him, but dispite this, he was finding it difficult to make any effort to slowing it down at this point.

The conversation with Claire at breakfast placed an astounding sense of appreciation for his family but, at the same time a strange sence of loss. It was the latter that convinced him to ring them. Paul new that his father would leave home around nine twenty to be at the church at nine forty, so he should catch them. The thought of being able to tell his parents about Claire was a real draw card. He picked up his cell phone and rang home. The phone rang longer than expected, then:

'Hello?'

'Hey Squirt, It's me, Paul.'

'Hey Big Fella, how ya going?'

'Good! Tired but good. Hey, it is so good to hear your voice little sister.'.

'Yeah, you too um, what's with the little sister thing? Everything OK?' she asked.

'Oh yeah everything is wonderful, nothing wrong, just wanted to say I arrived safe and sound. I know Mom was a bit concerned when I left you guys at the airport.'

'Yeah, she was, but you know what she's like. Her spirits picked of on the way back home though. By the time we got home she was her usual fun loving self. Anyway ... so everything is wonderful?'

'Oh yes,' he assured her, 'never better.'

'Not jetlagged?' she asked.

'I have hardly slept the entire trip. The trip from hell, rough as guts most of the way from Manila.'

'Really?...You've hardly slept on the flights from hell and everything is wonderfull.'

'Um yeah.' The Doctor laughed under his breath

'Boy you really do need a holiday.'

'Yep.'

'Are you sure someone wasn't smoking that herb on the plane?' Lynn asked.

'Oh ha ha.'

'Paul, what's going on ... somethings going down. What? Tell me,' his sister said now concerned.

'Well, um.'

'I knew it ... yes?'

'Well, I have met this girl.'

'No way,' Lynn screamed.

'Yes way.'

'Tell me, tell me... how old , what does she do, where's she from.' She began to babble.

'Hang on old girl ... one question at a time. OK, first, she's from the States, but working in Sydney'.

'The States?'

'Yep.'

'As in the good old US of A, type States.'

'Yes as in America.'

'There's a problem already.'

'What?'

'Well they don't like Vegimite ...'

'What?'

'The Americans don't like Vegemite,' she said, 'and you are an addict.

'Rubbish.'

'What's the rubbish refering to , The Americans or your addiction.'

'The latter.'

'Yes you are,' she said insistantly.

'Oh garbage,' Paul said more interested in talking about Claire than vegemite.

'Oh really, I bet you have got it with you in your bag ...'

'What?' he asked incredously.

'Come on ... come on fess up!'

'Hey do you want me to answer your questions or not?'

'Doctor, that sounded like a yes to me. Has she tried it?' she said laughing.

'Has she tried what?' Paul said now slightly annoyed.

'Vegimite!'

'I don't know, probably... who cares.' The doctor was now a little frustrated.

'Tell her I said she has to try it ... Her reaction will show you what she's made of ... it's a good test,' Lynn said laughing.

'Hello, I said do you want me to answer your questions?' he repeated, ignoring her point.

'I thought the bit about Vegimite might qualify as a question,' she said giggling.

'Forget the vegimite! Do you want to hear about Claire or not?'

'Oooo Claire be her name hey?'

'Yes Claire be her n.... um..is her name,' Paul said quickly realising his accendental mimickery of her mockery.

'Will you stop that?' he said a little firmer.

'Sorry ... it is good to hear your voice again Paul ... please continue ... you have my undivided attention ... but I am concerned about the Vegimite,'she said now giggling.

'You need medication ... anyway she has a PHD in economics a masters in education or is it around the other way and..'

'How old?' she asked cutting him off.

'Well, she's twenty one ...'

'What?? She's a baby!' Lynn yelled.

'Nearly twenty two.' He re-enforced.

'Still a baby ...That's twelve years difference.'

'Not quite,' Paul insisted.

'Well close enough,' she softly laughed.

'Well she is very mature for her age and she reminds me a bit of you and Mom.'

'Ooo she sounds wonderful,' Lynn said.

'I think so.'

'But Paul, is she a Christian?'

'Actually she is very committed.'

'Mm ...Well then, she's irresistable,' Lynn said softly.

'She certainly is,' Paul said again, getting a little emotional.

'Ooooo listen to you good doctor,' the sibling replied, now becoming a little too condescending for his likeing.

'Does she feel the same way?'

'I think so.'

'You think so?' she said laughing.

'Well no actually, I am sure.'

'When are we going to meet her?'

Paul gave his sister all the information, including their schedule, Claire's plans back in the States and concluded with a possible date for the meeting.

'Paul, you need to be careful. Three weeks together on a yacht ... you know?'

'Sure. I intend to keep it steady.'

'Yes indeed ... anyway she sounds lovely Paul ... wow.'

'Yes she is Lynn, but I think prayer might be in order.'

'Prayer? Sure ... of course ... you have it. Hey Paul? ... how's your faith going? ... with all this in mind ... I mean, you said she's a very committed Christian woman ... you know what I mean?'

'OK ... you got ten minutes?'

'Good sir, I've got all day for this,' she chuckled softly.

Paul began to share his story in Manila ... every thought, every emotion and everything that Claire had said to him at that International Airport. Paul's sister was joyous and he was sure, that during the course of his testomony he had heard her crying softly on the phone.

'You OK if I share this with Mom and Dad?'

'Yep, absolutely.' the doctor said laughing given her recent conversation about her son's biological clock.

'Anyway, I better hang up and get some sleep.'

'Yeah, of course. You rest well,' Lynn said lovingly. 'Hey big fella, I won't stop praying untill you come home to us raised up on wings of eagles ... you know, safe and sound ... All of you.'

There was an unsettling quiver in her voice at that point. Paul thanked his sister, they said their goodbyes then, he hung up the phone, feeling confirmed, feeling at peace.

CHAPTER TWELVE

⁓

T he phone rang.

Paul sat up in bed. A momentary state of shock greeted his travel weary body.

He reached over, made clumsy contact with the sonic intruder and answered.

'Hello,' he said with a husky voice.

'Wow! Listen to YOU, sunshine,' the American voice on the other end of the line offered bright salutations.

'Hey, how ya doing … Claire?' Paul answered with his mind battling with the sudden reality confronting him. 'Um, it is Claire, isn't it?'

'Sure is, sleepy head, are you OK?'

'Mm yeah, a bit wacked in the head, but OK. Why?' he said still trying to bring balance back to his cognitive processing.

'I was getting worried.'

Paul laughed under his breath. 'You think I'm going to stand you up on our first date. Oh, ye of little faith,' he said trying to bring a little humour into his foggy situation. The Doctor sat himself up in bed whilst organizing the pillows for comfort sake.

'Oh, the thought had in fact crossed my mind,' she said now playing with him, 'and what about our date?' she continued.

'Yep. All good. I'll meet you downstairs at six thirty. I think that was the proposed time.' He rubbed his eyes.

'Mm really?' she asked laughing softly.

'Yeah Why?' he said now with a serious tone.

'Well just a small detail … that was last night. We were going to meet at six thirty… last night?' she said laughing.

There was silence on the line.

'Sorry. I don't understand.' he said with his head now spinning as he began passing his left hand through his ruffled hair.

'Good morning sunshine it's six AM … the next day,' Claire said, 'fancy some breakfast?'

Paul looked across at the bedside clock to read its' bright red message.

'Six o'clock … in the morning? I've slept … twenty hours or so?'

There was further silence on the phone.

'Strike! I'm so sorry,' he said trying to make sense of his recent comatose state.

'Don't be.' Claire said 'as long as you are OK. I was getting a little worried.'

'I can't believe I slept that long,' Paul said humbly.

'Well you wouldn't have gotten much sleep in the last twenty-four hours prior to your … sleep. I slept quite a few hours if you remember?' she said, 'a good effort I would say on your behalf,' she said laughing.

Paul took on board her logic but there was something else. He had known many a long shift in the hospital, never had he experienced such aftereffects that would cause him to have slept that long.

'You should have rung me. I would have woken up,' the Doctor said now looking for more information.

'Oh, my goodness,' Claire replied laughing. 'I did that ... and more.'

'You did?' Paul said now feeling rather vulnerable.

'Oh yes I did! I rang twice over a period of an hour or so. That would have been between ... maybe seven and eight thirty last night, I guess. Then I was getting worried, so I spoke to management and they rang the room and then we came into your room to check.'

'You did what?'

'We knocked first and called out to you before we entered,' she said laughing.

'You came into my room?'

'Well yes. I needed to know that you were OK Paul. I am so sorry, but I was worried and besides I was with the manager,' Claire said now defensively, 'actually, I didn't know what else to do. You might have been sick,' she said caringly, 'and management said I did the right thing ... you know letting them know.'

'Yes of course,' Paul's reply was soft and thoughtful.

'We saw that you were fine, and we just left you to it. Maybe we should have woken you, but I thought ... hey you were sleeping like a baby and obviously OK so, yeah, thought you must have needed your rest,' Claire explained a little awkwardly, trying to pay careful attention to detail.

'Yes, I see. Under the circumstances you did well. I'm so sorry that I caused you such anxiety,' he replied, slowly 'I can't believe I slept that long,' he said now perplexed. 'Odd.'

'Well you did and no, don't be sorry, and by no means odd. I was just so relieved that you were fine. I just hope you're not secretively offended by my intrusion into your personal space.'

'No, not at all and no offence taken. In fact, thank you for your concern,' Paul replied in a professional tone.

Claire heard that tonal direction and began to doubt her actions.

'I could have stood outside your room and let the manager check on you, but ... I just ... I just wanted to see for myself ... you know, that you were OK. I am so sorry Paul. My intentions were ... You were all covered up, quite decent and looking a picture,' she said with a giggle.

'Mm, well that's comforting,' he said releasing his dry humour into the equation.

'So ... interested in my invitation for breakfast, or would you like to keep your distance given these new developments?' she asked now presenting a little more professional posture to match his.

'Absolutely,' he said softly.

'Absolutely that you would like to keep your distance or absolutely that you would like to have breakfast ... Um ... with ... with me?'

'Absolutely ... breakfast with you would be an honour, especially with these *new* developments in mind,' he said deliberately.

'Awesome, will I meet you downstairs in ... ten?' Claire's relief came with a rush.

'Um can we make it twenty? ... I don't have your gift,' he replied laughing under his breath.

'Twenty it is,' she said excitedly, 'I'm so relieved, that you're awake ... and OK.

See you in twenty. Bye.'

Paul sat quietly on the bed resting on the pillows packed up against the bedhead ... thinking. He then slowly placed the receiver on its mount and shook his head in disbelief.

CHAPTER THIRTEEN

⁂

After breakfast, the morning was spent checking emails and then a swim just prior to lunch. The two travellers were sitting at the edge of the hotels perfect pool with their legs dangling in the water. 'Excuse me Mr Langley?' A hotel employee approached them.

'Yes.'

'I do apologise for this interruption but, you are required at the desk.' He pointed toward the lobby.

'And would you be Claire ...?' He was immediately cut-off by the young American woman.

'Yes, is there a problem?'

'I really couldn't tell you. They would like to speak with you.' The lobby boy promptly excused himself with a broad smile across his face and left their side.

'Wonder what's up?' Paul said as he smartly sprang to a stand, quickly followed by Claire. They took their towels that were carelessly thrown across the adjacent pool-side chairs and wrapped the soft white material around themselves.

'Hope everything is OK.' Claire said softly as they made their way to the place of business.

Once at the desk Paul took charge with Claire standing at his side.

'Hi, Paul Langley and Claire…'

'Oh, Mr Langley, thank you for coming so quickly.' she said looking across at Claire, 'We didn't know where you were,' she said rustling through a collection files in front of her.

'Is there a problem?' Claire asked.

'We were advised an hour ago that there has been a mix up with your booking for the Pacific Fair. The ship is scheduled to leave at 2pm this afternoon. It seems that your arrangements from Australia had the ship leaving tomorrow. Now, we have a shuttle bus ready for you. It is only a fifteen-minute drive away, so you won't be late.' The young lady revealed the news as she continued the process of printing documents ready for the couples check out.

'But we have paid for another night here.' Paul exclaimed.

'Oh yes, we have credited you both for tonight and have changed your booking here for your return. You will need that extra night as the Pacific Fair arrives a day earlier. We have rooms available for you both so that will work out well,' she quickly included.

'OK.' Paul said somewhat bewildered.

'Oh, thank you so much.' Claire reached across the counter and touched the hand of the young attendant at the desk. 'We really appreciate your efforts.'

'Oh, you are most welcome Miss Chandler, but you will need to hurry. I will have all the documents ready for check out when you come back down. Please come straight back to me after you have packed.'

'We'll be back in ten minutes,' Paul said.

They quickly turned and moved towards the lift.

'Ten minutes hey?' Claire said looking at Paul with a challenging face.

'I'll race ya,' he said with a twinkle in his eye.

'You have no chance boy,' Claire mocked.

Paul threw his head and laughed to with Claire joined with her characteristic giggle.

They waited at the door of the lift.

'You know what's good about being here... on the ground floor that is?'

'Mm what?'

'You can't get on the wrong lift... it's only going the way you want ... up,' she said with face brimming.

Paul answered with his face screwed up slightly at her. Paul continued his response with a half laugh then said: 'Chandler.'

'And?' Claire quickly replied to his strange return.

'Your surname is Chandler.'

'You didn't know that Chandler was my surname?' she asked incredulously.

'No, you never told me your surname,' he said defensively.

'I didn't?'

'No...' He said looking her straight in her blue eyes.

'Doctor Claire Chandler ... I like it. Are you ever addressed by the title of doctor?'

'Not so much.'

Paul continued to look at her ... studying her intently.

'Where did you get your blue eyes?' he asked, lingering his gaze.

'Umm, dah! My parents.'

The doctor laughed softly, but continued his stance demanding a civil answer. Claire quickly took his cue.

'My grandparents on my fathers' side were from Germany. Blue eyed blonds, both of them.'

'And the olive skin?' he asked now summing up the total package standing before him.

Her hair was a light brown colour with natural blond streaks and her eyebrows were a darker brown.

'Well, my father is blessed with olive skin but the real culprit we think, is my mother,' Claire said watching for Pauls response.

'Really? Spanish?'

She looked at this genuine man standing in front of him.

'Oh probably, there's quite a mixture on Mom's side,' she replied, readying herself for her next point.

Paul smiled whilst maintaining his stare at her face.

'But, no, the olive skin comes from the Sioux Indian on Mom's side,' she said, now waiting for him.

'Really?' The doctors' face blossomed with excited interest.

'Yes, really.' Claire moved her head back just a little in surprise to his sudden reaction.

'That's awesome!' Paul continued, 'do you know much of the background? How far back? Wow that's amazing! Do you have any photographs?' The doctor's rattled response set Claire back a little more.

'Actually, I do to all of the above,' she said now eager to share.

The lift door burst opened with its usual sonic herald, to which the two took its cue and filed in. With a speedy selection of the third-floor button, the conversation continued.

'The line comes from my grandmother's side. It seems that my great, great, grandfather, Charles Alexander Eastman was in fact a Sioux Indian. His indigenous name was Ohiyesia. or maybe, *Ohiyesus* or something like that. Apparently, his name meant, *the Winner* in the local language. In fact, he was a winner indeed, because he ended up a Santee Dakota physician and author,' Claire said displaying much pride.

'Really? A doctor.' Paul announced with interest.

'Yes sir,' a prompt reply was offered by Claire.

'As I understand it he was born in the late eighteen fifties somewhere around the Redwood Falls area, Minnesota.' Claire was interrupted by the lift door opening at their floor.

'Redwood falls, where's that?' Paul asked as they made their way out of the lift.

'Um, Redwood Falls? ... Um it's a city in Redwood and Renville Counties in the state of Minnesota. Anyway, his father name was *Many Lightning's*, How cool's that?' Claire said as she stood at the door of her room.

'Very cool.' Paul laughed.

Claire was now well focused and continued.

'His mother was the half-blood daughter of a well-known army officer.'

'Really? Who was he?' Paul continued his interest.

'You know, I have absolutely no idea,' she replied. 'Mom has the details and from what I understand his mother died soon after she gave birth to him and he was reared by his grandmother and an uncle, I think. It's all a bit fuzzy as far as accurate information is concerned, but we think they fled after the Minnesota massacre in 1862 with the boy into Canada. From what we can understand he lived the life of a wild Indian until he was about 15 years of age or so. It seems his father ...' Claire was interrupted again by Paul.

'The lightning bloke ... what was his name?'

'Many Lightning's' Claire said looking up at Paul just to check that he wasn't being funny.

'Ah yes, Many Lightning's' ... interesting name that one. I wonder why they called him that?'

'Oh, I don't know,' she said thoughtfully 'maybe he was born in a thunderstorm or something ... anyway, his father, who in the meantime had become a Christian and civilization, sought him out and brought him home to Flandreau, South Dakota., where a few Sioux families had transitioned to farming. My great, great, grandfather, Ohiyesa was placed in the mission school at Santee, Nebraska. He was a very bright student and eventually went on to become a medical doctor. He worked with the US government on Indian matters and was very well respected in his field.' Claire looked at Paul waiting for a response.

'Wow, and hence your olive skin'.

'Yes sir.'

'Most interesting'. He looked down at his watch. 'Well we had better get moving'.

'Meet you downstairs... in ten,' she said with a sparkle in her eyes.

'As said downstairs, I'll race you,' he said with a smile on his face.

'You're on boy.' With that she opened the door and closed it without looking back to Paul.

Paul was first out of his room and felt confident that he had won, when at the point of passing Claire's room, her door opened.

'OK it's a draw.' Paul explained between his muffled laughter.

Claire looked at Paul with surprise then joined in the merriment and they journeyed together to the lobby.

With all the necessary paperwork completed they found themselves on the shuttle bus and venturing towards their five-star floating adventure.

CHAPTER FOURTEEN

L ord we thank you for your goodness to us. We give you thanks for this food set before us. Bless it to us we pray in your service and Father, we ask your protection on Paul. May he know your journeying mercies, your hand of purpose in his life and may he rest in you during his time away. We ask these things in Jesus name, Amen.' The head of the household looked up gazing at the two women seated at the table with him.

'Well doesn't this look good?' he said with great expectation of a delicious lunch of baked lamb.

'Hey, I forgot to tell you.' An interruption from the opposite side of the table commanded attention.

'Paul rang this morning, just after you left for church,' Lynn said with excited eyes dashing between her parents.

The two older adults suddenly focused on their daughter's face as she readied herself to release further news.

'Is everything … all right?' Lynn's mother asked with concern.

'Oh, he's fine,' Lynn said, displaying an expression of *I know something that you don't* darting around her attractive face.

'He rang to say that he had made it to Palau,' she said still with that look commanding attention.

'Well that's very thoughtful of him,' Lynn's mother said looking at her husband searching for a cue of some sort.

'Yes, it is. But he's OK?' The man of the household inquired as he began to slice hearty servings from the meat set before him.

'Oh yes, he's doing just fine,' Lynn said nearly bursting with the need to confess the news.

'Lynnette Langley, what's with that look?' The lady of the household said now responding to her daughter's almost smug countenance. 'What's going on?' she said with an interested look, laced with a hit of a smile.

'Well, he has met a young lady on the flight and, she sounds ... wonderful!' Lynn released the news with a burst of enthusiasm.

'OK, and why does she sound wonderful Lynn?' the Rev Langley inquired calmly.

Lynn went on to inform her parents all that Paul had told her. The two were captivated by the news and by their daughter's impressions.

After their daughter's detailed exposition, her father looked around the table.

'Well she does sound interesting indeed. Mom and, I have always thought the Paul would be an *outside the square* type of person and this is certainly in keeping with his character I feel.' He said laughing. 'But I am more encouraged that he seems to have come to grips with his relationship with God. He's been concerning me a bit lately. From what you say Lynn, this young lady, Claire?' He questioned Lynn. She nodded confirmation. 'Yes, this Claire has played a part in Pauls change of heart?' The head of the table continued.

'That seems to be the case Dad,' she said briefly, waiting on her fathers' impressions.

'Mm, well that is interesting,' he said thoughtfully.

'Let's see what the Lord does here,' the Pastor said now focusing on his duties as carver of the meat. 'Yes, very interesting.'

An air of confidence had come upon him, if not a lighter countenance and, it showed.

'What are you thinking Mom?' Lynn noticed her mothers' posture.

'Oh, I don't know,' she said. 'Maybe it's just a mother's concern'.

'Mom, I think Claire not only sounds wonderful but in fact is wonderful. There is something right about this and I haven't even met her... how crazy is that? I haven't heard him sound like that since ... oh, I don't know ... maybe when he came back from the Philippines, all those years ago,' she said slowly reflecting. 'Remember that Mom? Yes, I think there's something going on and it's good.'

'Oh, I agree she does sound lovely. Mind you, its early days for goodness sake,' the lady of the house said laughing.

'True,' the Pastor said thoughtfully.

'However, I just can't help worrying ... for some reason.' Lynn's mother shrugged it off and, suggested they start eating before lunch got cold.

'Well may I suggest that we all leave them in God's hands? He'll keep them both safe. In that I am confident.' The man spoke and the women all agreed.

'Mom, I do think this is a little exciting though, don't you?' he said reaching under the table and squeezing his wife's leg.

Lynn noticed her father's movements.

A surprised yet delighted appearance suddenly came across the woman he loved.

'Ooo Dad!' Lynn said with mischievous intent. 'I saw that. Would you like me to leave the room?'

'Oh, stop it girl,' her mother said enjoying the Moment.

Pastor Langley laughed with great gusto and the rest around the table took his cue and joined in.

CHAPTER FIFTEEN

———— ⧆ ————

The warm sea breeze rushed through their hair as they stood on the deck watching the sun slide beyond the tropical horizon. The golden light washed its' influence across the glassy water, as the Pacific Fair cut clean through the water's resistance, keeping its' course true for this fair-weather adventure.

Paul watched as the afternoon's sienna light bathed its' radiance over Claire. She was dressed in a one-piece dark blue bathing suit with a loose fitting unbuttoned shirt draped over her and a pair of board shorts. On her feet, where a pair of brown leather sandals. The two, along with some of the guests had just enjoyed an experience of a lifetime. The ship had anchored off a coral atoll where they snorkelled around some of the most beautiful coral Paul had ever seen.

Claire looked at the horizon and breathed in deeply the pungent salty air.

'Oh, my goodness,' she exclaimed softly as the wind caressed its way around her face. 'Look at this!'

Paul scanned the watery sight set before him and turned back to her.

'Stunning,' he said smiling, making reference to her, but playing also on the spectacle of the beautiful sunset being painted before their very eyes.

He was more captivated by the miracle of the beauty standing next to him than he was by God's momentary handy work in the heavens.

They stood together for some time and said nothing, enjoying this open solitude, a solitude, that began to make its home in their hearts, a solitude that was binding them together while surrounded by this mass of water.

'Isn't this perfect?' Claire said, turning to look up at this man who was quickly winning her favour.

The dinner gong suddenly broke the magic with its' intrusive clang.

The couple walked together toward the tables covered with the evenings offering of gourmet delights. Four tables were set apart presenting a full array of tropical fruits, a table offering fresh reef fish cooked various ways, a presentation of side salads a plenty and another table with a selection of fresh nuts, chees trays, crackers, and homemade breads. All drinks from fresh fruit juices, a selection of beer, a generous offer of wines, and all free of charge. Such a smorgasbord was more than adequate to feed the twenty adult guests and two minors.

The guests clamoured around the tables, helping themselves to the night's feast. Paul noticed the woman who he saw in the lift back in the hotel. She was talking to the head waiter who stood aside from the tourist's ready to attend to any needs that may arise. Tonight, she appeared to have had a much better disposition than the previous time Paul had seen her in action and stood with purpose pointing to the different tables of food as though she was giving him instructions.

After her authority was displayed, the gentleman in charge of the evening nodded his head and politely repeated her instructions to him, to which she gestured her approval by smiling and saying thank you. After which, she then returned to their luxury VIP room. It wasn't long before a generous selection of the night's delicious offering was on its way to the executives' apartment.

That couple were hardly seen on deck for the remainder of the trip, however, their children seemed to be able to do whatever and go wherever they liked. The minors on board were treated with a little contempt by the other guests, due to the children's lack of respect paid to any adult.

Paul and Claire kept to themselves that night as they ate modestly; in stark contrast to the other guests, who seemed to be well acquainted with such occasions and made no small effort to consume as much as possible. The alcohol was flowing freely, and it wasn't long before inhibitions were cast aside and the real people were released from their masters' control.

The two traveling from Australia carefully retreated from the group and made their way to the open deck where they were greeted to a sparkling display of cosmic brilliance.

'Oh, look what God has done for us tonight,' Claire said as she gazed heavenward.

The sun had set, leaving the darkness to feature billions of stars flung across the universe.

'Yep that's some spectacle,' Paul said quietly as he joined Claire in her gaze at the heavens splendour.

'That lot don't know what they're missing,' he said slowly gesturing towards the other tourists.

A burst of laughter chorused its way from the partying guests in the top deck. Music was now being piped into the room where dinner had been offered and voices were getting louder.

Paul placed his arm around Claire's shoulder and directed her away from the encroaching volume to the bow of the ship where a sonic reprieve was found.

She accepted his encompassing arm and his proposed direction.

'Would they really recognise what we are seeing if they saw this?' Paul continued, as they walked to the bow still looking up to the divine story board in the sky.

'You mean Gods' glory?'

'Yes ... Isn't it written, 'The heavens declare the glory of God?' he said.

'I believe it does.'

'Will you look at this?' he said softly, waving his stretched-out hand across the expanse set before them.

'How could anyone say there isn't a God after seeing this.' Claire posed her question as she breathed in deeply.

She looked back at the developing party. 'How sad ... How really sad they seem,' Clair said now looking at Paul. 'Have you noticed that?'

'It's interesting. You know that family with the kids? ... They are pretty wealthy, but they're not happy ... as far as I'm concerned, they seem miserable. Money sure doesn't make you happy.'

'No, it does not, and I think most of the guests are pretty wealthy also and from what I heard tonight, those hockey players have come from well to do families,' Claire said continuing her gaze at the small crowd now starting to pair off to commence a night of dancing and frivolities.

'How do you know they're hockey players?'

'I heard them talking. They're a top national team and celebrating their winning of the grand finals or something. It appears that eight members of their team couldn't come for some reason.'

'Wow that's a bummer.'

Claire glanced at Paul and laughed. 'Well yes I guess it would be'.

'They certainly don't seem to be upset tonight about their teammate's demise.' Paul looked back at the young women dancing wildly in the ships large lounge.

The moon had made its' presence known with a brilliant white light that spread its wonder across the shimmering glassy ocean. The two talked for some time under the stars.

Paul noticed that Claire had begun to wrap her arms around herself, rubbing her arms slowly.

'Are you cold?'

'Actually, yes I am a little. You know, I might turn in for the night. What time is it?'

'Um ... 'Paul looked down at his watch. 'wow! It's nine PM,' he said in disbelief.

They slowly proceeded to walk to their respective rooms. Passing through the lounge, the party was in full swing and Paul stopped at the table where tropical fruit was laid out.

'Hey, do you want to take some fruit down to your room? Might come in handy for a midnight snack,' the doctor said smiling.

'No, I'm fine, but you go ahead.'

'OK sleep well.'

'Goodnight!'

Paul looked around at the fruit on display and spotted some freshly cut watermelon.

He took two pieces and placed them neatly on a plate.

'Can I help you with anything sir?' The waiter had approached him from behind.

'Oh,' Paul exclaimed with surprise. 'Um, no I'm fine thank you.'

'Let me know what you would like sir and I'll have it sent down to your room. Your wife isn't in need of anything sir?'

'Ah, no she's fine thanks ...' Paul suddenly cut of his sentence realising what the waiter had just said.

'Oh, Um, no, no she's not my wife.' Paul spluttered out his need to clarify feeling slightly foolish.

'Oh, of course, I do apologise, and I understand sir,' he said taking liberty with interpretation.

'And might I say sir, if you or your partner are in need of anything, we are here to serve and to make your stay with us a wonderful experience.'

'No, we're not together, just met forty-eight hours or so ago,' Paul said, now really feeling rather odd.

The waiter laughed. 'Oh my, now I really do apologised sir. I see I have put you to some discomfort, I hope you can forgive me,' he said now rather embarrassed.

'Forgiveness not necessary,' Paul said, 'all good.'

'Thankyou sir, but I must say you had me fooled.'

'I did?'

'You did.'

The waiter looked at him inquiringly.

'Is it that obvious?' Paul said leaning across to the waiters' ear.

'Yes sir, just a little,' he said nodding his head and leaning across to mimic.

'And might I say I think there may be similar persuasions from the young lady's perspective as well,' he said with a large smile.

'You do?'

'I do,' he said with quiet authority.

They spoke further on the subject of Claire for a few more minutes, then Paul bid the waiter goodnight.

'You're not staying for dessert?' the man in waiting asked.

'No, I think I'll hit the sack.'

'Pity, it's such a beautiful dessert on such a beautiful night. Chefs' speciality, trifle,' he said with a tempting look on his face.

'No, I think I'll pass, but it is a beautiful night. Is it always like this?' Paul asked.

'No sir, quite the opposite for this time of the year. Normally we way anchor for the night, but there is some less than pleasant weather possibly on the way and the captain wants to get to the primary holiday areas as quickly as possible. There's very safe anchorage in that area as well.'

'Really? What sort of weather? You not talking a typhoon, are you?' Paul asked with a perplexed frown across his forbid.

'Oh, it's very unlikely it will reach here.'

'So, there is a typhoon in the area?' Paul asked

'Oh well, it's around the northern part of Luzon in the Philippines. It will take a month of Sundays to get here, if it comes this way.

In fact, last report, said that it was likely to cut across the northern part of the Philippines and move towards the south China sea, which is the other side of the Philippines.

We are fine sir, but it could make the seas a lot rougher. It's a big one and its influence might make things a little uncomfortable for the guests. There's nothing to be concerned about sir.'

The waiter said with most comforting tones. 'Our Captain and his staff are some of the best in the world.'

'Really?'

'Oh yes sir.'

Reassured, Paul made his way to his five-star room. He opened the door to be greeted by a bottle of champagne packed with ice in a container that looked like it was made of gold.

His king size bed had been turned down revealing sleek satin sheets, with complimentary chocolates placed on his pillow. The air conditioner had been set to 25 degrees which made for perfect sleeping in this tropical humidity. He could hear a slight hum which he concluded must have been the sound of the engines dutifully turning the shafts propellers, thrusting this magnificent ship through the water's liquid blackness.

His suitcase was placed on a stand made of mahogany situated next to a large, clothes cupboard. He moved towards the bathroom, opened the door and set before his eyes was the most luxurious ablutions area he had ever seen. The shower drew him like steel to a magnet.

It was walled off by an inch think sheet of hardened glass, that reached the ceiling. Drawn to the invitation, he dropped his clothes to the floor, opened the glass shower door with its golden' handle, stepped in and just stood there. He was overwhelmed by the opulence. There was Chinese slate perfectly laid on the floor of the shower. The walls were full length mirrors. The golden fittings were polished, sparkling their brilliance under the ceiling lights.

The shower head consisted of a two-foot disc that hung directly overhead and strategically placed on special ledges at the end of the shower were growing two magnificent orchids in full bloom. He turned the tap to the setting that said 'Warm' and instantly warm water landed on his welcoming body. The soap lathered over his body with full foam due to the softness of the water that seemed to take for ever to rinse off all traces of this natural scented soap. He had never smelled soap like this. He turned off the water and stood there not wanting to leave this *garden of Eden* environment. Finally, he opened the perfectly balanced shower door to reach the towel that was hanging just to the left and stood there drying off. As he dragged the soft towel over his wet body, he began to review the day and this American woman, Claire. After his reflection, there was a moment, an epiphany. He stopped the drying process and looked heavenward and said, 'Lord this is all going too fast but, I really love her.'

A clean and now very dry man stood looking at his reflection in the full-length mirror.

He was well built, with good skin and clear complexion. He turned and walked out into the room, leaving his clothes abandoned behind him.

Paul looked across at his locked bag. Upon their arrival, the ships stewards took their bags and placed them in their respective rooms while they completed their guest registration.

After which they were ushered to a *get to know* the other guests function which was a Chicken a Champaign affair. Little time was on offer to unpack before an early dinner was offered.

It seemed all too hard to find the keys, unpack, hang up clothes, so he walked over to the closet and selected the bath robe. Paul then walked over to his bag looked down at its secured position, but still couldn't be bothered and decided against all the trouble it would offer. He was never in the habit of sleeping naked, but that night he didn't care.

Exhaustion was quickly overcoming his personal standards. He made his way toward the bed dropped the robe and slipped between the cool Saturn sheets.

'This is perfect!' he said softly to himself.

With a flick of the switch at his bedside all the lights were off and darkness took over for the night.

CHAPTER SIXTEEN

After the table had been cleared, the dishes washed and put away, the adults of the household tucked their children into bed. Following the nightly ritual, Claire walked behind her husband as they made their way out of the girl's room with her hands massaging his shoulders.

'Hey, can we have a talk'? she asked.

'Sure, what's up?'

They sat down in the living area and with a low voice Claire began her difficult subject.

'It's Tiff.' She said looking her husband squarely in the eye.

'Yeah? What about Tiff'? he asked now fully focused on his wife.

'Well, I think you should back off a little my love.' She said in the gentlest way she knew how.

Paul was astute enough to know what his wife was talking about. Earlier that evening Tiffany was told by her father to put some clothes on, however the youngest complained advising her father that the only dry piece of covering was scratching her. Her father was insistent and the obedient child did as she was told, though reluctantly.

'I think you were a little rough on her tonight and it might have been better not to have discussed the matter in front of Jess. I think that was a special time that we missed with our Tiff.'

'Claire, if Tiffany had her own way, she wouldn't wear anything ... ever!' he said pushing his point with conviction.

'Well, so what?' Claire matched his conviction.

Tension between the two suddenly began to build.

'What do you mean ... so what? She needs to learn that there's a time and a place.

Standards Claire ... standards,' he said now with heated authority.

'Well, this is *the time* and this is *the place* Paul.' she said calmly.

'What'? Paul replied with sharp annoyance. 'What are you talking about?' he asked feeling the frustration and trying to decipher his wife's logic whilst endeavouring to maintain the integrity of his authority. He was suddenly angry and had every intention of cutting her down. He waited for her reply. Claire hesitated, sensing the gravity of the moment.

Paul looked deeply into his wife's face. A horrible flash came across his heart. He had now entered into his first fight with his wife. He had never been angry with the love of his life before. His heart sank.

Claire reached over and took his hands in hers.

'Look, God has put us here, at this time for whatever reason and Tiff has just turned five years of age. She's only five Paul. What she said tonight was true. They're just kids, so let them be kids and let Tiff enjoy her innocent freedom. Don't force her to grow up too quickly. This will work itself out, but just let it happen naturally. It's her time. Let her have it.

That goes for Jess too. This is *the place*: the place for us. Look where we live Paul? It's paradise. It can be tough sometimes, but our girls are in no moral danger. They are safe from all the rubbish and all the social dangers the kids are faced with back home. You know what I'm talking about. This is 'the place' where God has put us. He washed that ship down there high up on dry land on this island, a type of Noah's ark if you will.

I don't know why He has done this, but as I watch our children growing up, you know?... sometimes, I really thank God that we are here ... even if it's just for the sake of our little girl's,' Claire said, then stopped abruptly.

With that there was silence. Paul dropped his gaze from his wife's face to the ground.

He was tired and stressed. The responsibilities of caring for his family on this remote place cut off from all the safety nets of modern society was wearing him down.

'Do you get where I'm coming from?' she asked softly pressing his hands for a response.

'Sure' Paul said, 'sure ... I'm sorry for my anger, but I just ...' He paused still processing all she had said. 'But, I just think it's also important that we don't drop our standards.'

'Hey, I know and I understand. I understand that you want the best for the girls, and I agree regards the standards thing. Paul, you're a great Dad ... I mean a really great Dad.

You're an awesome husband for the girls to watch.'

'Really?'

'You have always said the best thing a man can do for his kids is love their mother.'

'Mm, sure, of course and I really believe that, but ...'

'I know you do and don't think that your daughters don't see how much their farther loves their mother.' Claire pushed her face towards him to emphasise her point. She paused then continued to bring her case to rest.

'You are teaching your children how to love and how to be loved. You are teaching them the true love of the Father. Oh, and by the way, your daughters think the world of you.

You are their provider, their protector. You are their example of who to look for in a future spouse. They read who God is and what He is like, through you and because of you. I've seen how they watch you Paul, how they respond to you. They love you so much. You are their hero and it's so healthy, but please my love, let them grow the way they need to grow here.

This isn't Australia.'

Paul looked deeply into the face of his wife again.

'Sure. But, let me process this. I see your point, but please consider mine,' he said quietly.

'Oh, and by the way, I think we are faithfully maintaining the right standards before God,' she said as warmly as she could. Claire took a breath, paused in thought, then continued.

'You know, we are so blessed to be set apart in this place. I can't see any other way of interpreting our situation other than we have been set apart for our kids, to give them our full attention ... our full influence. Think about it. They have no distractions here.'

'Yep, sure,' he said continuing to think on all her points deeply.

'And just keep in mind, there are three girls in your family and ...' Claire was interrupted

'Hang on, their hero?' Paul asked with slight humour to his question.

'Yes, their hero. I can see it.'

'Mm, OK. Didn't know that.' he said still deep in thought. 'That's a bit scary,' he concluded.

'Well of course you are. Sometimes I think you are so focused on worrying about the *what ifs*, that you can't see the *what is* ... right here. Anyway, where was I ... '

'Something about females,' he said scratching his head.

'Oh yes ... there are three females in your family.'

'Mm, yes ... and your point?'

'Simply this, it just so happens that I happen to be one too.'

Claire stuttered.

Paul looked up at his wife.

'You know I've noticed that,' he said with a stupid look on his face, trying to lighten the mood.

'Hey, I'm serious,' she said brushing off his soft merriment.

'Sure. Sorry,' he said looking back to the ground in calm defeat.

'I'm a girl too, and I think I can speak from the female side of things better than you ... yes? she bargained.

'Sure.' Paul said looking back at his wife.

'So, I have no problems nor can't see anything wrong with my daughters and I swimming in our natural state. After all, we are girls, we are family and we are alone on this plot of dirt and if you haven't noticed lately our clothes are rotting on our backs and, our clothes being exposed to that saltwater is adding to the problem,' she said softly still holding his hands.

'Well yes, all good points, but that was probably not my primary objection. My concern is Tiffany's seeming need to... 'Paul stopped in midsentence as a crack of thunder interupped the tension as it rumbled its way around the island. A heavy down pour followed its crescendo.

'Just let them be kids.'

'Sure.' Paul paused, then slowly, he focused back on his wife.

'Maybe deep down I'm battling with the thought of not being able to provide for my family and, the thought of the kids running around with no ...' He stopped.

'What are you saying Paul? You are a great provider ... the fish, all your ideas ... you're a doctor ... I would have died with that infection ... Tiffany was a breach birth. You knew exactly what to do … remember that time? What about the solar power for our home here in the rock … oh man, I could keep going … there's so much. I can't believe you're downing yourself like this … stop it … please.'

The doctor nodded.

'And if you're really worried about the kids running around naked … well bucko, your vision for maintaining standards is soon to be challenged and will need to be deeply contextualised in the near future, as we'll all be forced to be like Tiff, given how quickly our clothing is deteriorating. That is if God doesn't intervene soon.'

Claire ran her fingers through her hair and tucked it behind her ears

'Frankly, we should stop trying to make things holier than they are. It is what it is. Do you see what I'm saying? If God wants us to run around butt naked well … so be it. Frankly I couldn't think of a better place to do it.'

'Oh, really? Come on Claire,' Paul placed his hands behind his head frowned and stretched. 'Joy.'

'Yes. As I said before, the Lord will work it out. He will have His way. We'll be fine … butt naked or draped in grass skirts.' She waited for a response.

'Yeah, fair enough. Matthew chapter six. Don't be anxious about what you'll wear … etcetera.'

'Yep, as I've said before, the Lord is at work and maybe this is all about trusting him right down to our very fibre … you know?'

'Yeah right … right down to our bear backsides hanging out of our shorts … all of us.

I can't accept it Claire … sorry. The morality of the whole thing.' Paul's tone changed.

'There's got to be a way Claire,' he said looking through his wife as though she didn't exist.

'Paul?'

The doctor breathed in deeply, only to follow his action with a hissing exhalation, as though expelling his full frustration.

'Oh boy, you are really battling with this, aren't you? I didn't realise … the extent …' Her husband interjected.

'Hey, I'm OK … all good … sorry, just spitting it out. It's hard for me to stomach it. I guess, I should be thankful that I'm not … Isaiah.' The doctor chuckled under his breath.

'Isaiah?'

'You know the prophet?'

'Sure, and what about Isaiah?' Claire frowned softly, awaiting his response.

'Well, the Lord told him to walk around naked for a few years prophesying to the people … or against them actually … regarding the nation's sin.' He shrugged his shoulders.

'Naked … Go figure.'

'Oh, yeah … he did too. Was it that long?' Claire looked at Paul and laughed.

'Yes mam.'

'Well, the way things are shaping up, I'll be calling you Isaiah soon.'

'Oh, Ha Ha.' Paul was sombre.

'Hey, I think you've got it easy … in comparison … hey?' She giggled and slapped his shoulder.

'Sure, maybe.'

'Maybe? Come on dude.'

OK, maybe the Lord's telling us to get over ourselves,' he said deep in thought.

'Us?' Claire pointed both her index fingers at her husband.

'Right. OK ... me. He's telling ... me, to get over myself ... maybe.' The doctor shook his head slowly.

'No maybe about it ... mister.' She reached up and kissed him. 'You're such a hunk.'

'Man, I can't believe we are being forced to even consider this subject. Life can really offer some interesting twists ... can't it? Who would have thought? Wow! We are becoming so base ... unbelievable ... unbelievable,' the doctor said ignoring her last points shaking his head again with a smile growing across his face.

'But this is our live here and we can either live in victory or in defeat. We can accept His circumstances or reject His circumstances for us. The choice is ours. So, I choose victory and that's ... real life and real life in this beautiful place ... bare backside or not.' Claire's face shone as she delivered her final point with conviction.

'Yeah, sure. Hey, let's invite God into this situation? What do you think?' he said with a sudden softness overcoming his person.

'Yes lets, and by the way. I believe God will look after us. Really, I do.'

The pair bowed their heads, hand in hand and committed their topic of debate into the creator's hands. They spent but minutes in prayer when another crack of thunder pounded their living space. This time it seemed the lightning had hit their mountain again, causing a distinct vibration throughout the cavern.

The couple lifted their heads, looked at each other, then were about to return to their heavenly objective when they heard a small voice.

'Dad?' Tiffany walked straight to her father.

'Hey Tiff. Did the storm wake you?' Paul said to his frightened five-year old.

'I don't like it when it's that loud,' she said holding out her arms to receive her father.

Her small face unashamedly showed its fear as she looked to her Dad, throwing her desperate arms around her protector.

Claire watched the spectacle unfolding before her. The parents made eye contact.

Claire winked at her man followed by a smile.

'Hey, baby its fine. It's just thunder and, besides God is with us, remember? So why are you scared?' Paul said receiving his daughter's need for comfort.

'But I can't see him Daddy, so … that's why I'm scared.'

'Is that so.' Her father said warmly as he held her close.

'Tiff? There's and an old legend of the Cherokee Indian youth's rite of Passage.'

'What's that mean?' Tiffany asked her mother.

'It's a time when a Cherokee Indian boy becomes a man and has to prove he's ready to be a man, he has to do something difficult or even scary.'

'Do I have to do something scary to be a grown up?'

'No.' Paul said smiling at Claire wondering how this was going to work.

'OK, good, because I don't like scary.' Tiffany sat back against her father, listening to her mother.

'Anyway, his father takes him into the forest, blindfolds him and leaves him alone.'

'Mom?'

'Yes.'

'What's a blindfold?'

Paul held back his emotions watching intently.

'Um, it's a piece of cloth that's wrapped around his eyes'

'Why?'

'Well so he can't see.'

'But you said it's dark.'

'Tiff, how about you let Mom tell her story and ask questions after she's finished.'

'OK, but why does he have to have that thing on when it's dark. You can't see in the dark. Remember when we went down in the engine room Dad and the flashlight stopped working?'

'Tiff, let Mom finish and ask your questions after, OK?'

'OK.'

'Right, now, where was I?'

'He was in the forest wearing that blind thing when he couldn't see anyway because it was dark,' Tiffany said quickly.

Her father held back a laugh with great difficulty.

Claire cleared her throat and started again.

'OK, he is required to sit on a stump the whole night and not remove the blindfold until the sun rises the next morning. He cannot cry out for help to anyone. Once he survives the night, he is a man. He cannot tell the other boys of this experience, because each boy must experience this in due time. The boy is very scared. He can hear all kinds of noises throughout the night, but he can't touch his blind fold. He must trust his Dad and prove that he is worthy of being a man. It would be the only way! Finally, after a scary night the sun appeared and he removed his blindfold. It was then that he discovered that his father was sitting on the stump next to him.

He had been watching out for his child the entire night, protecting his son from harm.

We, too, are never alone Tiff. Even when we don't know it, or it doesn't feel like it, God is watching over us, sitting on the stump beside us. When trouble comes, all we have to do is reach out to Him. -So, just because you can't see God, doesn't mean He is not there looking after you in the storm. Sweetie, when you really understand that and exercise it, you become a champion in God.' Claire reached over and kissed her daughter.

'That's called Faith Tiff and God's Bible says to us that *we walk by faith, not by sight*. OK?' Paul added, now composed.

'OK'

'You alright now?' Claire asked.

'Yep …' The five-year old looked into the faces of her parents one by one.

'But I still don't like storms.'

'OK.' Paul hugged his daughter.

The intimate time lasted for but a few minutes when Claire noticed something on Tiffany's shoulder.

'Paul, what's that just below her neck?' she asked moving forward to pull down the top of Tiffany's T shirt.

'Tiff, let me have a look,' he said turning his daughter around on his lap.

'Mm, there seems to be a significant irritation here,' he said looking closer.

'I told you Dad, this T shirt is scratchy,' Tiffany said in her defence.

'Do we have a clean shirt?' Paul asked his wife.

'Nope, all wet,' she said, 'I can't get anything dry with this rain,' Claire said looking at the doctor sitting before her.

'OK, well she can't keep wearing this.'

'Right blossom, your wish has come true,' he said with tones of adventure.

'Off you hop and off with that shirt. I'll get some of that coconut oil. That'll fix this rash,' the Doctor said lifting his daughter off his lap and walking over to a cupboard where the medical supplies were kept.

Tiffany needed no further prompting. She pulled the shirt over her head and dropped her bed clothes immediately on the floor of the cave.

The problem was attended to quickly and their youngest was back in bed somewhat happier than when she left her room.

'I should have checked that when she complained about it. That could have broken out into something serious ... I feel so bad,' Paul said dropping his head. Disappointed in himself.

'Come here.' Claire moved to her husband with arms wide open and held on to her man.

'Hey, this is all right,' he said, 'This is the second hug in ten minutes,' he said laughing softly.

'Aren't you special?' she said squeezing him tightly.

'Yes mam, must be,' he whispered.

Paul suddenly picked up his wife and carried her into the bedroom where the dim light washed over the island lovers.

The night was a restless one for the household.

The man of the house had gotten up later in the evening to continue his writing.

Jessica woke up screaming and Tiff began to cry as a result of her sister's outburst. Paul moved towards the girl's bedroom as Claire shot out of bed to attend to the unsettled hearts of their children.

'Oh, Jess sweetheart, what's the matter'? Claire said still trying to wake up from a deep sleep.

'Mommy, there were bad people,' Jessica mumbled.

'Where were the bad people'? Paul asked picking up Tiffany who just wanted her father's arms again.

'They were running up our path to the cave Dad,' Jessica explained.

'Daddy, I'm scared. Why is Jessica crying like this'? Tiffany asked.

'She's had a bad dream love,' Paul responded holding his youngest daughter whilst moving alongside his eldest.

They had never seen Jessica complain of bad dreams, only Tiffany. Both adults agreed that the only option that night was to bring both girls into bed with them. Jessica remained unsettled and finally Claire brought her eldest daughter out to the kitchen area so as not to disturb the other two. A glass of water was quickly consumed, and soothing words were constantly offering encouraging messages to Jessica. After some prompting Claire was able to understand what the dream was all about.

'Well it was just a dream. There are no bad people here, are there?' she softly said holding her daughter close.

Jessica didn't respond, but held her mother tightly around her waist with her head nestled against her mother's warm chest. Within twenty minutes Jessica was fast asleep in Claire's arms and she carried Jessica back to bed for what was left of the night. As she carefully manoeuvred between the mosquito net and the Saturn sheets, Paul rolled over to face the pair.

'Hey, all good?' he whispered.

'Yeah, she's fine now,' Claire returned the whisper, settling her eldest in next to Tiffany.

'OK, that's good. Wow, what a night!' Paul said now surveying the sight set before him in their bed.

'Hey, I might get up and do a bit of writing. I'm wide awake,' he said as he carefully navigated his way out of the king size luxury bed.

'Sure ... night,' whispered Claire.

Paul walked to his living area sat down at his desk and began to write.

Chapter Seventeen

T he first three days on the yacht were just a dream. The weather was perfect although the captain had advised the guests that bad weather could be coming in our direction, but it was a fair way away. He advised our group that we were heading to a small atoll that consisted of a cluster of three small islands and we were due to reach our destination sometime after lunch. This was the further most point of our trip from Palau. It was very isolated but offered many spectacular sights. There was good anchorage there should foul weather come our way.

By the time we arrived at our destination the waves were beginning to get a little rough. Once in the protection of the atoll, the water was calm. It was decided that all the guests go ashore on one of the islands where we were treated to a swim in crystal clear water bedded by the whitest sand I had ever seen. There, littered across this vast area were large heads of coral to which were home to thousands of small, beautifully coloured tropical fish.

After our experience in the waters of this glorious atoll we were then offered a smorgasbord under a large tree that stretched its branches over a wide area growing at the edge of the beach.

I remember suggesting to Claire as we were eating our lunch that we should have taken our sunglasses with us as the glare was extreme due to the white sand and long-term exposure would lead to cataracts. Claire laughed and said that we wouldn't be there long enough, but she went on to say how wonderful it would be to live on an island like that one. I looked at her and said I could *think of nothing worse, to which she asked 'where was my sense of adventure'. In hindsight. I find it all rather ironic. From that point, our lives have been involved in one massive adventure ... of which I would have preferred not to have partaken in.*

After lunch, we were allowed to investigate the island. This proved to be an interesting time, as Clair and I decided to walk around it which took one hour.

We talked about a lot of things and it was there on that remote beach that we both came to the conclusion that there was a close relationship developing between us ... very fast.

I suggested that we invite God into this new thing and there on that beautiful isolated white sandy beach we stood hand in hand and committed ourselves into the hands of God. We opened our eyes and kissed for the first time, then, continued a new journey together, hand in hand back to the ship. There was a cool sea breeze that began to blow by the time we got back to the ship. The water in the lagoon was calm but beyond the reef was entirely another story.

Dinner that evening was a little more formal as we were seated in individual groups.

The hockey team were all placed together at a long table in the lounge area. The family were placed at the stern and we were positioned at the bow. The tables were well placed apart from each group to allow for privacy and each table was beautifully laid out. Our meal was prepared with all the professionalism of a five-star organization. Claire and I both ordered lobster, caught that morning and with this magnificent dish came a side salad. When the waitress came out with the meals I asked how they were able to offer such a fresh salad and she advised that the kitchen had its own hydroponics garden.

The evening was perfect. After the meal, I looked at our table and noticed a little wine left in my glass along with some bread sticks stacked neatly beside each other in a crystal glass. I suggested given our intimate dinner for two on the deck why not have an intimate communion for three on the deck referring to Christ's presence.

She was delighted and I went through the liturgy of the communion using the bread sticks and the remnant of the wine. It was the best communion I had ever presided over, probably because it was the only one I had ever done but, the presence of God with us that night was profound.

Claire sat back in her chair and looked around and then to the sky. She said that that was a great supper and she couldn't fit another bit in.

Little did we know that that was going to be our 'last supper' that we would have in a civilized environment for a long time.

As the dinner plates were taken away Claire and I remained at our table not wanting that night to leave us.

The family had turned in for the evening and the girls in the hockey team were beginning to ramp up the volume. More alcohol was being consumed than the previous evening and their language, was becoming more colourful as the night went on. This was soon followed by some unsavoury behaviour from some of the young women. Claire walked over to a small table to get some water and on her way back discretely mentioned to one of the young ones in question that she needed to be careful. I didn't hear everything Claire said but I could see she was really concerned for the young women. What followed was a shock.

The young lady being counselled laughed and verbally accosted Claire with more than colourful language. This sentiment was then echoed by some of the accompanying party.

Claire made no effort to reply but returned to our table. She looked a little stunned.

The tension was immediately abated by Claire's comment. 'Well that seemed to go well' she said smiling at me.

I burst out laughing but didn't realise at the time but found out later that some of the team were watching us with eyes inflamed.

It may have been my laughter was the last straw and with that the coach, who was also watching, a woman in her mid-thirties, marched over to our table.

CHAPTER EIGHTEEN

Paul stopped his writing and sat back in his comfortable chair taken from the captain's office of the 'Pacific Fair'. He rubbed his tired eyes. There was a chill in the air. With this year's wet season, came an unusually cooler temperature for that time of the year. He wondered if there was an early typhoon in the area.

As he leant back in his leather office chair, he reflected on that night: The second last night on the ship some ten years earlier. His thoughts were fixed on the coach of that hockey team. A frown came across his face as he recalled the words of the angry woman that night on the vessel. Sitting back in his position of comfort, he brought his hands up and clasped them behind his head. Leaning further against the high backed, black padded chair, his mind brought her face clearly to view. He could hear her words resinating in his head.

'Good evening. I'm the coach of this team,' she said in a cold matter of fact manner.

'Hi. I'm Paul and this is Claire.' Paul stood and offered his hand expecting hers as common course for greeting, but nothing came. 'Would you like to join us? I'll get another chair,' the doctor said eager to defuse a tense moment.

'No thank you. I'm happy to stand. Listen, mind your own business.'

The coach looked straight at Claire.

'Excuse me?' Claire said softly.

'Your little mother hen act back there.'

'Sorry I didn't catch your name,' Claire extended her hand, but received that same treatment as the doctor.

'That's because I didn't give it.'

'Oh, I see. Well, I was just concerned and ...' Claire was cut off.

'We don't criticize you and what you do. Don't push your *do good mentality* on these great kids ... Just for letting off some steam. These girls have worked so hard. They deserve it, so leave them alone,' she hissed her return, looking straight at Claire.

Paul felt let out of the conversation that night as he watched the spectacle unfold before his eyes.

'I am certainly not against celebrating and I am sure your team deserves it, but I think one has to be careful with the young ones,' Claire calmly replied.

The coach glared at her enemy. Her face beginning to show the red dawning of a heart that was filled with anger.

'I am sorry if I have offended you and your group but, I am sure given your professional standing, that you certainly wouldn't be condoning binge drinking for the teenagers in your team, would you? If you have any questions on the subject, I am sure Dr Langley here could offer sufficient advice on the dangers of the matter,' Claire's face was a picture of loving confidence.

The embittered coach looked at the doctor and began to calm down. She stood there with nothing to say. The silence was awkward. Paul smiled politely.

Embarrassed, the coach looked back at Claire.

'Whatever! Next time you have something to say. Say it to me. Do you understand?'

'Certainly, I do apologize.'

The leader of the group just nodded back at Claire, accepting her apology and walked off.

'Well ... that was interesting. Are you OK?' Paul asked reaching over to take her hand.

'Yes, thank you,' she said squeezing his hand.

'That was well handled,' Paul said.

'Thank you. You know there's something really sad about that group of girls. Like there's something wrong.'

'Really?'

'Yes. I feel for them. Do you see it?' she asked.

'Mm, not sure, but I know one thing.'

'What's that?'

'If they keep partying like this there will be some pretty sore heads tomorrow,' Paul looked over at the celebration developing before them.

'Ever wondered why you were put in a situation?' Claire pondered openly.

'Sure, so you think that you might be here for a special reason?'

'Well I don't want to get all melodramatic, but I really believe my circumstances are controlled by God. Don't you?' she said looking for a response.

'Sure.'

'Well maybe that is one of the reasons why I am here,' she said turning slowly to look behind her.

'You mean ... to talk to some of those young girls?'

'Well not just them,' she said pausing in thought. 'There's the coach ... as you saw,' Claire said making light of what just happened.

'Yes, well, you have obviously made a big impression on that one.'

Claire returned his sentiment with a smile, but he could see her concern. The doctor suggested they walk around the deck and with that they made their way to the bow of the ship. The lagoon's water lapped lazily against the side of the ship as the two tourists stood for some time, in silence, hand in hand, looking at another night sky peppered with billions of stars.

'They're beautiful, aren't they?' A voice from behind them added.. Both Claire and Paul jumped with fright as they spun around to witness the intruder. 'Hi,' The young woman said with a smile.

'Hello and, yes, they are ... beautiful that is,' Claire smartly responded surprised by the intrusion.

A teenager moved next to Claire looking heavenward.

'When you see this ... all this out here...' she said now pointing to the expanse above them. 'It's hard to believe it was all a gazillion to one chance of happening ... don't you think?' the teenager said.

'Hard to believe? Actually, I find it impossible to believe that,' Paul said.

'This was no accident,' Claire said looking skyward. 'All planned.' Her voice was soft as she maintained her focus on the heavens.

'You really think that?' the young girl replied.

'Yes, I do,' Claire said, slowly redirecting her gaze from the celestial glory to the young inquirer.

'When you see the stars, it sometimes, makes you think about God or something. I don't know,' she said questioning deeply.

'It does, indeed,' Claire said taking a deep breath.

'Why do you think that is?' the young woman asked with an absent-minded look as she gazed up at the awesome presentation of lights set before them.

'Well, when you look at a painting, like a masterpiece for example, you are seeing something of the character of the person who painted it and you inevitably at some stage start thinking about the painter, don't you?' the doctor paused, waiting for a response.

'Guess so. Never thought of it like that,' the teenager shrugged her shoulders in thought.

'Hi, Paul's the name and this is Claire,' he reached out and shook her hand.

'Jessica,' The teenager smiled, 'but everyone calls me Jess ... except Mom. As far my mother is concerned it is Jessica and that's it.'

'Hey, hi Jessica great to meet you,' Claire said warmly.

'I am sorry about tonight,' Jessica said softly, 'thank you for caring enough to tell Alisha to be careful. I heard what you said. She needed to hear that. She can be a bit of a wild one when she wants to be, but she had no right to talk to you that way,' she said still with a soft voice, not wanting anyone else to hear, particularly anyone from the team of drunken revellers. 'and sorry for your ear bashing from the coach. Celine, that's our coach ... she can be a bit too ... well let's say she's quite protective of the team,' Jessica continued trying to offer some defence for the coach's reactions.

'Oh, that's fine. No harm done,' Claire looked at this young girl standing in front of them and reached out and patted her arm.

'Are you out for some fresh air before turning in?' Paul said making conversation.

'No, I just wanted to get away from all the stuff going on in there,' she said thumbing back at the now wild party in the lounge.

'You're not enjoying yourself Jessica?' Paul said.

'Um you can call me Jess. I prefer Jess. And am I enjoying myself? ... Mm sure, but I just don't like it when they ... when they get drunk ... I mean ... It's no big deal really ... it's just ... Ha, I don't know,' she began to falter.

'Why don't you just go to bed it's around nine pm ... starting to get late,' Paul said offering a simple solution.

'Yeah right ... totally pointless! My roommate is Alisha ... you know the one you spoke to ... she comes in at all hours and messes around ... you know ... So, I'll wait till she goes to bed. Tonight, I think she'll just pass out on the bed. She's getting pretty drunk.'

'And you don't like it when she specifically gets drunk?' Claire asked digging a little deeper.

'No ... no I don't,' Jessica said now showing some reserve on the subject.

'And if you don't wait up and go to bed instead ... what then?' Claire asked.

'As I said she does stupid stuff.' Jessica said displaying some intolerance to Claire's probing questions.

'What sort of stupid stuff?' Paul asked.

'Oh, she wakes me up ... and... anyway, best if I stay up,' she continued trying to avoid any further discussion on that subject.

'Have you spoken to Alisha about it?' Claire asked.

'Yeah, as I said, totally pointless ... she doesn't listen to me ... I'm the youngest in the team ... And mostly on standby ... You know I sit on the sideline waiting to get a game. You know just a reserve. Yeah, I'm a nobody. I'm nothing in Alisha's eyes,' Jessica paused, looked down to the floor then continued.

'She complained when she found out that she had to share a room with me ... you know.'

'Have you spoken to the coach? Claire asked.

'Sure, but, didn't do any good ... you know. Alisha is one of the *star* members of the team. Hey anyway, no big deal,' she said with a sudden countenance coming over her that was far from happy.

'Jess are you OK?' Claire said lovingly squeezing the teenager's arm.

Tears welled up in Jessica's eyes. 'Oh yeah,' she said trying to show strength.

'I just ... Oh man ... I'm sorry. I'm really tired. I just ...' her voice began to quiver as she tried to hide her emotions with a smile. It didn't work and with that, tears began to flow down her face.

'Hey, kiddo?' Claire said softly, as a mother would to her daughter.

The youngster began to sob.

'Come here girl. What's really the problem?' Claire opened her arms and the troubled spirit welcomed the offer by throwing herself into the arms of this amazing woman standing before her.

'I hate it here. I miss my Mom so much. I just want to go home,' she said releasing her truth.

'I didn't want to come, but my step-Dad convinced my Mom that it would be a good thing for me,' Jessica said between her heaving sobs. 'he just wanted to get rid of me so he could go skiing with Mom ... didn't want me around. That's the truth. I hate it here. I'm such a freaking reject,' she said in bitter defeat.

Claire held the troubled teenager for some time as Paul placed his hand on Jessica's shoulder and waited for the right cue.

'I'm sorry,' The young girl said as she suddenly broke away from the safety of Claire's influence.

'I'm so sorry. Oh my God, I am so embarrassed. I shouldn't have done that,' the young woman said looking at the deck. 'I'd better get back,' Jessica looked to Claire.

'You're really nice Claire,' she said and began to walk away. 'Good night,' Jessica stopped, turned and took one last look at Claire totally ignoring Paul.

'Jess, don't feel embarrassed. It's OK. Let's talk,' Claire reached down and took her hand.

'No, I'd better go,' she said wanting to escape her foolish situation. Jessica had released too much information to total strangers and she suddenly began to feel grave regrets.

'Jess I want to help you,' Claire said beckoning her full attention.

'No, you can't help me,' the exposed teenager said wanting to run away in shame.

'Well I might be able to if you'll hear me out,' Claire said with the warmest smile that Jessica had ever seen.

She stopped her objections, being drawn to the possibility and looked deeply in the face of this special woman standing at her side.

Suddenly disbelief overcame her. It was all too confronting for the girl and tears now streamed down her cheeks.

'No, you can't. I don't know why I even came up to you. It was stupid. You can't help me. How could you?' she said with tears running over her lips. 'I'm just stuck and that's all there is,' she said now crying.

'I only have to put up with Alisha's crap for another nineteen days ... no big deal. I can do it,' she said with focus.

'Jess, I can help,' Claire said taking her hand.

'How?' Jessica snapped.

'Would you like to stay with me in my room? I have an extra bed in my suite. How does that sound? You'd be safe with me. I can assure you of that. You don't have to put up with whatever Alisha is doing to you,' Claire said trying to discern the depth of

Jessica's situation whilst holding her hand tightly. 'I will go and speak with Celine now, if you like?'

Claire said looking at this sad creature.

Jessica stopped her crying, wiped her tears with a paper napkin that Paul offered her which had previously been taken from their dinner table.

'I don't know,' Jessica said. 'I don't know if the coach would go along with that. She doesn't like you,' Jessica said, though seriously considering the proposal.

Claire turned to Paul. Their eyes met.

Paul placed his hand on the young teenager's shoulder. 'I'll go and speak to the coach. With your permission, of course,' Paul said with full authority.

Jessica stood motionless then nodded, looking directly to the deck in surrender to her new situation.

'OK. Thank you.'

'Claire can you stay with Jess?'

'It would be my pleasure,' Claire replied drawing Jessica to her side with her arm around the young girl's shoulder while she watched this man take charge.

Paul walked towards the party, entered the lounge area of the ship and soon brought Celine outside to talk, clear of prying ears. The conversation took some time. A serious, almost threatened look came across her face and she looked at Paul then back at Alisha while Paul continued with his mission. Finally, the coach seemed to appreciate Paul's interest and she explained Jessica's situation at home and some of the young teenager's behaviour, which explained, to a point, Alisha's attitude toward the girl. It seemed that Jessica was a last-minute inclusion on the trip due to her father's insistence that she go. The coach went on to explain that she and the club's board felt obliged to let this young player come on the trip, as her stepfather, a wealthy man, was a major sponsor of this elite hockey club. This brought ill feeling to some members of the team because they felt that she hadn't earned the right to come, and she was under the required minimum age. This was also reflected by some of the team member's parents. Alisha insisted on a room to herself but was denied this due to Jessica's last-minute arrival. Finally, after Paul had offered some more background regarding the treatment being offered to Jessica by Alisha, it was agreed that a swap might be appropriate.

'Claire has offered to share her room with Jess. It would no doubt take some heat out of the situation for you and of course Alisha. Maybe we review it all in a few days. With your permission, of course. What do you think?'

She thought for a while.

'This is very gracious doctor. Thank you so much.'

The coach shook Paul's hand and thanked him again.

'Well, it's Claire you should thank. She made the offer,' Paul said now remembering the rift between the two women.

'Mm OK. I will certainly talk to her but not now. I had better stay with the group, but please thank her for me and I will chat to her later and, thank you again doctor. Be assured I will speak to Alisha.'

'You're most welcome,' Paul said. A little more conversation took place then the pair parted company.

The doctor returned to the two admiring females at the bow of the vessel, who had been watching the events from the other side of the ship.

'All organised,' Paul said with a smile on his face.

Jessica threw her arms around Paul and kissed him on the cheek.

'Thank you,' she said.

'No problems, happy to help,' the doctor said winking at Claire whilst being clung to by an over enthusiastic teenager.

'Well done doctor,' Claire said softly to the man she secretly loved.

Paul simply smiled in return.

'OK, what's say we get your things and get you settled in?' Claire said.

'Now that sounds like a plan,' Paul announced, eager to untangle himself from a well-meaning teenage human vine.

The three moved quickly toward the girls' room. They walked into the lounge to make their way to the stairs leading to the deck where all the first-class rooms were located.

The coach was talking to Alisha on her own off to one side in the corner of the ships' lounge. She noticed the three and made eye contact with Claire and mouthed the word *thank you*, to which Claire smiled and nodded as they made their way down the stairs steadying themselves on the mahogany rail that spiralled its way down to the next floor.

CHAPTER NINETEEN

───────── ❧ ─────────

Paul woke early the next morning. He drew the curtains to welcome the virgin light of the day. The sun had just begun to make its presence known across the liquid horizon. The lagoon sparkled as the sun's light massaged its rays over the glassy water set before him. He watched as two large reef fish lazily swam past his window, flaunting their golden red scales in the morning's first light. The sight of the lagoon's deep turquoise blue beckoned his presence. With that, he changed into suitable attire, took his snorkelling gear and made his way to a set of external steps that hung off the side of the ship and led down to a temporary pier where three small boats with outboard motors were tired securely to their respective posts.

The vessel was originally purchased from a Greek company then, refurbished by its new American owners to bring it back to its five-star status. They renamed the vessel the 'Pacific Fair'. It was one hundred and seventy-nine feet from bow to stern, had a beam of thirty-five feet, powered by two, seven hundred and twenty-break horsepower Caterpillar engines and would cruse at a steady twenty knots. Initially its new owners intended it to be a tax deduction as it was to be used solely by the board's executives and upper management to entertain clients and perspective clients. However, due to the Global Credit Crisis, it was decided by the board that the ship, from an accounting perspective, needed to justify its existence as more of an asset than a liability and putting it on the open rental market was one of the best ways to generate necessary cash flow to qualify its reason for being.

As Paul made his way down to the temporary pier being careful not to slip on the dew blessed steps, he heard a voice.

'Well, good morning sunshine, care to join us?'

It was Claire's voice and it seemed to be coming from a distance.

Paul looked around but the sun was just peeking over the horizon causing a considerable amount of glare across the water, thereby hiding the position of the vocal intruder to the morning's peace.

'Over here,' she said, a little more insistent on being found.

He looked in the approximate direction of the sound of her lively voice.

Finally, he noticed an arm waving a hundred yards away. Paul quickly found himself in the tropical water, hardly offensive to the senses due to its warmth. He finally made his way to Claire only to be greeted by Jessica.

'Hi Paul. You should see the fish down there. So amazing! Come and see,' she said with a snorkel positioned half out of her mouth to ensure some semblance of vocal clarity.

'And there's a huge clam down there. It's so beautiful. Follow me I'll show you where it is,' the teenager said and with that promptly duck dived straight down in the crystal-clear water.

'Wow, do we have a different little lady here or what?' Paul said.

Claire laughed.

'Good morning,' the Doctor said laughing back as he slowly treadwater.

'Morning!' Claire replied beaming in the midst of the morning's brilliance. 'Yep, we certainly do, in fact quite a new creature swimming down there.' Claire said pointing to the slender teenager submerged beneath them.

Suddenly a splash and a 'whoosh' of water being blown out of a snorkel appeared next to them. Jessica surfaced with more exciting news.

'Hey, there's two lobsters down there. Come on guys, come and see,' Jessica yelled, adjusting her snorkel in readiness to submerge again.

'OK, lead on little lady,' Paul announced with equal enthusiasm.

The young girl disappeared under water as quickly as she appeared.

'Strike, this kid's a fish,' he said laughing.

'I'll race you,' Claire said excitedly.

'Have you noticed that we've been doing a lot of racing since we've met?'

Claire dove down, not hearing a word he said. In surrender Paul followed in chase.

He watched the two females below him in the twenty-foot depth. The doctor noted how graceful they both appeared as they moved around the coral heads searching for the creatures that Jessica spoke of on the surface. He soon found himself next to his fellow explorers in hope of new discovery. It was a world of beauty with some of the most amazing coral and colourful fish he had ever seen. With a sudden urge for oxygen he hastily made his way to the surface followed by the other two swimmers.

Reaching the surface first, Paul watched Claire as she approached his side from beneath. She was beautifully made by the creator, but above all the most beautiful aspect about this woman from his perspective, was her character. How he loved her. His heart began to pound in his chest. He knew that she was the one. He had to tell her how he felt.

Claire burst to the surface followed by the young Jessica.

'Isn't that amazing? Yes?' Jessica said, swimming around Paul in chase of a positive answer.

'I have to admit that was something else,' Paul said somewhat breathless, glancing across to Claire maintaining his equilibrium in the salty water.

'You know what? I think that is a miracle down there,' Jessica said, waving her arms in the water in sequence to her bright yellow flippers keeping her slim body buoyant in the water. 'Don't you think? It's got to be, hasn't it?' she said.

'Well, I have to admit, it's teaming with life. ... and that's certainly a miracle,' Claire said looking at Jessica with a sense of pride as she began to float on her back.

The three swam for another thirty minutes, exploring more coral heads populated by thousands of tropical fish in all their colourful splendour.

As they ventured towards the ship the water increased in depth and the coral was less plentiful until there was nothing but pure white sand on the bottom.

'Hey, I'm hungry anyone interested in joining me for breakfast?' Paul said to both of his companions.

'Race you back?' Jessica said.

'What's with the racing thing?' Paul looked at Claire.

With that Jessica started without them. Claire and Paul took chase but, she was a strong swimmer and it wasn't long before she was drawing away from the other two. Claire picked up the pace leaving Paul to be the straggler in the team. The doctor looked up to see Jessica already pulling herself up on to the pier and Claire would soon be at the same location. He slowed his pace admitting defeat and took a more leisurely pace.

'Come on Doctor Langley put some muscle into it,' he heard Claire call out now standing on the pier with Jessica.

The two women stood well in their one-piece swim wear as they flaunted their gestures of inadequate form to the man in the water still making his way to their side.

Paul finally reached his destination and dragged himself up on the pier and sat there somewhat out of breath.

'Hey, you two aren't bad swimmers,' he said looking up at the females who were smiling with pride at the man who had just come last.

As Paul stood up, his two companions began to navigate their way up the steep stairs to reach the ships' deck. Jessica led the way, talking about the wonderful sights the morning offered. She was quite nimble and easily climbed to the top of the stairs. Once on the deck she looked back down to the adults still climbing and continued to share her observations about the reef's beauty.

As Claire stepped onto the clean deck, Jessica took her by the hand.

'Isn't this beautiful?' she gestured suddenly releasing her mentor and, spinning around in a three hundred and sixty-degree rotation referencing the morning's glory.

'Everything is so alive this morning. I can feel life,' she said as she gazed at the beauty set before her. 'I feel so alive,' she continued, 'can you feel it Claire? Can you?' she asked with a final crescendo of emotions.

Paul looked in the direction of her gestures agreeing with her observations yet still wondering about this change that had come over her since the previous night.

The sun had fully risen and was bathing is pure white light over the picturesque lagoon.

'You can feel it, can't you Claire?' Jessica asked again.

'Oh, I certainly can Jess,' Claire said warmly, hugging her.

Paul was a little surprised by such a reaction from Claire towards this junior from the Midwest.

'Come on. Let's get cleaned up and ready for breakfast?' Clair asked equalling Jessica's excitement.

'Amen!' With that Jessica ran ahead.

'Strike, I'll have what she's having,' Paul said in response to the puzzling change that had come over the teenager.

'You've already got it,' Claire said softly.

'What?'

'Never mind. Tell you later,' Claire said as she reached up and kissed her man on the cheek, then ran off to catch the ball of energy.

'Hey, wait you,' she said reaching Jessica's side.

Paul watched as the two females ahead of him hastily made their way to their room.

Claire and Jessica were chatting away as though they were inseparable sisters. There was some whispering between the girls, followed by Jessica turning back to look at Paul then muffled a girlish laugh.

'What are you guys saying?'

'Wouldn't you like to know,' Claire said throwing her head back to at least direct her voice to him without looking at him.

Jessica giggled followed by a softer mimic from her new-found friend.

They moved through the lounge area and down the spiral stair-case on their way to their rooms.

'I'll meet you two at breakfast in ten?' he said now standing at the door of his room.

'Ten minutes? Let's make it twenty,' Claire said, softly looking squarely at Paul.

'Wow, what happened to the ten-minute wonder woman,' he said laughing.

'Hey, wait up buddy, there are two in this room now,' she said playing with him with such confidence.

'Yeah!' Jessica said placing her hands on her hips.

'Of course, I'll see you both in twenty minutes,' he replied smiling and with that all parties went into their respective rooms.

Breakfast was served on the upper deck and Paul was the first of all the guests to arrive. It seemed that the wealthy family had decided to eat in their rooms and the population of the previous night's party hadn't been seen at that stage. Paul waited for the other two and made conversation with the head waiter, who seemed a little worst for ware that morning.

Paul discovered that the festivities the previous night went well into the early part of the morning and the head waiter had to remain on duty until all had retired for the evening. It was also revealed that there may be some changes to their various stop overs as the typhoon was heading in their direction and it would be unwise to head back to Palau, nor was it wise to stay in their current location as the storm was already a category four and likely to be upgraded to a category five by that evening. The captain and his team were already on the bridge in preparation for a ten-thirty departure to a more appropriate lagoon with an island that offered a small bay further south from their current position. This would offer safe harbour during the storm.

'So, what's the name of the island?' Paul asked.

'It's an uncharted island,' the waiter replied, 'no name to my knowledge. There are so many uncharted Islands and atolls around here, but the captain and the first officer are well acquainted with the area. It's further south than our intended boundary but it will be worth-while ... you'll see ... just beautiful,' he added.

'So, we've got the Captain, his second in command and a trainee officer?' Paul asked with interest.

'Well not exactly a trainee officer but she is just starting her career in this line of work. But I can assure you sir she has all the necessary qualifications to be on the bridge.'

The head waiter said with smooth authority.

'OK, would it be possible to go up on the bridge at some stage and have a look?' Paul asked.

'Of course, sir, I could inquire for you after breakfast if you like.'

'I'd really appreciate that. Thank you.'

'You are most welcome,' the waiter said now taking the metal lids off the warming containers that house the hot portion of the buffet breakfast.

'Would you care to start your breakfast sir?' he invited the doctor. The waiter's facial expressions offering a lure of wonderful things to discover on the table.

'I might wait for the others,' Paul said now looking at the tempting morsels on display.

'Very well sir, but what about a coffee while you wait,' the waiter said as he made his way to the coffee, tea and fruit juices table to make some last-minute adjustments.

'That would be great.'

With that, the man in charge of breakfast made swift work of a half strength flat white coffee just as the doctor liked it.

Paul stood on the top deck slowly sipping his coffee while waiting for Claire and looked around enjoying the perfect day. The thought of a typhoon began to trouble him, but the assurance of the waiter was compelling and, he tried to push the thought aside.

The small island looked perfect in the mornings new light but, the idea of a typhoon forced its way back into his imagination. What would it look like during a typhoon? A sudden slither of fear pierced his heart. *It would indeed be a dreadful thing to be caught out in the open ocean in a typhoon,* he thought. He could see how such a lagoon could offer safety during such a storm but what of a category five storm?

'Good morning!' The words accompanied a familiar voice breaking the spell of the encompassing concerns in his heart.

Claire stood close, next to his side looking up at him with a beaming face. She had washed her hair, and the scent of this clean woman wisped its way into his nostrils. A sudden intoxication filled his head and drove away all sense of fear. He experienced the strongest desire to put his arm around her, but his head found clarity, and quickly felt it improper to do such a thing in front of the teenager.

Jessica was close behind Claire, greeted Paul, the waiter and walked straight to the table filled with the vessels breakfast offering. A generous spread was on offer with fresh tropical fruit looking most appealing to the three hungry travellers.

With plates nearly full, they found their table to break their nights fast and sat down.

'Jess, we are in the habit of saying grace before we eat. Would you be OK if we were to do that?' she asked.

'Sure!' Jessica said, shrugging her shoulders. 'That would-be kind of ... cool,' she added.

'OK great ... Paul?' Claire said, gesturing to the Australian man seated next to her to take the lead.

'Absolutely!' he said, throwing up a quick quiet prayer for guidance for the sake of Jessica.

They all bowed their heads, and as their eyes were closing, Paul reached over and held Claire's hand, to which he felt her positive response. His heart thrilled.

'Father, we thank you for your goodness to us, and for your presence with us, never leaving us nor forsaking us, and we give you thanks for this food. Bless it to us, and us to your service, and Lord we thank you for Jessica being with us. We thank you, in the name of our Lord Jesus Christ. Amen.'

He opened his eyes and immediately noticed two things. Claire had Jessica's hand in hers, and Jessica's had a tear flowing down her right cheek.

'Are you alright love?' Paul asked with an unintentionally strong Australian accent.

Jessica quietly stared at the table.

'Jess?' Claire said lovingly.

The young girl slowly looked up at the two seated with her.

'You guys are really nice. I've never met anyone like you before,' Jessica said wiping away her tear. 'When you were saying grace, I realized I was meant to be on this ship, just to meet you Claire,' the teenager declared looking back and forth to both adults. 'And you too Paul ... I know this sounds a bit weird but, I feel ... that in some way, I have been a part of a miracle, just by meeting you guys.' Jessica said still holding Claire's hand.

'Well, actually I think you might be the miracle little lady,' Claire said shaking Jessica's hand gently.

'Come on let's eat. I'm starved. Anyone else hungry?' Claire said lightening the situation.

Jessica looked at both the adults and said, 'This is the best day of my entire life.

Thankyou ... I have never known life to be like this. Wow. I can't wait to tell Mom about this,' she said bringing her attention to her plate and its contents.

Paul noticed Claire's look when Jessica made that confession.

The three talked, laughed, and the girls began to make plans of what they wanted to do during their vacation. Paul broke the news about the typhoon and the necessary move to safer waters. This didn't faze Claire and Jessica as they were more focused on the fact that they would be together, during the rest of the trip. The girls swapped their addresses in the States, and emails were given.

'Wow. I would really like to see Australia,' Jessica said. 'I want to see kangaroos,' she continued, 'They are so amazing. Don't you think they're amazing?' Jessica asked looking at her captivated audience.

'Yes, they are,' Claire said.

'Have you seen them Claire?'

'Yes, I have.'

'Do Australians think that they're amazing?' Jessica asked Claire.

'Well I think the native here might be better suited to answer that question,' Claire gestured for the doctor the take the floor.

'That depends on who you're talking to,' Paul replied with a slight smile on his face.

'Really?' The American teenager said. She slowly took her napkin, wiped her mouth, and sat back in her chair.

'Why?' Jessica inquired.

'Out west they're a bit of a pest,' Paul continued.

'Oh,' the young girl said quietly as though to herself.

'Can you keep them as pets?' she asked.

'Sure, I have one at home.'

'Really? Where do you keep it? In a cage?'

'No ... just in the back yard,' Paul said with a straight face.

'Shut up! You don't do you?' Claire said in total disbelief.

'Wow,' Jessica said wide eyed.

'Yeah, he's a big fella ... a big red. He'd be a good six foot tall I'd reckon.'

'No way,' Jessica exclaimed in total wonder.

'Yep.'

'How long have you had him Paul,' Claire asked, watching his every move.

'Um, got him when he was a little Joey. He's got real personality.

Sometimes the way he looks at me, I'd swear he's about to say G'day,' Paul said, cementing in his absorbed listeners with his now over the top Aussie accent.

'Awesome!' Jessica said. 'What's his name?'

'Well ... He's known in the neighbourhood as Mr Roo, but family and friends call him Kanga,' the Doctor said ready to explode.

'Wow, how cool ... that's like Mr Kanga Roo,' Jessica said, basking in the revelation.

'Yep ... You got it. Sort of fits nicely, doesn't it?' Paul said with a wink.

Claire began to frown.

'Wow, that's awesome. Do you like ... take it for a walk ... like a dog?' Jessica said now completely sold.

'No! No point.'

'Why?' Jessica asked.

'He gets his exercise every day when I ride him to work,' Paul said, now with a ridiculous exaggerated Australian accent.

'No way!' Jessica exclaimed. 'You ride it to work?' she questioned incredulously.

'Oh, my goodness! He does not Jessica! Look at his face. He is playing with you,' Claire said unmasking the scam.

Paul couldn't hold on any longer and released a laugh that resinated across the ship.

Jessica reflected on Claire's point and ... Paul's outburst.

'You rat ... I can't believe I fell for that.' Jessica lashed out laughing hard.

'Mr Kanga Roo ... Oh, how dumb!' she said, as she began to lose it. 'You rat!'

Claire joined in to the infectious merriment, and all three had tears beginning to well up.

As Claire looked across to the place where the breakfast food was laid out, she noticed the head waiter joining in on the moment. He had been listening to every word.

Claire motioned Paul to look across at their waiter who was by this time laughing as heartily as they were.

The waiter gestured his thumb up in the air as an indication of his favour with the joke played on Jessica.

'Miss, you have to watch these Australians sometimes,' the waiter spoke with a loud voice from the other side of the upper deck.

CHAPTER TWENTY

The rest of the morning was spent on their own as the team of girls didn't rise until after lunch. Claire and Jessica had developed a close relationship. They sat in the lounge and talked. Jessica had a new-found thirst to know all about Claire, her life's story and what she believed. The young teenager was captivated by her mentor. There were many questions about life, about spiritual matters and Claire was eager to satisfy her new student with the truth.

Paul soon saw his presence wasn't required and excused himself. He went back to his room and spent some time reorganising his wardrobe, placing his valuables in the small safe situated in the closet in his room. The doctor took out his laptop and sized it against the safe … there was just enough room. With that in mind he squeezed it into the safe and locked it.

Paul placed his limited amount of clothing in the cupboard and after entering his valuables in the private safe encased firmly in the cupboard, he walked casually back to the girls.

The Australian tourist walked to the lounge of the Pacific Fair. The doctor's vantage point was perfect. He decided to sit in the corner and watch the woman he wanted to marry.

He sat on a stool situated in the corner of the ships lounge listening to the two young women talking.

'Claire, I want to know more about him.'

Paul listened intently.

'Well, he is so amazing and so loving. He's a gentleman's gentleman. He doesn't force himself on anyone but eagerly waits to be asked.' Claire stopped and looked at Jessica.

'So how does he make you feel?' Jessica asked.

'How do I feel? Well, loved. Really loved Jess and I love him so much because of what he has done for me.'

Paul's heart thrilled, but not quite sure what he had done to turn this woman's head in such a way.

'Me too.' Jessica's face lit up.

'Really?'

'Yes, I don't know Claire, like, after last night when I woke up this morning, I was different. I felt alive and it's all because of meeting Him and what He did and, I realised I have met this most amazing beautiful person. Thank you so much. I can honestly say Claire I really love him too just like you. I know you understand. I can't believe I'm saying this. This is so weird and cool at the same time. I never thought it possible.'

The doctor's emotions calmed down as he listened further, a little concerned. A frown began to form across his brow.

'When did you know that you loved him Claire. Like really loved him?'

Paul stretched his neck out to soak up every syllable.

'Well, actually, when I first heard the story of what he had done, I realised I needed him so badly. I just surrendered and I guess that first night He just poured his love into me, so full, so powerful, so loving, so deep. Wow Jess! I've never been asked that question before.'

Claire stared out at the ocean reflecting deeply.

'Wow, that's so cool. I so want him in me like I can see he's in you.'

The doctor began to question what he was listening to. He kept his focus, suspecting that he may not have been the centre of the conversation.

'He is Jess. When you asked the Lord into your life, He came into you by the Holy Spirit, whispering deeply in your heart ... *I will never leave you nor forsake you.* He is so there Jess I can see it ... and you have changed ... overnight.'

Disappointment and elation hit the doctor's heart at the same time as he listened to a confirming conversation regarding a much higher dimension than that of his own reputation.

'Really? Claire, I can feel it, but you can see it?'

'Oh yeah girl, I sure can. Paul has seen it. Hey, even the coach has seen it.'

'Shut up,' the young teenager's face looked surprised.

Claire just nodded her head with her face beaming.

'It's the authority of God in action saying Jess arise and you came to life.'

Jessica's faced was fixed to her mentor.

'Like what Jesus did with the young girl who had died?'

'What young girl?' Jessica asked as though an urgency was the high priority for her life at that point.

Claire explained the background of the biblical story.

'... and there were people crying and wailing and Jesus came along and said why make all this commotion and weep? The child is not dead but, sleeping.'

'So, the girl wasn't really dead?'

'No, she had died.'

Jessica looked at Claire strangely.

'Problem Jess?'

'But you said that He said that she was sleeping ... sorry, I don't get it. Why did Jesus say she was sleeping when she was dead? Dead. Sleeping. Big difference,' Jessica said with a giggle.

'Well, Jesus used the image of sleep to show the people that her condition was temporary and that she would be restored to life.'

'Oh, OK.'

Their conversation deepened as Paul began to feel that his ease-dropping might be considered a little intrusive. With that, he walked back down towards the staircase only to be beckoned by the waiter who was walking up towards him from the deck below and advised him that he was cleared to go up to the bridge. Paul walked up the external stairs and knocked on the window of the well painted wooden door. The second officer, a young woman, came to the door.

'Yes,' she asked, in a cold, yet professional voice.

'Hi! I'm Paul Langley. Was just told that I could come in and have a look,' he said, noticing the captain now looking across at him from his command position.

The second officer said nothing but looked closely at his face. She slowly turned her head to look at the captain for confirmation.

'Hey Yeah, come on in.' The captain, a man in his late fifties called from his leather chair positioned high for optimum visibility.

'Peter Chapman,' he said, reaching out to offer his hand. His thick southern American accent gave away his nationality in an instant.

'Paul Langley,' was the quick response as he reached out to match the captain's offer of a handshake.

'Ah yes, our Aussie doctor,' the captain said with his face beaming.

'So glad to finally meet you,' he said, 'I haven't made my rounds with all of the guests yet. Normally do that the first night but we've been a little busy. Hey John, take the chair,' Captain Peter Chapman asked.

'Yes sir,' the bright, enthusiastic Chief Officer replied.

'Let me introduce you to my team up here.'

'This is John Donaldson, my Chief Officer,' the Captain said gesturing to the young man, now seated in command.

'Paul Langley,' the doctor said stretching out an eager hand.

'Hi Paul. What part of Australia?' the young chief Officer asked with great interest.

'Brisbane.'

'Really? I have been to Brisbane,' he said, 'It's a nice city. Very clean and real friendly people,' he said cementing a common bond.

'Really? Interesting observation ... the clean part, I mean,' Paul said with a smile on his face.

The captain laughed. 'Oh, he's from LA. and he's right. I've been to Brisbane too and, in comparison to LA, that little city of yours ... it's as neat as a pin.'

His southern accent was more than a fascination to the doctor and Paul hung on to the Captain's every word.

'And over here is our brand-new second Officer, A'ishah Kadesh.'

'Doctor,' she said, nodding with respect.

'Um, just call me Paul,' the doctor said humbling his status before the onlookers on the bridge.

'A'ishah has just recently passed her exams and this is her second trip with us ... and might I say a fine officer in the making indeed,' he said with genuine intent.

Her face lit up with pride responding to the Captain's honour.

'Thankyou sir,' she said with a soft voice. Her English was very clear and, she was obviously well educated.

'We normally only have two up here but, I've been called on deck due to a possible distress call. We're trying to decipher the vessels position. If we can get the coordinates we can try and help or call on other ships who might be closer to help.' The Captain said, almost making conversation as his attention was drawn to a faint signal coming from the HF radio.

'Did you get that?' he asked his second officer.

'No sir, sorry sir,' she said.

'Keep on it then,' the captain replied.

The Second Officer went back to her efforts of trying to contact the vessel in distress.

'Station calling, this is The Pacific Fair, your signal is very weak. Can you use channel sixteen? I repeat, your signal is very weak. Can you use Channel sixteen?'

'They must be some ways away,' the chief officer announced.

'Why's that John?' Paul asked, now being drawn into the potential emergency.

'Well they're not using channel 16. They are probably outside of VHF coverage,' he elaborated.

Suddenly the radio crackled into life.

'PAN PAN PAN.'

'Wow, maybe not so far away after all,' the young officer shared.

'This is Crystal W ...' Serious interference came over the broadcast which masked a clear understanding of the vessel's identification. Even though it was repeated three times, little could be deciphered to clarify its identification and authenticity. The Captain looked across to his Second Officer. She shook her head.

'Sorry Captain.'

The voice faded back into prominence over the frequency's static.

'. . . our position is Lati . . . one . . . six . . . Longit . . . thirty four . . . ,' the broadcast began to cut out completely only to return with a burst of clarity.

'We have had an explosion in the engine room and we ha ...' more dominant static married it's influence over a strong accent.

'That sounded like an Australian or a New Zealand accent,' the young Chief Officer said looking at Paul for confirmation.

'No, that's not a Kiwi accent and definitely not Australian,' Paul demanded, now straining to catch another sample from the speaker mounted high up on the wall above the plethora of technology that made the impressive looking bridge.

The static cleared as suddenly as it arrived, revealing the same voice pursuing its urgent message.

'... repeat. We h . . .e one man down with a serious ... of the leg. Request urgent assistance. 'Do you have medical crew on board? Number of souls on board thirty...' The signal went to static again.

'Why would they require urgent attention for a broken leg?' the captain asked Paul.

'Well, it might be a compound fracture. If that's the case, then it's serious, but we would hardly be able to help other than offer medication for pain management. They would need to get to the nearest hospital for surgery as soon as possible.'

'Could this interference be as a result of the typhoon?' the young woman interrupted the two men with a look of concern and frustration across her face.

'Maybe, but they could be having radio problems. It's hard to tell,' he said looking out to sea.

'Keep on that radio. Let's get their position confirmed.'

'Yes captain,' the Second Officer replied, picking up the hand help microphone.

'Station requesting assistance, this is the Pacific Fair, we have a doctor on board, I repeat we do have a doctor on board. Please repeat your current position, I say again, please repeat your current position?'

The radio burst into life with the clearest signal yet, allowing the crew on the bridge to ascertain the position of the vessel in distress. With the new information at hand the troubled ship's position was easily plotted on the digital charts.

'Copy that. Please stand by,' the second officer replied then looked to the captain.

Paul watched as the captain and the chief officer studied the screen and talked between themselves.

'So, glad to have you on board Doctor Langley,' Captain Chapman said as he began to walk over to his second Officer.

'Just out of curiosity, where are we headed?' Paul asked.

The captain looked up at the doctor and walked over to a bundle of technology.

'Right ... there.' He said pointing to a spot on a small computer screen. 'Should be there in two hours and thirty -five minutes and that's our track, straight ahead. Coincidently, if we kept going in this direction, in a few days or so, we would be entering the Darwin harbour. It's just shy of one eight zero degrees magnetic, as can be seen on the monitor.'

The captain addressed the touch screen and a broader map appeared. Paul came closer to look at the screen.

'And there's Darwin,' Peter Chapman said with his index finger pointing to its position.

'Now if I press here it will give us the information about Darwin, the Latitude and longitude.' His finger traced under the longitude and latitude numbers of 12.4667° S, 130.8333° E.

'All the necessary port information, hey and we can even get the frequencies for the Darwin airport … not that we would ever use that, but it's there,' he said.

'Really?' the doctor said with renewed interest.

'Yep,' the Captain said eager to display the information of the said subject.

The screen opened its information in a flash and Paul was drawn closer to investigate.

'Ah yes, ATIS one one two decimal six, clearance delivery one two six decimal eight, tower one three three decimal one,' Paul said mumbling the various frequencies to himself as his finger traced over each line across the cold face of the computer monitor.

'Have an interest in aviation Paul?' the captain asked.

'Yes, I remember these frequencies. Went into Darwin a number of years ago.'

'Really? How come?'

'Had to get my hours up to qualify for further training for my commercial and a group of us decided that we would take a month off and fly around Australia and Darwin was one of places we checked out. A lot of fun,' he said as his face lit up with the recollection.

'So, you're a pilot as well?'

'Yes!'

'OK. How far did you go with your licence?' Captain Chapman asked honouring Paul's interest.

'I got my basic commercial, got IFR rated.'

'That's instrument flying I gather? What aircraft did you do that in?'

'Yes, that's correct, IFR rated. I did that training in a Beachcraft Baron, lovely little twin that one, sweat as a nut.'

'Yes, I have flown in one of those.'

'Do you fly?' Paul asked.

'No, my brother does. In fact, he owns a Baron. So, have you taken your licence further?'

'No, but I went ahead and got my study done for my LAME ticket,' he said, releasing his obvious passion for aircraft again.

'Your what?' Peter said pulling his head back in surprise.

'Oh, sorry, Licensed aircraft maintenance engineer.'

'Really! Wouldn't have thought you would have had time for that, what with all your medical work and all?'

'I pulled back on my hours in the hospital … just worked weekends in hospital and spent four days a week getting the necessary hands on.'

'So why did you do that?'

'Well, needed to come off the boil a bit from medicine at the time and had aspirations of buying my own aircraft. Thought it would be good to be able to do my own maintenance work. Save a lot of money in the long term and besides I was interested in how it all worked so, thought why not jump in?'

'So ever get to do any work on jet engines?'

Paul laughed. 'No, just the little stuff, you know piston engines, but I have had some experience with radial engines. Got a friend who owns a World War II T28 Trojan. Now, that's a lot of fun,' he said with his face now lit up with excitement.

'Ever flown it?'

'Sure have. Got a rating on it in fact.'

'My Lord, will you look at this mans' face. Beaming like a kid with a new bike,' he said beckoning all on the bridge to see what he was observing.

The radio splattered back to life with an inaudible signal, closing the subject of aviation.

'Did you copy any of that?' The captain asked the only female in the room closing his mind rom his previous pleasant interlude.

'No sir. I don't think that is our contact. It could be someone else broadcasting.'

He walked over to the monitor and stared at the screen.

'So, do you rely totally on digital technology for your charts?' Paul asked.

'Mm? Oh no, we have our chart room next door. Got a full complement, even some aviation charts,' the captain said. 'Quite comprehensive,' he added.

'Captain, should I tell them we are coming to their assistance?' The second officer interrupted.

'Get their vessel's serviceable status, if they can make way, we'll meet them at our destination. We will at least all have safe harbour there. That typhoon is coming down fast.

We can't jeopardise the safety of our ship and the passengers,' The captain replied with a distinct frown across his face.

'Paul normally I would ask you to leave the bridge but under the circumstances we may need your assistance. Are you OK to help?' the captain asked.

'Certainly, but it would be helpful if we can get some more information regarding the injury.'

'We have a well-stocked clinic downstairs ... never been used. Well, not for serious stuff,' he said now turning to his chief officer.

'Maintain our heading John,' the captain ordered his man in the command chair.

'A'ishah, stay in contact with these guys, confirm their status. If they're good to go, give them our coordinates for tonight's harbour, get that information that the doctor wants regarding the injury and I will take our doctor down to the clinic. Ring me in the clinic if there's any new developments.'

'Yes sir.'

'Walk this way Paul. Wait till you see what I have for you,' he said making his way down the internal stairway to the ship's medical clinic.

'You could deliver a baby down here. We have all the swabs, bandages, all the medical instruments you know. You want medication? . . . We've got antibiotics, pain killers . . . large and small. We've got the stuff you inject. Hey, we even have happy gas.'

'Well, we're going to need more than Nitrous oxide if that injury is a compound fracture,' the Doctor elaborated, 'and I can see no other reason why they would be contacting us for assistance,' the doctor said pondering deep concern in his heart.

CHAPTER TWENTY-ONE

━━━━━━━ ⌦ ━━━━━━━

Claire and Jessica had been lost in their conversation until a stern presence stood in front of them.

'Hi Jess. I hope you had a better night sleep last night.' It was the coach. Her harsh, alcohol-driven tones of the previous evening had softened considerably.

'Hey Coach. Yeah, I did thanks.' Jessica's face was bright and full of life.

'Hi, Celine,' Claire said, holding out her hand. 'Claire's my name.'

'Hi Claire. Look, um, can I have a word with you?' Celine asked still focusing on Jessica.

'Sure.'

'Look, why don't we go for a walk outside?' the coach asked releasing her gaze from her young team member whilst directing with her hand to the breeze swept deck.

'Of course,' Claire said softly. 'Jess, do you want to wait here?'

'Mm, actually Claire, can I go down to our room? Might take a nap,' she said eager to leave Claire to her conversation with her sporting authority.

'Sure. Good call,' Claire said standing up, 'I'll see you down there later.'

Jessica nodded. 'Hey, see ya Celine,' the teenager said as she sprung up from her chair.

'Yeah, sure kiddo. Rest well,' Celine said watching this new creature walk confidently toward her room.

'Wow. Jess seems the happy one today. You seem to have had a good influence Claire,' the coach said still fixed on her youngest team player as she made her way down the spiral staircase.

'Oh, I'm not sure I'm the one who can take the credit for the change,' Claire said also watching the centre of attraction disappear down to the second floor.

Celine turned to study Claire's face in response to her answer.

'Well, whoever it was, needs to be thanked. Anyway Claire... I just want to apologise for my out-burst last night. I was out of line,' the coach said, as they began to make their way outside into the tropical salt air disturbed by a steady breeze.

'I have had a serious talk with the alleged offender and, she has confessed up, as it were, to what she did to Jess. It's unacceptable. I don't tolerate bullying, and I seemed to have had missed the seriousness of the situation,' she said taking charge.

'But Claire, I not only want to apologise, but I want to thank you for offering to have Jess stay with you. That was big of you. I do appreciate it. However, I'm not happy that we are disturbing your vacation, and with that in mind, I have spoken with the Captain, and he has agreed to organise another room for Jess, so you won't be disturbed any further. The main-man upstairs is preparing a place as we speak,' Celine said, making reference to the Captain as she pointed up to the bridge.

'By the time the sun sets, Jess will be set up in her new home and you won't be bothered,' the coach said frankly.

'Well Celine, she really isn't an imposition, and it was my privilege to be able to help.

Jessica is a wonderful young lady, and actually we're getting along quite well,' Claire said with such a gentle voice that it stopped Celine's focus.

'Yes ah, well yes she can be a good kid. A lot of baggage though,' the coach said still looking deeply into Claire's face.

'Don't we all,' Claire replied.

'Mm,' Celine replied in agreement looking back towards the staircase.

'Look what did you say to her last night? That kid's different. I've known her for a couple of years now ... Frankly, ... Let's just put it out there ... spoilt brat. Like, let's put the cards on the table hey? ... she's got a mighty chip on the shoulder, you know real problem child. Mind you, if you knew what she's been through, you'd understand why she is like she is, or ... or was ...You know what I mean? Celine said a little more forcefully.

'So, what did you say?' The coach looked back at Claire with her head slightly tilted to one side.

'Oh, we just talked, confessed a few things, shared a few things. We did some laughing, and, did some crying ... You know. Hey, we even asked God to help out with a few things, and then more talk, you know, girl talk stuff. I think it might have helped,' Claire said looking gently back at the coach.

'Yes, well I don't know what you said, but it seemed to work. I've never seen this kid like that before ... Yeah,' she paused in deep reflection, then shrugged her shoulders.

'Keep up the good work,' Celine said slowly as though she had been moved by something ... deep in her heart, something that she could not understand.

'Anyway, thank you.' She said softly. 'Hey, I'd better go,' the coach said continuing her deep reflection.

There was silence between the two. The coach stood there motionless. Then, she looked straight into Claire's eyes.

'Did she actually open up to you?' the coach asked.

'Yes, she did. She did most of the talking. I just listened,' Claire said.

'Painful stuff?' Celine asked, with what seemed to be a new caring spirit.

'Yes,' Claire said. 'very ... Lots of tears, lots of questions, some hugs with lots of quiet moments during those hugs,' she continued.

There was more silence between the two women.

'Hugs?' The coach asked with a frown slowly developing on her face.

'Um ... Well yes. I hope you're not concerned about me holding her in the midst of her distress,' Claire asked.

'Oh no. Of course not,' Celine said lowing her gaze to the deck.

'Actually, the truth is, she instigated the initial contact,' Claire said displaying her professional voice with a hint of a laugh. 'She just threw herself into my arms and sobbed. It took me a little by surprise, to be honest,' Claire elaborated.

'And she hugged you?' the coach asked.

'Yes,' Claire replied, curious as to what the significance of Jessica's hugging could be.

'Mm. I can't believe she hugged you. I mean, I do believe you, but, ...' She looked back at the stairwell where the young teenager had only just walked down some minutes before.

'So?' Claire added requiring clarification.

'Well frankly Claire, that's not ... that's just not Jess. She's a ... *keep your hands off me* kind of kid. You know a bit of a cold fish ... she's an island most of the time. As I said before ... a major chip on her shoulder. You know, she's built big walls around herself. She wouldn't let anyone in,' the coach said, now raising her eyes to Claire expecting a return.

'I've tried many times,' Celine added.

'Well she did,' Claire said.

'Mm, Yes, obviously. But I wonder why she picked you?' She said pondering. 'I mean no offence, but she won't even let her mother in. Why has she let YOU in? A total stranger.' The coach asked with deep searching.

'Well I'm not sure that I was the one she really let in,' Claire said slowly.

'Meaning?'

'Well I think she let someone with much higher authority into her life.'

More silence was shared between the two.

'Really? You mean like God or something like that?' the coach proposed.

Claire nodded. 'The job was too big for me.'

Silence was again the monument at that point in time.

'Well from my perspective, you are the one, and I thank you Claire. I really thank you,' she said and with that put her arms around Claire, kissed her on the cheek, and hugged her tight, then let go quickly.

'I love my girls, and everyone is important to me. Thank you,' the coach repeated.

'You welcome,' Claire said reaching out to hold her hand as confirmation of her sincerity.

The coach nodded, smiled, and proceeded to walk away slowly letting Claire's hand slip from hers. Suddenly, she spun around to face Claire again.

'Hey, I enjoyed our talk ... really. I can see why Jess opened up to you. You're a good person,' Celine said, wanting to savour more of Claire's personality yet also recognizing awkward feelings beginning to well up in her heart.

'Maybe you and I can have one of those chats sometime ... you know,' she said thumbing back towards Jessica while backing away.

'Sure. You tell me when.' Claire said with a gentle smile.

'OK, sure ... I'll get back to you on that one,' the coach said suddenly feeling a little embarrassed, wishing she hadn't mentioned it.

'Look forward to it Celine.' Claire said recognising the coach's sudden embarrassment.

'Yeah sure … Um, maybe tonight or tomorrow. Tomorrow would be good? …. Hey, we got plenty of time, I guess no need to rush things … Is there?' the coach said finally, as she turned to make her way back down to the rooms below. She looked back to Claire to see her response.

'Sure. Tonight, tomorrow, it's your call,' Claire said starting to feel a little rejected.

CHAPTER TWENTY-TWO

⟨≈⟩

T he phone rang.

'Yes?' Captain Chapman answered the device in the clinic situated deep in the bowls of the ship.

Paul looked across to the man in charge. He could hear clearly the voice of the second officer blearing from the receiver.

'Sir, have made contact with the stressed vessel and they have advised that they can make way to our destination'.

'OK, very well and what of the information for the doctor,' he asked looking across at Paul.

'Yes sir, it seems that the patient definitely does have a broken leg. The break is high up near the hip, but it doesn't seem …' Paul interrupted the conversation.

'Did they mention anything about bleeding, bone protruding out?' Paul asked the captain.

'Stand by,' Captain Chapman asked of the second officer

'Sorry Paul?'

'Did they mention anything about bleeding, bone protruding out breaking the skin,' Paul reinforced.

'Um, the doctor is asking did they make mention of the nature of the break, for example bleeding or bone piecing the skin?' Peter inquired looking back at Paul.

'Ah no sir. They just said that the break seemed to be near the hip joint. However, they did say that the patient was in a lot of pain and they weren't able to reduce that pain due to insufficient medication.'

'Very well, I'll pass that on and I'll be back there as soon as I can.' He placed the receiver back on its mount slowly.

'So, Paul, I guess you heard that. Do you think we can help this guy with what we have here?'

'Well it sounds as though it's not a compound fracture which is good. We can immobilize it with the resources we have here and from what I've seen looks like we have adequate medication for pain management, so I'll be able to make him comfortable. But frankly Peter, it might be better if I go on board their ship and, do what has to be done. It means less discomfort for the patient and let them get to a hospital as soon as possible.'

Paul looked at the captain and noticed a hint of strain in his face.

'Mm, OK. I'll look into it. I see your point.'

'Is this all the medication on hand?' the doctor said pointing to a small cupboard that ran all the way to the ceiling.

'Ah, no Paul. Walk this way.'

They moved out the door of the clinic and moved to the next door. The captain pulled some keys out of his pocket and quickly unlocked it. The door opened outward and into the narrow hallway.

'Here you go doctor, come on in, knock yourself out. This has to be a separate lockable room. Some serious drugs in here.'

The light was turned on and there before Paul was a well-equipped medical store room. He was a little overwhelmed if not mystified as to why there would be such medical supplies on that ship. He surveyed the room and spotted a small sterilizer unit.

'I thought this was a tourist ship. More like a floating clinic, if you ask me.'

The captain laughed. 'Well the main reason for this vessel is business, big business Paul. Clients and potential clients are entertained here while multimillion-dollar deals are written. The company's resident doctor and nursing staff will be on board when business is on. Every detail is catered for including their medical needs if required.'

'Fascinating. I believe the head of the company is also on board,' Paul said with a grin appearing.

'You are indeed correct, actually he's the founder of the dang company.'

'Don't see much of him or his wife. Have seen the kids but not Mom and Dad. What's with that?'

'Oh, they stay to themselves. However, whilst on the subject the lady of the manner is not feeling well today. I think she may have partaken a little too much last night.'

'Along with most of the other guests.' Paul said smiling as he went through the various shelves of medical supplies.

'Do you have an inventory of what's on hand?'

'Yes sir re bob, surely do. Should be in this cupboard.' The captain replied with his broad southern accent as he bent down to open the small cupboard door and retrieve the document of interest.

Paul took the ship's medical inventory and moved toward a comfortable looking stool, with its padded black leather seat and high back rest.

'Do you mind if I sit? I need to go through this.'

'Sure, but you will need to close the door. Can't leave it jutting out into the walkway. Engine room is down the hall so can be a major source of human traffic going back and forth. Don't know why they designed it that way. Anyway, you'll be fine. Here's the keys for this room and the clinic. Now this is the only key for the medical storeroom. When this door is closed, it is locked so don't leave the key inside here.'

The phone could be heard ringing from the clinic.

'That'll be for me no doubt,' the captain said as he walked out the door. 'Remember keep this door shut.'

'Actually, I'll follow you. I'll come back here in a minute.'

Both men walked out of the medical storehouse and, closed the door. They walked back into the clinic where the phone continued its insistent demand for attention.

'Yes?'. The captain's face formed a frown.

'Sir we are entering harbour now.' The Second Officer's voice could be heard clearly over the phone in the room.

'We've made good time. Any sign of our visitors?'

'No sir.'

'Very well … updates on that typhoon?'

'Yes sir, category five, with winds now reported up to 250 knots. Expected to hit us late tonight given its current track.'

'Damnation, OK I'm coming up now. I want an all hands on-deck in thirty minutes.

Let's make it the lounge.' The captains face cemented concern for all to see.

'Doctor, breakout the seasick tablets, we're in for a wild ride tonight. We'll assemble all the guests and I'll brief them. Maybe, it wouldn't hurt to get some medication into them, but I'll leave that to be your call. This typhoon,' he said shaking his head.

'Bad?'

'Very.'

'Couldn't we run from it.'

'We could try, but that isn't going to be nice out there,' he said referring to the open ocean. 'And this is the best lagoon to harbour the vessel that I know around here.

No, I think we're better to batten down the hatches here and ride this little puppy out. Do you get seasick Paul?'

'No, not usually.'

'Good ... but might be an idea if you take the medication as well, just in case. I can't have you out for the count over the next couple of days. I think you'll find that you could be busy tonight. You might need to give a few people injections. We have the stuff in the refrigerator, I think. Anyway, you'll find it.'

'Sure,' the doctor said shrugging his shoulders.

'Paul, I'm so glad you're with us. You're a God send,' he said, reaching out to shake the doctors' hand. Captain Peter Chapman looked Paul in the eyes and just nodded his head, turned around and walked out the door.

Paul searched for further appropriate medication, finally found the supply and, promptly took the suggested dosage. He spent the next fifteen minutes laying out the necessary materials for this inbound emergency case.

The phone rang again.

'Paul Langley.'

'Doctor, I'll be addressing the guests in five minutes in the lounge, could you be present as well please?' the Captain asked abruptly.

'Certainly, on my way.' The receiver was placed back on its mount and the doctor made his way to the lounge.

Paul finally reached the top deck after navigating his way through the tight passage ways of each floor only to be greeted by the humid salt air and the signs of deteriorating weather. The company of passengers had already gathered in the lounge which included the wealthy family impatiently standing to on side trying to keep their distance from the rest of the people. The captain stood waiting about to give his address.

'Ah, there you are doctor,' he said with a face that showed no emotion.

Paul walked over to the small crowd and took his place between Claire and Jessica.

'Well, hello lovely ladies. What have you two been up to in my absence,' he whispered softly, putting his right arm around Claire's shoulder.

Jessica beamed at his compliment and her companion discretely moved in closer to him placing her left hand up to meet his hand cupped around her shoulder.

'Ladies and gentlemen, I have asked for this gathering to bring you up to date regarding the typhoon.'

All the souls in the lounge were dedicated to the Captain's every word.

'We have a category five Typhoon in the area.'

The groups attention was broken momentarily, as some looked at each other for a reaction.

'And if it maintains its course, then we can expect the full force of this storm to hit us around eleven or so tonight.'

Paul watched the reactions of the group as the Captain briefed the passengers on a number of issues including what to expect during the storm, their need to go to their rooms, secure any loose items, other various safety requirements, and also the news of Paul's newly appointed command as ship's doctor.

Jessica looked up at this Australian man next to her and smiled with pride, to which Paul acknowledged her honour with a wink.

'Now, I have things to attend to, so I'll hand you over to our doctor and he will talk to you about a few things.' The Captain had no sooner spoken when a voice sounded behind him.

'Excuse me sir.' It was the second officer softly requesting his attention.

'Yes.'

'We have the vessel in bound in sight.'

The captain looked toward her indication of passage as did Paul. This move proved to be infectious as the rest of the guests followed suit.

'Hey there's another boat coming,' an excited exclamation was uttered from one of the hockey players.

'Ah yes,' Peter Chapman replied turning to face back to his audience.

'I neglected to advise that we will be sharing harbour with another ship tonight. We have an emergency on board that vessel requiring our doctor's attention. Anyway, as I said I'll leave you in his capable hands and after he is finished with you, I want you all to secure your rooms. This is going to get a bit rough later. Now after you've secured your rooms, I want you all back here in one hour to be issued with life vests. That's one-hour sharp. Thank you ... Paul?'

The captain turned to his second officer and they walked off together.

'Excuse me captain, can I have a word with you?' The owner's wife carefully made her presence known.

The man in charge made his way to the exclusive couple while Paul began advising the group of the captains' wishes for the administering of motion sickness medication. He suggested that this could be done when they assembled back in the lounge in one hour. He dismissed the tourists and looked at the two women between him.

'OK you guys, get that room secure and I'll meet you in one hour back here,' he said and with that, he bent down slightly and kissed Claire on the cheek. After the point of impact, he whispered, 'I love you.'

Claire spun her lips to his. They lightly met. 'You too,' she said looking at him deeply.

Paul broke away from his love and, focused on the observer to his left.

'And as for you ... you're just irresistible,' he said holding her shoulder with one hand and roughing up her hair with the other.

A squeal of delight was Jessica's response as she escaped from her humorous admirer and ran down to her room.

'Are you coming, Claire?'

'Right behind you, kiddo.'

'OK' Jessica said with her face beaming because of the attention just received. 'Claire loves Paul.' The young teenager sang out melodically.

'I heard that,' Claire responded.

A squeal of laughter was given from the merry maiden as she raced down the spiral staircase.

'Ratbag.' Paul laughed.

'She sure is but, a wonderful ratbag,' Claire said looking up at her man.

'Yeah, she is. Been a big change in her. Care to share?'

'Of course, but later? Hey, you need help tonight?'

'Sure. Got a strong stomach? It could get messy.'

'Solid as a rock.'

'OK, you're hired. We'll see how you go. Meet you here in one hour.'

'It's a date,' Claire said with eyes sparkling.

'I'll stay awake this time.'

'You better buster.' Her hands came up to his face gently holding him and looked deep into his eyes. 'One hour.' She carefully brought his face to hers, paused, then kissed him quickly.

'I know I keep saying this but, I feel so safe with you. Why's that?' she said and ran off to her room.

Paul stood there, stunned. His world had stopped ... again. He had revealed his feelings, but he had not revealed his commitment.

His euphoric splendour began to fade as unsavoury sentiments slowly seeped into his world.

'I don't God dam care if his head was hanging by a thread. This is just not right and besides I do not have a good feeling about this. Why couldn't they get help somewhere else?

You should have conferred with my husband.' Mrs Susan Stafford lashed her words at the stone-faced captain.

'Mam, it seems that we are the closest in the area and we have a responsibility to aid other seafarers who are in distress. If you were injured and we had no means of helping you for whatever reason, I think you would be very happy to receive assistance from anyone.'

'I don't think so and oh, by the way in case you haven't noticed Captain, I'm not injured and therefore I don't need assistance. In fact, I don't care. It means more of them on our vessel and I don't care for it. Did you hear me? I don't care for it. I don't care for these tourists and I don't care for them whoever they are, in fact, to hell with them. This is disgraceful, Ronald, disgraceful.'

'My dear, I think you're over-reacting. I believe our Captain's point of view is correct, and I feel he has made an appropriate ethical decision, the right decision. If we can help I think we should. Go ahead Peter lets help this poor fellow,' the chairman of the board discretely declared.

'Oh well, that is just charming. I am going to my room,' she spat furiously, staring into the very soul of her husband.

'Susan, pour yourself a drink, and calm down. In fact, have that drink and draw yourself a hot bath and relax. We'll get some of the staff to see that the children's room is secure. I'll stay here and see if I can be of any help.'

The woman turned and lifted her head in disgust and walked away in silence.

'Apologies Peter. I wanted to ask if I could be of any help?'

'Follow me Mr Stafford.'

'Peter, call me Ron.'

The captain nodded with a twinkle in his eye. The two walked up to the bridge leaving Paul alone in the lounge.

The head waiter appeared from the lower deck, greeted the doctor and asked if he required anything.

'Actually, can we get some water up here for all the guests and the staff, say within twenty minutes?' Paul explained his request and the attendant moved immediately to cater for the occasion.

The doctor looked around at the horizon. The weather was building, with the clouds looking darker in the direction of the typhoon. Further out to sea he could see the incoming vessel cutting into the troubled ocean. The ship was making good time despite the oceans' swell and he estimated that it would be entering harbour within the hour.

Paul returned to the clinic to make final preparations for the soon to arrive patient. He spent some time making sure everything he thought he might require was laid out systematically on one of the benches. He checked the examination table then, he looked for blankets in case the injured seaman needed to be treated for shock.

After finding the inventory journal he moved to the storeroom, unlocked the door but neglected to close it, therefore leaving the door exposed to the narrow hallway. Paul spent some time getting himself acquainted with the variety of assets found in the large medical storeroom. He even found a collection of body bags. His focus was locked to the work at hand, when a mechanical grinding sound commanded his attention. He turned to its perceived direction and jumped with fright. Two men stood at the door.

'You must be the doctor,' a young man said with another standing behind him peering over his shoulder to see the man with the medical reputation.

'Hi, Paul Langley.'

'Alan Picton, Chief Engineer and this is Roby Dawson Chief Grease Monkey and troublemaker, but he's really the technical officer for all that hi-tech stuff up-stairs on the bridge, the radar and radios, you know,' he said with a broad Cockney accent. His partner stood to one side of the engineer, smiled and gave a peculiar wave.

'Hi guys, good to meet you,' Paul said, holding back a laugh after seeing the interesting response of the engineer's mate.

'So, Roby why are you working down here with Alan in the engine room?'

'Well it's all brand-new tech equipment. No need for maintenance so far. Got to do something, so Captain has kept me out of trouble and made me engineers assistant till something stuffs up upstairs.' The technical officer presented his case with educated clarity.

'I'm told you're an Australian.' The chief engineer asked.

'Yep. Born and bred.'

'You don't sound like one.'

'Sorry to disappoint you,' Paul said now releasing a laugh.

The response wasn't duplicated.

'No, not disappointed, just don't sound like one.'

'Right,' Paul said now feeling a little baulked.

'Anyway, the ship is in harbour Paul.'

'OK. What was that grinding sound?' Paul asked.

'Oh, that's the anchor dropping,' the engineer said, looking at the doctor with a face that appeared as though it needed to learn how to smile.

'There's another to drop soon.' He continued.' Oh, and by the way, make sure you keep this door closed, gets in the way … totally stupid design.'

The doctor agreed and the two went on their way to the upper deck. Paul followed soon after with a box filled with the medication in hand for dispensing to the guests and staff.

On arrival, all were waiting in the lounge with the exception of Mrs Susan Stafford who according to her children wasn't interested in participating. The guests were dispensed the doses followed by the staff. The Australian doctor advised that they take another dose before they went to bed. He then asked the children of Mrs Stafford to give their mother the medication to which they agreed. Paul watched the two children closely. They appeared quite subdued.

'You guys OK?' he asked.

'Sure.' The older one said with her less than attractive tone.

'She is so not. She's scared shitless,' the younger of the two blurted out to the doctor.

The Doctor muffled a laugh.

'Hey, we'll be fine. Just make sure to take this medication again before you go to bed.' The doctor advised as a strange sense overcame him.

Claire and Jessica came over to the doctor.

'Hey, there you are,' he said affectionately to Jessica. 'Got that room of yours all moved into and secured?

'No, we thought it might be wise if we stick together tonight?' Claire said, putting her arm around the young teenager.

'Coach, *A OK* with that?'

'Yes sir,' Replied Jessica with a broad smile admiring her new-found hero.

'When do you require my help?' Claire asked, releasing her arm from the girl to tire her hair up in a bun.

'Let's go down now and I'll brief you on a few things. -They want to bring the bloke over, so he'll be brought down to us in the medical centre. By the look of that, it won't be long,' Paul said beckoning attention to the incoming vessel. 'Mind you, I can't see much point in it.'

'Why?' Claire looked at Paul with her head cocked to one side.

'Makes more sense me going over to them.'

'OK, Yes, I guess if he's got a broken leg, he won't feel like hopping into a little boat and bounce all the way over here. Mm, can see why a house call might be in order.'

'Exactly ... Odd.'

'Can I help too?' Jessica asked.

'Um, probably not blossom.'

'Why not? I could help Claire ... help you.' A frown came over the teenager's face, as she realised that separation from her new-found mentor was now pending.

'Well given the nature of the injury Jess and where the injury is, I'm probably going to have to cut off his pants, including his underwear... maybe,' Paul said, using this probable procedure as a hopeful deterrent to her participation. 'So, if you're OK with that then ...' The doctor was cut off.

'Oh gross,' she said with sudden shock waves emulating from her face.

Claire laughed. 'Maybe better you stay up here Jess. Don't think you need to see that. Besides he will be in a lot of pain, could be a little stressful.'

'True enough,' the doctor reinforced.

'OK,' a simple reply from a compliant young lady was on offer immediately after the explanation.

The doctor and his assistant left Jessica standing in the lounge as they made their way down into the lower deck of the five-star vessel.

CHAPTER TWENTY-THREE

aul left the lounge and ventured outside to check the status of the impending weather. As he did so Claire lagged behind watching his every move. The cool air hit his face as the afternoon grew older. He looked around at the sky. A considerable change had occurred over the last few hours. Grey clouds were mounting overhead giving a sombre feel to the beautiful area. The wind had begun to show itself, whipping up choppy seas beyond the reef.

'Here comes that weather that the captain was talking about,' Claire said walking up behind him.

'Mm, hard to believe that it's going to hit around eleven tonight. I mean, you'd think it would be really blowing by now. I wonder if there's a change to its estimated time of arrival, or better still, maybe it's heading in a different direction,' Paul said as he looked around at the sky.

'Hey, that boat has made good time. It's coming into the lagoon,' Claire mentioned pointing to a much larger vessel.

Its sleek shape sliced into the calmer waters of the islands lagoon and presented a beautiful picture in the crystal-clear water. Paul, more concerned about the incoming typhoon hadn't noticed the new arrival into their safe harbour.

'OK, we'd better move. I need to brief you before we see this patient, but first let's get up to the bridge. I want to have a word with the captain.'

'Lead on good doctor,' Claire said drawing her attention back to the incoming ship.

Its markings could now be seen clearly. A black dolphin, riding a turquoise blue wave painted on its bow, pushed the waters aside as it made its way to its charted anchorage.

The captain turned and saw the doctor at the door of the bridge and asked the Second Officer to let both the guests in. She opened the door with a new-found twinkle in her eye.

'Doctor,' she said brimming with confidence.

'Hi.'

'Paul,' the skipper called 'Come on in.'

'Captain, this is Claire. She'll be assisting me downstairs.'

'Hi Claire. A nurse I presume?'

'Ah, no Captain, an economist working in banking education actually.'

'Oh OK … works for me,' he said, raising his eyebrows at the doctor, smiling.

'I'm all he's got.' Claire smiled broadly at the captain.

'Lucky you doctor,' Captain Chapman said winking back at Paul. 'Oh, how rude of me. Paul, Claire, this is Ronald Stafford, the owner.'

Paul turned around and noticed this unassuming man sitting on a high stool in the corner of the bridge.

'Doctor, good to finally meet you. We're so glad to have you on board. Sorry to take you away from your vacation.'

'Not a problem. Just hope I can help. This is Claire.'

'Yes, your assistant. Good to meet you Claire. Thank you for your willingness to help.

Interesting qualifications for the job required though. I guess it's a case of not what you know but who you know,' he said, laughing.

'Oh yes. What can I say, he needs me,' she said shrugging her shoulders with a cracking smile across her face.

'Indeed.' The captain interjected.

Paul looked back at the captain and smiled.

'Now Paul, there has been a slight change. It seems they are also requiring some technical help as a result of the accident on board, so they are coming over to pick up our engineer and technical officer. Apparently, they want us to bring some of our gadgets to help assess the extent of the damage. Anyway, our boys know what they are talking about.'

'Right and the patient?'

'Yes. They agree. Moving him might be a big problem and they see the sense in you making a house call.'

'So, you don't need me?' Claire said placing her hand on his shoulder.

'Probably not over there, but I would appreciate a hand downstairs getting things together.'

'Sure.'

'Peter, is there an update on the typhoon?' Paul asked, looking outside at the sky.

'Yes indeed,' The man in command said, looking across to his Second Officer.

She looked up immediately, recognised her cue and reached over to a bench that was home to a number of documents. She picked up a sheet of paper with the forecast freshly printed.

'It came in ten minutes ago doctor. Looks like its slowing down. Um, ground speed that is ... still a category five and still expecting up to two hundred and fifty knot winds, but due to its slower ground speed, won't get here until around three tomorrow morning.'

'OK, well let's hope the thing heads off in a different direction,' Paul said with a faint expression of concern washing over him.

'Never can tell with these dam things. Within a few hours it can be a whole different story.' The Captain said as he looked over at the beautiful ship now in the lagoon.

'The slower they are the more damage they can do,' The Chief Officer said.

This led to some time being invested into the subject of typhoons. Various stories were shared of the experiences had by the men on deck and of known stories of others. The second officer was silent through it all, constantly monitoring the incoming vessel whilst showing little interest in the stories being passed around the bridge that afternoon.

'Ah sir? Looks like they are about to drop anchor,' the Second Officer interrupted.

All heads turned to the subject in question.

'She's a pretty one,' the Chief Officer said, with binoculars now to his face pouring over the sleek lines of this fine vessel now harboured five hundred yards away.

'OK. Well, we had better be getting to work. Can we use the internal stares?' Paul asked.

'Yes certainly. Oh, and by the way that key I gave you, remember it's the master key.

It will open all the doors, just in case you have to make house calls later on tonight due to the weather. The other key? The medical storeroom … that's the only one so, don't lose it.'

Paul thanked him and they made their way down into the lower deck of the ship. The owner said his goodbyes and left the bridge to venture down to the lounge.

Paul and Claire navigated through the narrow passageways that lead to the lower deck and the clinic.

'Wow. Who's special, the master key and the only key for the storeroom?' Claire exclaimed holding on to the arm of the doctor.

'Yep, they need me what can I say,' he said smugly in gest, mimicking her comment previously to the owner upstairs.

'Well, I guess it's not what you know it's who you know,' she said giggling softly.

Paul smiled and looked at Claire.

'You know, something tells me this is going to be one heck of a night,' the doctor mused softly.

They spent thirty minutes in the medical storeroom finding the various medications required, packing them in one of the two small medical back packs found in the storeroom and briefing Claire on what to expect should they have to transfer the patient to the Pacific Fair. Paul was thorough, succinct and spoke with a calm, *matter of fact* voice. Claire had difficulties focusing on the details due to the doctor's professional posture. Her heart thrilled.

'OK, can you take these up-stairs to the bridge? I've got a few more things to organise and I want to have a quick read about some of these drugs. I'm not so familiar with some of this lot. This is all American standard, bit different to home. Here you go … see you up there shortly,' he smiled handing her the backpack.

'OK Doc,' she said whisking the bag away from him and swinging it around to land comfortably on her back.

She walked out the door stopped, then swung back around to face him.

'You know something? You really sound good.' She said laughing 'You can be my doctor anytime. Thinking of moving to Sydney?

'Sorry?' He changed his focus … to Claire.

'Sydney! Ever thought of moving to Sydney? I said, you could be my doctor. Weren't you listening?'

'Well, of course I was.'

'Yeah, sure you were,' she said with hands on hips expecting an answer.

'I think you moving to Brisbane is a better idea.'

'Excuse me?'

'Brisbane ... you,' the doctor said pointing at her as he released a faint smile.

'Oh really, and why would I want to move to Brisbane?'

'Well, so you could see your doctor ...every day.'

'Every day?' she said mystified.

'Yes, every day ... till death us do part.'

'Excuse me?' Her countenance was suddenly flawed. 'I ... what ... Excuse me?'

Claire's thoughts were scrambled.

Paul enjoyed the preface to this potential meltdown set before him.

'Hey, time is marching on ... you, have a package to deliver. We'll talk later,' Paul said, coming back down to earth feeling very satisfied with himself.

'Um ... Yeah sure,' she said as she turned and walked back to the bridge processing deeply.

Within minutes, Claire was standing at the door to the bridge.

'Ah, Claire there you are! how's the ... Claire? Are you OK?' the captain asked as all heads on the bridge turned to the person in question.

'Um yes, Well no, I ...'

The Chief Officer came over to her taking her by the arm. 'Do you need to sit down?' he asked warmly.

'Yes ... um no, no, I'm fine, really ... I'm so sorry, just got a shock. That's all.'

'A shock?' The Captain asked.

'Um the doctor. ... ah Paul ... he ...'

'He what?' the Chief Officer asked now concerned as all on deck were studying her reactions.

'I think he just ... proposed,' she said slowly, as though the last piece of the puzzle had just been placed home.

'You think?' the Captain asked laughing.

'Well yes, I think that ... well yes ... he did. Oh, my goodness ... till death us do part. I didn't get it. Moving to Brisbane. That's what he meant.'

The chief officer's face sprung with life. 'No way!'

'And?' the Captain questioned.

'What?' Claire said vaguely.

'What is your answer?' the young man on the bridge asked.

'Well yes ... of course!' she said laughing with tears welling up in her eyes.

'And how did he react?' Captain Peter Chapman inquired further.

'React?'

'Paul ... how did he react when you said yes?'

'Well ... he didn't.' Claire's reactions were proving more humorous for the Chief Officer.

'Why the heck not Claire?' the young man spat out his question laced with a laugh as he looked at the Captain, seeking a cue.

'Um, well he doesn't know.' Claire's disposition began to find normality.

'What? Why not?' the Chief Officer asked, now laughing heartily while the Captain stood there mystified.

'I didn't quite get it ... then he told me we would talk later and that I had to get this up here and I ...' She pointed to the backpack, then quickly passed on the instructions given to her by the ship's temporary doctor.

'Claire there's the phone. Push nine. That's the clinic,' Peter said with a broad smile.

She looked across at the Captain.

'Ring him. Tell him ... unless you have doubts,' he demanded.

'Oh no. Oh dear me ... no!' she softly exclaimed, as she rushed to the phone.

Claire looked to the Captain still partially lost in the moment.

'Nine?' she asked him.

'That's it.' he said, winking at her. Peter Chapman folded his arms, looked across to his Chief Officer and raised his eyebrows.

Paul was underlining points about certain drugs from the thick hard bound reference book sprawled across the bench. He jumped as the phone next to him squawked. He reached across and picked up the receiver.

'Paul Langley.'

'Did you just propose to me back then?'

'There's no doubt about it ... you're quick girl,' he said making light of her new- found revelation.

'Did you?'

'Yes ... and?'

'Oh Paul!'

'Am I to take that as a yes? … yes?'

'Oh my.' She said holding on to her surreal situation.

'And?' He laughed, listening to her breathing. 'Claire?'

'Yes, oh my goodness, Paul ... yes!' Her voice was broken by deep emotion.

There was a sudden explosion of cheers from the bridge pouring out of the receiver to hich Paul reacted by pulling the loud explosion away from his ear.

Back on the bridge, the Captain and Chief Officer both heartily congratulated the young woman.

'Captain we have two boats in the water coming our way,' the Second officer said shattering the mood.

The skipper looked across to the anchored ship and frowned.

'Um actually, correction … There's another one … We have three boats. The chief officer said with the binoculars being focused against his face.

'There's quite a few people in each boat,' the Captain said.

'What's that all about,' the Chief Officer asked.

'Don't know! Can you get Alan and Roby ready? They might need a hand with the gear. I'll stay here.'

'Yes sir.'

'Mam, take the chair,' he said to the Second Officer.

'Yes sir.' Her face was sombre.

'Are you … all right?'

'Yes sir. Just a headache.'

'It's been a big day,' he said studying her.

'Yes sir, very big. Sir, could I quickly go and get something for this?'

'Of course.'

'Yes, thank you sir.' The Second Officer walked off to address the problem.

Claire was still talking to Paul being totally engrossed with her man on the other end of the line.

'Excuse me Claire,' the Captain abruptly interrupted the bride to be.

Claire turned to the intrusion.

'Can you tell Paul that he might have to wait a bit for his visit to the other side. It seems we have three boat loads of visitors coming. Why the heck ... I have no idea. Tell him we'll ring him when he is required.'

Claire passed on the message, said goodbye and hung up the phone.

'Captain, I'll go down to the lounge if you don't mind. Thank you for your kind ... assistance,' she said and walked straight over to the man in command and kissed him on the cheek.

'Wow! You're most welcome little lady. Hey and congratulations ... he's a good man.'

'Yes, he is.' Claire smiled, then made her way down to the lounge, where Jessica sat, now watching the small craft making their way closer to the Pacific Fair.

CHAPTER TWENTY-FOUR

The Captain looked down from the bridge as the visitors boarded the Pacific Fare one by one. All were being welcomed by the chief officer. The chief engineer and the technical officer stood at the side waiting to board the small boats to take them to the neighbouring vessel. The captain watched as three of the visitors walked over to the guests in the lounge while the engineer and technical officer over saw the loading of the equipment into the ferry craft. The Chief Officer stood at the edge of the stair way leading to the boats moored at the temporary pier speaking to the leader of the newcomers.

'Ah there you are,' the man in command spoke to the Second Officer who had just arrived from below deck 'Did you get what you needed?'

'Oh yes sir,' she said with a strange smile on her face.

'You know this is a strange lot. Take the chair. I'll go down to meet these guys,' he said, looking down at ten men on the deck. 'They seem to be making themselves at home,' Peter Chapman suggested, continuing his focus on the events on the main deck.

'Why don't we go down together?' she announced with new-found authority.

He spun around to be greeted with a high-powered pistol.

'What the ...?'

'Move, American pig,' she said, with an accent he had never heard come from her before.

'What have you done?' he said softly to her.

'Move.' she pointed the handgun with such familiarity, indicating the proposed direction she would have him take.

The intruders looked up at the bridge. At the sight of their female infiltrator now in command, the visitor's leader whipped out his hand piece aiming it directly at the Chief Officer and with that the rest of his motley crew followed his lead.

'Surprise,' the South African sang his announcement while twirling his pistol in the face of his new hostage.

'Pirates.' The Chief Officer yelled his warning as he foolishly endeavoured to disarm the immediate threat set before him by seizing the held pistol and smacking it into the face of the blond marauder. A brief tussle proved fruitless and in one defensive move, the painfully dazed criminal shot the Chief Officer in the head. A fine spray of crimson mist appeared from the young man as his body cascaded over the ships rail into the water below.

The Engineer's face instantly filled with rage.

'Mongrel!' His Cockney accent was heard across the deck, as he squealed his last word. He ran to the murderer, throwing the piece of equipment that he was carrying in his arms, straight at the man in question, reaching its target, slamming its mass against the leader's chest. This further injury, caused the South African to buckle to one knee, holding his upper torso with newfound priority. Possessed by anger, he haphazardly aimed his pistol, and fired. The Engineer froze, then, looked down as his chest opened due to the bullet's merciless track through his body. Alan's lifeless form fell backwards into the shallow waters of the lagoon, causing a crimson wave to wash its declaration of death against the small boat tied to the vessel under attack.

The Technical Officer screamed in horror. 'No!'

His fate was quickly duplicated as he received a bullet's point-blank impact from the thin Asian man standing next to him. The hot lead missile possessed its mark, leaving a hellish stare on Roby's face. His mortal remains awkwardly tumbled into the ocean, adding further to the blood flow in the water.

Screams were heard, followed by a rush of demands, then more screams echoed across the vessel's deck. The men, strategically positioned in the lounge took control of the horrified onlookers. Peace had been conquered and terror now commanded the Pacific Fair.

Susan Stafford lay still as the warm water lapped its calming liquid over her shapely body. She sipped casually on her glass of champagne enjoying the sensual combination of the water on and the alcohol in her earthly temple. Her deep bath was found in one corner of its opulent surroundings. A double shower was situated on the other side of the large bathroom.

On all the walls were mirrors, from floor to ceiling, Chinese slate was intricately laid on the five-star floor. A light grey marble bench with two thick white porcelain basins with gold taps were centrally positioned to present the perfect touch. Her mind wondered as she lay in her liquid luxury. The smell of the scented water tantalised her senses. She opened her eyes slowly and focused on the mirror strategically placed above her on the ceiling. She admired her form and studied her shape with pride for some time. Another sip of champagne washed down into her belly as she closed her eyes to enjoy her perceived right to be rich ... her universal right and with that concept she was very comfortable. She had chosen the right husband with the right connections. He was handsome, intelligent, ran after her every whim and most importantly, he came from the right family with more than suitable means to support her expensive expectations.

Susan also came from the right family with assets to impress, was very beautiful, mixed in the right circles, knew how to entertain the right people and presented her husband with two perfect children without physical blemish. In her mind, her life was as it should be.

Slowly, her attention was drawn to noises. She casually focused. There was a crack, then another, a sound as though someone screamed. Her pulse began to beat a little faster.

'Those stupid girls. Why are they here?' she wined a whispered complaint under her breath.

She blocked out the annoyance by focusing on herself, her comfort, her feelings, her body. She released her grip on the crystal Champaign glass leaving it securely standing on the edge of the bath and submerged her arms into the warm tranquil water. Susan's hands strayed down the length of her form, caressing, enjoying the effects of her touch.

More distant cracks, more faint screams then, the sound of voices began wafting from afar into her private domain.

'Oh my God, can't a woman take a bath in peace?' she whispered the intolerant words.

'NO.'

The word ripped into her world of pleasure. Her eyes flashed open and darted straight to its source.

'Get up, bitch.'

'Oh my God!'

The horror of what stood over her was crippling. She lay frozen in the warm water, totally displayed, totally vulnerable, and now, totally submerged in lethal danger.

Suddenly her arm streaked across her chest in a vain attempt for modesty, leaving a tidal wave of water to crash over the side of its enclosure. The only available hand left latched itself to the remainder of her womanhood, hiding as much as possible from the terror hovering above her.

'I said, get up, you stinking-bitch, or I will blow your brains out,' the intruder said with a Sig Pro semi-automatic pistol placed to her head.

'Oh my God.' A pathetic whimper trickled from her lips. 'Please, please don't hurt me. I have money. Oh God please.'

'Get up!' he yelled. His words oozed with hate. The Asian face glared its evil intent at the woman. He poured his prefaced intention of villainous intrusion up and down the length and breadth of the sight set before him. The pirate grabbed her by her hair with one hand, whilst maintaining the cold nose of the pistol against her temple with the other.

'Move it.'

She winced with pain and tears now poured down her face as she clumsily climbed out of the bath still maintaining her right for modesty by clinging on to those areas of priority.

'Oh my God. Oh, who the hell are you? You bastard. I have rights. You have no idea who I am,' she snapped as humiliation and pain turned into anger while being dragged upright by the hair and directed to the door of the bathroom.

Forgetting her dignity, she released her need for modesty and began swinging her fists and elbows making painful contact in the face and ribs of the evil controlling her.

'Help. Someone help me. Oh God please...anyone,' Susan screamed as she continued her pointless fight, but no one came.

In one swift move her intruder retaliated by pushing her over the opulent bathroom basin, while smashing her face up against the crisp cold mirror. With his body firmly pushing against the full length of her nakedness, he placed his face up to her ear.

'You have no rights infidel pig,' he hissed, 'I hate pigs. I kill pigs.'

The heat of his stinking breath rushed its way around the contours of her right ear reaching her nostrils with its stench. Her stomach convulsed. Fear owned her, as it shot its sharp chill up her spine and pieced her heart.

'Oh God, please don't ... please don't kill me ... I'll do anything. Oh my God.'

He hesitated, maintaining his weight up against her body, pinning her to the bathroom bench with his hips.

'Anything?

'Yes, oh yes ... anything, anything.'

'Mm, so, you want to live, infidel bitch ... do you?'

Yes, don't kill me. I beg you ... Oh God. Oh God please, oh please ... I don't want to die.' The woman of importance's desperate lust for life took control. She surrendered. Susan began to shake uncontrollably as she sobbed silently against the unforgiving glass of the cold, hard, mirror.

After a quick personal adjustment, he pulled on the handful of hair and yanked her head toward him. She had no option but to arch her back, pushing her behind toward him and with that he reached his mark.

A gasp of air thrust itself into her lungs as the intruder began to violate her womanhood with merciless intent. She cried out in pain. She cried out in shame ... but, no one came.

Paul sat in the medical clinic waiting for the phone to ring. He had completed all necessary preparatory procedures in readiness for his departure. Needing an update, he picked up the phones receiver and rang the bridge. It rang for some time, but there was no answer.

After another unsuccessful effort, the doctor decided to make his way to the bridge and then spend some time with Claire before leaving the ship to attend the patient in need. The question of why no one had answered the phone bothered him as he walked along the narrow corridor to get to the stairs that led up to the next level. As he began his assent, he heard an Asian language being spoken by a number of voices. It sounded a little like the major Philippine language but there were some considerable differences. As he journeyed up the steps he achieved partial view of the next level. He was suddenly fixed with an incomprehensible image. There, directly in front of him, at the end of the passageway were men moving in and out of the rooms, looting. He stopped immediately, frozen, confused. His heart began to pound in his chest. Reality hit him, bringing its truth home relentlessly. These men were modern day pirates. Each intruder had a handgun, some had their weapons tucked in their shorts, some in their back pocket of their jeans. One man had his weapon secured in a holster hidden under his shirt that had lost a few buttons. All were carrying money, passports and other items of value that had been stolen from the various rooms. As the men stuffed their pockets with their ill-gotten gain. Two other intruders of middle eastern appearance were making their way along the corridor, unwinding what appeared to Paul to be a cord.

One carried a large backpack full of packages, with some sort of pouch strapped around his waist and both men were coming in his direction. Suddenly he heard the unmistakable sound of distant gun fire, then screams coming from the upper deck. Ducking his head so as not to be seen he rushed quietly back down toward the clinic.

Murder was in the air. Panic began to seep into his heart and anger poured through his veins. He arrived outside the clinic. He needed a place to hide, but where? He looked to his left in his desperate plight and the words of the captain came to mind.

'Now this is the only key for the medical storeroom. When this door is closed, it is locked, so don't leave the key inside here.'

Paul took the key out of his pocket, silently slid the item into the slot, opened the door of the storeroom and, rushed in closing it softly behind him. Turning on the light he looked around for a secure spot. With mind racing and heart thumping he noticed a cupboard that made no impression on him previously. He opened it and there before him was an empty space just large enough for him to stand in. He could think of no reason as to why it was there. There were no shelves, no hooks on the wall of the space, not even boxes stacked, just an empty space big enough for him. He climbed in and closed the door as he heard the muffled sounds of men coming along the corridor. Suddenly the words *the light*, flashed into his head. He rushed out of his shelter, switched off the potential beacon and felt his way back through the blackness to his hide out.

On deck, chaos reigned supreme. Jessica was holding on tightly to Claire's side. They were both quiet as they watched the unfolding horror, frozen in fear. One of the hockey players buckled to the floor as the effects of the fear in the tropical air sapped her of her strength. Two of her teammates came to her rescue, comforting her as they all watched a small team of men carry the high-tech equipment ripped from the bridge's console.

The ship was being gutted of anything that could be easily carried and the small boats were being ferried back and forth to deliver their booty. Anything from ships radios, radio hand pieces to communication dishes, tools, ships computers, laptops, cell phones, handheld GPS units. Emergency locator beacon units were also taken.

Susan Stanford entered the Lounge being practically dragged by her conqueror. Her eyes were filled with defeat and horror. Her children were holding on to their father, set off to one side by the afternoon's murderers. When Susan's girls saw their mother they cried out, to which she snapped from her daze in response and rushed to their side, ripping herself from the clutches of her molester and almost herself from the covering of her robe. She ran to her family now haphazardly clad, partially revealing her gender for all to see. Her cruel companion stood still, surprised by her escape. He was an impulsive man, with a reputation of being a greedy braggart, with no respect for anyone, particularly women.

There in the centre of the action was the second officer standing next to the chief of operations of the afternoons plunder.

'You've done well my love,' he said in clear South African English clutching his aching side.

He was a tall, thick set man, with blond hair. It was clear that the couple were close, given her response to his compliment. He bent down and kissed her fully on the mouth. She responded warmly as all the captives watched on in disbelief.

Susan's attacker walked around the couple, smiling at the two on centre stage. He then looked at the prisoners as he stood next to the second officer and said to all the women in the lounge.

'Don't worry, you will get your turn soon beautiful ladies,' he laughed with an evil laugh waving his handgun casually in the air.

The Second Officer broke her face away from her lover.

'Abang, shut up you idiot,' she said glaring at the Asian spokesman.

The Captain stood by, powerless, but consumed with bitterness as he watched the present discourse between what he considered as worthless people.

'You'll get your reward soon enough,' she spat out her cold demands.

'You dam Jezebel,' the enraged captain suddenly cried out losing all control. He lunged at the man's weapon, with full intention of causing his treacherous Second Officer harm.

The young woman spun toward the pending danger. Before she could respond further, the Asian braggard aimed his pistol at the captain, eager for a kill. The gun released its payload point blank and, the captain dropped to the floor, dead.

The room erupted with screams as some fell to the deck huddled together in a desperate attempt to protect their lives.

Jessica suddenly gripped her American mentor.

'Claire?'

The desperate sound of Jessica's voice broke Claire's attention from the hellish sight that had just danced its damnation before her. She looked down at her frightened friend.

Jessica was clutching her chest with one hand as blood was oozing out between her dainty fingers.

'Claire?'

'Oh, my Lord,' Claire screamed as she took Jessica's weight, guiding her failing body to the floor gently and holding the injured in her arms.

The bullet had passed through the captain's body and lodged itself directly into the young teenager's chest.

Jessica held on to Claire's arm with desperate focus.

'Claire, help me?'

Claire, gasping, cried out aloud. 'What have you done you ape of a man?' she said, as she turned to the one, that perpetrator of destruction.

The second officer spun around to meet the action with intense distain. She turned her icy stares to the retched bungler.

Jessica's face grew as pale as ash. Internal bleeding began its deadly outcome.

Claire looked down at the beautiful teenager who was slowly fading in her arms.

Claire's head was spinning, her heart crying out to God for her new-found sister in Christ, crying out for desperate mercy.

'Help me! ... please Claire. Save me,' Jessica's panicked face looked at the woman who cared. The teenager began to cough.

'Jess, I can't help you baby girl, only Jesus can help you now. Remember what we said last night. Those who call on the name of the Lord will be saved. Jess call out to Jesus ... Oh Lord, come to Jess! ... Oh Lord,' Claire said, with emotions now at critical point, tears flowed freely down her face as she watched an incomprehensible sight.

Jessica heard her voice, closed her eyes and spoke softly. 'Jesus, help me, save me, save ...' Her voice grew softer as she seemed to sleep.

'Jess?'

Every soul on the deck was glued to the spectacle set before them. Silence was fitting, as though all sensed a profound presence.

Jessica's eyes opened. She looked straight up and smiled.

'Jess?' Claire watched as the young girls faced changed from the colour of ash to a healthy glow.

The teenager opened her eyes wider and lifted up one arm, reaching out as though to accept a hand from a close friend. A close friend she hadn't seen for a long time, a close friend who was about to lift her up.

'Jesus,' Jessica spoke the name ... the last word on her earthy lips, then, she was gone.

There was a faint glimmer, like a ripple of light, a twinkling, just beyond her face, just for a second. Claire saw it.

The weight of death began to settle its presence into Claire's arms, as the youth's earthly shell relaxed to lifelessness. Claire held Jessica's body closely to herself sobbing deeply, then, with focused presence of mind, she slowly laid the body gently on the floor.

'No!' she cried out loud, as a plethora of emotions began to well up from her soul.

Remorse, confusion, disbelief, but the greatest of all, was anger, and all being welcomed into Claire's heart building an ugly picture of intent about to be acted out. Her vengeful heart suddenly took its cue aiming to murder the murderer. She looked up at the killer.

His eyes had no place for mercy. Her cold intent equalled his atrocities. She stood up in a flash as though possessed by a power beyond understanding and lunged straight for the killer's throat.

She cried out again in anguish as she reached her target well but, she was over powered by his strong arms. He speedily swung her around and smashed his pistol grip into the side of her head. The gun went off as she was thrown down hard against the edge of a coffee table. Her limp body bounced helplessly off the furniture and slapped hard on the polished parquetry floor next to Jessica's lifeless form. Her right arm flung into the air and came to rest over the teenagers remains. Claire's face landed hard on its side in a pool of blood seeping out of the fresh kill.

'You ... stupid fool,' the voice of authority squealed. The Second Officer ran over to Claire, knelt down beside her now pale face and put her fingers on Claire's throat searching for a pulse.

'Swen, he's killed another one,' she yelled looking up at her partner.

She stood upright with a threatening finger pointing straight at the culprit.

'You have cost us big money! Idiot. That young one would have fetched a good price.

The captain ... the company would have paid good money for him and this woman another company executive,' the female officer said looking straight at the careless murderer. 'You, stupid shit.'

The offender smirked with his defiant eyes squinting at the woman he had little respect for.

'These things happen in this business bitch. Get used to it,' he said with cold antagonistic tones shrugging his shoulders in angry defence.

Suddenly, the South African leader spun into action and with just a few strategic movements had the accused disarmed, immobilised and being dragged to the rail at the ships' edge. A guilty declaration was declared with the sound of gun fire as the offender, fell lifeless to his watery grave.

'There my love, we've just made up for the loss. We'll take his share,' he said rubbing the side of his face, now feeling the effects of the Chief Officer's offensive actions.

The tension escalated with the sight of another murder and the young women screamed and huddled together around the coach who tried desperately to console her team.

The Second Officer began to yell out orders to the foreign crew.

Swen, wincing in pain, rubbed his chest as he looked at their captives. 'Where's the doctor?' he said spinning around looking for him.

No one offered any help but stood frozen with fear.

She called over two of the pirates and gave them orders to find the last man.

'He will be down in the clinic. Bottom deck ... follow those stairs,' she said pointing to the spiral staircase. 'And I want him alive. Do you understand ... alive?' she snapped.

They nodded, then dutifully followed orders and ran down to look for their final prize.

The guests and the remainder of the crew were herded up and packed in the small boats. All their belongings were taken and placed in a separate boat. One by one, each small vessel and their cargo were transferred to the sleek ship waiting and the new arrivals were greeted as captives.

The wind had picked up as the weather deteriorated at an increasing pace and the Pacific Fair rocked gently in the lagoon waters.

Paul stood still in the blackness of the storeroom's cupboard hearing the sounds of men walking into the clinic next door and talking to each other. They walked out and stood at the door of the doctor's place of hiding. There was more chatter then the sound of the door being shaken, then kicked, then silence.

Back on the deck the officer swung to her man. 'Swen,' she said, bringing his attention to a good-looking young man coming on board. The South African lifted his head from his efforts of reloading his weapon and focused his attention to the slender young man who had just boarded the Pacific Fair.

'What's up?

The newcomer looked at the boss a little nervously. 'Just received communication from our appointment. They want to bring forward our rendezvous by six hours due to the typhoon.' He stopped and waited for the reaction.

'And if we don't make it within their time frame?

'Well we can, but we need to be under way within thirty minutes.'

'Answer the bloody question. I asked if we don't get there in time, what then?'

'Well, we will have to find another buyer. Deal's off.'

'Shit,' he said spitting on the floor. His face went bright red with frustration and he beckoned a private dialog to one side with his lady. 'We can't afford to lose this deal. It's top dollar.'

'What were you able to negotiate?' she asked her partner in crime with soft voice.

He moved his face close to her ear as he motioned her to come away from earshot of the newcomer. 'Ten point-five million. Two point-five in cash and the rest to our Columbian account with confirmation of arrival. It's top grade stuff and they know it and our price is good.'

'How did you get that?'

'Shall we say I acquired it from a now ... deceased estate.' He smiled close to her face. 'Nice and clean.'

'What will you ask for the people?' she said offering further pressure.

'Well for all these lives, we'll go for five, maybe ten million, the company will pay up. Got some inside information. Should be sweet,' he said brimming with confidence.

'What will you accept?'

He laughed and shrugged his shoulders. 'five maybe two. No, maybe lower, but let's reach for the stars first and see what they'll pay. Pocket money for you and me. It's cream.'

'And if they don't pay?'

'Well, the company will pay for their founder and his family.'

'And what do we do with the girls, if they're not interested?'

'They'll pay for them, but if not there's always the sex industry. Some very nice merchandise here,' he said, raising his eyebrows and smiling broadly.

She smiled back at him then kissed him quickly.

'OK, well we better get under way, yes?' she asked.

He nodded.

'What about the Australian doctor?' she asked.

'We haven't got time. Let the Aussie rat go down with the ship,' he said with a scowl.

'OK.'

He walked back to the young man waiting for an answer. 'Tell them we'll be there.'

'Well, we need to be evacuating this ship now Swen,' he said reinforcing his point.

'OK, let's get out of here. Hey you two! Get downstairs and tell everyone to get off the ship. We're about to blow her,' he said, yelling at two men carrying a large box full of technical equipment.

'There's a big storage area down there. We'll get it all first,' one of the pirates demanded.

'What aspect of GET OUT OF HERE don't you understand ... MOVE IT,' the leader screamed back in total frustration.

A large bead of sweat ran down Paul's back as he remained in the stuffy environment of his cupboard hideout. He opened the cupboard door slightly to gain some fresh air when he heard a voice yelling in English with a strong foreign accent.

'Hey, you two, get off the ship, she's going to blow soon. Is there anyone in the engine room?'

'No, they have finished laying the charges. They've just left maybe five minutes ago.'

'OK. Let's go.'

'What about the Doctor?'

'Forget about that Christian pig. Swen said let him go down with the ship.' He laughed. 'Got better things to do now than to waste time on him. Come on, move it!'

The men ran up the passageway leaving behind them, silence. Paul stood in the dark, with his heart pounding. The thought of drowning attacked his senses. He walked out of his hiding place and felt his way to the door of the room, listening. There was complete silence.

He slowly opened the door with senses fully alert. His eyes fell on the chord on the floor that ran down the hallway towards the engine room. Given what he just heard outside that door he realised that the chord on the floor was in fact a fuse line. He quietly moved into the clinic, found a scalpel and cut the fuse in two places then threw the severed fuse to the side. He ventured up towards the deck where he found charges strategically placed for maximum damage. Again, he cut its line and threw the fuse away from the charges. As he continued his journey toward the top deck a strong smell of sulphur hit his nostrils. Ahead he saw the burning fuse hissing its threats toward him. It then met a junction and split its fiery, furious journey into two paths. He ran to the end of the hallway where the junction ignited. He cut the line that ran behind him just in case he missed a junction in his panic. He raced after the hissing mischief snaking its way up another corridor to an area he knew nothing about.

Catching up to the ignited fuse he noticed the charge just a few feet away. He lunged at the menace and began to cut the fuse only to fine that his scalpel had received damage as a result of his diving at the fuse. He cut furiously a foot away from the charge and finally won the battle. Dropping the scalpel, he threw the oncoming threat away from the charge.

With the stinging effect of the sulphurous smoke biting into his lungs he ran to the bridge tracing the burnt-out trail of the fuse while looking for any further evidence of other explosive devices.

At the bridge door, he listened and again there was silence. Then he heard a faint sound of a small boat in the distance, then it stopped. Using the key, he was given, he slowly unlocked the door, then opened it. All the instrumentation was ripped out leaving large gaps.

Only the ships compass remained as it wobbled slightly in its mount as a result of the ship moving in the rougher than normal waters of the lagoon. He remained behind the door as he looked out for the marauder's vessel. It had already raised its anchor and was making preparations to be underway. The doctor looked out to the open ocean. The waves were rough as a result of the oncoming typhoon. Looking back at the criminal's ship, he noticed a slight plume of black smoke shoot from its exhaust indicating the diesel engines had fired up, followed by a churning of the water at the rear of the ship. The propellers spun in obedience creating the thrust required for velocity. The vessel was under way and Paul was left behind, alone, abandoned but … alive.

CHAPTER TWENTY-FIVE

To remain inconspicuous, Paul had to retrace his steps and the doctor ventured back towards the lower decks with the view of clearing all the explosive charges from the ship's bowels.

As he passed by the spiral staircase that led up to the lounge he paused, then looked up. His thoughts echoed in his head. He had passed by that spot an hour or so previously ... when life was wonderful. He was with the woman he loved, the one he believed God had given him... Claire. What had become of her? Suddenly, panic filled his soul and a deadly anger followed only to take control. He took a step towards the staircase, placed his quivering hand on the steady rail and stepped up ... one step at a time, drawn to an outcome.

Each step offered a heavy payment for his efforts ... one by one. As he moved slowly, cautiously up the winding way, he lifted his gaze to see the horizon of the lounge's floor coming down to greet his eyes. A whirl of disbelief met his soul as it fingered its cold intent round his senses, pulling the very breath out of his lungs. Jessica, the captain and Claire lay together in a pool of blood. Forgetting his vulnerability, he rushed to the scene of the crime and suddenly stopped, standing above the horror. His heart missed a beat, as his world moved around in a timeless bubble. Grief smashed through his veins. A sudden dry mouth beckoned his favour for a drop of comfort. He tried to swallow but his tongue couldn't perform. The stench of death raped his nostrils, as he stood and looked at the faces. All things important had gone, stolen. There in that lounge he was faced with truth laying before him, crying out with lethal silence. He was faced with life and death ... his life their death. Why was he spared? His thoughts echoed a new declaration. *It should have been me, not Claire*, he thought. Why Claire?

The doctor turned his head looking for a current fix on the position of the other vessel.

It had made its way into the open waters, running from its lucrative atrocities.

His eyes dropped from its thunderous attack on the growing swell of the ocean, to a strange wash spreading its message through the water in front of him.

In his state of stupor, his legs moved with great effort, eager to retreat from the imposing, gruesome reminder of human frailty. He walked outside replacing deaths unmistakable sent with clean salt air only to be accosted by more brutality. The empty stare of the chief officer, looked pointlessly up to the heavens, as the body floated on its' back with arms outstretched, as though eager for embrace. Then more bodies, this time, all floating face down some thirty feet apart from each other. The water was stained crimson, circumnavigating its message around each victim, declaring the need for justice to a much higher authority.

A strange feeling shot into his very soul. Paul spun around feeling a presence behind him, expecting to see someone, only to be shocked. There was ... nothing, nobody, just the sound of the water slapping against the side of the ship and the unmistakable sound of wind and rain, now heralding the onslaught of a typhoon. His eyes darted back and forth, but there was no one to be seen.

Sudden vulnerability screamed a needed retreat to the lounge. The doctor ran hunched down as though someone was about to shoot him too. Fear forced its way back into his soul sapping him of more strength and he returned to the perceived protection of the lounge with a stumble, bringing him to his hands and knees just feet from the departed. He looked across at his love. Her lifeless, beautiful body, lay motionless. How he wanted to know her. He scanned her ash grey face. There was a gash just above her right temple. It had been bleeding heavily, but, no longer. His heart burst with heavy emotion.

'God, WHY?' he screamed out, as his body collapsed in surrender, face down on the cool parquetry floor and there in the fellowship of death he broke down and wept bitterly.

With fists beating the floor, he cried out to the God of Abraham, Isaac and Jacob.

'WHY, WHY HAVE YOU LEFT US?' he pathetically questioned between deep heaving, as his lungs demanded copious amounts of oxygen to cater the demands of hyperventilation.

Then, there was a voice, a small ... soft voice. He looked at the bodies. He heard something, but what? He listened in sheer exhaustion. Suddenly his heart rang with a profound authority. A welling up within his very being, filled him, as though a flood had declared itself as victor over his soul. '*I will never leave you nor forsake you.*' The words thundered in his heart and peace offered sound companionship. His thoughts raced back to his youth group days, to his youth leader and a devotion given by the leader about God's commitment to His people never leaving then. Paul lay there in timeless submission, drinking in the profundity of his creator's presence.

More words thundered into his soul. '*Why make this commotion and weep? The child is not dead but, sleeping*'. They were the words he heard earlier that day, as fresh as that morning. '*The child is not dead but, sleeping*'. His head stopped spinning. He looked straight at Jessica. He hadn't checked anyone for a pulse. He moved straight to Jessica.

'*The child is not dead but, sleeping.*' It haunted his mind.' ... *not dead, sleeping.*'

Paul's heart pounded with great expectation as his hand was quick to slide down at the side of the young girl's neck. To find a pulse would be a greater discovery than finding Solomon's mines. He waited for the signal, a pulse, even a faint pulse ... but, nothing.

He took her wrist and placing his finger on the spot, he focused searching for … anything, but nothing was found. There was no pulse. He concentrated harder. There was nothing. His heart sank.

No, no! The thought, screamed in his head. T*he child is not sleeping, the child is dead, shot dead.*

He looked over at the Captain and there in the middle of his back was a gaping hole where the bullet had passed through leaving the evidence of heart tissue pushed through the bullets exit point. Death would have been instant for the captain now relieved of his command.

Paul drew his gaze to Claire. Something triggered his attention to a small detail. He noticed a slight effect on the now cool pool of blood just under her nose. It was the same effect as ones' warm breath on a cooler surface. He gathered his senses and focused, looking closer. She was breathing, though shallow, none the less, she was alive. Hope began to enter, if only for a moment. Still in disbelief, he called out.

'Claire?'

His hand moved to her neck and checked for a pulse.

'Yes!' he whispered. A strong indicator of life thumped its love against his two fingers.

God's child, Claire, was not dead, she was just sleeping indeed. A soft confirmation swept through his heart.

'Claire?' he hushed her name as he bent down to her ear.

'Claire, it's me Paul.'

He searched her body carefully for any more wounds but, none could be found. With the exception of a nasty gash on her forehead, she seemed to be clear of any other wounds.

'Claire? It's me love, Paul.'

She moved her hand, then groaned. More signs of life crept into her form, as she opened her eyes. With the sight of the blood, Claire moved her hand quickly away. She sat up slowly, wincing in pain.

'OK, steady girl, you've got one nasty bump on that head of yours.'

The young woman wasn't listening as she stared at the floor. Claire glanced around, then looked at her clothing covered in blood. She lifted her head to the direction of the voice.

Her dazed state demanded slow movements. Finally, her visual focus steadied, but her cognitive state left much to be desired. Her right eye closed in response to sudden pain coming from her wound on her forehead and she brought her hand up to comfort the spot.

'Hey careful, don't want that wound any more contaminated than it is,' he cautioned pointing to her hand covered in blood.

She turned the palm of her hand around in front of her face and with a sudden jerk of horror, rejected its presence by thrusting it away and wiping the contents on the side of her shorts. She looked back at Paul and began to shake. There was the man she loved. Her arms flung themselves around his neck and she sobbed.

'Oh Paul, don't leave me,' she cried.

The doctor held her close, feeling her every jolt of convulsive grief radiate its presence through his body. He held her tighter, confirming his commitment as the common emotion of the moment welded them together. They were one in spirit as the power of the event consummated their common covenant to life.

Paul finally broke the physical bond.

'Hey beautiful, let's see if we can get you standing. Want to try?' he asked with gentle tones looking directly into her eyes.

She nodded and slowly moved upright.

'Well done. OK, do you think you can walk downstairs?'

'Yeah,' she replied looking down at Jessica.

'Oh Jess,' she whispered, clinging on to Paul with greater need as she stared down at the empty shell that was once a beautiful young teenager.

'Hey, come on, let's get this head of yours looked at.'

'We can't leave her here.'

'I'll attend to it later. You first.' He held her close.

'Come on love. You right to go?'

'Sure,' Claire surrendered.

'OK, good. We'll get you cleaned up, but first we better go down to the clinic and have a look at that gash. I think it might need a stich or two. Then, once we've got you patched up, then a shower, fresh clothes and bed my girl,' he said eyeing her injury a little closer.

She glanced at Paul.

'I must look terrible'

'You look pretty good to me,' he winked, 'but, you do have a nice old bump on your noggin.'

'On my what?' she said with slightly slurred speech.

'Your 'noggin, you know, your head.'

She smiled as he tightened his steadying arm around her shoulder.

The walk down to the medical room took longer than expected as Claire struggled with the distance and had to rest on each flight of stairs. The concussive shock of the afternoon's events had taken its toll on the young American woman. Renewing her strength, whilst seated on the step, she looked ahead to the end of the corridor.

'Paul, what's that cord in the hallway?' she said sitting on the third step from the bottom of the stare case.

'Commonly called fuse wire.'

Claire looked at the bearer of the outrageous news and frowned questioning his answer.

'Yep, they were going to blow the ship. Why do that in this shallow water you might ask? Frankly, I don't know.'

'OK, but, why? Didn't they light the fuses?'

'Well they did.'

'Excuse me?' She squinted in pain again.

'They lit the fuses but, they failed,' he answered smiling at her with an over exaggerated cheesy grin.

'How?'

'It's called a scalpel. Works really well on a fuse line.'

'You didn't?'

'I did.'

'And where's the explosives now?'

'Well, exactly where they put them. Unless they came back to collect them, but I don't think so.'

'Paul, stop joking! You mean they are still set to blow?'

'Mm, guess so. Puts a whole new meaning on smoking or non-smoking, doesn't it?'

'Not funny,' she said trying to understand his perspective.

'Really? I thought it was, anyway, it's all good, Once I get you patched up, I'll attend to the fireworks. OK?'

'Good.'

They reached their destination. The doctor cleaned the wound carefully and confirmed it needed three stitches. The clinic had everything he needed to achieve the objective. Within the hour, Claire's wound was cleansed, closed and bandaged.

'Well that was fun, all done and looking beautiful,' he suggested feeling quite satisfied with himself and with the woman set before him, full of life.

'Thankyou doctor,' she said slowly, 'that didn't hurt a bit, except for the initial needle.'

'Give it time. Once the sedative wears off it might be a little uncomfortable.'

'OK, now for those explosives,' she demanded, feeling a little more in control of her circumstances.

'What ... now?' he said with surprise.

'Yep, off you go. I'll wait here for you.'

'Right, yes mam,' he said saluting.

She screwed her face up at him and waved him off.

Paul followed the lines and immobilised them all, wrapping the charges in separate coverings and threw them all overboard. He ventured back down to the clinic only to find Claire lying down waiting for him.

'How ya doing?'

'Fine. All done?' she asked with her face beginning to swell around the wound.

'Yep.'

'Where did you put them?'

'Under your bed, they should be safe there,' he said with a straight face.

Claire studied the man before her.

'You didn't.'

'No, I didn't, threw them overboard.'

'Good.' Her relief showed physically.

'OK let's get you to your suite.'

They reached her room, only to be greeted by chaos. The ransacked quarters cried out for attention, as clothing had been thrown everywhere.

'Well looks like house-keeping need to pull their socks up in this establishment,' he said again in an effort to make light of the trauma within sight.

'Oh, this is awful Paul,' she said as she sat on her bed looking across at the bed that Jessica used only hours previously.

She dropped her head into her hands ignoring the bandage and sobbed again.

'I can't do this. I can't stay here. Oh Jess. Why Lord why?'

Paul sat down next to her and just held her. She dropped her head lower toward her lap and she began to rock back and forth crying.

'Oh Claire, come here, please come here.'

She responded to the tender sound in his voice and threw herself into his secure arms.

The force took him by surprise and, he was thrown back with his chosen on the bed in the midst of the strewn clothing. He drew her up fully onto the bed and there they lay close together for some time. She moved in closer to him as he held her tighter.

'Paul, don't leave me. Can I sleep in your room, please? I can't stay here.'

'Sure, when you're ready we'll get your things together.'

After a little time, they gathered all the necessities and before long the two tourists were walking into Paul's room. The doctor's room had received little interference, just cupboards opened but nothing thrown around.

'OK, you have your shower, try not to get that dressing wet,' he said pointing to the bandage on her head.

'I need to wash my hair.'

'Really?' he said trying to understand the logic given that her hair was clear of any blood.

'Yes.'

'OK, but I don't want that dressing to get wet. Will you be right in there?' he said pointing to the bathroom.

'Sure. How long will you be?'

'Mm, maybe an hour, maybe less. Once you've finished your shower, I want you resting. OK?'

'OK. Please don't be too long Paul.'

'Shouldn't be.'

Claire moved to the bathroom and closed the door while Paul went to the medical storeroom, collected the body bags, some surgical gloves and made his way to the lounge deck. Once he arrived at the scene of the crime, he laid out the devices for the confinement of the bodies. After he had taken any personal belongings out of the pockets of the deceased, it took less time than thought to get the bodies concealed in the bags. He dragged the dead weight to the corner of the lounge where there was a large cupboard for the housing of brooms and other implements for cleaning. In that domestic area, was found plenty of room to lay the remains of the captain and Jessica securely on the floor.

The doctor looked across the horizon. There was no sign of the pirate's ship. The weather was beginning to take a turn for the worst, with the wind picking up, making the ship move to the command of the water. Paul made his way back to Claire. He walked into his room expecting to see Claire in bed sleeping, but to his surprise she was still in the bathroom with the water running in the shower.

'Claire?' he said knocking gently of the door of the bathroom. 'You OK?'

He listened but only the sound of the shower greeted him.

'Claire are you OK?' he repeated as concern mounted.

He stood at the door fearing she had passed out.

'Claire?' he called, now more insistent. The doctor knocked louder on the door.

'Claire, I'm coming in,' he said turning the handle of the bathroom door.

As he entered, he heard the soft sound of sobbing, deep breathless sobbing. There at the end of the shower, the young woman sat naked, crouched up in a ball on the floor with her head buried between her legs, rocking back and forth.

'Oh girl.'

He took a fresh towel, threw it over his shoulder, then snatched the soft bathroom robe off the gold-plated hook on the wall, opened it out wide and walked towards the distraught creature, protecting her dignity as best he could from his sight. He wrapped the luxury covering around her foetal shape, reached over, turned off the shower, then picked her up in his arms and moved towards the bed. The dressing on her wound was soaked. The instant Claire felt his touch, she threw her arms around his neck and cried bitterly.

'It's OK, I'm here.' Paul said whispering.

His presence was her only comfort and she held on to him as though her life depended on it.

The Doctor sat her slowly on the bed speaking words of conformation close to her ear.

She listened to every syllable, drinking in his sound, feeling his strength wrapped around her.

With her robe loosely covering her nakedness, Paul took the towel from his shoulder and proceeded to dry her soft brown hair as he continued to share gentle, comforting words.

She had calmed down considerably as a result of his favour in her time of distress.

The doctor stood up and looked down at the wet dressing on her head.

'I think I had better redress that wound,' he said tenderly, looking into her eyes.

'Won't be long. I'll just go downstairs and get the necessary materials.'

She suddenly snatched his arm with a shaking hand.

'No, please don't go, it'll be fine,' she said with her face filled with fear.

'No, we need to put a dry dressing on that love.'

'I'm sorry.' Claire replied full of failure.

'Hey, it's OK.'

'Maybe I can come with you to the medical room, I just can't stay here on my own, sorry,' she apologised again, standing clutching the robe across her front.

'Well OK, if you think you can make it down there and back again.'

'I can. I just need to be with you.'

'OK, but it might be an idea to put that robe on properly, don't want the neighbours to get the wrong idea,' the doctor said, pointing to the robes precarious position. He turned his back and Claire quickly slipped into it securely.

She took the belt and tied it carefully around her waist, straightened the material around her body, tightened the top across her chest and looked up at the back of this special man.

'OK, you can turn around now,' she said smiling with blood shot eyes. Security was her constant companion from the moment she had met Paul. His last gesture of chivalry honouring her need for modesty drew her closer to him right there on that spot.

'OK beautiful, let's get that bandage replaced,' he said taking her hand.

'Paul?'

'Yeah?'

'I love you so much.' Claire placed both hands on his face and kissed him quickly.

'And that's a ditto, my dear lady, but come on, let's get downstairs and get you attended to,' the doctor said smiling, keeping it as professional as he possibly could.

They walked down hand in hand for a time in silence. Paul's thoughts were for Claire and her current mental state. Grief and shock had taken its toll on his wife to be. He was watching her emotional highs and lows during this early stage of her affliction, being also conscious that he too was on a journey. He searched for a topic that might help lift her spirits a little. The voice of his sister came to mind and the topic of Vegemite. It was a stupid topic, Paul thought at the time, but given the circumstances, it was possibly perfect for the occasion.

'Hey, here's a question for you,' the doctor said, looking at Claire with a comical look on his face.

'Yes, what?' Claire looked up at him with her face continuing to swell around the wound and over one cheek.

'Do you like Vegemite?'

'Vegemite? Oh no,' her response was intense and immediate.

'I thought that might be the answer. I haven't met one American who likes the stuff. Just out of interest, why do you think that is?'

'Easy question, I'll tell you why,' she said with a new purpose.

'Yes, go on,' he beckoned, eager for distraction.

'It tastes so foul.' Her case was full, to the point and offered no mercy in light of cultural differences and potential offence.

'Really? That bad ha?' He laughed under his breath.

'Oh man, you bet. I mean, we put that stuff on our roads,' she said with a focused look.

Paul threw his head back and laughed. Claire realised her point could have been softened just a little.

'Sorry,' she apologised with head slightly bowed.

'I bet our kids will like it,' he said looking deeply at her with full intent.

She paused and looked back at him.

'I so want that,' she declared softly, looking into his eyes.

'Me too.' He smiled back. 'A bunch of happy little Vegemite kids.'

Her face broke from the romantic notion.

'Oh, no, God forbid,' she laughed hard then winced in pain.

'Where does it hurt?'

She pointed to her cheek bone and her jaw.

'OK, might take a look at a few things when we get to the clinic.'

'It sure feels strange,' Claire replied gently, probing the area with her right hand.

CHAPTER TWENTY-SIX

⁓

T he typhoon approached, proving its tropical influence, by whipping up large waves on the open ocean and causing considerable disturbance in the lagoon.

To amplify matters, there was a king tide due sometime after midnight, thereby, allowing the force of the waves to rise above the protective barrier of the reef, bordering the small group of islands.

Paul had redressed Claire's wound, and diagnosed a suspected fractured cheek bone as a result of the assault by the assassin's pistol grip. Pain killers were administered to his patient, along with a cold ice pack found in the clinic's small refrigerator. Motion sickness medication was prescribed in anticipation for the rough weather ahead. The only passengers were seated in Paul's room on the two leather-bound armchairs eating a light dinner of cold chicken, a side salad and washing it down with some bottled water that Paul found in the well-equipped galley. Apart from the considerable upheaval found in the rooms and the bridge, the ship seemed to be reasonably secure, as the crew had battened down the ship in readiness for the onslaught of the storm, prior to the arrival of the pirates.

The sun was setting. Paul was preparing himself for a long night. They had searched the ship for any means of communication to contact the outside world, but their unwelcomed visitors had stripped their new home of all necessary technology. All radios, communication dishes, antennas, handheld local communication devices, were all taken. There wasn't even an EPURB on board. They were cut off from the entire world. Paul did, however, find in the ship's storeroom a handheld G.P.S. that was carelessly stuffed back in its original packaging. He suspected, however, that it may have had problems. The doctor was surprised that he found another laptop. This was discovered in the ships chart room, that the thieves overlooked, however such pieces of equipment, were hardly useful for the purpose of rescue.

Paul watched Claire as she ate with difficultly due to her injuries.

'How's it going?'

'Yeah, OK. It's hard to chew on this side though,' she said pointing to the side of her face. 'But this is tasting good. Man, not only has God given me a neat doctor, with a great accent, but a good cook too. Something tells me, I'm blessed.' She smiled, then winced, due to the pain that was now her constant companion.

'I hardly cooked anything.'

'Well, I appreciate your efforts,' she paused tilted her head slightly to the left. 'Hey, and I appreciate … you,' she declared, reaching over and lightly squeezing his bare knee.

Her touch ignited a warm glow throughout his entire body.

'Shucks mam, it was nothing,' he said trying to imitate the southern accent.

'Paul?'

'Yeah?'

'That was pathetic.'

'Really?'

'Yes.' A laboured smile came over her face.

OK. Um, try harder next time?' the doctor said, with a straight face.

'No, quit while you're ahead,' Claire said, trying not to smile too much.

Paul threw his head back and laughed as was customary for him when something triggered his sense of humour.

They both drank in the lighter dynamic, as the waves were beginning to make their presence known around their floating shelter, with the three dimensions of pitch, roll and yaw beginning to enter the evening's equation.

'Man, I'm tired,' Claire noted, as she placed the cold pack back on her face.

'The medication I gave you will make you drowsy. I want you to get some sleep tonight. It'll be a big day tomorrow.'

'Paul?'

'Yeah?'

'You OK ... Um sleeping with me tonight? I don't mean ... you know,' she said feeling a little uncomfortable. 'I just don't want to be alone. I'm really sorry.'

'Sure, I understand.'

'Thank you.' She placed the remnants of her meal down on the floor next to her armchair, stood up with the ice pack still on her face and walked over to the bed and began to lie down.

'Hey, might be an idea to use the toilet now.'

'Really, why?' she asked.

'Well, high winds and big waves make for unstable conditions and possible plumbing problems on a ship I would imagine. I might be wrong, but seems a logical possibility ... if you know what I mean.'

'OK, makes sense, good call.' Claire stood up, moved to the bathroom and closed the door.

By the time Claire had returned back into the room, Paul was navigating a mattress from the room across the hallway and securing it on the floor against the wall opposite her bed.

'What are you doing?'

'The floor's a bit too hard for me.' He laughed.

'Oh, um, OK, actually I was thinking ...' She was softly interrupted.

'Well for your sake, it might be better if I sleep here. I'll probably be getting up and down tonight given the weather. Don't want to disturb you. You need your sleep, old girl.'

'Hey, steady with the *old* bit, buster,' Claire smiled and looked at her man. 'Is that really the only reason? The bed thing that is,' she said pointing to the mattress on the floor.

'I'd be fine if it wasn't.'

The doctor chuckled to himself. 'Bed girl, get some sleep.'

'Paul, can I say something? I think I should say it before the storm hits. Just in case we don't ... you know.'

Claire walked over to Paul. As she passed her bag on the bed, she picked up a long-sleeved shirt sitting neatly at the edge of the bed to place it on top of the bag. A small sapphire ring flung out of the shirt and hit the floor spinning in front of Paul. The doctor bent down picking it up thereby cancelling its brilliant dance before him.

'Loose something?' he asked, holding up the simple white gold sapphire ring with two small diamonds mounted on either side of the deep blue stone, making a glistening cross.

'Oh, my,' she said, holding her hands over her mouth in disbelief. 'That's Jess's ring.'

'It's beautiful.' Paul held it up to the light. It sparkled its radiance, in Paul's hand under the bright light of the rooms L.E.D down lights.

'Jessica's Mom gave it to her the day Jess left for the trip.' Claire was staring at the ring set in Paul's hand as he was holding it up to the light scrutinizing its craftsmanship.

'This is no Wal-Mart special. An unusual bon voyage gift, don't you think?'

'It was Jess's grandmother's wedding ring. Her grandmother died recently and Jess was really close to her. Her mother wanted her to have it and felt it appropriate to give it to her before she went away for some reason.'

'But how did this get in there? Paul asked, shifting his scrutiny from the focus of brilliance to the shirt.

'I guess, it was thrown on the floor with everything else by those monsters and it got tangled in my shirt. I really don't know.'

Claire looked at the piece of clothing now sitting neatly in her bag.

'Oh, no, no its' not, … It's Jess's shirt. That's why.' She broke down and wept.

The doctor stepped forward and held her, in part for comfort but also for fear that she may weaken and fall to the floor incurring more injuries. Within seconds, he felt her full weight fall into his keeping and he lowered her gently on the mattress holding her closely in silence. Minutes went by in his arms, when gradually she regained her composure and asked her doctor for a tissue to wipe her face. He returned quickly sitting her up with the necessary request in hand.

'Here you go.'

The lady in the room exercised its purpose with accuracy and quickly focused.

'Paul, where's the ring?'

'All safe and sound in my pocket, here.' He brought it back out into the light.

'Can … I, have it? … I want to return it to Jessica's Mom, but I'll be its guardian in the meantime.'

'Are you sure you want to receive it?' Paul said softly.

'Excuse me? Well of course I do,' she questioned him softly.

Paul looked at the ring.

'Then, I give you this ring as a symbol of my love.'

He reached down, took her left hand and slid the ring on her third finger. It was a perfect fit.

She watched the event unfold before her very eyes, then looked up into the face of her carer, but said nothing ... stunned.

'I think that's probably the best place to put it in the meantime,' he said with a straight face. 'Or until death us do part'.

Paul moved his lips to hers and, slowly kissed her. Her response was immediate and, she pressed into him warmly. Releasing himself, he looked deeply into her soul.

'Oh Claire, I love you so much. This has all been a bit of a whirl wind, to say the least, and I could have thought of better places to do this, but, ...' he paused.

'Just in case we don't make it ....?' She finished what she thought might be his words.

He nodded slowly looking into her beautiful yet blood shot eyes.

'Claire, will you do me the honour of being my wife?'

She brought her hand up toward her face, looked at the miracle on her finger, then with both hands she touched his face softly.

'Oh Paul.' She kissed him then wrapped herself around his neck.

'I take it that, that's a yes. Yes?' he whispered feeling a stirring throughout his body.

'I've said before and I'll say it again ... Yes, yes, yes,' she said with tears flowing down her face and on to her mans' neck. 'I love you so much mister.'

'Wow, getting a bit wet here,' he noted, laughing softly.

'Never thought I could be so happy, in the midst of such a calamity.' She burst out with laughter followed in succession by Paul.

'Paul? What's going to become of us?'

'Don't know love but, God does and He is good.'

They spoke together for some time on that makeshift bed on the floor as the ship moved to the demands of the wind and the motion of the water.

CHAPTER TWENTY-SEVEN

A massive jolt woke Paul from his sleep. Sitting up, he slowly gathered his bearings back in the conscious world. The doctor glanced down at his watch. It was one o'clock in the morning. He decided to keep the lights on in case quick actions had to be made in the middle of the night.

The ship was pitching and rolling in the midst of the tempest. The storm had hit its full fury on the small atoll with its judgment being pronounced on all things in its way.

Another massive jolt was felt, this time, it seemed to permeate its way into the very fibre of the ship and its occupants, causing the doctor to be thrown to the side on the mattress on the floor. The lights in the room flickered and Paul quickly looked across at Claire. She was securely placed in the middle of the king size bed where she began to stir, moving her hand slowly up to her head. Paul felt the boat rise up again above the ocean swell, only to be stopped with another jolt and the ship came crashing down back into the watery blackness.

'Paul?' Claire cried out. She sat up from her deep sleep looking to her man. Her eyes were puffed from lack of sleep and her face a little more swollen than the previous night.

'What's that sound?'

'Well, if you're talking about the concussive crashing, I think it might be the resistance of the anchor holding us firm, or it is being dragged along and getting snagged on coral outcrops. I'm not sure.

If you're talking about that constant screaming, or wining sound, that's the gale force wind. Anyway, how's the head?'

Claire took stock of her injury, placing her hand on her cheek.

'A little tender.'

The ship heaved again throwing both its passengers on their backs.

'Claire, get over here now!' Paul's voice was urgent.

Claire rolled across the bed, easing herself over the edge and crawled awkwardly over to her doctor.

A violent shudder rattled the ship, causing the cupboard door to burst open, spewing out its draws as though convulsing from the effect of the relentless attack. The ship rolled dangerously to one side, sliding its human cargo up against the wall.

Seeing the potential tragedy ahead, the doctor reached over and gripping the edge of the mattress he pulled it over them, wedging its protective cover between God's chosen and the oncoming projectiles. A crash was heard then a thud as the furniture collided its full force into the bedding. Another jolt was felt as the ship righted itself in the rolling seas and then the sound of something deeply metallic breaking, resinating throughout the entire ship.

'Oh Paul. What was that?'

'Who knows, but it could have been the anchor giving way.'

'Are we sinking?'

'Well, there needs to be water to sink a ship. Certainly, there's plenty outside to do the job, but I can't see any inside so, no, I don't think we are sinking ... yet,' he said looking around as he stood up. 'Come on, let's get out of here,' he said, pushing the furniture away from them.

'Where are we going?'

'Up somewhere higher where there's no furniture trying to kill us. Maybe the bridge.

Are you up to giving me a hand with this mattress?'

'I'll try.'

Paul pushed the furniture off the mattress with reckless abandon and they awkwardly navigated their way to the bridge. The doctor climbed the steps that led to the place of command, dragging their bedding with much difficulty. Breathlessly, the man opened the door slowly. He was greeted by a secure area offering a horrible sight. As they entered the bridge, the spectacle of the waves and their size caused Claire to gasp. The island group could not be seen but as the waves brought their ruthless attack, the lights from the ship's decks revealed their hideous perspective. The Pacific Fair was a drift in the open water in the midst of the full fury of the tropical typhoon.

The bed was thrown in the middle of floor of that lofty position where the full effect of the motion was felt. They laid down huddling together in the midst of the terror that surrounded them. Looking up, they watched the huge swell of the ocean coming and going in and out of their sight.

The rest of the night offered little sleep as many monstrous waves crashed over the bow of the ship. Like a discarded cork, the Pacific Fair was tossed and thrown by the merciless anger of the sea.

As they lay prostrate in each other's arms, Paul looked at his fiancé and yelled out.

'You know this is going to sound stupid in a sense... because it's pretty obvious but, we are in a huge battle here,' he said, sinking deep within his thoughts.

'You think?' Claire incredulously exclaimed as she tried to keep herself on the mattress as all three axes of movement were being tested.

'I mean ... spiritual battle. You get the feeling that someone wants us dead?' He cried out directly in front of Claire.

'Oh, the thought has crossed my mind,' she yelled ... terrified.

'Claire, I think we need to pray. I think we need to praise God and I think we need to thank the Lord for our situation. The pirates meant it all for evil, but God has meant this for good ... I just know it. It's written in Isaiah somewhere ... um, where it says, *my thoughts are not your thoughts and my ways are not your ways.* And somewhere else it says, *in all things give thanks,* it also says somewhere else, *Render unto God a sacrifice of praise* and somewhere else in the bible, Um, ... *All things work together for good, for them who love God who are called according to His good will and purpose,* or something like that. So, given everything, do you want to pray with me, to put this stuff into action?'

Claire kissed him and nodded. The waves pounded their relentless hatred against the hull of the luxury yacht as the wind screamed its threats of violence to the only guests left on board.

The two held each other, and the man prayed thanking the Most-High God for their trial and for His presence with them. Such a prayer felt a little contrived at first, but as they persisted, their stand in faith began to make a difference. Their hearts slowly awakened to their creator's powerful presence, which overshadowed their calamity. *To live is Christ and to die is gain,* thundered its defiance into the darkness. Claire suddenly broke out in song, singing a hymn of praise to the one who was in fact the totality of ultimate authority and the one who reigned over all things ... even over this storm ... singing to the one who was the ultimate caring authority in their situation. The command was given, power was released and the victory was declared by unseen heavenly warriors, released to stand against an unholy realm, not familiar to mortal eyes.

The constant violent motion of the ocean, caused considerable nauseous symptoms in both riders of this aquatic roller coaster from hell. The ship was suddenly lifted by a gigantic wave and thrown as it were, by menacing angry hands to the unforgiving water beneath its now naked, vulnerable hull. The raw metal of the ship smashed against the sea waiting below.

Screams could be heard from the bridge as the redeemed cargo battled to remain on the cushioned safety of the bedding of the floor of the bridge. Both lay with ashen faces in the centre of that room, dressed in their life vests. The desperation of their situation caused Paul to remember that he had some medication in his pocket and offered it to Claire.

'Can you swallow this without water?' the doctor yelled with difficulty due to his sickness.

'What is it?' Claire said awkwardly, sitting up to take the drug on offer.

'Medication for sea sickness... might help,' he screamed out.

Claire obeyed her doctor's wishes, but quickly lay down due to her illness.

Eventually, exhaustion and the effects of the medication caused the two travellers to pass out as the tempest continued its horror around them. The eerie blackness of that night enveloped them, as the ship was ripped along by winds that exceeded two hundred and fifty knots, journeying to an unknown place, on a track perfectly plotted by the omniscient, omnipotent, omnipresent navigator.

Hours later, the most hideous sound sunk its screeching horror into the hearts of the sea farers, waking them suddenly. A massive jolt, then, a sudden violent tilt of the hull demanded their mortal shell to be cast up against the door that lead to the outside world, reviving the unconscious travellers. An explosion of colliding materials hitting the hull thundered its way throughout the ship, followed by a massive tilt of the ship to the opposite side. The two guests were flung across the other end of the bridge. Claire screamed as she smashed into the wall with Paul close behind her slamming his body into hers.

Her cry of pain drew her man to reposition himself against his woman to investigate, as the ship slowly brought itself back into the upright position. The waves thundered their efforts for a time against the bow, but something was different. The sound of the wind had changed almost immediately. It was still strong, if not stronger, but there was something new about their horror.

CHAPTER-TWENTY EIGHT

T he sun had risen.

The howling wind of the previous night seemed to have lost its significance. Paul listened. The medication had taken effect, he thought, as there were no symptoms of nausea.

This noise was loud and continuous. Still half asleep, Paul lay there on his back on the mattress in the bridge, coming to grips with everything that had happened. He was alive. His eyes remained closed and his thoughts suddenly came to Claire. Where was she? The doctor rolled over with his arm extended to embrace her. There was no one there. He slowly pried open his tired eyes to be greeted by an empty space. Rolling on to his back he turned his head and looked in the opposite direction. There in the corner, standing just in front of the door that lead to the outside world, was his love. Her face appeared blank as she stared straight ahead. Paul quickly noted how steady she stood. There was no adjustment in her stance for the violent motion of the ship. He could feel the motion, but she wasn't responding to the movement that he was feeling. He looked around and noticed the captains wind jacket hanging over a hook mounted on the back wall of the bridge. The garment was casually dangling freely, but not swinging to the demands of the tempest. The ship was stationary. *It must be my middle ear that's causing a phantom effect*, he thought. He brought his watch up to his face. It was one PM. He looked back at Claire.

'Hey beautiful. Boy did I ever sleep in. How're you feeling?' he said, yelling over the raw noise coming primarily from the roof, as he tidied his ruffled hair.

She turned her head slowly and acknowledged by nodding.

'Head not too sore?'

Claire just shrugged her shoulders.

'Are you all right?' he said, sitting up watching the strange behaviour of the young woman standing in the corner.

She simply shook her head pointing outside.

'Feels like the waves have really calmed down, that's good. Man, I've never seen anything like it. I'm so glad I had that medication on me. It knocked me out. Did you sleep any? Wow, is that rain? Man, its thundering down.'

Claire shook her head again and pointed back outside.

'Paul, look!' Her tone struck fear into Paul's heart and he stood up quickly, directing his focus to her suggested bearing.

'Oh Strike!' he said, mumbling under his breath.

His first impression was confusion. The sight was too much to comprehend. There in front of him ... was devastation ... palm trees, some stripped, some, had been blown over across the deck of the luxury ship which was covered in other debris from its bough to its stern.

The waves could be seen thirty feet below, away from reach of the ship. The Pacific Fair had been beached high up on a sandy hill, carried to its resting place by the huge storm-surge early that morning.

'Where the heck are we?' Paul looked around from their place of observation. The ship had settled to one side of a bay approximately two miles wide circling around to an opening between two rocky points.

'Maybe we're on one of the islands? You know yesterday?'

'Maybe ... but doesn't look like it. Where are the other two islands?' Paul asked, rubbing the soreness in his lower back.

'We might be on the other side of one of them.'

'Yep ... could be. Man, it's stuffy in here. The air-conditioning system looks like it's not functioning.' He walked over to the door that led outside and tried to open it. The wind hampered his efforts. A burst of tropical air accosted his senses and the driving rain rushed in to deposit it's offering on the floor of the bridge. He closed it with great difficulty and turned to Claire.

'No, might wait till later,' he suggested, looking back behind the ship through a rear observation window.

'Oh Wow! The doctor looked in disbelief.

'Your point about being on the other side of one of those islands? Ah, I don't think so ... look!' He pointed to a large igneous volcanic plug stretching some hundreds of feet into the cyclonic sky.

Claire turned, moved toward Paul, took his arm in hers and looked out the window that was beaded with hundreds of drops of rainwater joining forces and cascading down the smooth surface. The ship's bow was buried up to its rails in sand and debris.

'Oh, my goodness.' Claire placed her free hand over her mouth and tears began to flow again.

Paul felt the uncertainty of his wife to be. He turned to his only companion and wrapping his arms around her, he held her tight. They stood motionless for some time, alone, bewildered, but together and very much alive and well.

'You hungry?' he gently whispered into her ear.

'No.'

'Well, care to come for a walk with me down to the galley?' he asked, kissing her on the forehead.

She nodded, not wanting to be left alone on their somewhat battered and bruised nautical prison.

'Bathroom first?'

'OK, of course. Let's go,' he said, using positive tones for her sake.

They walked down the internal stairs that lead to the lower decks.

'Hey, look! The lights are still on.' Pauls' spirits lifted.

'And that means?' she asked slowly, whilst carefully rubbing her injured cheek.

'That means the generator is still working. Wow, now that's a bit of a miracle, after last night's ride from the dark side. Hopefully, that's going to mean the refrigerator will be still working.'

Claire made no comment but stared blankly ahead as they made their way to his room.

'It will be interesting to see if the plumbing is still working,' he said as he opened the door of the room.

The small table was haphazardly leaning up against the wall next to the bed, with one chair on the bed and the other found damaged in the bathroom.

'Well, well, a little disturbance occurred in here last night it seems,' he declared, taking any opportunity to lift the mindset of the group. Paul moved the chair out of the bathroom.

'There you go my dear, all clear,' Paul said gesturing the way with his hand.

The young woman acknowledged his offer with a nod of her head and a faint smile, walked into the bathroom, then closed the door.

He repositioned the table and chairs in their respective places, picked up his clothing that was strewn over the floor, then sat on the bed reflecting on their situation. A flush was heard and the bathroom door opened.

'I think all is well with the plumbing.'

'Another point of interest, given our ride last night and our rough arrival.' Paul quickly entered the bathroom, turned and looked back at Claire.

'You traveling OK?'

'Yeah, I'll just sit here for a bit. Take your time.' She sat on the chair and looked out the window.

'Be out in a jiffy, then breakfast,' he said, closing the door.

Claire didn't acknowledge his point but remained fixed on the outside world. The small bay took her interest. Waves were breaking on the white sand of a generous beach and through the teeming rain she could see much larger waves breaking on the outer reef that boarded and protected their harbour. Another flush was heard and, the doctor walked out.

'OK, let's get some breakfast, or lunch or whatever.' He laughed.

'Sure.'

Their walk to the galley brought home some truths of the severity of the ships condition. Walls were buckled in places, doors were cracked as a result of the door frames being bent out of shape and one area of the floor on the galley's deck had been risen six inches. They pried open the kitchen's door and all seemed to be in order inside. A large pantry with secure compartments was well stocked with tinned food, copious amounts of flour, rice, noodles, powdered milk and other condiments that made for healthy living.

The walk-in refrigerator offered ample storage for a wealthy compliment of a wide variety of fruits and vegetables, packaged meats such as bacon, salami, sausage meats and fresh meats that would have been set aside from the freezer for the previous night's meal that was never prepared. Within the generous refrigerator another door was present. Paul walked over to it.

'OK, wonder what's in here?'

He opened it easily and a wall of freezing air fell from its blackness on to their warm bodies.

'Wow, strike, it's cold in there,' he exclaimed, turning to Claire who was directly behind him.

'Freezer, no doubt.' Claire's voice reflected a trace of her unique humour and for Paul, given the circumstance, that was a joy to hear.

'No doubt ... now where's the light switch?' he said, fumbling around the cold walls at its entrance.

'Um, would this, be it?' she asked, pointing to a switch on the outside wall just inches away from the Australian explorer's face.

'Well well well, who put that there?'

'A logical designer ... no doubt,' she replied, with a bright smile, offering a gentle sense of mockery to her onlooker. She reached over and turned on the switch.

The freezer light bathed its surroundings with its yellow glow.

'Wow, better not go in there. Not with bear feet,' he announced as he glanced down at their lack of foot ware.

From the entrance, they feasted their eyes on secure compartments filled with what appeared to be chickens, fish, vegetables, frozen fresh milk and in the corner, were hanging two hind quarters of beef, four lambs and two carcases of pork.

Paul closed the door, turned off the light and looked at Claire.

'Well we're not going to starve, at least not in the near future.'

'As long as we can keep the power up to the ship,' Claire said, looking around the kitchen.

'Yeah, should go down and check out the engine room, but something to eat first,' he suggested.

Claire continued her gaze on her man. His confidence was infectious. She could feel an overwhelming sense of security flowing back into her spirit.

'Maybe I will have something to eat,' she said, noting the well-equipped galley.

'Hey, now you're talking. So, what would you like mam?'

'Surprise me.'

'OK, stick around and let me dazzle you,' Paul said with new interest, given their surroundings.

Claire approved as she raised her eyebrows and nodded her head.

A hearty lunch of cold chicken, sliced ham with tomato and cheese with mustard placed between two thickly sliced pieces of multigrain bread baked the day before, was enjoyed by both parties.

This was followed by a piece of passionfruit cheesecake and the doctor suggested they both drink a litre of bottled water.

After lunch, they moved down to the clinic to check the wound on Claire's head.

Despite the fresh bump received early that morning, the stitches were still intact. The wound was washed with an antiseptic lotion and a new dressing was administered.

'OK, all clean,' he declared, washing his hands and looking back at his lady.

'Might be an idea if you go back to the room and get some rest. I'll go to the engine room and check out this generator.'

'No way buster, I'm coming with you.'

'Sure.'

They made their way down to the engine room in silence. Upon reaching their destination Paul stopped at the doorway of the ships power-plant.

'You're interested in generators?' he asked, with his hand on the latch.

'And what if I am?' she snapped lightly back.

'Fine,' he said laughing.

'What's with the laughter dude? I might be one of those *kinda gals* who likes to get her hands dirty ... with grease and stuff ... you know.'

Paul looked at Claire then laughed harder.

'Yeah right.'

A quick punch to the upper part of his right arm was offered by the woman, not wanting to leave his side.

'Ow!' Paul winced and laughed simultaneously. With the latch engage the door gave way and opened to a sight set before him.

'Wow! This place is as neat as a pin.' The doctor looked around with renewed vigour.

'So, these are the generators?' Claire pointed to the two main engines.

'No, they're the ships engines. This is the standby diesel generator.' He walked over to the unit in question slapping it on its side.

'This is the little baby that's providing electrical power to the whole ship and recharges the yacht's batteries. For yachts engaged on long-range cruising, such as our ship, we also have wind and solar-powered generators that can perform a similar function.'

'We have wind generators?'

'Yeah, sure do, didn't you see those four small propellers on top of the bridge spinning around?'

'Oh yeah. Is that what they were?'

'Yep, they help to keep trickling extra charge into the batteries. Quite handy when the solar cells aren't as functional for example when there is cloud cover, or in the evening.'

'So, if we were to turn off this diesel generator the wind generator would kick in or the batteries or something?'

'Um, no, they took down the wind generators when they battened down the ship in preparation for the typhoon.'

'So, those batteries … would they be able to run the freezer?' Claire's curiosity began to mount.

'I doubt it. They'd need a lot of batteries to power that cold room.'

'Oh, OK,' she acknowledged, soaking in every word.

'Now, here is the Inverter,' he pointed out, patting its face.

'So, another type of generator?'

'Ah no, beware of confusing an inverter with a marine generator, each is a separate electrical power producer. This inverter will convert the vessels battery power, which is direct-current or DC power into a weak alternating-current or AC to provide power. A generator, on the other hand provides constant AC electricity independent of the batteries.'

Claire maintained her focus.

He went on to explain the systems in the engine room and began to quote all his knowledge regards the performance of the engines and their associated power systems, even explaining the purpose of the small portable gasoline generator secured in the corner of the heart of the ship.

'Wow, whatever dude! I have no idea what you are talking about. Man, how do you know all this stuff?'

'Oh, just experience, I guess.'

'Yeah, right! A medical specialist, AC DC, engine performance and whatever … Sorry, don't buy it. Something you picked up at University maybe?'

'Not quite.'

'You have my attention … again. So, how do you know all this?'

'Ah, just mucking around with stuff.'

'No, not good enough … what's the deal?'

'Well, if you must know,' he said, pausing, while he smiled at her inquisitive face.

'Yes, I must know.' She laughed. 'Tell me, tell me,' Claire asked, shaking his arm with both hands

'I have a light aircraft engineer's licence.'

'What?'

The doctor humbly nodded his head slowly.

'You don't.'

'I do.'

'Really?' She studied his face wondering if she wasn't dealing with another *kangaroo story* of sorts.

Yep, and I helped a mate rehab an old boat of his. Nothing like this of course, but the same principle.' He replied, nonchalantly turning away and soaking in his surroundings.

'Shut up, I can't believe you, you're an aircraft engineer?'

'Well, just light aircraft,' he said, turning to investigate her surprise. 'Didn't I tell you? Maybe I didn't. I took a break from full time medicine … just worked on weekends in the hospital and got my commercial pilot's licence. Flew, or trained at least, during the week and practiced medicine on the weekend…a lot of fun. A few of my medical associates have done it, but I went one step further and got my engineers ticket.'

'Commercial pilot,' she asked.

'Yes'

'Light aircraft … engineer,' Claire added.

'That's right.'

'Really? Why become an aircraft engineer?'

'Well, thought I might buy my own aircraft and would save a lot of money if I could do my own maintenance and besides I'm really interested in how things tick I guess.'

'Are you sure you're not pulling my chain. Like I do remember something about riding a kangaroo to work... do you remember that?'

Paul laughed. 'No, I'm ridge-didge'

'Excuse me? You're what?'

'Ridge-didge! How long have you been living in Australia? It means I'm for real.'

'Really'?

'Really.' He stressed his case.

'OK, I believe you ... I think. What a pity this ship isn't an aeroplane. You could fix it up and fly us home.' She stopped. The nightmare of their predicament had come home to roost.

'What are we going to do Paul? Does anyone know we are here? How do we get out of ... wherever we are. What's going to happen to us?' Her voiced quivered.

'Hey, woo girl. I think we need to live one day at a time and besides let's count our blessings so to speak.'

'Count our blessings? Excuse me?'

'Yes indeed, count our blessings.'

'Like?' she asked with a challenging tone.

'Well, like ... well, firstly, we're both fine. We are alive Claire. There are two bodies upstairs in body bags. That could have been us, but we are fine, except for a bit of a bump on the head. Second, we have a roof over our heads. Did you see how much water is falling from that sky outside. Man, like that's Noah's ark stuff, unbelievable. Third, we have dry, clean beds to sleep in. Fourth, good food and .... Fifth, we have God with us, who is promising never to leave us nor forsake us. ... just to mention a few points.

From my perspective, things are looking pretty good. What do you think?'

She paused and reflected.

'Yeah, sure, no, you're right, thank you.'

His words instantly offered a balanced perspective. Those words were a calming gift and security flooded back into her life. As she was thinking the young American woman casually played with her nails on her fingers and her focus began to centre on her left hand.

The ring glistened on that finger. She looked up at this tower of strength standing right in front of her.

'Mm, and the God of Abraham, Isaac and Jacob has given me .... You. Yes, ... yes, yes indeed, things are really looking good,' she said deeply.

Paul reached out and took her by the hand.

'Amen, same here.' He reached his arm around her shoulder and quickly squeezed her, kissing her cheek.

'Now, before we go back upstairs let me show you around the room here, there are lots of interesting things in here. Come on I'll show you.'

'Oh, really? I can hardly wait,' Claire said, with slight sarcastic tones made in gest.

'Oh, come on, look at it as a new module in your continual education.' He smiled.

She enjoyed his enthusiasm as he moved around items of interest in the engine room.

A flashlight was discovered hanging on the wall.

'Now this might come in handy.'

'Really why?'

'Well I am going to turn the geny off shortly.'

Claire looked up at him, puzzled.

'Um, geny, as in generator?' he advised, walking over and reacquainting himself with its metal by patting its casing.

'Yeah, sure, but why turn off the generator?'

'Well I want to see if the batteries kick in and if so, which lights come on and which don't. I'm assuming there will be emergency lighting throughout the ship. We'll check out the galley and see what's powered etcetera and the same with the rooms, you know, see what's working and what's not. If the batteries don't kick in, well, without this flashlight it will be pitch black in here. Might be a little hard to see what I'm doing and might be a bit hard to get back to the top' he said laughing. 'Pitch black.' he reinforced his point by turning his flashlight on into her face.

She squinted her eyes and pushed the unit away.

'OK, you're the engineer, pilot, um, slash doctor, I suppose you know what you're doing. Is there anything else you can do that you haven't told me?'

He laughed. 'Ah, many sings, mine little angel,' he said, in a rather poor German accent.

Paul had studied the language during his high school years and, he achieved high grades however, the doctor could never perfect the accent. His face had a stupid look displayed just for her entertainment. She played along with him.

'Ooooo really? Tell me, mien liebschkin,' she said, in a mischievous manner breaking into the German language.

'Ah vell, dat's for me to know unt for you to find out.'

'Vell, vee have ways of making you talk, buster,' Claire said, displaying her best German accent which surpassed his rather poor effort. She began to dig into his ribs with her fingers.

'Ouch! You don't have Nazi in that blood of yours, do you?' He laughed, as he investigated the generator and its power plant.

'Excuse me, no way, in fact quite the opposite.'

'Really? Care to elaborate?' he asked as he continued his mechanical investigation.

'Sure. My great grandmother on my father's side survived the Ravensbrück concentration camp in Germany, but that's another story.

'No way,' Paul's attention was captured by this news and he turned his head swiftly toward the source of interest, wanting more information.

'Yep, she was an amazing woman, so I've been told.'

'You never met her?'

'There's a picture of me sitting on her lap when I was, oh, I don't know, maybe six months old, but I don't remember her. She died a year or so after.'

'So, the concentration camp ... Jewish?' Paul asked looking closely at Claire.

'No, I don't believe so. She and her husband were Jewish sympathizers. I'm told she was a very committed Christian woman and she had a real gift with people. Mom really loved our great nan. When they got together they would talk for hours'

'OK, interesting'

'And you? What's your background?' Claire shifted the focus deliberately.

'Oh, nothing as exciting as yours,' he offered, searching around the generator looking for power controls. He looked up at the wall next to the diesel power-plant.

'Ah, this is what I'm looking for.' Standing up, he reached across and turned off the generator. Instantly the engine room was thrust into darkness. With the flashlight switched on they made their way out of the room. As the marooned couple approached the door, two small L.E.D. down lights suddenly burst into life.

'OK, that's a good sign,' Paul said, turning back toward the room noting the lights position in the ceiling.

Ahead, more down lights could be seen strategically place in the hallway to offer minimum, yet sufficient light for safe passage along the hallway. It took some time to check all rooms, including the clinic and the galley. All offered sufficient lighting for adequate human functionality.

They made their way back to the bridge to check the weather.

'Wow! This is bad Paul. Just look at it.' Claire yelled back to her partner. The wind had picked up since they had initially left the place of command.

'Yep ... but I think the ship is pretty secure stuck up on this hill. Man, that must have been a mammoth storm surge that hit this area ... I mean to get the Pacific Fair this far up the slope. Huge.'

Claire agreed. 'Not much point being here with this noise. Let's go back downstairs. I can't stand this wind.'

They made their way back to the kitchen with the view of an early dinner. The damaged door was opened and, the battery powered L.E.D. lights were turned on again.

'OK, I think we should cook that steak sitting in the refrigerator. What do you think?'

'Sounds good to me'

The doctor got to work, making himself familiar with the placement of the necessary utensils. Claire collected the meat, some vegetables and other condiments required for the nights' meal.

'Hey, there's a lot of meat here,' she observed, placing aside the required amount and holding the balance up in her hands.

'Should I place the rest in the freezer?'

'Mm, probably the best place for it, I guess. Though they say you shouldn't re-freeze meat after its been thawed. We can only assume it came from the freezer, but I guess what option do we have under the circumstances. What do you think?'

'Agreed!'.

'OK, but don't walk in that room with bare feet, remember?'

'Oh yes, of course, though might cut this meat up into meal size portions and place it in freezer bags, if I can find some, or something as an alternative'

'Good idea.'

The team worked well together that late afternoon. The hotplates were fired up and a nutritious early evening meal was prepared and placed on two white china plates. Paul opened a bottle of red wine while Claire poured herself a long cold glass of fruit juice and the two bowed their heads and said grace. There was an 'amen' to finalise the moment and the two appetites were well satisfied on that tropical wet evening. The galley was finally cleaned up. All the plumbing in the ship's kitchen seemed to be working well, including the pressure pumps that pumped the water up from the twenty-thousand-gallon water tank housed deep in the bowls of the buckled ship.

'Hey, are we going to start that generator for tonight? I guess I'm thinking of the freezer,' she inquired slowly, as she scanned the engine room.

'Yeah, I'll give it a whirl later on but only for an hour or so just to get that freezer back down to temperature and the batteries recharged and I'll let her rip again tomorrow morning for a while. If we keep that door closed and the refrigerator as well of course, I think the unit should keep its chill in place. My objective is to preserve the diesel as long as we can.'

'OK, great, hey, you didn't answer my question about your background,' she asked.

'Oh yeah, sorry, well as I said, nothing as exciting as yours.'

'You think my background is exciting?'

'Well, yes I do.'

'Oh, OK.' she paused. Claire had never known such appreciation of her background.

'Anyway continue.'

'Well basically, England, a little Scottish on my father's side and English and Norwegian on my mother's side.

'No way, I have Norwegian on my great nan Tina's side. She was from Norway.'

'Tina? That was her name?'

'Yes, Tina. Not sure what her surname was.'

'OK, Mother or father's side?'

'Um, as I said before … on my Father's.'

'Of course, interesting.'

Considerable time was spent talking whilst sitting on the two uncomfortable chairs in the galley that evening. They then ventured back to the engine room and let the generator run for an hour while they prepared themselves for the evenings rest. The weather had not eased and the wind continued its relentless persecution of the area.

Their rooms plumbing was checked and found still to be functional. Claire was the first to use the facility. After ten minutes Paul heard the shower turn off and the thick glass shower door open.

'Paul?' Her voice cut through the bathroom wall.

'Yeah, what's up?' he asked, standing up quickly and moving to the bathroom's door.

'Hey, my head is really starting to thump.'

'Mm, OK I'll get some medication, back in a tick.'

'OK, thankyou *hun*,' she yelled out from her secure enclosure.

Paul stood surprised, as though pinned to the floor outside at the bathroom door. His heart thrilled as he mentally replayed her words.

'What did you just say?' he asked. He suddenly felt odd, if not slightly false, as he knew exactly what she called him, but simply, he wanted to hear it again.

The door suddenly opened slightly and, a bandaged head peaked around the corner with a bright smile hiding the rest of her from behind the barrier.

'I said thank you, *hun*.' She looked expectantly at the man she loved.' Is ... that OK, or would you prefer doctor?

'That's more than OK,' he replied softly.

'Come here?' she asked, stretching up to him whilst still maintaining her modesty.

She kissed him quickly.

'I'll get the medication,' the doctor said smiling broadly. 'And I'll turn off the generator.'

'OK, I'll be waiting,' she said confidently.

'Oh, by the way, just a heads up ... remember, when I turn off the generator the room will go black ... but the standby lights will come on very quickly ... I hope.' He smiled, pointing at the two seven-watt lights strategically placed in the room. 'Better get on the bed sooner than later.'

'OK, will do.'

By the time the ship's doctor returned to the room Claire was in bed.

'Here ya go beautiful.' He placed the two white tablets in her hand accompanied by a fresh bottle of water as he sat on the bed.

'Hey, it's a bit dimmer in here with the L.E.D lights.'

'Mm, sure is,' she confirmed, swallowing down the tablets. 'But still adequate.'

'Did they take long before they came on?' he asked looking up at the ceiling, showing more interested in the ship's systems than his patient's headache.

'Almost immediately,' Claire replied closely watching her doctor.

Paul nodded his head slowly, deep in thought.

'OK great ... Yeah, Good.' He nodded again, frowning slightly. 'Are you sure you still want me in here with you? I'm more than happy to buzz off into another room,' he said, suddenly navigating to a new subject.

Claire pulled her head back in surprise. 'Am I making you uncomfortable?'

'Hardly, but if you still need me here that's fine, but I don't want to cramp your style ... or more to the point, invade your privacy.'

'How could you invade my privacy?' she said smiling, handing him back the bottle of water. 'You are my very own personal doctor. There's no invasion when you are invited in.' She kissed him again.

Her very own personal doctor smiled, backed away slightly on the bed, then stood up maintaining his smile.

'Thank you love, I'm thrilled. Really, I am but, even so ...' His smile was dampened. 'I will stay here with you for professional reasons. You understand?'

Her smile slowly left her face.

'Yes of course, I'm sorry but, please stay Paul. I understand what you're saying and you're right but when you're around I feel so secure. I don't want you out of my sight.'

'Well I was when I went down to turn off the generator. Out of your sight that is,' he laughed softly questioning her logic.

'Yes, you were, weren't you ... and I did, didn't I? Stay here on my own that is. Thought I would be brave. Well, try at least.'

'Did it work?'

'No. I nearly ran up the hallway after you.'

'But you didn't.'

'No. But, I won't do that again. Well not until I settle ... if you know what I mean.

Please stay Paul.'

'Sure, no problems. Now you have a good night's sleep. By the way how's the cheek?

It looks a little better.'

'Mm, still uncomfortable, but it's the headache.'

'Yeah, suspect you have a slight concussion. That medication will help with the pain and make you sleep soundly tonight. If you have any discomfort later on, wake me up, OK? I want to know about it. I want you to rest well tonight. You need it.'

'Yes doctor.'

'I'm serious.'

'And so am I ... seriously in love with you,' she said, with mischievous eyes looking all over her man.

'OK, you, bed, sleep ... good night,' he said, laughing under his breath.

'I think I need a kiss goodnight doctor.'

'I don't fraternise with my patients,' he replied. A humorous expression came over his face. His emotions were stirring. It would be easy to take advantage of what appeared to be an open invitation, however he knew the consequences. At that moment, he was thinking for both of them.

'But doctor I want …. No, I really need a good night kiss. I'm sure you could prescribe that because I really need it.'

'No, you don't. Do you know what you really need?'

'What?' she asked, with a confident, expectant look.

He stood upright.

'You really need a cold shower.'

She gasped. 'Oh, how rude!' And she proceeded to throw a pillow at him.

He laughed softly. 'Good night.' With that he turned out the dim L.E.D. lights and with his flashlight bringing meaning to the sudden darkness with its brilliant white light, he made his way over to the mattress on the floor.

He lay down, feeling the relief as his head nestled into the cool pillow. Exhaustion began to seep into his soul. The last twenty-four hours had been more than anyone should have had to cope with. His thoughts were on Claire. Despite her injury and all the other events that had recently transpired, she was maintaining reasonable social skills, with the exception of considerable insecurity. He switched off the light in his hand and darkness flooded in all around them. The room offered blissful silence, except for the patter of heavy rain which could be heard against the window of their room.

Though exhausted, he lay there soaked in the profound knowledge that their plight was for a purpose, but what was the reason for all this? The profundity was overwhelming and he pondered the point for some time, then slowly drifted off to sleep.

The weather continued its warfare with the surroundings throughout the night. Early in the morning, a sudden blast of wind pounded against the couple's bedroom window. A scream accompanied the ruthless buffeting and Paul sat upright at the ready.

'Paul?'

'Mm?' he replied, trying to wake up and take action against the unseen enemy.

'Paul?'

'Claire, I'm here,' he assured her, fumbling around in the darkness trying to find the flashlight.

'Paul?' Her voice was desperate.

Finally making contact with the instrument of light, he released its glory with a simple push of its button.

'Hey, here, I'm here.' He quickly made his way to her bed and sat on the edge stroking her ruffled hair away from her face.

Claire opened her teary eyes and focused directly on the face.

'It's all right.'

Her panic stopped. She sat up, threw her arms around the doctor and sobbed.

'I think you might have had a bad dream, yes?'

Claire nodded her head as she buried her face deep against the base of his neck.

'I dreamt they were after us and they sailed into the bay and came through the window.'

Her voice vibrated its urgency into his neck offering a strange tingle to his larynx.

'It's just the wind. It's a bit rough out there again, but you're safe. It's all good.'

She held her man tighter.

'So how about you try and get some more sleep, hey? It's …' He brought his watch up to his face from behind her back.

'Two thirty in the morning. Still pretty early.'

'Paul, don't leave me. Please don't leave me.' She burst into a fresh round of sobbing.

'Sure, but I haven't left you love. I'm sleeping just over there,' he said, pointing to the mattress. 'You'll be fine.'

'No, just hold me. Don't let me go.' Claire's grip around Paul began to tremble.

'OK. OK, I won't let you go. Let's just lay down, hey? Now, I want you to relax Claire. You're safe.' He gently coaxed her down onto the bed and turned off the flashlight.

'No, leave the light on,' she demanded, as her voice increased towards a measure of panic again.

'No, we'll leave it off. You're fine. I'm here. I want you to listen to my voice. I am here and I have you in my arms and your safe,' he confirmed softly, as he began to lightly stroke her arm.

'You're safe OK? Hey, and by the way, have I told you lately how much I love you?' Instantly he felt her ridged form relax against his body.

She moved closer to him, as he took the displaced sheet and threw it over both of them. Within minutes his female companion had drifted off to sleep. In a short period of time the rain and the wind had stopped. Claire's breathing could be heard clearly. Paul lay there for some time listening.

He was deeply conscious that in his arms he held a wonderful person, but he was equally aware of her vulnerability. She moved her body even closer to him, Claire took a deep breath, then, released a slight groan of pleasure as she snuggled into his chest. Paul began to see his future, just a glimpse. He had been made responsible for Claire and he could see that she was bowing to his headship over her. In the blackness of that early morning, Paul stood before the highest authority, understanding his responsibility and his accountability for this woman. His heart began to pound again as he focused on the closeness between them there, in the darkness, he saw it.

The most-high God was watching his every move. Her scent was intoxicating. Her comfortable body was warm, it was soft and, it was close ... too close for his comfort. He was responding to her again and knew he should not. He pondered further their situation.

Why had this happened to them?

Paul was so thankful for Claire but, not so thankful for their situation. '*In all things give thanks.*' were the words from that chapter in the bible and he knew he needed to work on his attitude. It seemed a cruel verse given their plight, but none the less that's what it said.

Such a verse was perfect for the right mindset required to function there on that ship. Where were they? Would they be rescued? If they weren't rescued how long would the fuel last to run the generator? How long would the food last without refrigeration? The questions continued to pour into his head, as sleep began to slowly overtake him. He sank gently into the purity of peaceful rest.

CHAPTER TWENTY-NINE

ynn had just arrived home from the university that overcast
Friday afternoon. She was talking to her parents in the kitchen,
when a series of knocks burst loudly against the Langley's door.

'Goodness!' The lady of the house jumped with fright at the
seeming severity of the pounding coming from the front of the
house. The pastor turned to move toward the front door.

'I'll get it, Dad. I'm expecting something from Uni. They said
they would send someone over when they've compiled the documents.' Lynn began to move towards the front door.

'Oh, does that mean you'll be working tonight?'

'Afraid so, Mom. It might be a late one too. Got to get everything in place by Monday. It'll probably take me through to the
weekend as well.'

'Oh, really? I was hoping you could help me with something on
Saturday.' Lynn's mother raised her voice as her daughter walked
away to the front door. 'But that's OK; we can do it some other
time.' Mrs. Langley was a lively woman, and her daughter was
blessed with a similar character. Her life had revolved around the
teaching of children and her husband's ministry, but her devotion
to her children was paramount.

'Well, we'll see, Mom. If I can get stuck into it tonight, I might
have a fair bit done, and we can do whatever you have in mind.
So, what's happening tomorrow?' she yelled out with her head
slightly turned in the direction of the kitchen.

Lynn opened the door. There was a reply from her mother, but the voice had no impact on her daughter.

'Mrs. Langley?' Two well-dressed people stood, stone faced, on the paved walkway outside the residence.

'Um, actually, no, Miss Langley. You want to speak to Mom? Dad's here, too.'

'Both might be more appropriate,' the tall man said.

Lynn turned and called out to the authority of the household in the kitchen.

'Dad, it's for you, Um and Mom, you too,' she yelled and returned her gaze to the sight before her. The two at the door looked past Lynn, noting the man of the household now walking to the door.

'Yes, can I help you?'

'Reverend Langley?' A tall man dressed in a dark suit posed the question.

'Yes.'

'Sir, I'm John Huchinson and this is Vicky Allan, federal police.' They presented proof of identification, giving their observer plenty of time to soak in their official authenticity.

'Hi, how can I help you?' he asked, as he shook their hands.

'Would you like to come in?'

'Thank you.'

The two visitors were ushered in and offered a seat in the large lounge area.

'Mr. Langley, we believe that this is the residential address of a Doctor Paul Langley.'

'Yes. He's our son. Is there a problem?' the pastor inquired, just as his wife entered the formal lounge.

'This is my wife,' he said, as the parents sat together. 'Love, these are federal police.'

'Hello.' Her greeting sounded uncertain.

'Hello, Mrs. Langley, we're sorry to disturb your day.'

The tension in the room began to increase.

'We've come to inform you that the ship that your son was on in the North Pacific has been reported missing.'

Lynn stood watching the words come from the mouth of the attractive man in the dark blue suit.

Her world began to slow down as she looked across at her mother who had placed her hands over her mouth in shock. Mrs Langley moved closer to her husband who accommodated her need by placing his arm around her shoulder.

'The last scheduled report from the ship was a few days ago, just before a category five typhoon moved through the area,' the officer said without any obvious emotion.

Lynn moved over to her father's side and sat down, taking his hand in hers.

'Wouldn't they have found safe mooring in some harbour?' Lynn begged the question. 'Their radios might have been put out of action or something'.

'Well possibly, Miss Langley, but ...'

'Lynn ... please call me Lynn.'

The female police officer took the cue and leant forward.

'Lynn, Mr. and Mrs. Langley, we have come to advise that the ship ...' She looked down at her information placed neatly in a folder. 'Um, I believe its name is the *Pacific Fair*?'

'Yes?' the word was sharp coming out of Lynn's mouth.

'We have been led to believe that the *Pacific Fair* has fallen in the hands of pirates.'

'Oh, Lord, no.' Lynn's mother whispered her prayer.

The woman of the household brought her hands down from her face and placed them in her lap. Her husband slid his arm from behind her and reached over to confirm his support by slightly squeezing the hands of both women.

'How do you know this was his ship?' Paul's father gently asked.

'Yes, it could be any ship. Couldn't it?' Lynn inquired softly.

'No, Lynn, there is a ransom request in place for the ship's passengers. It was sent last night to the American company that owns the ship. It definitely is the *Pacific Fair*.'

'A ransom? But we have no money to pay a ransom.' Lynn's mother advised with a quivering voice.

Both officers looked at each other, and again the female officer took the cue.

'Mrs Langley, they're not asking a ransom for your son Paul.'

The conversation paused, and the room was filled with a sombre silence.

'I'm sorry. I don't understand. Why wouldn't Paul be included? He is one of the passengers.' Lynn said as the strain began to show.

'Well, for some reason, Paul isn't on the list, and this is where it begins to get confusing. We have been advised that people have been killed.'

'Oh no.' The reverend sat back in his chair.

'But Paul isn't one of them.' The officer confirmed quickly.

'Do you know who they are?' Lynn asked.

'Do we know...?' The male constable's words were cut off.

'A list, do you have a list of the names of the passengers?' Lynn clarified.

'Yes, we do. Those names can't be divulged, but we can assure you that Paul isn't one of them. He seems to be missing, I'm afraid.'

'Constable, there was a young woman named Claire on board. What of her? Is she all right? Is she on the list?' Lynn moved forward to the edge of the black leather lounge chair.

'How do you know this lady?' The female constable moved her head slightly to one side, expressing interest.

'Paul rang me from the hotel and spoke of her. I suspect there was something romantic going on.'

The male constable looked at his neatly dressed female partner seated next to him and nodded.

'Lynn, she isn't on the list either, but ...' She looked back at her partner. He nodded his approval.

'We believe that she may be one of the ones killed; however, there is some conjecture,' Officer Hutchinson elaborated further. 'Things are moving quickly as there has been a handover of two of the ship's crew early this morning as proof of cargo in hand and, therefore, assurance of payment. The extortionists intend to hand over the cheapest hostages first and leave the most valuable till last. This insures their cash flow, so to speak.'

Officer Allan took the next point.

'Folk, the two hostages released have conflicting stories when it comes to Claire.

One of the released hostages says she was shot in the head and was left dead on the top deck of the ship. The other said that she was hit in the head with the pistol grip, and the gun went off, but there was no way that the bullet entered her. It seems, according to the second witness, the bullet went into the ceiling directly above the head of the observer telling the story. She said she knew that was the case because there were particles of the ceiling that fell on her as a result of the bullet's point of entry. Both, however, do agree that the doctor, your son, was nowhere in sight, and he definitely didn't board the other ship.

Their stories both confirm that the doctor ...'

'Paul—his name is Paul,' Lynn interrupted.

'Um, yes, both stories confirm that Paul was still on the ship somewhere when the rest of the passengers were taken off the *Pacific Fair* as prisoners. We can therefore, only assume that he was left on the ship for whatever reason and was still alive at that point.'

The three in the Langley household sat frozen to their seats, soaking in the horror of the moment.

'Both of the released hostages agree that the ship, the *Pacific Fair*, was left at anchor in a small, sheltered atoll, which was in fact the last point of contact with the ship's bridge. However, we were advised two hours ago that a search-and-rescue aircraft flew to the location. Nothing could be seen except a lot of damage as a result of the typhoon.

We are very sorry to have to be telling you this. Obviously, we have to advise you given that you are next of kin. We'll be in contact when we hear any new developments.'

'Thank you. What do we do now?' Lynn asked.

'Lynn, we pray, and we activate the prayer warriors in the church and beyond,' a stone-faced pastor spoke softly.

'Sir, and I will be praying with you,' Officer Allan spoke softly standing up and, walking over to the upset mother, placed her hand on her shoulder.

'Mrs Langley, I WILL be praying,' she reinforced her point with a gentle whisper.

The female officer turned, shook Pastor Langley's hand, and met Lynn as she stood up.

'He's in God's hands,' she whispered again but this time into Lynn's ear. 'But they that wait upon the LORD shall renew their strength; they shall mount up with wings as eagles; they shall run, and not be weary; and they shall walk, and not faint.'

284

Lynn looked straight into the face of the young federal police officer.

'Thank you. For some strange reason, I see him on wings of eagles,' the sister of the missing doctor whispered back with full belief.

'Amen. Don't let that vision fade.' Officer Allen whispered back. She smiled turned and walked out behind her partner in law.

Lynn followed and stood at the door, watching the two officers move smartly towards the unmarked police car. The female officer opened the passenger door, turned, looked back at the house, saw Lynn, nodded slowly, and then quickly entered the vehicle.

CHAPTER THIRTY

Paul stood on the sandy hill overlooking the stranded ship. Two days had passed since their savage arrival. With sweat streaming down his face to his naked shoulders, he dug the brand-new shovel, acquired from the ship's storeroom, into the saturated ground next to a deep hole he had just finished excavating. The sun had been above the horizon for an hour. Though the weather was still overcast, there hadn't been a drop of rain since late the previous day. A whisper of warm breeze chilled his chest as he wiped the remnants of sand from his hands onto his dark blue board shorts. The view from his vantage point was pleasant to the eyes. The small bay set before him was a tropical picture as the sun broke through a thin patch of cloud, bringing to life a burst of brilliant colour. The crystal-clear, turquoise-blue water sparkled beyond the condemned vessel, and large fish could be seen swimming lazily around submerged coral heads within the protection of the bay's sanctuary.

The beauty of the moment was instantly shattered, as he turned and looked down at the sight lying on the ground just a few feet from his tall slender form. Paul bent down and taking the corners of the first body bag, he dragged the remains of the captain down the earthen ramp leading into the base of the six-foot grave, followed by the bag containing Jessica's body of. A hint of stench from the decomposing bodies could be smelt, as both bags were placed side by side in their sandy resting place.

As the doctor made his way out of the grave, another fresh wash of morning breeze caressed his tired face. He took the upright shovel in hand and stood beside the pit. Looking down into its opening, he reflected on the events over the past few days. It all seemed so surreal, pointless, and his heart began to pound in his chest as he pictured the two people he once knew.

'Lord, I really need you right now,' he whispered.

He had never buried anyone before. Reality thrust its horror into his heart. His emotional pendulum began swinging wildly. Thoughts of panic rushed through his mind, psychotically raiding his peace.

'Lord?' he whispered again.

As he stared into the grim hole, another glorious burst of sun-light suddenly bathed the area with brilliant light.

'Hey, I've been looking for you everywhere. What are you ...' the voice stopped just as its owner reached the crest of the sandy hill.

'Wow, um, Morning! Didn't really expect to see you so early. Thought you might have slept in for a little while longer,' he said slightly startled by her sudden arrival.

'Hey, no, I think the sun might have woken me ... um ...' She stood motionless, fully focused on the dismal display laid out at the bottom of the grave.

'You dug this on your own? Man, it's deep,' she said with vague intentions.

'Excuse me?'

'Oh, da! Sorry, Paul. Like you're going to call the local hole diggers association around here to help you. I'm so sorry for that stupid question.'

The doctor smiled.

Claire walked over to her husband to be and wrapped one arm around his bare waist, looking up at him.

'You look tired.' She placed her free hand on his face and stroked it gently.

'Actually, I'm stuffed. It took a bit to get the bodies off the ship and up this hill.'

'How long have you been up and … working?' She pointed to the excavation in front of the pair.

'A few hours. It was dark when I started.'

'Why so early?'

'Well, it had to be done, and I thought the earlier I got started, the less chance of you seeing this,' he said looking back at the sad sight below him.

She looked intently at the speaker.

'Paul, thank you. You're a wonderful man, but I'm fine.' Claire reached down and took a handful of sand.

'Which one is Jess?'

The doctor pointed to the appropriate body bag, and Claire sprinkled the contents from her hand across the length of the body from her elevated position.

'Rest well, sweet Jessica.' Claire paused, then looked upward. 'Lord, I know Jess is with you. Say hi to her for me?'

Paul reached down, gathered a small handful of sand and threw it over the body of the captain.

'This was a good man. Unfortunately, I don't know where he stood with God.'

A sudden lump developed in Paul's throat, and holding back his tears, he began to shovel the moist sand into the grave. Each thud of heavy sand could be felt in their hearts as gravity directed the sand's course onto the silence below. Slowly, the depth of the dual grave decreased. Within thirty minutes Paul was patting down the surface as Claire gathered loose volcanic rocks to mark each person's place.

'Hey, hun, do you think we could make two crosses?' Claire was composed, as she wiped sweat from her forehead.

'Of course, but not today.'

'OK.' She looked deeply in the face of her exhausted man.

'Hey, are you OK, boy?'

The tables had turned. Paul stared at the mound of sand at his bare feet and sighed.

'No. I feel filthy. Dirty business this,' he said under his breath. 'Might go for a swim.'

Paul turned with shovel in hand and began to walk down towards the ship. Claire took his arm and stopped him.

'Want company?'

'Yeah,' he said wiping copious beads of sweat from his brow with his free hand. The two walked down the hill toward the white sandy beach that was peppered with debris.

At the stern of the stranded vessel, Paul thrust the shovel into the sand, looked out to the beautiful picture before them and took the hand of the woman next to him.

'Let's go.' He winked at her.

'I'll race you.' With that, she broke free from his hand and ran like the wind toward the water. Claire jumped over the obstacles littered over the ground.

'Hey,' the doctor laughed running behind her with the greatest intent of catching her.

He watched her run with great agility. Her body easily navigated around the storm-ravaged beach front.

Claire had reached the edge of the water first with every intention of diving in. She pounded into the deeper water, ready to feel the full delight, only to be held back by a cry from behind.

'Claire, don't!' the doctor yelled.

A little fear prompted her heart to listen to the advice. She stopped and spun around.

'Don't get the wound wet.'

'What?' She laughed.

'The stitches, you need to keep them dry.'

'Oh. darn it, Paul; surely, it'll be OK. It's been how many days now?'

'Not enough days yet. A few more, and I'll take them out.'

'Man, this ... sucks! The water is so beautiful. Wouldn't the saltwater be good for the wound?' the patient said, slapping the water in frustration, then bobbed down up to her neck in the bay's peaceful water.

'Just another couple of days,' he said wading out to her.

Claire studied this man closely. *For a doctor*, she thought, *he was well built*. She gently massaged the side of her face. Her neglect to consider her suspected fractured cheek bone was beginning to pay its dividends. A dull ache reminded its owner of the injury.

'Hurting?' Paul said, watching closely.

'Yes. I forgot about ... the fractured bone ... thing. I ...' Claire looked down at the water and then back to the doctor. 'I really hate this,' she said now given over to total frustration.

'You need to take care, Claire.'

'I try to, but, it felt OK up there at the ... you know.' She looked sadly at Paul.

'The graves,' he said, helping her.

'Yes.' Reflection possessed her, then passed as quickly as it came.

'And this water is so beautiful, and I just ... forgot.'

Paul waded out to her side. 'You are just like a kid. You know that?' he said as he shook his head.

'Well, maybe, being here is bringing out the kid in me.' She giggled and skimmed her hand across the surface of the water, directing its mass in front of her hand to his chest.

Paul welcomed this sudden liquid onslaught.

'You are so right; this is nice.' With that, he dove under the crystal clear tropical water and surfacing next to her, displayed a broad smile.

'All clean,' Paul said, displaying his liberty. He wiped the water from his face.

'Ooo, that was cruel. You did that, just to spite me. Didn't you?' She screwed up her face at him.

Paul gave a cheeky grin.

'You rat,' she said, pushing him away.

Claire quickly took his head and pushed him under the water, only to see her man bob back up, laughing.

'I hate you,' she said laughing, pushing him under again.

He surfaced again, blowing a large breath of air out of his lungs and spraying a fine mist into the morning's brilliance.

'You hate me?' He laughed hard.

'No, ... no, I don't. You know that,' Claire said, suddenly pinning him to herself by wrapping her legs around his waist and holding on to his shoulders.

'Not one bit.' She laughed. 'I just think you're a bit tough.'

'Really?' His eyes were smiling as they explored her face.

The doctor submerged further into the water with his new passenger. The water was cool, and the intimacy was perfect. He kissed her on the lips, to which she responded fully to his intimate proposal, wrapping her arms around his neck. Finally, with a quick release, she looked him directly in the face.

'Paul, what are we going to do?' she whispered.

'Well, we are going to get rescued. They'll be out looking for us, but first we'll investigate where we are. Thought we might climb that mountain to get a better view. Might do that after breakfast. What do you think?'

'Umm, yeah sure, but ... Paul, what if we don't get rescued, you know, what will ... *we* do?' she emphasized.

'We will.' The thought of not being rescued was too much to consider at that point in time for the doctor.

Claire kissed him again. 'That's not what I'm talking about.'

'I'm sorry, what are you saying?'

'You know, for a doctor, you are rather thick,' she said kissing him again.

'Excuse me?' He pulled his head back from her face trying to pick up her logic.

Claire took his face in her hands and kissed him deeply again, then released her captive audience.

'Now, do I have your attention?'

The doctor laughed. 'Oh yes, you certainly have my attention.'

'Good, so given that last little display of passion ... What are *we* going to do ... you know? ... *for better or for worse* ... etcetera?'

Paul stood still looking at every aspect of her face. They were so close he could feel her warm breath on his lips.

'*We* need to keep focused on our rescue, love,' he said slowly.

'But what if *we* don't ... get rescued, that is. What then?' she asked. 'You know, for better or for worse, richer or poorer and so on. So? ... What are *we* going to do?'

'Oh, OK, well if we don't get rescued ... And I'm sure we will, but, if we don't. Um.'

Paul looked out to sea thinking deeply.

'Paul?'

'I'm thinking.'

'Can you think faster?' She lovingly looked squarely at him.

'Well, the scriptures teach that it's better to get married than to burn, if you know what I mean'.

'Yes, yes I do,' Claire replied, studying him.

'So, I guess we'll get married,' he concluded, bringing his hands under her behind for added support as she continued to grip his waist with her legs.

'Well that sounds just Jim dandy to me,' Claire said, with a slight smug look on her face.

Paul studied his fiancé.

'So, let's see ... Mm, OK, so who's going to marry us? I know, Pastor Allan! Oh no; he's in San Francisco ... pity. What about Pastor Roberts? You'll love him, such a funny guy. Oops no, he's in Kansas City. Oh yeah, I've got it ... the perfect man ... why didn't I think of this before ... haven't met him, but I'm told he's a wonderful guy ... Your Dad ... What do you think ...Mm? Oops, oh darn another problem—he's in Brisbane, you know? ... Down under? ... In Australia?' she said slightly frustrated.

Her point was too much for Paul, and he began to laugh silently under his breath.

Claire realized her unintentional humour. His shoulders beginning to shake, then his eyes started to water and finally an explosion of laughter bathed her face.

'Not funny, bucko,' Claire said, meeting his onslaught, but only to catch the infectious emotion and joined her partner in the blessing of the joy now spilling throughout their hearts. The release was sweet, and both moved around in the water enjoying their new home in this tropical paradise.

'Breakfast anyone?' Paul said, preparing a way of escape from the subject at hand.

The doctor walked out of the morning's salt washing. His arms adjusted to her weight as the waters released its welcoming support.

Claire sprang out of her love's arms and ran out of the water, sending spray in all directions, but this time more carefully, not wanting to aggravate her fracture any further. Once she reached the beach, the fine sand squeaked under her as the tiny particles massaged her feet. She turned around in jest, as though looking for her audience.

'Is that a yes, ma'am?'

'Oh, you mean me. What a lovely idea. Thank you for the invitation.'

'You're welcome,' Paul said, going along with the role play.

'Have you been here long?' She laughed a little.

'Me?'

'Yes.'

'Oh just a few days,' he said, continuing with her playful antics.

Paul walked slowly out the water.

'Oh, OK. So, how did you get here?'

'Mm, an interesting question, actually by boat.'

'Oh, that's great. Sounds exciting.'

'It certainly was.'

They both burst into rapturous laughter as they exited the water. A strange relief had overcome the two as they walked hand in hand back to their first-class beached accommodation.

CHAPTER THIRTY-ONE

B reakfast was very simple that morning: a serving of fruit, consisting of two slices of cold pineapple, a mango each, and a large helping of watermelon of which there were ample supplies in the cold room. This was washed down with a cup of coffee.

The weather was clearing, with patches of blue skies scattered across the tropical canopy.

'That was a good breakfast.'

'It was, wasn't it?' Paul said, as he helped Claire over the rail of the ship.

They had each packed a backpack with adequate supplies, including plenty of water, for a day's walking.

'How long do you think the food will last us?' Claire asked, as they stepped off the back of the ship that was buried up to its safety rails in sand, fallen coconut trees, and other foreign matter.

'Not sure. Might be a good idea to take stock just in case we are here a little longer,' he said. His heart sank.

'Yeah, good idea. You never know.' Claire's thoughts were searching for security.

'But, off the top of my head ... providing we can keep that refrigerator going, I estimate we would have, maybe a year's worth of supplies, providing we are careful,' Paul said, keeping a positive tone in the conversation whilst taking a mental stock of what he had seen in storage.

'Really?'

'Well think about it, there's all that beef hanging up in that freezer, chickens, and other meats. There's a stack of food, and if we are careful and eat sparingly, I really think we could make it last a year.' The doctor paused. 'Maybe even longer. We could have meat every second day. That would give us twice as much time, regarding protein, using that simple strategy … so we have a while, I think, if we budget our food intake.'

Claire was relieved.

'It's the generator that's the key to our longevity. So, we'll have to work out the most economical way of operating that freezer and cold room … therefore conserve as much diesel fuel as possible.'

'Mm, OK.' An overwhelming peace overcame Claire as she watched this man.

'You know, I didn't see much fish in that freezer. I love fish. Do you like fish?' she asked her captivated audience.

'Yeah, it's OK. Prefer a good steak.'

'Oh, you are just like my Dad. He loves his steak. It must be a man thing,' the young American said, looking up at the Australian, smiling. 'Mom and I love fish. Actually, so do my brothers come to think of it. OK, maybe it isn't a man thing … Just personal taste,' she giggled.

A wave of desire came over the doctor as he listened to this woman weave her thoughts, wrapping him in her intoxicating character. A hint of sweat began to bead its presence on her forehead, just above the bandage covering her wound.

'Did you see much fish there? You would have thought they'd have stocked more fish, wouldn't you? I think I saw five fish in that freezer. They were pretty big. I think it was five. How long do you think our fish supplies will last?' she asked, now fully in the spirit of conservation.

Paul looked bewildered, as she chatted away like a little girl. Her character was a delight to the doctor as he continued to wonder where she was going with her logic.

'I guess, not long, given that there is only five,' Claire said not giving her audience a chance to answer. 'Seems rather odd that we are marooned here, on this tropical *wherever*, and we have no fish or not much at least. Life can throw you some interesting curve balls, can't it?'

Paul nodded, amazed at her conclusion.

'Anyway, I'm trusting that we will be rescued before we run out of fish, or that God miraculously provides more until we are rescued. If He does ... I wonder how He would do it ... you know, provide the fish. He could, given that He's God, but the question is will He?' Claire said. Her mind was totally absorbed with her pondering, not noticing that they had entered the lush undergrowth on their way to the summit. She stopped and looked around.

'Hey, this is nice. Looks like the typhoon didn't do too much damage in here,' she said looking up to Paul. She saw the strange look on his face.

'What?'

'Claire?' he said, preparing himself to break the news as gently as he could.

'What, Paul? You don't agree that ...'

The doctor pointed to the expanse of water set before them.

'Yes ... and?' She stopped talking and looked to his reference. Silence owned them as she soaked in his context.

'You mean the fish?'

He nodded his head slowly.

'No way!' She giggled like a child.

'Yes, way.'

'No way!' she yelled, then proceeded to laugh hard.

'Yep.' The doctor chuckled under his breath, struck by her simple naivety.

'You mean, we have to catch them from there? In the ocean ... really?' She pointed at the watery expanse.

Paul nodded his head at his doubting audience.

'Like, that's going to happen.' Her laughter abated gradually. Claire looked back out to sea.

Paul watched curiously.

'Get out of town! You're not going to tell me that you think that you can go out there and bring home dinner?'

Paul shrugged his shoulders.

'It's worth a try.'

'Really? How do you intend to do that?' She laughed, still looking out to the horizon.

'You don't know how to fish?'

'No,' Claire insisted then paused. 'but ... you do ... right?'

'Well, it seems I might have a better chance than you.'

'OK,' she replied slowly. They resumed their walk up to the igneous monolith towering up in front of them. 'Don't you need all the stuff. You know like hooks, worms ... and things?'

'Bait and tackle... yep.'

'Well, where will you get that?'

'The ship will have the fishing tackle and as far as the bait is concerned, I'm sure we can find something suitable in the galley,' he said smiling.

'Oh, um, OK.'

'Where do you think those fish in that freezer came from?'

'They caught them?' she questioned.

'Yes.'

'OK.' Claire thought for a short time. 'Paul?'

'Yep.'

'Um, do you want an apprentice?' she asked laughing softly.

'Fishing?'

'Yeah, why not?' She shrugged her shoulders.

'Sure, sounds good to me. How are you at gutting fish?'

'Oh gross.'

'OK, well that doesn't sound so positive, but hey, by the time I'm finished with you, old girl, you'll be able to write it up on your resume. Big plus, if not only a handy talking point at parties,' he said, taking her by the hand as they navigated their way up the steep slope to the impending rocky outcrop set before them.

Within fifteen minutes they had reached their destination. With sweat now streaming from their bodies, soaking their shirts, they sat on a large rock and looked back down at the landscape before them. The ship could be seen clearly nestled on its sandy platform just below the fresh gravesite. The two pulled out their water supplies, and each drank heartily from their own bottle as they gazed in silence. The picture was perfect, as a gentle breeze greeted their hot bodies, offering much relief.

'You know, the ship is a little like Noah's ark.' Claire looked down at the stranded vessel, then turned quickly to her man. 'Don't you think?'

'Yeah. I wonder if Noah and family went through the ride that we did?'

'We'll never know, will we, but one things for certain, they were on that ark a darn longer time than us.' Claire smiled back at the doctor. 'Pretty sure I couldn't put up with that.'

'If you had to, I'm sure you would.' He looked at his fiancé and noticed her wet shirt as the result of prolific sweating. The garment was sensibly modest and well chosen for the day's journey. However, once soaked, it clung to her chest revealing her shape.

'Hey, you want to be careful. That shirt is pretty wet. Don't want you getting a chill.'

'You are such a worry wart.' Claire patted him on the shoulder 'But thank you all the same.'

'You're welcome and … um, it's also a little see through,' he said taking closer notice.

'What?'

'Might need to be careful, don't want the neighbours to get the wrong idea … again.'

His eyes lifted from her shirt to her surprised face.

'Excuse me?' she said, holding her arms across her chest. 'Look the other way.'

The doctor laughed.

'Seen it all before, remember? Come on, lady, let's check out this mountain. See what we can see on the other side,' he huffed as he stood up, stuffing the water bottle back in his backpack.

'I bet you have,' Claire said shaking her head.

'Come on,' the doctor commanded briskly.

'No doubt about you, doctor; you can be full of surprises,' she said under her breath, as she adjusted her loose-fitting cotton shirt to release its cling from her bare skin beneath.

'Lead on, good sir.'

'By the way, why aren't you wearing a bra?' Paul spoke louder as he led the way.

'Oh, Man,' she said softly. 'Well, if you must know, I have a rash around the bra strap line, and it's rather uncomfortable. That's why. Didn't think you'd notice,' the woman said, sporting a prominent frown over her brow.

'Might be a bit of heat rash,' he spoke, in a matter of fact way, ignoring her previous point. 'When we get back, I'll give you something for that. Need to be careful with things like that in the tropics. It could fester before you know it, and that could be nasty.'

'OK. Thanks for the info, doctor.'

'You're most welcome.'

The temperature had dropped five degrees due to the trees protecting the area from the hot tropical sun. Claire noted something in the rock face ahead and ran on to investigate.

'Hey look!' She moved closer to the point of interest. Within fifty yards of their initial resting place, a cave entrance could be seen.

'Wow, look at that,' Claire cried out as she made her way to the entrance. As she approached the entrance, the American turned to the doctor.

'Paul, come and have a look at this. It's a cave.' Her voice reverberated as she walked within the cavern's depth.

'Wow, it goes in a fair way. Oooh ... it's really dark further in, Paul. Hey, there's no dirt on the floor ... it's rock ... wow come on.'

'Yeah, yeah, hold your horses, lady.' The doctor carefully made his way to the opening in the rock.

'Come on, old man, speed it up,' she called out. This newfound discovery had brought her to life.

'Careful with the old man thing, kid,' he said, delighting in her excitement as he entered the room of rock.

'Careful with the kid thing, old man.'

Claire was blessed with a transparent personality; what you saw was what you got, and Paul found that to be just one of the traits that attracted him to this woman. The temperature was much cooler than outside, and the pair walked around the large room, enjoying each other in their newfound reprieve from the heat of the day.

'I wonder how far it goes in?' Claire said, as she gazed into the blackness.

'Not sure. Might bring the flashlight next time and have a good look,' Paul replied, as they moved back outside. The humid atmosphere hit their bodies.

'It's better in there. Man, this heat is pretty oppressive,' he observed, looking around at their surroundings and wiping more sweat from his face. Claire walked beside him, soaking in the beauty of the area. She looked up at Paul and took his hand.

'You know, I really like it. I hate the cold, having to get all bundled up with heaps of clothing. I much prefer this,' she said. 'The less clothing the better... within reason.' Claire giggled.

'Yes, I'm beginning to see that about you,' he said smiling.

Claire hardly heard a word but continued to drink in the emerald green surroundings.

'I'm coming to the conclusion that there's something good about this place. Don't you think?' She continued her visual appreciation as she looked around.

With the doctor's hand still in hers she walked in front of him.

Claire began to walk backwards, looking directly into his face.

'There's like, a freedom here, or is it a presence? Oh, I don't know ... Can't you feel it?' She released her hand from his and twirled around in front of him taking in the sight of the lush foliage.

'Well, we've only just arrived but ....' He was cut off.

'Look at this place.' She stopped and breathed in deeply, smelling the damp sent of the tropical atmosphere. The doctor watched this somewhat euphoric creature, direct his attention to the nature of their new environment. Her emotions were infectious, nonetheless.

Paul began to see what she was saying. Both stopped and just looked at the pristine sight set before them. A breath of wind washed over them and swirled their senses, only to be pounded further by the beauty of it all.

'OK, I think you might be right.'

'I'm absolutely sure of it, Paul.' She turned to her fiancé.

'I think what you might be experiencing is the presence of God.'

'Excuse me?'

'I think, this is … His place for us.'

'Really?'

'It sounds odd I know but, … you know? … for the moment, I think this is where God wants us. Why? I don't know, but …' Paul shook his head in surrendered disbelief.

'God's presence.' Claire thought deeply. 'This is a little scary,' she said, overwhelmed.

His words gripped her with a sudden fear, a fear of knowing one's comparative failings against the perfect of perfect, the Holy of Holies, a fear that understands the undeserved favour in one's situation.

A noise suddenly interrupted the moment. Paul turned his head to the direction of this new declaration.

'Did you hear that?'

'What?'

'That sound.' He looked around and stopped, straining to hear It again. 'It sounded like a chook.'

'Like a what?' Claire laughed.

'A chook.'

'What's a chook?'

'You know, a chicken or rooster actually.'

'No, I didn't hear a rooster. You call chickens chooks?'

'Yeah,'

'Aussie vernacular kicking in again?' she asked.

' Sorry,' he said, listening intently to the sounds of the area.

'Don't be. ... Chooks... most interesting.' Claire giggled again.

A distant sound of a rooster, heralding its presence, was clearly heard by both new arrivals.

'Oh yes, I heard that,' she said, as Claire's head spun toward Paul for confirmation.

The doctor nodded his head.

'That was indeed ... a rooster, or a chook as you call it.' She laughed.

'Yes, it was, and you know what that means?' he asked, with further enthusiasm.

'Um, eggs?'

'No ... people.'

'People?'

'Yeah, where there's chooks, there's people.'

'Oh, da, of course. Paul, I knew it. We'll be home sooner than we think.' Claire took hold of the doctor's arm with excitement and shook it gently.

'Actually, it'll be kind of sad leaving here. Don't you think? So, lovely here. As you say, wherever *here* is.' She laughed softly.

They moved toward the direction of the bird's beckoning, which brought them to the other side, around the base of the rocky outcrop. The two explorers stopped as they looked at the damage set before them. The typhoon had struck a heavy blow to that side of the rock, and trees had been ripped out by their roots, laying haphazardly over each other offering a clear view ahead. Claire was first to see it. She gasped, bringing her hands to her mouth in sudden disbelief.

'Paul?'

He spun to her, then to her point of reference. The sight was more than he wanted to take in.

'Oh, Lord,' Claire whispered.

There, from their new-found vantage point, was the sea, as far as the eye could behold, ... nothing but water. The doctor placed his arm around her shoulder. The pair stood on that small tropical mountain, for some time ... silent. Not a soul could be seen.

CHAPTER THIRTY-TWO

———— ⌇ ————

A rooster crowed again.

'It's just an island, Paul. We're on an island, in the middle of the Pacific Ocean.' 'So … it would seem,' he said, softly.

The positive heavenly revelation just experienced, vaporised with the reality of isolation. The truth of the sight raped their emotions, and Claire buried her face into her man's chest.

'We're not going home.' Claire held on to him as thought her life depended on it.

The man responded immediately by folding her in his arms. His embrace poured assurance into her soul, and she greedily stayed there for some time, not wanting to leave for fear of further disappointment. The doctor was lost for words. His professional posture was weighed and found wanting. Claire's corporate competence was taken captive by the simple needs of life.

The midmorning's breeze played with Claire's silky brown hair, as she lifted her head up to face her protector. Her eyes were red from soft crying, and her words spoke a volume of hope to her listener.

'I thank God that He has saved us Paul. I thank Him that He has seen fit to put me here with you, my love,' she said, her face focused fully on his face.

Paul kissed her lightly on the lips. Claire responded holding him to her for a little longer than he had initially planned. He quickly separated himself from her and lifted his head.

'You know, Saint Augustine once said that saints pray as though the outcome depends solely on God and work as though it depends on them,' he said looking around and gesturing at the panoramic view displayed in all its tropical splendour.

'And in Him ... this is our work,' the doctor spoke slowly, softly as the gentle revelation settled itself upon the man.

'Our work?' Claire stood back a little with renewed interest.

'Yes, our work. God put Adam and Eve into the Garden, didn't He? He put them there not only to live in it but to tend it. He put them to work ... within a perfect framework, so to speak. I think, God has put us, or transferred us, here.'

Claire watched the doctor intrigued by his quiet insight.

'A wild ride to get here, though,' he continued.

Claire hushed a laugh.

'Whilst this is no perfect Garden of Eden, I guess I see a similarity here with us,' Claire said, softly. 'but what's our work here?' the new woman of the island asked with deepened interest as she turned to scan their part of creation set before her.

'I don't know, beside staying alive, maybe planting a garden or ...'

The sound of a rooster crowing attracted his attention again.

'Or breeding chooks ...' he laughed. 'That's definitely a rooster. Let's go find him; what do you think?'

Claire ignored his question and maintained her stare at the view below.

'Paul, what's that?' she pointed to an area at the end of the island.

He saw her reference immediately but, said nothing.

'That's a road,' she said slowly. 'What's a road doing on a small island? But ... it doesn't seem to go anywhere ... just stops out in the ocean.'

'Actually, Claire, that's not a road.'

'No?'

'No ... That looks more like ... in fact, a lot like an old runway.'

'No way.'

'Looks like it.'

'No way. What's a runway doing here?'

'I have no idea. Could be an old, World War II runway.'

'Makes sense, I guess,' Claire replied softly.

'Come on, let's check it out,' Paul suggested.

They made their way down the hill. Claire noted her man's face. It beamed with excitement.

'What about the chook?'

'It can wait.'

'OK, chook can wait, possible airstrip now new priority,' she laughed as she followed her doctor.

He pounded down the slope.

'Hey, speedy, wait for me.'

Paul stopped his pace, turned, and waited for Claire. His enthusiasm was difficult to contain, as they navigated their way through the tropical undergrowth and fallen trees. The battered coconut trees towered over the thick foliage with their fruit all over the ground as a result of the typhoon's attack. Broken branches had been ripped off and mercilessly thrown everywhere.

The two travellers came to a clearing half the size of a football field. On the other side were some buildings. Behind these old constructions, a wall of excavated earth the height of the buildings could be seen.

'What is this?'

'Claire, this definitely looks to me like it's of World War II vintage.'

'OK, but what is it?'

'This is an old airfield.'

'What?'

'Yes, what … indeed.'

They walked up to one of the igloo-shaped structures. Peering through the weather-soiled window, beds could be seen all positioned in a row with small locker-style cupboards standing neatly next to each bed. Another building contained fewer beds, and the last structure had only one window that was crusted with a moss-like substance, making it difficult to see what was inside. Paul went to the door to open it.

'Mm, OK,' he exclaimed, as he vainly tried to operate the aged handle, 'It's turning but not happy.' he said as beads of sweat ran down the back of his neck.

'Maybe it's locked?'

'Could be.'

The doctor pushed against the door, causing one hinge to come clean out of its wooden connection. At that point, the lock slipped from its bolted position, and the door was brutally opened.

'Wow, that was easy,' Claire declared humorously, 'I think my man has some muscle.'

'No, our door here has some rusty screws in some rotten wood.'

Paul lead the way, as the two squeezed into the dark enclosure.

'Hey, love, turn the light on, will you? It's dark in here.'

Claire turned towards the old light switch, then stopped, realising the problem with his request.

'Oh, ha ha,' she said, with a broad smile blessing her face.

He chuckled with immense satisfaction, as he stood still waiting for his eyes to adjust to the dimly lit area. Directly in front of him was a large engine.

'Don't tell me ... Um, generator, right?' Claire looked to Paul displaying her confidence.

'Well done. That's exactly what this is.'

'Do you think it still works?'

'I doubt it, but, ... well, it probably wouldn't take much to get this old girl going, I'm sure. The fuel would be the big challenge ... but being diesel ... might be OK. Just look at it.

It hasn't been used much. And look at this ...' Paul moved across the room, where in the corner, was a much smaller old engine.

'How exciting,' Claire laughed, 'I'm sure you're going to tell me, but allow me to get in first ... what is it?'

'Well ... I'm not sure but what I think we might have here is ...' He moved around the unit in the darkened corner of the generator building. If I had better light, um ... hang on a tick.' The doctor walked outside to the moss-covered window and wiped the years of growth from the glass, then smartly pranced back to the unit in question.

'How's that? ... Ah, Yes, that's better,' he said looking around the room.

'You astound me.' Claire said, watching this man with his new toy.

'Thank you,' he laughed, realising her subtle sarcasm, 'are you finished?'

'Mm, I think so.' Her smile was even broader than her previous display.

'Now, what we have here is a Chore Horse Generator made by Johnson of Canada ... This is a 12-24 volts DC or 120 volts AC unit.'

'How do you know that?'

'Well it's written here.'

'Oh, OK, glad I asked ... and this big fella?' Claire indicated by cocking her head towards the monster in question that she was leaning on, 'You didn't tell me what this one is.'

'I have no idea.'

'Oh, disappointment consumes me.' Claire released a sarcastic grin.

Paul gave her a condescending look and walked around the large generator again, searching for make and model details. 'OK, here we go ... it's a ...6-71 Detroit GM 60KW 1200 RPM Diesel Generator ... wow,' the doctor said as he stood in awe next to the ageing piece of engineering.

'I knew that would be worth the wait,' she said looking at him with a nonchalant expression. 'So, what's it all here for? ... it sure isn't for all the people,' Claire asked with her hands gesturing the question.

'Mm, well, I'd say your countryman built this during World War II, my dear. This is definitely an old airfield, and what we saw from up the hill is a runway.'

'OK, so where are the airplanes?' She laughed looking around.

'Well, there won't be any aircraft, but there's got to be a hanger somewhere around here, surely or what's left of it.'

'Hey, I've got a great idea.'

'What?' Paul looked straight at his love, soaking in her perceived interest.

'Let's go look for the hanger.'

'Are you having a go at me?'

'Who me?... never!' She threw her head back and laughed out loud. 'Come on, handsome, let's go find your hanger.'

'You're such a ratbag. Have I told you that lately?'

'Yes, you have.'

The couple were quickly becoming more at home with each other, and Paul reached over to grab her, but she bolted out of the engine room with lightning speed. He took chase, following her closely as she ran around the earthen wall darting in a zigzag pattern, barely escaping his grasp.

'Hey, watch out for objects in this long grass,' he called out suddenly becoming aware of the possible dangers.

With screams of laughter coming from Claire, Paul was just about to catch her when they both stopped. With heavy breathing matching their exercise, they both looked up. There, directly in front of the pair was a large hanger with huge doors securely slid across the entrance.

'Well there's your hanger, bucko. Now, let's go find Wal-Mart,' Claire whispered breathlessly.

They walked over slowly to the giant structure.

'It looks all locked up to me.'

'Sure does.' Paul's voice seemed pensive.

'If it's all locked up, one would think that there's something in there that they don't want anyone to play with ... yeah?'

'Sound logic there my girl,' Paul whispered as though this secret had to be kept from prying ears.

'Thank you, ... Um, Paul, are you sure you want to go in there?'

'Of course, why?'

'Oh. Nothing. Just thought ... the Wal-Mart idea might be a safer option at this point.'

'What?' Paul turned to Claire.

'Never mind. What if there's something in there that we shouldn't see ... you know top secret.'

'I hardly think it matters now.'

'Mm, OK, good point.'

The hangar door offered no vantage point to sneak a view of the contents inside, so they walked around the perimeter of the construction.

'You know, for something so old, this building is in remarkably good shape,' Claire said, with hand over her eyes, protecting herself from the sun now well into the sky as she looked up towards the roof.

'Another good point, Claire,' he said, as they made their way through the long grass.

'Maybe it's not that old.'

'Well the style is right for that era, and they built things well in those days.'

'How do you know that?'

'What, the standard of building, or ...'

'No, the style,' she asked, now genuinely interested.

'Well, there's a World War II hangar up at the airport in Toowoomba. It's ...' His words were cut off.

'Where's that?'

'Just west of Brisbane, and the hanger there is a pretty sturdy construction, but, this is a serious building here, very sturdy materials used and a lot bigger than the one in Toowoomba. I wonder why they built it like this. Man, it would have cost a pretty penny.'

'OK, well, if that's the case, then I think good old Uncle Sam wanted to protect something important. What do you think?' Claire turned to her man.

'Maybe.'

They continued their journey and came to a single door placed in the middle of the back wall of the hangar. Paul tried the door handle.

'Another rusty hinge?'

'No, I don't think so.'

'Could it be kicked in?' Claire asked.

'No, it opens to the outside.'

Paul got down on his hands and knees, bringing his head down to the bottom of the door where it met the concrete floor of the hangar.

'What are you doing?'

'Seeing if I can see anything through the gap at the bottom of the door'

'And?'

'No, looks like there's some sort of barrier, or seal, or maybe one of those guards that stops the weather coming in. Anyway, can't see a thing.'

'A reputable Fort Knox,' Claire said, looking up at the structure.

From that door, they followed a concrete path, cracked in many places, but still useable. It led to another building. From that building another concrete path, in a worst state of repair, which led to another larger building. This building was constructed with the same materials used to build the hanger and attached was a separate construction.

This appeared to Paul to be what might have been be a garage. All buildings were locked and sealed well.

'Well, what now?'

'I guess, we're getting nowhere here. We can't get into that hangar, so let's check out the runway. You up for it?'

'Sure, got nothing else scheduled for today.' Claire took Paul's hand. 'Come on, show me an overgrown World War II runway, dude.'

Claire took the lead as they retraced their track along the cracked concrete path that led to the back door of the large hangar. The tall grass brushed across their legs as they made their way toward the runway. As they approached the rear of the hangar near the concrete path's intersection, a sudden rustling was heard in the long grass, then a scurrying sound that heralded potential danger to the young woman. She stopped dead in her tracks.

'What's up?' The man behind her call out.

'Shh.' Claire motioned with her hands for him to be still. 'There's something in the grass ... right, there,' she whispered, as the young woman pointed to a place a few feet ahead and to the right of their path.

'Might be a snake,' she whispered a more solemn warning.

'Don't move,' Paul demanded.

'Um, I thought of it before you did,' Claire hushed her words, as she strained every fibre of her being to catch a glimpse of the potential menace.

The two explorers stood still, held captive by a sound and their imagination. Suddenly a small hen escaping from its rich green herbage hideaway ran along the path with four, small chicks desperately trying to catch their mother with insistent cries of help. Claire jumped back, mouthing a muffled scream.

Paul burst out with a rush of laughter.

'Oh, so not funny.' Claire spun around at her infectious audience trying not to prove him right about the comic relief on offer.

'That nearly scared the sh ...' Claire stopped her sentence before regrets took hold.

He laughed even harder. 'That nearly scared the ... what?'

'Put a sock in it, buster,' she replied with a distinct smirk beginning to appear.

'Come on; she's gone this way.' Claire raced ahead following the hen and her lightning-fast chicks.

The birds speedily followed the path along the back of the hangar and around its corner, with Claire in hot pursuit. Paul reached the young American only to see a dejected face.

'They've gone. For goodness sake.' She looked around a tree that had grown directly against the hangar wall, breaking open the concrete path and causing the hangar's steel sheeting to buckle leaving a small opening at the base for the bird and family to escape inside.

'I think the mother has gone inside the hangar, here, look,' she advised pointing to a small opening at the base of the wall next to the tree.

Paul bent down and peered into the chamber.

'See anything?'

'No, can't see a thing ... pitch black.'

'Where have these chickens come from?'

'Beats me. I can only imagine that they've been here for a long-time interbreeding.'

He said, still looking into the black hole at the base of the hangar wall.

He stood up brushing the dirt from his hands and knees.

'Well, we've confirmed one thing today.'

'What's that?' Claire looked at her man, expecting something stupid given his expression.

'We are not alone on this island.' He looked at Claire and raised his eyebrows.

'Joy.' Claire took his hand and spun around facing the runway.

'Come on, bucko, let's check out this runway of yours.'

They walked together away from the hangar in silence for a time.

'Claire?'

'Yes.'

'Back there, with the chook in the grass ...'

'Yes.'

'You were going to say ... That nearly scared the shit out of me, weren't you?'

'Not saying.'

'That's a yes.' He laughed 'Um, Ma, you said the S word.'

'I did not.'

'Well you thought it.'

'Oh, grow up.'

She went to hit him, but he quickly ran from her reach, and a merry chase began until Claire finally caught her accuser and delivered a swift blow to his upper left arm.

'Oh, Man, you're fast.'

'Sure am, so don't mess with me, mister,' she prattled back as her face fixed on the man, smiling broadly, declaring her victory.

They spent the next hour walking to the end of the runway, then back to the hangar and the abandoned settlement. The runway was made of crushed coral. It had been extended out into the water. This made a large point that jutted out from the end of the island.

There was some grass growing over the edges of the airstrip, but most of the surface was serviceable. The ocean side of the strip was packed with volcanic boulders protecting the edge from the ocean. Along the entire length of the five-thousand-foot airstrip, at the water's edge, oysters could be seen growing on the rocks in the crystal-clear water.

Just as they returned to the hangar, Paul took stock of their surroundings.

'This is amazing. Really amazing! I'm coming back tomorrow and see if we can't open that back door. I'll see what tools the ship has on board.'

'OK. There's something in that hangar isn't there?'

'Well, I think you're right. The way it's all locked up, there could very well be, but we'll see tomorrow. Let's get back to the ship.'

'OK, hey, can we walk around that way?' she said pointing to a clear path that seemed to lead around the water's edge.'

'Sure.' Paul looked across to the suggested route.

'I don't fancy having to walk back up that hill,' she confessed, wiping the sweat from her face.

'You know, that looks like an old road. It's a bit overgrown but it certainly looks like it might have been one once.'

'Why would there be a road here?' Claire was overwhelmed by the existence of such a facility on the island.

'Why would there be a hangar with a bunch of chickens?' Paul turned to her with a humorous look on his face.

Claire laughed and patted his arm.

'God has put us in a most peculiar place.' She shook her head and giggled softly.'

'Sure has. Amazing!'

'Maybe that road might lead to something else exciting?' she said taking him by the hand.

'Don't know, love; maybe they made it to get the coral over to this side, you know to construct the runway.'

'That runway is made of coral?'

'Sure is. Didn't you see the stuff under your feet. That's what you were walking on.'

Claire shrugged her shoulders.

'Probably explains what looks like a channel cut into the outer reef that leads into the bay where the ship is.'

'I didn't see a channel.'

'Really? The coral has grown back to some degree, but it looks like that's what might have happened, now I've seen all this. They probably cut a channel through the coral. Man, that would have taken a bit to do. I'll show you when we get back to the ship. I noticed it this morning up at the gravesite.' He paused. Reality washed over him for a split second as he looked back at Claire. They were marooned on a tropical island in the middle of the Pacific Ocean, and his heart sank.

'Anyway, I guess there's not much else to see. We're on the other side of the island.

Do you want to go back to the ship?' he said, snapping out of his sudden depression.

'Sure do. I would like to take a shower, then a nap. Are you tired?'

'Yeah, a little. How's the head?'

'Mm, slight headache.'

'OK, let's go. Might take another look at that wound when we get back, hey?'

'Sure.'

The road was an easy walk and, though covered with a wide variety of ferns, brush and small coconut trees, it proved a favourable trek back to the stranded vessel.

The shade from the sun was welcome as both noted a little sunburn on their arms and legs as a result of the little protection during their walk over the runway. The old road meandered its way along the edge of the water, cutting its way through some rocky outcrops to reach a much smaller bay. The beach was less attractive than the bay where the *Pacific Fair* was stranded, but it seemed a lot more reef was to be found in this confined, well-protected area.

A few trees had fallen due to the storm, but in general this area had been protected when compared with the area at the top of the small mountain.

'Wow! Will you look at this?' Paul said, in a hushed tone as he scanned this place of wonder.

They walked together to the narrow beach that framed the lagoon.

'Oh, Man.' Claire stared across at the water. 'Hey, looks like there'll be some interesting swimming in here. In fact, great snorkelling, I would think. Look over there Paul. Can you see those beautiful fish swimming around the large head of coral? Oh, this is so beautiful, isn't it? And it's so private,' she continued. Her excitement was reaching fever pitch. 'Oh man.'

'Claire, the whole island is private.' He laughed.

'Well, this could be our very own private, *private area*. You know, like our own natural bathroom,' she said, as though in a stunned stupor.

'OK,' he said, studying her reactions closely.

'It makes you want to just strip off and jump in, doesn't it?

'An interesting reaction, to say the least,' the doctor said enjoying her transparency once again.

'Oh, come on.' She looked Paul squarely in the face. 'You mean to tell me that you wouldn't just jump in. Doesn't it have this effect on you?'

'No.'

This time, it was Claire's turn to study her doctor.

'You've never gone *skinny dipping*?'

'No.'

'Really?'

'No.'

'Why not?' she said laughing, expecting him to surprise her with something stupid.

'Don't see the point.'

'Come on. Really?' Her laughter faded to a smile.

'Yep.'

'OK.' Her smile changed to a slight frown.

'I take it you have,' Paul said, softly.

'Well ... yes. When we were kids, we used to visit Dad's brother a lot. They had a big ranch. My brothers, and cousins, we'd all go up the mountains and swim in the beautiful creeks. It was so good. We were all very young. Just kids ... you know. When I was at university, I would visit my cousin at the ranch. She was the only one left at home there by that stage, same age as me, and we'd both go up and swim ... just the two of us ... so lovely.'

'OK, um, I'm not judging you, Claire, but for me, I don't see what all the fuss is about.'

'Right, OK ... You're telling the truth, aren't you, Paul. You've really never done anything like that ... have you?'

'No, sorry to disappoint you.'

'No ... not disappointed, just surprised. I hope you don't think that I'm immoral or ... if you know what I mean.'

Paul shook his head. 'Not at all.'

'OK, but, I just thought ... you were looking at me like ... you know. I don't want to disappoint you, but that's who I am, Paul. I guess, that's how I've been brought up and without getting too hyper-spiritual before the Lord, I believe I'm OK with Him about the subject.'

Claire stood silent as she looked back over the crystal-clear lagoon. Some time passed in silence as they both took in the beauty set before them.

'Penny for your thoughts?' The doctor said, a little concerned that he may have been too blunt.

'Mm, no,' she said, thinking that this conversation had probably gone too far.

'Please,' he said lovingly.

'Well, OK, Paul ...' Claire braced herself. 'I love you so much, but I think that you are such a prude.' She giggled and began to tickle him around his ribs.

'I see no problems with such a condition,' he said warding off this sudden delightful attack.

'Well, I'm sure things will change when we are married. Especially if we are forced to stay here for any length of time.' Claire giggled harder as she continued to work at his side with her insistent fingers.

'I'm sure they will,' the doctor said, holding off his attacker. 'Come on, let's get back,' Paul continued, looking up at the sky with slight concern.

Claire noted his change of demeanour.

'Storm?'

'Maybe. There certainly is a build-up of significant clouds. Better move.'

The two resumed their trek back to the ship, stranded in their beautiful turquoise blue bay.

Tiny ferns and delicate moss with small leaf-like shoots were growing from the cracks in the rock face of the cutting. Finally, at the bay, the road merged with the beach due to erosion of time and weather. The pair took off their shoes and slowly walked along the beach hand in hand. The clouds were building to a dark display of potential storms for the afternoon, and the humidity was more than either had experienced before. Paul took off his shirt and wrapped it over his shoulders, appreciating the immediate relief it offered.

'Oh, I wish.' Claire said looking up at the man's freedom. 'You guys are so fortunate, you know.'

He laughed. 'No argument there,' he said raising his eyebrows. 'See, may be not such a prude after all,' he continued.

'Well, it's a start.' Her faced beamed back at him.

Their return to the *Pacific Fair* was a welcomed relief, and as they walked through the upper lounge, Claire took hold of the doctor's arm.

'Paul, you know, I feel like this is home.' Her face looked content, as that of a woman who had just moved into her own house for the first time.

'You mean the ship?'

'Well, yes, the ship, the island, all of it. This whole setting and our private, *private bathroom* back there.' She turned around with, out-stretched hands, then paused in quiet reflection.

'Really?' Paul watched Claire as she searched for her words.

'I mean this could have been worse, couldn't it?'

'Sure.' Paul continued to study this fascinating creature, standing next to him.

'We could have been washed up on the beach half drowned. You know? With no food, no shelter.' She laughed and pointed to the cave's location. 'Just that cave up there, the coconuts, the chickens and the fish out there, probably all hard to catch.' She giggled as she looked out to the choppy conditions of the sea beyond the reef.

'True enough.'

'Anyway, I really don't know where I'm going with all that, but I just feel ... I don't know ... at home. Um, did you want to check my stitches?' She asked, changing the subject quickly.

Paul nodded and took her hand as they moved directly to the clinic where he redressed Claire's wound, then to the kitchen where they ate a late, light lunch and then to their room for an afternoon sleep.

The door of the cabin took a little longer to open due to the ship settling on its new earthly foundation. Once inside, Claire went straight for her bed.

'You don't want a shower?'

'Oh, um, no, I am so tired, What's wrong with me. It's like one minute I'm full of energy, and the next, I'm ready to drop. What's with that?' she asked, carefully putting her head on the pillow.

'Think you'll find it's a combination of shock, grief, and a pinch of concussion ... not to mention the stress of our trip getting here, all rolled into one emotional rollercoaster ride,' the doctor placed the answer squarely to Claire. His reply satisfied her. She relaxed.

'How are the feelings of insecurity? A little better?'

'Yeah, a little better, but I still feel odd when you're not around. You know?' she replied almost mumbling into her pillow. 'Why do you ask?'

'You seem to be a lot better. I was wondering if you think you'll be OK on your own tonight?'

There was silence.

'Claire? Are you asleep?'

'No ... I'm thinking.'

'OK, well, anyway, sleep on it and see what you think later.'

'Yep.' Her words accompanied her intention for unconsciousness.

The room went silent again.

'We can wait till tomorrow if you like ... OK?'

There was no reply.

'Claire?'

The faint sound of heavier breathing replaced all communication from the woman curled up on the bed in front of the doctor. Paul lay in their warm room. Though their balcony doors were wide open, there was little cool air to be found.

His thoughts began to focus on provisions and longevity, especially that of their water supply on the ship. How long would it be before this essential commodity would run dry?

It seemed obvious from that point that they would have to stop using their water for showers and the toilets.

The reality of their situation continued to seep into his very marrow. It wasn't long before all of the human population of the island were sound asleep.

A sudden crash of thunder woke Paul with a fright. He had slept for nearly an hour.

With heart thumping in his chest, he sat up taking stock of his surroundings. Another loud explosion, this time much closer than before, rattled their room. He looked across at Claire on the bed. She hadn't moved from her initial position when her head, first nestled into her pillow on the bed. The doctor, feeling slightly unwell, stood up. His head began to spin a little. Another crash of thunder was sounded across the island, only this time to be accompanied by a torrential downpour.

The sound of the rain was deafening just as it was the first morning of their arrival.

He felt quite uncomfortable, and he looked down at his clothing and noted that he was wet due to sweat streaming from his body. Dehydration had possibly set in, which explained his slight headache. He stood up slowly and felt strangely dizzy. During their time walking around the island, they hadn't drunk a great deal of water. He became annoyed with himself.

Feeling the need for a shower and not wanting to use the bathroom any more, he took soap and his towel out of the bathroom room, walked over to the windows, closed them and, proceeded upstairs to the lounge.

From there he stripped down to his underwear and walked out into the warm, thundering rain. He threw his face up to the downpour and opened his mouth. Due to the amount of water falling from the sky, the doctor's mouth was filled with clean, pure water within seconds. He swallowed his mouth full and returned his stance for another free helping.

The sweetness of the atmosphere's offering was intoxicating, and he stood there with eyes closed and arms held up as though greeting his new baptism. He drank some more of nature's juice, then proceeded to use the soap in the biggest shower he had ever experienced.

Paul stopped his activities, turned to look back into the lounge, seeking his privacy, and with careful reckoning, he then walked further around to a more secluded corner of the ship where he dropped his water-logged underwear, releasing them with a thud on the deck of the vessel. There in this private place, he attended to his personal needs amidst his newfound tropical freedom.

Prude, indeed, he thought and proceeded to chuckle to himself.

CHAPTER THIRTY-THREE

C laire moved slowly on the bed. She stretched her arms out by her side, opened her eyes, and looked across the room. She focussed slowly as her unsettled heart began to return. The young American woman sat up quickly, then moved to the door. Standing at its opening she called out.

'Paul?'

There was no answer. Nothing could be heard but distant thunder and heavy rain.

'Paul?'

Panic began to torment her as she walked swiftly along the corridor. She stopped at the stairs that led to the upper lounge, looked up, then straight ahead. The thought of walking the corridors of the vessel shot bolts of further panic into her heart. The claustrophobic humidity below deck beckoned her to move upstairs for fresh relief. At the summit of the stairs, disappointment was her reward. He wasn't there.

'Paul?'

Her eyes fell to the floor. There in an untidy pile was the doctor's shirt, his shorts, and his towel.

'Paul?' she cried against the raw of the torrential downpour she cried out pensively, as she walked towards the door that lead to the open deck.

The doctor was consumed by his new experience.

'Are you out there?

Paul Langley froze suddenly, realising his potential predicament.

'Shoot!' he whispered, 'Um, hang on,' he called out, spinning on the spot as he turned his back and bent down in panic to retrieve the only chance of modesty at his disposal.

His voice assured her immediately of safety and not heeding his message or any pending tone of warning, she rushed out into the warm pounding rain to be reunited with her protector.

'Paul? What are you doing out ...' As she walked around the corner, she froze. Her proposed words lost any point for further expression. There was her doctor, with his back towards her, clumsily trying to get one leg into his saturated and uncooperative covering while still holding on to his soap.

'Oh my.' Her hands quickly covered her mouth. 'I am so ... I just ...' She began to giggle. 'What are you doing, Paul?'

He resigned any thought of wearing his wet underwear and thrust the wet fabric firmly against his manhood, turning quickly to face his intruder.

'Claire ... do you mind?' The soap suddenly slipped out of his hand, skidded across the deck and over the side onto the sand below, the sight of which caused Claire to explode with a gush of laughter.

'Paul, what are you doing?' She laughed harder.

'What's it looks like I'm doing?'

'Well I know what it looks like ... But why are you doing this out here?' Claire gestured with her hands now dripping with the afternoon's blessing from the heavens.

'Do you mind, woman? Turn around.' His voice wasn't at all friendly.

'Sorry.' She obeyed his request slowly while giggling like a young teenager, now soaked to the bone.

'Claire, what are you doing out in this rain with that wound of yours?' His tone softened as he quickly dressed in his wet underwear.

'I think your explanation would be more interesting than mine.' She giggled again.

'Claire.' His tone changed again.

She ignored his cue.

'And, if its' any consolation ... I didn't see anything ... of any consequence.' She laughed hard. 'Except your ...'

'Claire, behave.'

'Butt ...' She placed her hands over her mouth trying to hide her intense humorous reaction.

'Claire,' Paul snapped.

'Very cute,' she said provoking him further.

'Are you listening to me?'

'No.' She shook her head laughing fully at his expense.

'You are incorrigible.'

'Yes, I know.' Her laughter continued.

'Oh man.' What little pride he had left, was now washed away.

Alright, I'm sorry. Can I turn around now?' she said trying to display a little discipline.

'Yes, you can,' he said. His vulnerability was at its peak.

She turned around, trying desperately not to laugh.

'If it's of any consequence, I do have brothers you know.'

The sight of her man standing with his pride in tatters was too much, and she just stood there in the torrential rain.

'Oh, to be the centre of such merriment,' he said, trying hard to make sense of the situation.

'Look at you. You're like a little boy caught with …. his pants down.' With that she burst into laughter again.

The doctor smiled, his pride still stinging.

She calmed down to just a giggle as she watched his awkward stance while he managed to keep his wet, drooping underwear on his hips.

He had always considered himself the owner of a healthy sense of humour, but he could see no reason for the depth of such jocularity given the circumstances and was fascinated with Claire's perspective regarding his lot.

'Oh Paul, I'm so sorry, really I am, but I can't help myself … You have to try to understand it from my end. Oh, sorry, I mean from my perspective. There you were, all …'

'Yes, I think I get the picture,' Paul said humbly.

'Oh, you are sooo … 'she said trying to compose herself. 'You are just …'

'I am what?' His curiosity began to show on his face. With a faint smile began to develop, as small streams of water poured down his face.

'Oh … you are just perfect … come here.' She moved straight to her source of security with arms open and face beaming.

Paul braced himself by holding on to his flimsy, water-logged covering with one hand while meeting her embrace with the other arm. She threw herself into him, meeting his hesitant half embrace and kissed him in total surrender. Their awareness of each other blossomed, and he returned her kiss more passionately than ever before. With nature's blessings showering them with cleansing confirmation, their bodies began to melt into each other.

Paul suddenly broke away.

'Wow, hang on,' he said breathlessly.

She opened her eyes, and her flushed face looked up at Paul waiting for his word.

'No, not like this.' The moment offered conviction for both parties, and they resigned themselves from the near-lost innocence and walked back into the lounge.

Claire took the towel and wiped his face and chest, then turned around, honouring his privacy. He dropped the wet underwear and proceeded to quickly dry his remaining wet areas and wrapped his towel around his waist. He picked up his shorts off the floor of the lounge and hastily put them on, followed by his shirt. Then, throwing his towel over his shoulders, he declared *all clear* to which his love turned around and looked up at him.

'Can I borrow your towel?'

He handed the wet towel to the soaked spectacle now standing in somewhat see-through clothing. She attended to her needs, then wrapped the towel around her upper body.

'Thank you.' She said, with a newfound deeper respect for him. She had caused him discomfort to which there was genuine regret.

'Thank you?' A slight frown came across his forehead.

'I'm sorry, Paul. That was my fault. A beautiful thing nearly destroyed. Thank you for taking a stand for both of us.'

'Well, I should have been more careful ... I mean, with the open-air shower thing. You were fast asleep when I left the room. I needed a shower, heard the heavy rain, and thought ... well, we need to conserve water, so why not.'

'Cute.'

'Cute?' He smiled wondering what her angle might be this time.

'Your idea, you know ... conserving water, showering in the rain ... very cute,' she giggled.

'Well, it seemed a good idea at the time,' he said softly.

'No, no, good idea, good idea.' She reached out and touched his arm, confirming her sincerity, softening her humour to a deeper mindset.

'We ... we need to conserve water,' she said absent-mindedly, focusing more on what had nearly happened rather than the issue of water.

'Mind you, if this is the sort of rainfall that we can expect around here, we certainly won't go thirsty.' He chuckled as he looked out across the small tranquil bay.

What had just transpired continued to trouble Claire.

'Oh, Paul, I'm really sorry. I'm so glad you ... I'm so glad we didn't ... Oh this is scary. I mean our situation here ... you ... me ... you know what I mean? This is so not good. What are we going to do?'

The doctor stood in silence thinking. He combed his fingers through his hair and for a few minutes he looked around at the topography surrounding them, deeply contemplating her question.

'You're right; it's not good at all.' He looked out to sea, deep in thought. 'We are in deep ... you know what ... here, for lots of reasons,' he said softly to himself.

Claire didn't hear him due to the continued roar of the heavy rain.

'I've been revaluating the situation... and I'm now of the opinion ... well, as I said, this is a whole new dynamic here, and if we are not rescued, well, what then? In fact, to be honest, I'll give them another ... maybe, seven days and I think that's it. I doubt if they'll continue looking for us after that. If that's the case, I think we might be here for a long time ... you and me possibly, for a very, very, long time.'

Claire froze right in front of him.

'I think we have to accept this as more than a possible ... more like a highly probable.' Paul's sombre face stared at his love.

'You mean … they will stop the search.'

'Yes, without a doubt. In my opinion, that is exactly what's going to happen. So, with that in mind and given our strong love for each other … well, that's why I am suggesting we get married … soon.' His stance was very awkward, but she hardly noticed.

The reality of his suggestion began to birth questions of accountability and feasibility.

'Paul, how can we do that?'

'Well, I'm not going to suggest that we hold hands and jump over a hollow log'

'What?'

'Never mind. We'll have a proper ceremony, and there'll be witnesses … eventually.'

She looked at him closely.

'I know we got a little carried away out there in the rain, but don't you think we've lost just a little perspective. I think there are a few things missing … like a pastor for one and what's with the witnesses … *eventually* thing?' she said carefully.

'OK, if you agree, we will be married before God. We will video the ceremony for people to see … later.'

'If there is a later,' she said solemnly.

'Yes, true enough but … well let's assume that there will be a later … sometime in the future … so not *if* … but, *when*.'

'Yep, OK …*when*.'

'But in the meantime, I propose that we will each write our vows and say them to each other, just like a normal wedding. I can preach … just a simple message. We'll draw up a wedding certificate to be signed by us and the pastor and witnesses … eventually … and besides, doesn't the scriptures say the we are surrounded by a crowd of witnesses? So, looks like it's going to be a big wedding.' He laughed under his breath.

She ignored his humour and looked deeply into his face. 'You're serious, aren't you?'

'Yep ... Big wedding.' He smiled broadly.

'Still not laughing and ... I don't know. Is this right? I mean ... Oh, I don't know.'

Paul subdued his humour.

'Well, if you have doubts, then we wait ... I'm happy with that, but we have to put some strict rules in place.'

'Rules?'

'Well, yes.'

'Like?'

'Well like, um, no physical contact ...' He thought for just a moment. 'If that's possible ... we should probably split ... you live this side of the island, and I'll live on the other side.'

'What?'

'Hey, you and I are on a tropical island .... Alone, just you and me ... hello ... we both know how we feel about each other ... don't we?'

'Yes.'

'Well?'

'Well, what?'

'Well, we need to split or ... you know what will happen ... and it will Claire, just like it almost did, just a few minutes ago.' Paul paused in thought. 'If we're going to wait ... and I'll honour you in that but, I think we need to put some distance between us ... really. I know that I'm labouring on this point, but this will insure us against regrets.'

'No way.' Claire's focus fell to the ground in deep contemplation. 'I can't be on my own yet; I just can't ... really, Paul, please ... and besides ... well, what if we get rescued within the week.'

'OK, normally they would search for a week maybe a bit more, but then they'll stop.'

'Yes, you mentioned that before, but why ... would they stop?' She said insistently.

'Because, it cost a lot of money to have aircraft flying all over the Pacific looking for us, Claire.'

'Oh, I see.'

'As I said, I'll give them a week ... if that, then they'll register us as missing presumed dead.'

Her silence was profound, then she whispered. 'Oh, Lord, this is bad.' Their reality came crashing down upon her again.

'But, they might find us, Paul.'

'Claire, I said it before and, I'll say it again. It could be a very, very, long time. I really think that we need to surrender to this ... to our new lot in life.'

'Well, OK then but, I can't be separated from you ... Really, I can't.' She spat out the words in sudden desperation. 'Not after what's happened. I can't.' She looked up at the small hill to the burial site. 'I need you, really, I do. Sometimes I just want to hold on to you ... for security, ... not ... you know.'

'OK, I understand, but there are other deeper emotions, deeper dimensions, playing out here, and we need to recognize them, wouldn't you agree? I mean, if there wasn't any of these issues playing out here, then what was that outside before? A need for security or a need for something else, possibly a burning desire?'

'OK, point taken. Yes, you're right. It's certainly something else all right.' She looked down at the floor, pondering deeply.

'It's better to marry than to burn, isn't that what is written, and something tells me we're burning, aren't we?' Paul looked at her lovingly.

Her face blushed. She suddenly looked back at Paul with her eyes beginning to mist over.

'Yes' her whisper quivered in her throat, 'very much so,' she confessed.

'Well, seven days and in that seven days, we separate, instead of moving over to the other side; I'll move into a separate room.'

Her face became troubled.

'You'll be fine. As we have seen, there's no one else on the island except for the chooks. I'll be in the room opposite. We can keep the doors open if you like.'

'I don't know, Paul, I still ….' Claire thought deeply maintaining her focus. 'I don't know, not sure I'm ready to be without you yet.'

'You're not without me; I'm here. OK, look; why don't we try it and see how you go?'

'OK.' Her reply was brisk but not convincing.

CHAPTER THIRTY-FOUR

H e looked around at all in the room.

'Ladies, gentlemen, thank you for coming.' The Vice Chairman, Alan Talbert, had worked with the founder of the company since the inception of the organisation. His tired, strained eyes complemented his grey hair that night, as he sat next to the empty place at the head of the boardroom table.

The large oval table was populated by stone-faced executives seated at their respective positions and focused on the speaker.

'I apologise for making such an urgent request without any explanation, and of course, I regret dragging you away from your families this evening; however, I felt it wise that we deal with this immediately given all the information now in hand. Of course, this needs to be kept within these four walls. I am afraid that I am a bearer of serious news.'

The board room oozed with conservatism. The large room offered a hint of the scent of old wood due to the rich display of the oak-clad walls. With its thick, dark-green carpet, the corporate area was the centre of great business decisions which had forged its company admirably and projected its place well into the twenty-first century.

The executive spokesman cleared his throat, paused, then spoke.

'The company's vessel, the *Pacific Fair,* has been attacked. Most of the guests and crew have been taken captive and are currently held for ransom.'

The concussive news shot deeply into each and every heart in the room that night.

'I also regret to advise ...' He paused again, to regain composure and draw the necessary strength to continue.

'I apologise ... this has been a long day. I was advised of the news early this morning ... around three a.m., in fact. I have been in touch with our insurers. A gentleman has flown from London and is here to address us. I will call him in, in due course.' The vice chairman tapped his pen on his notes a few times and continued his difficult discourse.

'I regret to advise that we believe that one of the guests has been shot dead ... possibly two. Our ship's captain is dead and some other crew members. It would appear that we have fallen foul from pirates.'

'What the hell?' An astute middle-aged man spoke up from the other side of the long table.

'Allan, pirates, for God's sake.'

'Yes, Bill, pirates. Hard to believe, I know, but nonetheless, that's the report.'

'And what of Ronald and family?' An attractive soft-spoken woman raised the concern of most in the room.

'I'm afraid it seems that Ronald, Susan, and their girls have also been taken for ransom, along with the rest of the guests.'

'Ransom? My God.' Bill slammed his hand down onto the highly polished surface of the table.

'Yes, Bill, I understand your sentiment.'

'How do we know that this isn't just some sort of ... some sort of a Goddamn scam?'

'Bill, it was Ronald who rang me at three a.m. this morning and advised of the situation. He then gave the phone to a guy who

I assumed was the spokesman, ringleader of the criminals, and he laid out the demands. It's legitimate Bill.'

'Good God.' Bill gasped his words as he sank back into his high-backed boardroom chair.

'Ladies and, gentleman, I think it appropriate we ask the gentleman from the insurance company to come in and address the board. Are you happy with that?' The Vice Chairman asked the executives around the board room table. All agreed, and the secretary at the meeting was asked to bring the visitor in.

All sat quietly in shock as the tall, attractive Englishman walked into the tense environment.

The Vice Chairman stood up, greeted the visitor with a handshake and offered him a seat at the table.

'Let me introduce Mr Robert Simms. He has just arrived from London and I'm sure is better equipped with up-to-date information. Mr Simms, the floor is yours.'

'Thank you, Mister Talbort. First, just a point of correction, I am not from the insurance company. I represent Luther Pank and Grimes, an international consultancy firm based in London. We are working in conjunction with your insurance company. One of our specialities is working with security in crisis situations such as your case.' He stopped to take a sip of water from the crystal glass set adjacent to his seat.

'Excuse me, the air-conditioning on our company's aircraft was a little too chilled and has left me with a slight tickle in the throat. I might add that I'm a little jet lagged.' He cleared his voice and continued.

'I'm not sure if Mr Talbort has elaborated, but when your organization advised the insurance company, we were activated immediately with a full brief. We have already been in contact with the extortionists twice. They have been given a cell phone number dedicated to communication with me. Let's get some things straight in our minds. This is a game to these people. They have the merchandise, you have the money, so you are forced to play by their rules. What they don't know is that it's not all your money; it's the insurance company's money as well'

Bill sat still with face reddening as the young man set the scene.

'With all due respect, Mr Simms, can I call you Robert?'

The young man nodded respectfully.

'With all due respect, Robert, shouldn't we just call the FBI or the CIA or whoever the hell handles these things in this country?'

'Well, sir, firstly, the insurance company has a very tight handle on such cases, given that it's potentially their money that will be handed over, or most of it at least, and secondly, the extortionists have given strict instructions that no government agencies are to be involved.

If we breech their demands, deaths will occur. However, we have asked for proof of their claims, and they have offered two hostages as proof. These have, in fact, been handed over.

Now this is the sticky part; because they have handed over the people, we have no option but to declare it to the authorities.' He looked across at the chairman, searching for a clue as to whether he should elaborate on the issue of the plight of some of the passengers.

'Who have they handed over?' Bill asked.

'Two of the ship's crew.'

'And where are they now?' The vice chairman asked.

'They were flown to Manila from Cebu and are being questioned by our people in a hotel there.'

'Did your agency collect them in Cebu?' Bill burst in.

'No, the extortionists did that. We got word where the hostages would be, and our guys met them at the airport in Manila.'

'Well how much are these bastards asking?' Bill interrupted again, spitting his request across the table.

'Well, they began with an overinflated amount. This was to be split into certain bank accounts around the world and some cash at the point of transfer.'

Consternation was suddenly heard around the room.

'This is outrageous. If this gets out, our stock will plummet on Wall Street,' A quiet man sitting at the end of the table submitted his opinion.

'So, how much?' Bill demanded.

'Well, I have already been at the negotiation table with them and currently their latest demand is now down to three million. I am quite confident that we will be able to negotiate them down lower.' The young man quickly interjected.

'Down to what?' Bill stiffened his point directly at the visitor.

'Maybe a couple of million, possibly even less.'

'Well if it's the insurance company's money, why are we engaging in questions of how much?' a third female board member spoke up.

'Well it's like this, Alice, our policy dictates that we pay a percentage of the ransom,' Allan Talbert advised.

'And what's the percentage?' She asked, looking directly at the young English gentleman.

'Thirty percent.' The jet-lagged traveller replied.

'Mm, so at two million we are up for six hundred thousand,' she concluded.

'A lot of money.' Bill mumbled under his breath.

'So, do we know where the transfer will be?' Another board member questioned.

'No, nothing confirmed, but it will probably be the Philippines, given the first two have been delivered to us from that country ... However, first things first, we will continue to negotiate them down for the remainder of the people.'

'How do we know they haven't killed them?' Bill posed his question bluntly.

'A good question. We don't. However, given that the money will be transferred at handover time, we are confident that all will be unharmed. They want the money.'

'How do we know they have all the people? Bill pushed him further.

'Firstly, and unfortunately, there seems to be a number of the crew who are missing, including three passengers but, the criminals have emailed us a detailed photographic list with passports of the passengers who haven't been harmed.

Robert Simms stopped, took a sip of water then glanced over to the Vice Chairman.

'Allan, feel free to add anything if you think it necessary. Do you want me to go on?' Robert asked.

'I have nothing to add; please continue,' the exhausted Vice Chairman said softly.

The young man took another sip of water, placed the crystal glass down on the leather coaster and then continued.

'As suggested, it seems there have been a number of deaths on board.'

The tone in the room changed, and all eyes were darting around at each other, except the Vice Chairman who sat still with his eyes staring at the table in front of him.

'These are the people confirmed dead: The Captain of the ship, the chief officer, the chief engineer and the IT guy. In addition, it seems that two passengers are dead and one missing. I have confirmed that one teenager was killed and possibly a young woman. It would seem that all were shot. I have all the names of the deceased in a file and will pass a copy onto your legal department. Now, the one missing is a doctor, but it appears he isn't ith the hostages, and they have no idea where he got to. We don't have any further details.'

'So, where the hell is our ship?' Bill brought his next point to the table with similar vinegar in his tones.

'We have no idea, Bill. There is a full search in place as we speak, but so far, no trace.' Robert took his glass of water and sipped more of its contents to soothe his irritated throat.

'No trace? That ship has the latest satellite communications and navigation systems on board. It gives off position fixes to the satellite every hour. So, what the hell are you talking about? ... no trace! This is crazy! Who's not doing their job?'

The Chairman took the cue and spoke to the only source of irritation around the table.

'We must put some perspective in the picture here, Bill. Just prior to the ship's disappearance, a category five typhoon went through the area.' The chairman looked back at Robert.

'Yes, that's correct. It's quite possible, Bill, that the ship sank due to the weather, or it is equally possible that the pirates stripped her of all things of value and then blew her up.

This is common practice. The search aircraft checked around the island where the ship was last known to be have been anchored and saw no signs of the vessel, either on the water or under the water. There are no signs of wreckage or oil floating on the surface of the water and no signs of life on the island or on the two smaller islands nearby—nothing.'

'So where do we go from here, Robert?' Bill brought the question to the table.

'Well, I have another scheduled phone link in two hours. I think this will probably be the last stage of our negotiation, and then the fun will begin ... so to speak.' He looked across at Bill, realising his poor choice of words.

'And what aspect of this do you think is fun?' Bill sat back in his chair and glared at the straight-faced negotiator.

'Not one aspect of it, Bill, not one. I was being facetious, and I apologize for my poor choice of words. The point I was referring to, however, was where I personally will go to the site that they nominate and meet the representatives for the pirates. That is where I will put my life on the line, Bill.'

The irate board member stopped his attack and reflected. There was absolute silence around the table.

Bill North cleared his throat. 'I see ... This is all new territory for us.'

'Not for me, Bill.'

'Right, now that's been cleared up. Am I to assume that you will contact me when you have some constructive news?' Allan asked calmly.

'Yes, indeed. I am booked into the hotel down the road. Here are the details.' He passed a copy of the documents to the chairman.

'I expect a final figure by midnight tonight, maybe sooner. Once that is forthcoming, you will be the first to know, Allan. I have your details here. Allan, I ask that you also book into a hotel tonight, preferably that same one as mine for reasons of convenience. When the final figure is negotiated, we will have to move fast. Is that clear?'

Allan simply nodded, confirming his complete cooperation.

'Hey now, just a cotton-picking minute, young man, who the hell are you? You don't tell us what to do, is that clear?' Bill spoke up again, this time, with a crimson red face, beaming his indignation.

The English consultant sat back in his chair and studied his opponent for a moment, and he pounced back at this irate board member.

'No, you listen to me, Bill. I do tell you what to do and I tell you when to do it, and that is final. These are cutthroats, and if you want to see your chairman again and of course the rest of the hostages, then you will listen to me, and not only will you listen to me, Bill, you will damn well jump every time I tell this company to jump. Is that clear, Bill? I suggest you read your insurance policy, Bill. Do not jeopardise this process, or you will end up paying the full ransom figure—whatever, that figure will be. Is that clear, Bill?'

'Perfectly.' Bill resigned his case and sat back again in his comfortable leather boardroom chair, defeated.

Additional details were discussed briefly. The young consultant stood up, greeted the board, shook the Vice Chairman's hand and left the room, leaving a shaken group of board members, sitting in silence.

CHAPTER THIRTY-FIVE

⟨⟨⟩

The two castaways separated. Paul moved into the room adjacent to Claire's room, and each slept throughout the entire night.

There was a knock on the open bedroom door. Paul stirred, stretched and rolled onto his back. Opening his eyes, he lay still listening to the faint sounds of the breakers crashing over the distant reef surrounding their tropical home.

'Morning handsome.'

The sweet sound of her voice warmed his heart as he felt the bed move due to a welcome weight pressing up against him. He turned his head to discover Claire sitting on the side of his bed.

'Hey, morning, how'd you sleep?'

'Great,' she said, combing her hair back through her fingers looking down at him.

'How's the head?'

'The best it's been since your creative handiwork.'

Paul smiled. 'Good. We might take a look at that this morning after breakfast?'

'Stitches out today?' she asked, with a sparkle in her eyes.

'Maybe not today … a few more days, I think.'

'It's getting itchy.' she advised, scratching around the edge of the bandage.

'Yep, part of the process. Anyway, we'll look at it later. What time is it?' He threw the sheet off and sat up.

'Six thirty.'

'Wow, you're up early, lady. Got a plan for the day?'

She looked at the doctor. 'Well, didn't you want to check out that hanger again?'

'Hey, you bet.'

'I guess that's my plan for today,' she said laughing under her breath.

'Sounds like a good plan to me. In fact, speaking of that, I thought last night that there must be a key ... you know for the hanger. Thought we could look back in that generator room or that other building behind the hanger. There's got to be a key somewhere.' He sat up, kissed her on the forehead, and stood up stretching his torso to the left and right.

'Maybe they took it with them?' she asked, watching his movements.

'Possibly, but worth a look, though. I'll take some tools with us, just in case we find nothing.'

'Um, Paul?'

He turned to face her.

'You said yesterday, that we had to conserve water, which makes sense but, um ...' She thought more deeply about what she was about to ask.

'Problem?' He studied her face.

'The toilets, are they out of bounds?

'Yeah, probably. Another thing I was thinking about last night ... Maybe, we only use them when the weather is bad.'

'Sure, good idea, yes, good idea, so …. ah, where do you propose um …'

Paul moved to the balcony, opened the doors and gestured with a wide sweep of his arms.

'The choice is yours. Plenty of spots out there,' he said with a broad smile. 'Just take a shovel if you need to … You know. Got to keep up the hygiene.'

'And the shovel?'

'Oh yes, there's one in the storeroom among other tools. I'll get it for you. Interesting place—all sorts of stuff in there. I even discovered a bicycle pump … not sure why we'd need that, but it's there.' He stood there in the room marvelling at the fact.

'You know, I'm sure glad you shared that with me. It really lifts my day knowing that we have a bicycle pump on board, but a spade does seem to have a priority.

' She looked at him then, broke out in an infectious giggle.

'Oh, and there is something that you might need to consider while we're on the subject of ablutions and conserving resources.'

'Yes?' She waited for his next revelation.

'Toilet paper.'

'We don't have much on board?' she asked with a shocked look.

'Oh, no; we have plenty … boxes of the stuff.'

'Well, what's the problem?'

'If we're here for a long, long, long time, well, the toilet tissue … won't last that long.' He ended his sentence quickly.

'Let's pray that we'll be rescued before then.' She laughed.

'Sure.'

Claire paused, her reflection continued to move to the practical consequence of the depletion of the resource.

'If that were to happen, you know the running out of ... you know ...'

'Toilet paper?' he said, filling in her reluctant word whilst analysing her potential destination for her proposed topic.

'Yes. What do you suggest we ... um, do then?' Claire's reality was seeping into her soul.

'Banana leaves.' He smiled.

'But we don't have ... banana trees ... do we?'

'Good point, maybe not.' His sense of humour began to bubble.

'So?'

'Well, I would go for a swim in the ocean. ... very sterile,' the doctor spoke, his face showed no sign of emotion.

'Oh, I see ... the logistics of that ... let me get this straight. Your saying I walk from the jungle, forest, whatever you want to call that out there and walk down and clean up in the ocean?'

'Ah, yep. That about sums it up.'

'Fascinating.'

He laughed under his breath. 'It could very well be, but we'll cross that bridge when we come to it. In the meantime, there's plenty of the stuff in the storeroom. Hey, breakfast?'

'Actually, any chance of that spade?'

'Oh, yes, of course.'

They walked down into the bowels of the ship with the aid of the flashlight. A detour to the engine room to engage the generator and then the treasure house of the ship's well-equipped storeroom was next on the agenda. The necessary equipment was found and handed to Claire.

'There you go, enjoy.' His face beamed.

'Are you making fun of me?'

'No way, welcome to life in our new home. We have some basic home truths to come to grips with. It's going to be fun. Exciting stuff, wouldn't you agree?'

'You have some serious thrill issues, mister.'

'I hardly think digging a ... poo hole is thrilling,' he said.

'It's not exciting, either.' Claire said flatly.

'OK, off you go. You need some help?'

'Excuse me? Hardly, buster.' She looked at him with a smirk.

'You do realize that you will be on your own out there?' He smiled.

'I sincerely hope so, I am quite happy with my own company, under the circumstances.' That mischievous look surfaced again. She reached over and kissed him.

Claire looked up at Paul.

'Yes, I will be on my own, won't I?' She shook her head in thought. 'One minute I'm happy to be on my own, and the next I don't want to be on my own. This is so not me ... and this digging a hole thing ... we are becoming very base, aren't we?'

'Yep but, isn't that life ... we just cover it up in society ... no pun indented there. We are forced to accept the truth about who we are here.' He smiled. 'and what we are, for that matter.'

'And what are we here?' Claire pushed the point.

'Desperate.'

'Yes, I guess that's true enough. We tend to lie to ourselves, don't we?'

'Yep, we do ... we're all a bunch of pathological liars ... anyway ...' he said shrugging his shoulders.

'Well moving on to the nicer basics ... breakfast? ... what about bacon and eggs?

That will be good … when I get back. Love you.'

'Yes ma'am.'

Claire walked confidently along the passageway with her spade over her shoulder and then out of his sight.

Paul made his way to the kitchen, checked the refrigerator, brought out the food and required to satisfy Claire's request. He looked around the large pantry and saw a sealed container filled with flour, and his thoughts began to reflect on his time in the Philippines where an American missionary taught some of the Australian team of young people how to make flapjacks.

His gaze suddenly fixed on two ten-gallon barrels placed side by side, soundly secured on the middle shelf with a sign on their respective faces. On one, was written honey, and the other was maple syrup.

'Maple syrup. Can't have flapjacks without maple syrup,' he whispered to himself.

Little time had passed before Paul had made a batch of flapjack mixture ready for use. He placed four strips of bacon in one corner of the large hot plate, and the smell of cooking bacon quickly filled the kitchen and the adjoining hallway. At the opposite corner, he poured out some flapjack mixture, and with great satisfaction, he watched it cook. Then Paul picked up an egg and cracked the shell against the edge of the kitchen's cooker and emptied its contents on the hot plate. The raw egg landed on the hot surface with a crackling sizzle.

This was joined by another, and the cook carefully monitored the progress of all items set before him. He had set out the galley table with plates and other necessary utensils for the breaking of their night's fast. The doctor then diced two modest pieces of watermelon, discarding the seeds into the trash, sliced a mango, also throwing the large seed into the kitchen's tidy bin and sliced a piece of pawpaw, scraping the seeds into the bin as well. He then divided the fruit equally into two small bowls and emptied the contents of a passion fruit over the fruit contents as a garnish.

'Wow. Now that smells great.'

Paul, slightly startled, spun around.

'Oh, mission accomplished?' He asked, walking over to the check on breakfast.

'Thank you.' She smiled.

'And everything working well?'

'Excuse me?'

'You … are you performing normally in that area?'

'Yes, thank you very much.'

'No headaches?'

'No.'

'Difficulty concentrating?'

'No.'

'No dizziness, nausea?'

'No.' She watched him closely.

'Did you have any problems with the bright morning light when you went outside?'

'A little bright, but, no, not really.'

'OK, good.' He turned over the bacon and using an egg flipper clumsily endeavoured to turn over the flapjack.

'Here, would you like some help?' she asked, coming to his rescue.

'Thank you.' He watched her take over.

'So, did you go for a swim?' he asked, making conversation.

'No, I didn't.' She smiled.

'Really? I thought you might have, given our discussion.' He chuckled under his breath.

'Well, actually after what you said … to be honest, I nearly did.' Her cheeky face beamed.

'That surprises me … that you didn't,' he said making his way to where the coffee was stored. 'Can you flip that bacon?'

Claire nodded, agreeing wholeheartedly, as she took the utensil and turned one aspect of the morning's breakfast. 'There's a tiny little cove just over there on the other side.' She pointed to the side where the vegetation grew adjacent to the ship's hull. 'It's so beautiful, Paul, and there were these little yellow fish swimming everywhere … amazing.' Her eyes lit up during her description. 'and further around … not too far, there's a waterfall. It's coming off the big volcanic plug. There's a great swimming hole under the waterfall. This place, man … so amazing.'

'You should have gone in.' Paul said, making himself busy with the coffee pot.

'Well, maybe next time.'

'I not really opposed to it … just not for me.'

'Really? We'll see.' She laughed softly. 'Hey, so what's with the bright light, dizziness thing, etcetera?'

'Just checking for symptoms of concussion. That's all.'

'Oh, OK, thank you.' She flipped the first of the flapjacks.

'Oh man, I think you've made a slightly challenged flap-jack here.'

'Yeah, It's a bit too American for me. I'm an Aussie, only an American can make good flapjacks. I'm way out of my depth.'

'Oh rubbish,' Claire stopped and looked at Paul.

'Hey, that reminds me.' Claire's said, revealing a curious expression overcoming her face.

'You know, for an academic … given your medical background …' She paused and tapped the hotplate with the utensil used to flip the flapjacks. 'Well, you don't converse like one.' Claire continued her focus on the hotplate eagerly waiting for the reply.

'Sorry, I don't follow.'

'Well, you are like my father in this context, but I have never asked him. So, I'm asking you. Paul, you don't use the vernacular like other academics that I've known, like they're trying to impress people. You know what I mean?'

'Well that's because I'm not trying to impress. I think I express myself adequately. Frankly, simple can often offer eloquent sufficiency and thereby adequately stimulating cognitive relevance to the general market, as in contrast to eloquent linguistic complexity that can create barriers to cultural relevance and thereby negate constructive communication. So, I have found simple communication using the right, simple words to the general market works for me. It's my belief that Jesus Christ was like that. He kept it simple, using simple words. Mark Twain is reported as to have said, *"The difference between the right word and almost the right word is the difference between lightning and a lightning bug."'*

'Wow ... OK, well, I guess that certainly answers my question.' She raised her eyebrows and sighed.

Paul chuckled to himself.

'OK, moving right along ... now I'll get another couple of these guys cooking, and I think breakfast will be ready.'

She diligently attended to the task at hand. Before long, the two were bowing their heads, thanking their Creator for a new day and the provision set before them.

Paul watched Claire slap a couple of flapjacks on her plate, on top of which she placed two strips of bacon, an egg, sprinkled some salt, then put three heaping tablespoons of fruit on the egg and poured maple syrup over the contents of the plate.

The doctor looked on in cultural horror.

'You're kidding, right?' the words gushed from his person.

'What?'

'All that, all, together, on one plate, in a heap. Like that?'

'So?'

'That's like ... Hey there, and what can I get you this morning? Oh, I think I'll have a garbage heap ... actually make it a small one, and can I have extra syrup?'

'Excuse me? You don't do this?' She looked surprised.

'No.'

'Have you tried it?'

'Nope.'

'Well, how do know what it's like if you haven't tried it, buster?'

'Hey, whatever floats your boat, I guess.' He began to laugh, realising what he'd just said, given their situation. He was carried along further, and he began to laugh more, only to find that he couldn't stop. His red face was accompanied by tears sliding down his cheeks.

'Your boat isn't floating, is it?' The doctor was completely overcome with the odd concept that was lodged in his mind.

'No, it is not,' Claire joined in, and both enjoyed the joy together. Quickly, they calmed down.

'It's sort of stuck in the sand, isn't it?' he coughed out his point in the midst of a chuckle.

'Yes, it is ... really stuck.' She laughed hard.

'Yes.'

'Have you noticed lately that we're laughing at the craziest things?' Claire asked, breathlessly.

'Yeah, we are,' he concurred.

'Why?'

'I think you'll find that we're both dealing with grief and the stress of the ordeal. It's got to come out in some way. People can do funny things when they're dealing with this sort of stuff.'

Claire nodded her head, as she stabbed an assorted selection of the food on her fork.

'Mind you, my sense of humour could be considered a bit different, compared to others, I guess.'

'You think? Anyway, here try this.' She placed her offering on her fork up to his mouth.

'Wow, no thank you.' His eyebrows raised, as his head moved away from this threat.

'Hey, I tried your vegemite, so you try my far superior American cuisine.'

'In your dreams, girl,' he said now flatly refusing her offer.

'Excuse me?'

'Never mind.'

'Here I insist.' Claire pushed the fork closer to his face.

'I'm not eating that!'

'Do you think that I would feed the love of my life something that wasn't good to eat?'

'Yes.'

'Eat it,' she said mockingly with a stern voice.

Paul had a sudden pained expression come over his face. He had been looking forward to this breakfast, only to see its familiar potential drowned in the sap of the maple tree.

'Eat, dude,' she said, as she gathered more items on his plate by stabbing each one by one onto the fork and offering to her man.

'I think you need some serious counselling.'

'Eat!' she simply commanded.

'I'm beginning to feel sorry for our kids.'

'They'll be fine; now eat.'

He opened his mouth in surrender and ate slowly, giving serious consideration to the sudden experience accosting his taste buds.

'Good ha?' She looked on with great anticipation.

Paul swallowed and looked over at the galley's large pantry. 'Do we have any cornflakes?'

'Oh you, it's great. Come on, it is, isn't it?'

'Yeah. It's edible.'

'Edible?'

'Yeah, OK. It really is … um. I could get used to it.'

'See. I told you. Good, hey?'

Paul watched this woman, sharing her culinary joy with him. He sat there eating, listening to her constant chatter, her expressions of wonder of the day ahead and her delightful character constantly revealing a new dimension to him. He was simply intoxicated by this young American woman perfectly placed together with him in this new world.

CHAPTER THIRTY-SIX

After breakfast, the two cleaned the galley, Paul took the trash outside, and given his concern of attracting possible vermin due to the rubbish, he buried it in a shallow hole dug next to their grounded ship. The spade sunk deep into the soft fertile ground, and within minutes, he was patting down the buried material.

With domestic duties completed, they set off to the hanger with the perceived necessary tools for opening the building should they not find a key. They retraced the previous days' trek along the old road that snaked its way along the water's edge.

Once at the site, they left the tools at the back door of the hanger and ventured to the generator building. An exhaustive search of that building proved fruitless. There was no key to be found. They walked over to the large building back from the hanger. Behind the sound structure they discovered a grove of banana trees with a bunch ready for the picking.

'What are these doing here?' Claire posed the obvious question.

'Well, I think the only logical answer would be that your countryman planted them, I guess.' Paul said, pushing his cap back to scratch his head, while shrugging his shoulders at the same time.

'But one good thing out of this.' He said.

'What's that?'

'Your future in toilet paper is now guaranteed.'

'Oh joy. I think your idea of the ocean has more appeal.'

'Thought it might,' he said, his face vacant as he looked around the area.

They walked around the building, only to find an office tucked in the corner with a separate door that seemed not to have weathered the years very well. Paul went back to the hanger to get the heavy-duty bolt cutter, which made short work of the well rusted handle, and the latch was dismantled within minutes.

The door was then easily pushed open. Inside was a cacophony of empty filing cabinets, a number of desks and another door that led to another room. The room was the office of the commander of the base.

After a short time of searching, a secure cupboard was opened, using a rusty key found in the drawer of the commander's desk. There, in that cupboard, a full rack of carefully labelled keys were found hanging in a row on the wall of that enclosure.

'Hey, looks like we have struck gold. I'd say we'll find the hanger's key here,' Paul said, as he slowly opened the cupboard door. Paul fingered through the labels at the end of each key and finally discovered the words he searched for: 'HANGER'.

'Here we go.' He took the key in hand and rubbed the face of its corroded brass surface.

'Hey, well done, you.' Claire patted her man's back and followed it by a kiss on his cheek.

'OK, come on; let's see what's inside this place of mystery.' His face was filled with enthusiasm.

The journey back along the cracked cement path seemed to take forever as the new arrivals were eager to find the answer to the question of what lay behind those sealed walls of that hanger.

At the door, the key was poised in the hand of the eager man. He slid its metal into the brass keyhole and turned it. Resistance was all that was on offer. Paul tried harder, but it seemed the years of neglect had seized any hope of cooperation.

'Could it be the wrong key?' Claire placed her hand on her man's back.

'Doubt it,' he said looking at the label attached to the key.

'So, what now?'

Paul shrugged his shoulders.

'Is it rusted inside?'

'Doubt it; it's made of brass. Might need some lubrication.'

There was no handle on this door, just a flat keyhole that was almost flush with the door's metal surface.

'What about some oil? Would that do the job?

'Sure. We'll have to go back to the ship though.'

'But there was what looked like a small oil can in that generator room.' Claire looked directly into his face.

'No way. Really? I didn't see that.' He looked surprised.

'Sure was. Do you want me to get it?'

'Yeah, go for it.'

Claire moved quickly as Paul remained behind returning to his continual manipulation of the key in its place within the mechanism. As he applied a little more pressure a slight amount of movement lifted his spirits. Claire arrived with her find. She presented a small oil can with a long, slender spout. The unit was small enough to fit in a person's hand, and its operation involved one's thumb to push on the base of the small can being supported with the index finger and the middle finger over the front on the unit with the spout protruding between the two fingers.

The moderately experienced aircraft engineer liberally pumped oil into the small hole, then he continued his manipulative efforts in the small keyhole. Moving the key backwards and forwards in the lock, he felt a little more give. He looked up at Claire.

'This might take some time. I don't want to damage anything.'

'OK, hey, do you mind if I take a look around, while you're doing your thing here?'

'No worries, go for it. Yell if you find anything interesting.'

Claire left her man at the door and walked back to the commander's office. The doctor continued to carefully move the key back and forth with considerable force this time in the lock, taking time out to apply some more oil.

Within a fifteen-minute period, his finger was beginning to feel the wear and tear of the persistent force required to deliver possible success. Needing a break from his continual state of bending over at the door, he sat on the ground leaning up against the door looking at his red finger. A sudden twinge of pain shot through his lower back. He shifted his position on the ground but it seemed to make it worse.

Standing up he moved back to his challenge and after applying more oil he inserted the key and began his effort with this most uncooperative barrier. Another five minutes passed, and his back began to claim the prize as 'nuisance of the day'. He straightened up, stretched, then applied more oil and stepped back as though needing perspective.

Suddenly he heard a cry from Claire in the distance.

'Paul, come here.'

He spun around towards the perceived direction of her voice.

'What's up? You OK?'

'Yeah, fine. Come look what I've found.'

He moved as quickly as he could, given the disagreeable twinge in his back. He walked along the weather-worn and cracked concrete path stretching through the long grass.

'Where are you?' he call out.

'In front of the big shed up the back.'

Paul, moving as fast as he could, reached his love standing in front of the large door of the building that was made of the same material as the hanger. She stood with her hands cupped in front of her chest.

'What have you found?' He asked looking around for something obvious.

'Look.' She opened her cupped hands and there in the palms of her hand was a fluffy yellow chicken.

Paul smiled. 'I thought you might have found something important,' he jokingly said.

'Oh, come on; this little one is important.'

'Where's its mother?'

'Don't know; it was sitting in front of this door crying out. Can I keep it?' she asked, mimicking a child's voice.

'Sure, why not, but that means you have a serious responsibility. You have to feed and every day take it for a walk.' He laughed maintaining the point in her role play.

'Cool, hey, and by the way, this little one is important.'

'Really why so?'

'Well, because in a kind of way, she led me to this,' She stepped back and opened the large door in front of them and there before their very eyes was a World War II dodge fuel truck.

'Wow!' He stood at the entrance in awe.

'How did you get this door open?'

'Well, I went back to the commander's office and got all the keys to see what they opened. Didn't want to be outdone by my wonderful man.' She reached up and kissed him.

'And I heard this little cutie crying for help, and the rest is history. How cool is this?'

She pointed to the truck. 'I wonder if it goes?'

Paul looked at the relic and then back at Claire. 'You mean to say you just put the key in, turned it, and it worked? Like no oil, no effort?'

'No oil, yes, but forget the no-effort bit. But I finally got it opened. Pretty cool ha?'

Paul looked at Claire in amazement and laughed. 'Yes, very cool. What did you do with the chicken in the meantime?'

'Put her in here.' She reached down unfastened her top button of her shirt with one hand and carefully placed the small creature down her front. Paul stretched his neck, following the disappearing chicken. The tiny creature just sat very still and content in that warm place. It then closed it eyes and went to sleep.

They entered what appeared to be a large workshop with a full complement of tools, many of which were still wrapped in grease paper.

'This is bazaar.' Paul walked around the dim area.

'Why?'

'Well, look at these tools.'

'So?'

'Well, they're still wrapped. They haven't been used. Look at this truck. With the exception of the tyres, it's in mint condition. I mean a lot of dust, tyres are flat and in pretty bad shape, but man this is unbelievable ... what is this place?' He bent down and knelt on the cement floor to look under the truck at the engine, forgetting the condition of his back. He let out a faint painful cry.

'You OK?'

'Yeah, hurt my back over there at the hanger. It's OK, no big deal. Anyway, check out this engine; it's hasn't seen much work. This would fetch a small fortune back home.' He started laughing under his breath.' Come and have a look. This sucker is brand new. I can't believe it.'

'Um, pass, besides I have a baby on board.' She looked down inside her shirt at the sleeping bird.

'How's it going?' he said, slowly standing up carefully.

'Oh, our little chickadee's doing just fine. She's fast asleep … so cute.'

'How do you know it's a female?' he asked with an incredulous look on his face.

'A mother's intuition.'

'Right,' he nodded, not buying it at all, but enjoying his first sight of the potential mother in her.

'Anyway, let's close up shop here, and how about you and junior have a go at the big fella over there.' He pointed to the hanger.

'Why it would be our pleasure sir,' she said, helping secure the door and finally locking it.

'Don't know why we locked it. Like who's going to steal anything?'

'It'll stop the weather getting in.'

'Oh, of course.'

Paul led the way as they walked over to the hanger with Claire more interested in her newfound cargo. At their arrival, Claire looked at Paul, snapped her fingers and demanded the key.

'You're not serious?'

'Key, good sir.'

'OK, be my guest, but I think you'll find that what you experienced over there was Beginner's luck, as they say.' He shrugged his shoulders and handed over the key.

Claire stepped up to the mark and slid the oily key into its place. After a little effort, she pulled the item out of the keyhole.

'Satisfied? As I said beginner's luck. This needs a bit more oil. Might leave it overnight and let the oil do its thing.'

'Excuse me? I didn't say I had finished. Got a few more tricks up my sleeve. Let me continue.'

'Sure, whatever.' He stood by her, enjoying her tenacity whilst rubbing his lower back.

She placed her hand deep inside the pocket of her board shorts and pulled out a handful of keys. Squatting down on the ground she sorted them out on the concrete path in a neat row and checking each tag, selected one of similar shape with a faded hand-written label that said, '*HGNR BACK DOOR*'.

'Mm, interesting,' she said, as she stood up and slid its length into the lock.

Paul looked on with growing suspicion, a simple possibility that he may have overlooked. With just a little effort and a few internal squeals coming from the lock, she turned the key all the way round. There was a click. She paused and slowly looked up at the incredulous man standing next to her.

'Well, that was embarrassing. So, what's with this key that says HANGER?' he said holding it out. 'I think I've been had.'

'Yep, I would say so.' She placed a confident look in his direction. 'Wrong key, buddy.' She giggled.

She went to open the door, but the hinges were tight. With effort shared between the two and an intense sound coming from the aged hinges, the back door was pried open. Once inside the dark environment, the smell of an aircraft hit their nostrils, and as their eyes adjusted to the dim light in the hanger, a powerful feeling invaded their understanding.

'Oh … my …' Claire spoke the first words, after which she just stood there, silent.

She reached over and took the hand of her husband to be. Paul responded and stood hand in hand with Claire, looking up at the sight set before them.

'Paul, what is this doing here?'

'No idea, other than collecting dust like the truck, the generator, and everything else around here.'

There in front of the shipwrecked travellers was a 1945 World War II bomber in pristine condition.

They walked around to the front of the aircraft and stood directly under its nose. The skin of the vintage aeroplane was dull due to years of fine dust and what appeared to Paul to be a coating that was cracking in places revealing a well-weathered metal surface underneath.

'What sort of plane is this?

'My darling, what you are standing under is one of the most famous American bombers in the world.'

'Yeah, great, but what is it?'

'It's the B17 bomber,' Paul said absentmindedly. 'I need to sit down.' The doctor stood there, trying to make sense of what was parked in front of him. His shocked face began to be drained of its colour.

'Are you OK, Paul?'

'No.'

Claire frowned deeply, studying her doctor as he walked over to the large hanger doors and sat down on the cool concrete floor with his back against the warm metal doors.

Claire watched as his eyes darted all over the relic, lost in the vision of this mighty warrior that stood at the ready for battle. His eyes fixed on the nose art of the aircraft. It showed an eagle in the strike position. Its impressive wings poised high and its lethal talons at the ready for attack. Under the bird was written ... *On Eagles Wings*.

Claire came over and sat close to Paul leaning into him tenderly.

'Hey, handsome, any idea when you're going to come back to earth?' She stretched her neck up to him and kissed him on the cheek and took his hand. Claire's sudden movement woke the chick inside the front of her shirt, and it began to sound its concern loudly. Paul looked down in the direction of the noise.

'Hey, it's OK,' she said, in a motherly tone placing her finger against the bird, caressing it, and immediately the tiny yellow chicken settled.'

'I forgot all about the little guy.'

'Girl, it's a girl and welcome back to earth,' Claire said confidently.

'What.'

'Oh, what indeed, mister ... you were loopy for the past couple of minutes.'

'Was not.'

'Was too.'

'Well, whatever, but this is absolutely amazing.'

'Um, really? Paul, it's just an ugly old piece of World War II surplus to requirements junk.'

'What? Wash your mouth out, woman. This is priceless,' he said gesturing with his hands.

'Really? Priceless you say ... so how much?' She looked at him with that look.

Paul laughed under his breath and shook his head. 'Name your price, Miss Chandler ... name your price.'

'No way.' She changed her look.

'Yep.'

'How much?'

'Millions, Literally millions. There probably isn't anything like this in the world, in this original state? Actually, it looks a little different from the normal flying fortress though.'

He glanced at Claire.

'That's what they called them, the flying fortress. Oh, my goodness,' he continued.

Paul began to laugh slowly shaking his head. His laughter grew until he was slapping his knees.

'Claire!' he yelled out. 'Can you believe all this?'

'Paul?'

'Oh man.' He said, coughing as he settled down. 'I'm on the edge of a nervous breakdown, I go on this amazing holiday, I meet this beautiful American woman from God, American for crying out loud.'

'Steady,' she said in gest, watching his unusual behaviour.

'And ... I fall madly in love with her, so, I offer her a proposal in marriage, she accepts, then ... wow, life is amazing, then, within the hour, we get attacked by pirates, by pirates for goodness sake, left for dead on the ship together, only to go through a category five typhoon and ending up out to sea together on this ship, getting thrown around on the ride from hell. A category five typhoon for crying out loud, category five, end up shipwrecked together on a deserted tropical island and now, I am sitting in front of a B17 bomber with this beautiful woman on this deserted tropical island ... and all in a period of six days ... I trust on the seventh day God's going to rest because I know for certain that I need a break. Not sure I can take much more.' The doctor kept shaking his head in total disbelief.

Then there was silence.

'Feel better now?' Claire asked, totally amazed regarding his outburst.

'Yes, thank you,' he sighed, 'needed to get that off my chest. 'Unbelievable, a B17 bomber.'

'OK. That's good.' Claire said slowly.

'Um, now, where was I?' he said scratching his head.

'The price ... millions.' Claire said, still watching him intently.

'Oh yeah, millions.' He began to drift off back to his state of mind, when Claire dug him in his ribs with her elbow.

'Hey, gorgeous, don't leave me.'

'What?' He blinked and turned to Claire.

'I know this will be a mistake but, why don't you climb on board and check it out from the inside?'

He shot to his feet.

'Absolutely. Coming?'

'Hey why not? It's not like me and the kid here, have anything else to do today,' she said, opening the front of her shirt and looking down at the sleeping creature.

Within that minute, they had boarded the aircraft. The heavy smell of this instrument of war was too much for Claire, and she quickly turned around and walked out.

'This is different; look the waist gunners. They seem to be ... Hey were ya going?'

'How can you breathe that air in there?' Claire looked uncomfortable.

'Yeah, it's a bit stale,' he said, yelling deeper from within the darkness of the plane.

He reached the cockpit and slid the side windows open and yelled out for Claire to return.

'Hey, come on up. The air will clear in a bit with these windows open. Claire, check this out.' His excited request was only surpassed by his wild facial expression.

'Yeah, OK, I'm coming.' She ventured back with more complaints than he ever heard coming from her.

'This is brand-spanking-new, Claire. Well, it's obviously very old, but I don't think this old girl has seen any service to speak of.'

'Oh man, this is still stinking bad, Paul.' She made her way to the cockpit and sat in the right seat, where the air certainly seemed clearer.

'Wow, these seats are not real comfortable. They could have done with the woman's touch.'

'Those pilots would have spent many hours at a time in front of these controls on these seats,' Paul said looking from left to right, overwhelmed by what was set before him.

'Ouch … so uncomfortable.' She looked around.

'Check all these buttons, dials and things. Do you think the engines would work? Can you try and start it?' Claire asked, trying to find some common bond yet, slightly interested at the same time.

He laughed. 'Wouldn't have a clue, but give me time, though; I'll work it out. There must be a pilot's operating handbook around here somewhere.' He laughed under his breath.

'Just give me time.'

'Yep, OK, well, you've got plenty of that here, that's for sure,' she said.

Paul was muttering confirmation of instrument recognition to himself, totally ignoring Claire who was watching his every move.

'You know, this might be our ticket out of here,' he said, as he continued to search the cockpit for familiar instrumentation. The doctor's heart was filling with hope minute by minute.

'Get out of town. You're not serious?' Claire frowned in disbelief.

Paul seemed to be lost in his search and hardly heard a word coming from his co-pilot.

The young woman slowly shook her head.

'Yep. Something tells me he's serious all right, little chickadee,' she said, looking down her shirt addressing the sleeping chicken.

'Paul? I know I said the other day it was a pity that the ship wasn't a plane and you could fix it and fly us home; well, given these new developments, let's just forget that shall we? Paul?'

He still hadn't heard a word she said, but persisted with his muttering under his breath as he pointed to the various instruments.

'Altimeter.' He tapped the glass face twice and sat back. 'Wow, these are brand-new instruments, Claire,' he said, looking at the array of nineteen forties technology displayed in front of him.

Claire looked down to her right, and there in a compartment was something that looked important. She picked it up.

'Um, excuse me ... Paul?' Claire patiently called from the seat just a couple feet to his right.

He was completely consumed by this discovery from the aviation archives, and Claire was fascinated by the pure joy that was exuding from her Australian doctor. There in the cockpit, she was observing a different side of the man. The young woman had seen him first hand competently practicing his gift in medicine and now she was watching the very capable side of this man in a new area—aviation. His methodical approach to his discovery seemed to imply training to his observer, and his application of things already understood was manifesting before her very eyes.

The more she watched him, the more she felt secure, and the more she saw, the more she loved this man, this unique creature. Her heart welled up with joy and a sudden deep understanding washed over her. It was as though a gentle, yet authoritative voice spoke deep into her heart, '*Daughter, I give you this son.*' Her heart stood still as it soaked into her reality for that moment, a moment when time stood still, a moment when God spoke intimately.

A scripture flooded her heart. Something she had learned as a memory verse in Sunday School when she was a little girl. *"They will have no fear of bad news; their hearts are steadfast, trusting in the Lord"* (Psalm 112:7). That verse would become their own Bible verse.

Paul continued to survey his newfound toy, unaware of a Divine presence, unaware of intimate communion between the most high Creator and a very special daughter seated next to him in a nineteen forty-five B17 bomber. Claire watched her God-given man and desired him.

'Master and ignition switches, OK, number one, two, three and fourth engine, ah yes, on and off and down here the battery switches, let's turn on number one battery.' He pressed the switch down at his lower left side. 'Yep, just as I thought dead as a door nail. OK, let's try number two ... 'He switched it on. 'Yep, also dead ... no surprise there,' he continued his muttering.

Claire sat back in the less-than-comfortable co-pilot's seat and watched her man in action.

'Hello? Paul?' Claire called.

There was no response from this man still possessed by the spirit of flight.

'Hey, fly-boy?' she yelled.

He sat to attention and spun around to face Claire.

'Ah, there you are good doctor.' She waved the document in front of him.

'What's that?'

'Checklist?' She smiled.

'Where was that?'

'Just down here.' She pointed to its original housing.

'Well done.'

She handed it over to Paul. 'Thought it might prove interesting reading.'

'You can say that again.'

'Oh, by the way there's no way I'm flying in this thing, OK? Do you really think that you can actually fly this?'

'No.' He laughed.

'No? Well, isn't that interesting ...then there's definitely no way I'm getting in this bucket of bolts with you ... sorry.'

'I can learn, little by little. A lot of maintenance required though. It will take a fair while ... the maintenance that is ... probably ... well a while anyway, but first things first; we have to secure ourselves here on the island.'

'That's a relief,' Claire said, rolling her eyes in her head.

'But after ... well, interesting concept, you know, fly back home.' He laughed.

'Paul, read my lips ... no.'

'Well ... Claire, we may have no option. This could very well be God's provision for us.'

She sat back again in the co-pilot's seat for the second time and thought deeply on the matter. She looked across at Paul.

'Surely, God in all His awesomeness could provide something better ... don't you think ... really?

'Well, we'll see, but for now, this is it ... Don't you think?'

'Joy.' Her countenance dropped.

'Hey, come on. Let's get out of here. I'll come back tomorrow. Let's check out the other side of our island.' He reached over and took her hand and kissed it. 'Come on, beautiful.'

'It's a deal,' she said, somewhat relieved. 'Anything to get out of here,' she said softly.

They closed the side windows in the flight deck and walked out of the aircraft, being careful to making sure the bomber's door was closed, then they walked out into the bright light of the day.

Paul locked the back door and returned the key to the office cabinet along with all the other keys in Claire's pocket.

CHAPTER THIRTY-SEVEN

⁓

The chicken had been fed a hearty meal of bread crumbs, a drink of water and had just been tucked into its new bed which consisted of a small cardboard box stuffed with some hand towels and placed securely on the floor of Claire's room at the foot of the bed.

She stared at the small spots of white paint on her fingers. The stranded couple had prepared the two crosses to mark the gravesites for the next morning's memorial service. Paul had discovered a plank found in the storeroom and with the necessary tools, crafted the two markers of the place of burial. A generous coating of white deck paint was slapped over the surface of the timber, and Claire carefully and tearfully painted the relevant names on their handiwork.

The evening was hot and humid, and the couple had decided to sit in the upper lounge after dinner. The sound of the distant surf breaking off the outer reef caressed the early evening's peaceful stillness. Not a breath of breeze was to be found that night. Paul had opened a bottle of red wine and slowly sipped on its full flavour in a crystal glass, while Claire was enjoying a combination of the wine mixed with a larger proportion of seven up and lots of ice. It was decided that she might try a small amount of alcohol to calm her down due to the distress involved with the afternoon's funeral preparations. She was largely unaccustomed to alcohol, and though her intake was in fact quite minimal, the effects were beginning to be felt in this young American woman.

'You know I miss my Mom.' She looked up from her hands to a contented man sitting across from her in the comfortable lounge chair.

'Actually, I was just thinking about my Dad. He's a good man.' He looked across at Claire.

'Do you think our folks would have heard of our disappearance?' she asked reluctantly.

'By now? ... yes, I think so.' He looked down at his wine.

'It makes you feel helpless. Doesn't it? I mean, you can just imagine the horror that they must be going through. Like you just want to cry out and say it's OK, we're OK ... just stuck here and can't get off, but we're OK. Don't worry we're fine.' She looked across at Paul.

He didn't respond but seemed to be deep in thought.

'You OK?'

He shot his head up to face her as though he had just been snatched from a trance.

'Yeah, I'm fine ... Just thinking.'

'What were you thinking?'

'Well, I was thinking ... well, from our perspective, it could be worse, couldn't it?'

'I guess so ... of course,' she replied slowly.

'Can you imagine if we were shipwrecked on our own ... you know, just you here, or just me here ... alone.' Paul pondered.

'Yeah ... like that movie with, what's his name ... the actor ... Tom Cruise?'

'Oh yeah ... actually I think that was Tom Hanks ... what was that movie called?'

'Can't remember, but yes, you're right, Paul ... to be stuck here on my own ... I'd go stir crazy.'

She sipped her chilled drink and looked straight at her doctor.

'Oh, I thank God that we're together.' She slid across on the leather lounge and nestled into him.

Paul placed his arm around her.

'Who would have thought that we would meet ... and then end up like this ... here?'

He chuckled. The wine was having an effect.

She looked up at him and laughed.

'Shipwrecked on a tropical island and drinking wine in five-star surroundings ... and I don't drink.' Claire laughed hard.

The two joined together in an absurd outburst of merriment, partly a by-product of the stress, partly the result of their joy of being together and the alcohol.

'But, I do like this drink.' She twirled the ice around in her glass. 'My, I think you have corrupted me, Doctor.' She giggled.

'Well, that's hardly fair, my dear ... a little wine for the stomach's sake. Isn't that what Paul the apostle said?' He smiled broadly.

'Oh, he didn't say that.'

'He did too, First Timothy ... around chapter five, I think; go read it.'

'I will. I wonder if he used Seven Up?' They broke out with another outburst of laughter, then settled down quickly. Claire stretched back in the chair, looking out to sea.

'So, you really think it's good for you?' she questioned thoughtfully.

'Yes, a small amount is quite good for you.' Paul swirled his wine around in his glass and took another sip.

'Really?'

'One or two, but no more. The positive health effects are lost after two.'

'Paul, look!' she pointed across to a glowing horizon. 'The moon, oh how beautiful.'

The crest of a full moon was rising over the Pacific's dark horizon, blessing its surface with a golden shimmer, as it made its way to a dominant display for the night.

'Hey, let's go for a walk on the beach,' she said standing up, offering him her hand.

'Come on.'

Paul needed no further invitation. Placing his glass back on the coaster, he let himself be led by this most interesting woman. He stood up quickly as need would have it, given her forceful insistence and headed straight for the beach. As they navigated their way down the sandy embankment, a section of sand gave way under their feet and both softly slid onto their backs. A squeal of delight was heard from Claire as they lay back on the cool sand laughing.

With sand now traveling into their loose-fitting clothes they relaxed their resistance and lay together looking up. The tropical night offered a brilliant display of the stars as the couple looked as though mesmerised.

'Oh, Paul, will you just look at that sky,' she whispered into the silence of the night.

'The heavens declare the glory of God.' He brought his arm around her shoulder bringing her closer to his side. They lay there in wonder, bathed in the warm tropical atmosphere, looking heavenward in complete silence. The mood was peaceful, and the two human bodies were comfortably close, lying in the cool sand.

'Look, Paul, you can actually see the stars reflecting on that wet sand way over there … see?' She pointed to a section of the beach further away from the two marooned souls, closer to the other end of the bay.

Paul studied the anomaly she referred to. His face began to frown.

'What, don't tell me you can't see it. Look way over there. It must be wet sand, see the reflection?'

'Yeah, I see it but, I don't think it is any reflection of the stars.'

'Really?' She looked harder. 'Well, what else could it be?'

'I have no idea.'

'Let's check it out.' and with that she shot up and started to run, followed close by the doctor.

'Oh no!' Claire made a quick declaration as she stopped her race to the location of interest.

'What's up.'

'I have sand down my shorts.' She stopped and began to stomp around trying to shake the tiny grains from her clothing. 'I hate that. Oh, this is gross,' she said now annoyed. 'What about you?'

'No, I'm fine' Paul saw the funny side of what was set before him. Her movements were exaggerated.

'Oh, lucky me,' she said, looking back at Paul.

'You look like you're doing the Kangaroo dance.'

'The what? She continued her movements trying to free herself from her gritty bondage.

'It's an Australian aboriginal dance.'

'Oh really? You're kidding, right?'

Paul laughed, catching up to her. He began to wipe the sand off her back.

'No, it's a real dance, actually I might have it on my laptop.'

'Oh, come on, why would you have something like that on your laptop?'

'Good question. I went online to investigate this holiday-package, I saw a Northern Territory holiday package offer, and I downloaded it. There was a documentary that came with the download. I'll show you tonight if you like. Your hootenanny reminded me of that. Mind you, they do it better. Come on, do it again.' He laughed heartily.

'You are heading for a bruising, mister. Remember, I have three older brothers.' She looked up at him with a cheeky face.

They continued their walk to the mysterious lights on the beach. A warm breeze began to whisper its presence around these people bringing with it a stronger scent of the sea.

'Oh, Paul isn't this just perfect?'

'With the exception of the sand in my shorts.' He smiled, raising his eyebrows.

'Um, yes, besides that, this is wonderful, isn't it?'

The closer they got to the mystery, the more the doctor pondered on its presence.

'Hey, that might be phosphorescent plankton,' Paul said, as they walked up to the area in question.

'Oh, wow, will you look at this? Oh, this is just wonderful.' Claire stopped and stared at the wonder at their feet. Time seemed to stand still as they walked, hand in hand, through their land of light.

She suddenly broke the magic with an urgent complaint.

'Oh, I can't stand this.'

'What?'

'The sand in my shorts. I'm going into the water to wash this sand out.' She looked at her man. 'Won't take long.'

Claire walked out into the water, addressed the problem quickly and proceeded to swim under the brilliant sky.

'Oh, this is wonderful. Hey, you so have to come in, Paul. It's perfect.' She swirled around in the still waters of the lagoon.

He removed his shirt and waded out to her. An hour went by as the only human representation on the island leisurely swam in the liquid wonder of the lagoon's solitude under the moon-light. Finally, they simply sat in the water and talked about each other's family, naming each sibling, describing their character and many funny stories that had happened over the years within their respective homes. The more they talked, the more they drew closer together.

'Hey, you know what's missing?'

'What.'

'Mosquitos.' She put her arms up out of the water. 'Where are they?'

'Good point, but, I'm sure they're here ... although, I certainly haven't been bothered by any, and I don't recall seeing any mosquito wrigglers in any of the pools of water on the other side ... did you?'

'Well, I wasn't actually looking for them but, come to think of it ... no, I don't believe there were.'

'Yeah, OK, anyway, Interesting observation.'

A flash of light from behind the mountain, then, a distant roll of thunder announced a pending threat coming.

'Storm,' Claire said, looking toward the tallest point on the island, expecting more lightning to prove her point.

'Yeah, better get back.'

They moved out of the water and toward the beach. Paul picked up his shirt and tied it around his waist while Claire slowly turned back towards the water, looking at the glow of the moon as it peaked its face from behind a group of clouds.

'Beautiful.' She raised up her hands and readjusted her hair into a bun, then walked ahead. Her wet clothing clung to her skin and under the bright silver light of the moon, Paul observed her female form silhouetted perfectly before him.

'That was so much fun,' she said, giggling softly, then began dancing around him.

'Wasn't that fun?'

'Lady, you are a ratbag,' he said, laughing while watching her playful antics.

Claire's high-spirited nature had been brought back to life, and her zest for life was on fire that evening.

She giggled like a little girl. 'I'm beginning to like how that sounds. Do you think our kids will be ratbags?

'If they take after their mother, they will.'

'And your sister, you said your sister was a ratbag, so, I guess if I'm one and she is one, then what hope have our kids got?'

'True.' He tilted his head back and laughed softly, then put his arm around her shoulder. Claire responded by entwining her arm around his waist.

'Thank you, thank you, thank you.' Her heart was full of joy, as she danced around her man.

'Yeah? For what?'

'For just being you. Have I told you that I love you lately?'

'A few times today,' he replied, captivated by this sudden activity.

'Do you like how it sounds, Paul?'

'Yeah, sure do.'

'Good, well consider yourself told again, my Aussie doctor.' She kissed him softly.

'Wow all this attention,' Paul said, loving the attention.

The moon continued to bathe them in its silvery light, bringing the entire beach and surroundings into view.

'So, were you really serious about moving to the other side?'

'If we thought it necessary, yes.'

'Wow.'

'Should I?'

'Well, obviously I don't want you to leave me, but I understand what you were saying. This isn't easy... really isn't.' Claire settled and dropped her gaze to the sand in front of them.

'Problems?' he asked, studying her again.

She looked up at him but, said nothing. Her answer was in her look.

He continued to study her and, frowned just a little. 'That bad, ha?'

She nodded, and tucked herself into his side.

'I've never felt this way, ever. It's not wrong. It's wonderful, but I've never ... Oh I don't know.' She resigned her thoughts and kept walking close to the doctor. Her love for Paul needed to be expressed, but her commitment to her God held her back.

Initially, there was no further response from Claire. She just walked close to Paul. She then stopped turned to him, and picking up both his hands, she kissed them. First on the knuckles, then on the palms, then on the back of the hands, and then she proceeded to do it all over again. She cupped his hand tighter in hers and pressed them up against her cheek.

'Hey girl, what exactly are you saying?' he said softly, while studying her new antics.

Claire looked him directly into his eyes.

'I'm saying ... I want you so much, that it hurts, really hurts, but you're right, you know, what you said recently ... If we're not rescued within seven days, well … they'll call off the search, and we'll be given up for dead. I can see that now.' She looked away. The water was shimmering under the moon light as a gentle breeze began to blow.

'Yeah, well logically, that's what's going to happen, but … that's just my opinion, I mean it costs big money to have aircraft flying for a week,' the doctor reminded her.

Claire slowly brought her gaze back to the only other person on the island.

'Yep, I can see that, and I agree we should get married.'

'You do?'

'Yes, I do. I can see that we're stuck here, I know it … but, just never thought God would do it this way. Getting married that is.'

The two began their trek back to the stranded vessel.

'I had such a picture of what my wedding day would be like … you know big wedding, lots of guests you know. It sort-of messes with your head, the whole island thing, doesn't it?'

Paul nodded.

'I can see my friends in the States, years from now, you know, after we've been rescued:

'*So, where did you meet your husband Paul?* Oh, in an airport. *Really? And where were you married, in the States or Australia?* Oh, neither actually, on a tropical island. *Oh, how romantic.* Yeah it was, very special, unique if you will. *Wow, how exciting.* Exciting? You don't know the half of it. *I bet, how wonderful. Big wedding?* No, just Paul and me. *Excuse me?* Yeah, couldn't wait, you know. *Oh, I see. Which island?* I have no idea, somewhere in the Pacific. *Oh really? So why don't you know where it is?* Well, because we were shipwrecked on the stupid uncharted thing, you know, as they always are … uncharted … and everyone thought we were dead, so we thought. Ah hang it, let's get married, you know, as you do.'

It was too much for Paul who burst with thunderous laughter. Claire didn't join her husband to be with an equalled outburst, only a slight chuckle was offered as she thought deeply on the subject.

Another sudden veracious whisper of breeze swirled its way around the two lovers to be, offering relief from the sultry conditions.

'When did you know?' Paul asked, with a voice that almost quivered.

'Know?'

'That I was the one.'

She hesitated, then slowly released her confession.

'Well, I guess that time at the hotel in Palau. Do you remember? I asked you to come into my room, but you wouldn't come in. You remember that?'

He nodded

'Paul, I felt so honoured. I'd never experienced such ... I don't know. I guess I felt protected or something, anyway it was so special. You do remember that, don't you?'

He nodded again captivated by her enthusiasm.

'I saw ...' She paused again.

'Go on.' Paul asked.

'It was like I saw your soul. Weird ... but, that's what I saw. I saw you ... and I loved what I saw. I didn't mean anything by it ... asking you into my room that is. I have never done that, ever. I quickly realised that I shouldn't have, but ... you covered my thoughtlessness. It was then that I saw something in you that I had never seen before ... never seen it in anyone else before. Not sure how to explain it really ... It's like you woke me up ... strange.' Claire said, deep in thought again. 'And you?' she continued.

He laughed softly. 'Probably started when you dribbled all over my arm in that aircraft for half an hour,' he said, trying to lighten things and dampen his passion.

'Oh, gross.' She took her fist to his arm.

'You can say that again, all that saliva down my arm.' He chuckled and ran off ensuring no further blows could be delivered from this woman.

She began to laugh, as she chased after him around the beach with the view of delivering another blow. Paul let her catch up and with a quick movement, spun her around, encompassed both his strong arms around hers, holding on to her hands, protecting himself from any further friendly physical violence. He bent down slightly and kissed her neck while holding her from behind. She stood still, calming down immediately, and enjoyed his embrace, pushing her neck into his face. The two souls stood under the stars for a short time then, finally walked back to the ship arm in arm, silent. The approaching storm made its presence known with constant flashes and louder rumblings rolling across the heavens.

CHAPTER THIRTY-EIGHT

———— ∞ ————

It had rained all night. The morning dawn was a spectacular sight, with its golden rays of light piecing the darkness with brilliant authority as the remnant of the night's weather cleared.

Paul had been up for some time preparing for the remembrance service. His sermon was brief. He realised he knew very little about either of the people who died.

'Hey, you're up early.' Her question broke his concentration, and he turned his tired eyes to the woman standing at his door.

'Oh dear, problems?' Claire said, studying her lover to be.

'Morning. Yep, having trouble. I really don't know these people. Well, Jess?

... maybe a little bit, I guess, but the captain?' He shrugged his shoulders.

'Wish Dad was here.' Paul never thought he'd be leading a funeral service.

'I guess having a Dad like yours under such circumstances would come in handy.' She smiled lovingly.

'What exactly is troubling you?'

'Well, given that I don't know them, how do I focus it? ... the service that is. For example, was the captain a Christian? ... That makes a huge difference ... the difference between victory and ... just offering comfort to the living, if you know what I mean.'

'Well, it's not like you're going to get any criticism from the maddening crowds … is it?'

'I suppose not, but even so I want it to be right … you know.'

Claire's face lit up as she listened closely to Paul.

'Um, regarding your question … I can help you with one answer.'

'Really?'

'Jessica, she accepted the Lord that night she moved in with me.'

'Oh yes, I knew that, but what …' Paul was cut off.

'Actually, I don't remember telling you that.'

'You didn't. I was sort of eavesdropping on your conversation in the lounge a few days ago.' His confession was humbling but quietly satisfying at that same time.

'Oh, were you now?' Claire smiled at Paul.

'Yeah, quite innocently of course, so tell me her story,' he asked, eager to divert the attention from his minor humiliation.

Claire sat on the bed and explained herself. Paul listened intently to her detailed revelation. It took the young woman twenty minutes to tell Jessica's story, which included her background, the family situation, and the joy Claire witnessed when the young teenager became a Christian with such a full heart.

'Oh, Paul, you should have seen her after that prayer. She was so full of joy. There was such release. I had never seen that before in a new Christian … man, something else.

Remember the next morning when you made mention of her changed appearance, behaviour or something like that?'

'Yeah, I do, when we went swimming.'

'Even the coach noticed it … In fact, she practically grilled me.'

'Is that so?' Paul sat fixed on Claire.

'Yes.'

Paul reflected on that perfect morning as the three were snor-kelling in the crystal clear water. Life was perfect then. Jessica's bright face came to mind. He saw her clearly. She was indeed ... so full of life, so young, so fresh and so beautiful.

'Yep, Jess was a different kid that morning,' he said slowly transfixed to his temporary vision.

'Oh, Paul, it was wonderfully genuine. She's with the Lord, I know it.'

'Just out of curiosity, why didn't you tell me?'

'Well I was going to, but we didn't have a quiet time together to confidentially discuss it. Do you remember all the stuff that was going on before the pirates?'

'OK, fair enough.'

Claire went on to explain the scene that developed on the deck when the pirates arrived and the moment just before Jessica's death.

'I held Jessica in my arms. She looked up at me and called to me for help. I knew I couldn't do anything. I could see, oh, Paul ... I could see she was dying, and I told her to call on Jesus ... I didn't know what else to say.' Claire paused, reflecting on the horror of that day, bowing her head to look at the floor.

'You did well to say that ...' the doctor said very softly.

Claire quickly looked up at him.

'And she did, Paul ... right there in my arms. She called out to Jesus. Everyone would have heard it.' Claire paused, then continued.

'Her face instantly changed. Paul, she looked like ... like ... she was seeing someone who was her best friend or maybe even her Dad, you know, that sort of relationship. I swear that I saw her face light up ... I mean actually light up. I started to feel strange, like I needed to say sorry to God for stuff in my life. It was the purest time I had ever experienced.

Then Jessica's eyes became excited with joy, more joy, and she raised her hands up as though someone was taking her hands to lift her up off the floor and out of my arms, you know what I mean? Then, right there in my arms ... she died.' Claire's tears began to flow. 'Oh, Paul, it was so sad but so ... I don't know, beautifully pure or something.' Claire's face was filled with questions.

'God's presence ... a holy presence?' Paul offered.

'Yes ... holy, oh my goodness, yes .... Amazing. Paul, she's with Jesus, I really believe that with all my heart.'

Paul reached across to the bench next to his bed and drew out two Kleenex tissues and handed them to Claire. She gratefully accepted his gift and proceeded to wipe her tears away and blow her nose.

'You're the most amazing woman I have ever met. Listen to you.'

'What do you mean?'

'That story, what an awesome experience. You witnessed such a wonderful thing ... a difficult thing, of course, but with it a huge blessing. Wow, what a blessing.'

'Yes, yes ... it was. Have you witnessed anyone ...die?'

'Yep ... an old man.'

'Christian?'

'No.'

'Oh dear.'

'Rather horrible actually.'

'Really? Why do you say that?' Claire asked.

'Well, he was a wealthy man ... it was a car accident, rather gruesome, internal bleeding among other things. A Salvation Army pastor happened to be there chatting to one of his church members who was being admitted for suspected peritonitis. Why he was there at that particular time, I have no idea, but he was.

Anyway, the old guy was crying out for help. We tried to comfort him, you know, saying that we were there to help him and he was in good hands, but he wouldn't accept our reassurance. It was like … he knew he was dying.

A nurse came over and said that this pastor heard the commotion and offered his help. This pastor was great … he was brilliant with this fellow. While we were working on the old guy's body, the pastor was working on his soul … or trying to.'

'I take it that, it didn't go well.'

'No, to cut the long story short, the Salvation Army fellow presented the message of Christ really well, you know so carefully, so sensitively. We all heard it, sure impressed me, but the old fellow couldn't accept the message.'

'Why?'

'Well it was all very odd. The patient actually said that he wanted to believe, but he couldn't. He kept saying it. Then he cried out help, help me, I can't believe … he said some other things, anyway … all really bizarre stuff. It unsettled my staff a bit … Man, it certainly shook me up.'

'What happened then?'

'Well, he died shortly after… and this is the most sobering part. He died with the most terrified look in his eyes. It was like he was looking at something that was scaring the life out of him, something really terrifying. I'll never forget it.'

'Why couldn't he believe, when he wanted to?'

'Yeah, that really got me. I asked Dad, and he had seen similar examples. He put it down to a hardened heart. I'd heard of it but never gave it any practical consequences.'

'Oh yes, my pastor preached a sermon on that—scary stuff.'

'Indeed. Dad said many a person is given ample opportunities to accept the messiah, Jesus Christ's, offer of escaping hell, His offer of life with Him, but every time a person says no, their heart is hardened a little. It becomes habitual, and then after years of rejecting Christ's offer of salvation ... when they suddenly see their desperate need, they simply can't believe. They just don't have a heart to be able to do it. It's like their spiritual heart has become dysfunctional.'

'Horrible.'

'But you saw the very opposite with Jessica, much to be joyous about.'

'Well, yes, but so sad at the same time, and there was anger ... real deep anger, too.'

'Anger?'

'Yep, from my side, that is, so much so that I wanted to kill that murderer. The truth is ... I actually attacked him with intent to ... yeah, anyway, and I recall the guy hitting me with something, and this explosion next to my head. I think he must have hit me with his gun and it went off. I don't know. Then I woke up with a head-ache and saw you ... the most beautiful face.' She paused again, thinking deeply whilst her fiancé sat on the bed watching intently.

'Oh, poor Jessica. She was a wonderful little gal, Paul. She would have fitted in well here with us. Why did she have to ...' Her words stopped, and grief over came her soul again.

'Paul, she was so special. When God gets us off this island, I want to find her Mom and tell her what happened.'

'Good call.'

Claire sat still on the bed, processing her grief.

'Would you like to record the service? So, when we get off this island ... you know, for Jessica's Mom?' he asked carefully.

She lifted her head towards Paul, with eyes filled with great expectation.

'Could we? Paul, that's a great idea.'

'Sure. I saw a video camera in one of the rooms. The pirates must have missed it.'

'And regarding the captain, I didn't tell you, I found a Bible in his office up there next to the bridge. It had an inscription written just inside the first page. It said … *to my dearest, may the Lord Jesus guide you home through the darkest night as you fix your sight on and navigate your way by this instrument of light, His Word.* … or something like that. It was signed, but I couldn't read the handwritten name. Maybe his wife.'

'I saw that Bible but didn't open it … interesting …and he was from the deep South. Isn't that a Bible-belt area?' the doctor asked.

'Yes, it is., He might have been a Southern Baptist or something.' Claire offered gently.

'Yep … maybe.'

'There was something wholesome about him, I thought.' Claire tried to recall some of his characteristics that might have given any indication of his beliefs.

The doctor began to change his notes to accommodate the new information about Jessica and the captain.

'You want some coffee, handsome?'

'Sure … Oh the generator, I better go down and kick it into gear.'

They made their way down the dimly lit corridors of the *Pacific Fair*, started the diesel generator and headed straight for the galley. With the water in the coffeepot, it took no time to create a brew for the only souls on board.

After the welcome stimulation of the coffee, a search for any equipment that could take better videos than Paul's cell phone was undertaken in all the guests' rooms. Finally, a small camera with a tripod was discovered, batteries were checked, and final preparations were made for the morning's brief funeral services.

CHAPTER THIRTY-NINE

───────── ≈ ─────────

Robert Simms sat in a discrete corner near the hotel's swimming pool, waiting for his appointment. It was eight-thirty in the evening. The negotiations were promptly finalised four hours after Robert's meeting with the company executives back in the States, and the weary traveller was then rushed again to the corporate aircraft; destination, Cebu City, Philippines. Within twenty-four hours, he was to meet the third-party negotiators to organize the human transfer, and now he was waiting. His appointment was thirty minutes late.

The hotel was centrally located within Cebu's premier financial business district and conveniently found close to a large shopping mall. The extortionists chose this location due to its position, ease of access from the many islands in the area, and the international airport.

Simms keenly watched all the guests seated around this five-star pool. On the other side sat a well-dressed Asian woman. She'd been sitting there since Robert's arrival, reading a magazine.

Her cell phone suddenly vibrated on the table. She quickly picked up the unit, said nothing but, just listened and occasionally nodding her head. Finally, she looked up at one of the hotel rooms and said 'OK … yes, he is,' after which she placed her cell phone back on her table and continued her reading.

Simms looked down at his watch. It was now eight-thirty-two. He knew his time was being held to ransom. This was a common practice among extortionists, and he knew he was being watched.

'Excuse me, sir.' It was the pool attendant.

Robert was slightly startled by the intrusion.

'Oh, hi. Hey, can I have another tonic water? It's quite warm tonight,' Robert said, picking up his empty glass and politely handing it to the attendant.

The tropical air was thick with the smells of the city.

A bead of sweat trickled down the back of his neck to be welcomed by the fabric of his white cotton shirt.

'I'm sorry sir, there is a message waiting for you at the desk in the foyer.'

'Thank you.' Simms tone changed, forgetting his need for further refreshments. This was it! The stage was being set! His nerves were being tested due to lack of adequate sleep, a slight sore throat and jet lag. Leaving the glass on the table, he casually walked towards the five-star building. As he entered the chilled hotel atmosphere, he turned and looked back to the young woman with the magazine. She was nowhere to be seen.

'Game on,' he said softly to himself.

At the hotel lobby desk, he was handed a small white envelope. Inside a slip of white paper was found and typed on its surface were four words: GO TO YOUR ROOM.

The hotel was booked out due to a conference being held on its premises, and people were walking around everywhere with tell-tail wrist bands, tagging them to the weekend's excitement.

Robert squeezed into the crowded lift and stood there, listening to all the chatter filling the tight space. After two levels, the lift door opened only to be confronted by an equal number of eager passengers. Only refusal was offered to the pending travellers, and the lift door closed. Just one more level, and he would be free from the uncomfortable population in that confined space. The door opened with its customary chime, and freedom was his. He made his way to his room. As he entered his one-bed suite, the phone on the bedside table rang. Sitting on the bed, he composed himself for just a few seconds and answered.

'Hello.'

'We are ready to hand over your people or sell them into slavery.'

'They're not my people.'

There was a course laugh on the other end of the phone.

'You know, I really don't care.' The caller gravelled his words to the young English listener.

'Neither do I; now what's the next move?'

'You got the cash?'

'As agreed, you'll get the cash at hand over.'

'And you can transfer the balance, all divided up, one bank account per person?'

'As agreed. As each person is handed over, the money will be transferred into the designated account, but only after each person is identified and safely in our hands'

'You are doing good, English man.' The heavily accented voice gurgled its message.

'And each person must be handed over with their passports as proof of identity.'

'Of course, and you have organised the internet dongle for your laptop?'

'Change of plan.'

'What?'

'I make a call.'

'No.'

'Yes! My people make the transfer. Our research indicates the coverage around these parts isn't as reliable as you said. You seem to forget who you are dealing with. You seem to forget your cell phone is on the same system as the dongle.'

'I won't be using a cell phone.'

There was a small pause on the other end of the line.

'Very well, whatever, you could be using pigeon carrier for all I care. Just remember, no money and your people get sold on the market. Either way, we get our money'

'You'll get your money,' the Englishman said totally focused.

'Good, now at one a.m. tomorrow, you are to go to the desk downstairs and pick up a package. In that package will be a list of all the hostages and against each name will be a bank account number. There will also be a cell phone.'

'OK, and what then?'

'To be continued at one a.m. Good night, Mr English man.' The phone went dead.

'Hello?' There was no answer.

Robert placed the receiver at rest. He looked across at the digital clock. It read nine p.m. He set its alarm for twelve-thirty, then his cell phone alarm for twelve forty, ensuring he wouldn't sleep through. Simms slowly lay down on the bed fully clothed and promptly fell asleep.

The foyer of the hotel was quiet, with the exception of an occasional roll of thunder from a passing storm. A taxi squealed to a halt outside the hotel entrance. A thin man with grey hair and an untidy moustache exited the cab. He had a parcel tucked under his arm.

'Wait here; I'll only be a minute,' he said to the driver.

He walked swiftly towards the lobby and moved boldly up to the desk.

'Good morning, I am to meet my friend Robert Simms, but I see he's slept in. Can you ring him and tell him I can't wait, and I'll meet him later this morning. I've taken the liberty of wrapping the present. Do you have paper and an envelope?'

'Yes, sir,' the alert female desk attendant promptly replied. With that, she presented him a hotel note pad and an envelope.

The stranger slipped a silver fountain pen from his pocket, carefully removed its cap, scribbled an address on the sheet, tore it from the pad, folded it in half, slid it easily into the security of the white envelope and, sealed it. He then handed it with the parcel to the young Filipino lady.

'Please give him this with the parcel; the address and all he needs to know is in here.

Tell Mr Simms that we'll meet him there, with the guests,' he said, tapping on the face of the envelope.

'Certainly, sir.'

'Oh, and don't forget to ring him, and please give him my apologies. Thank you so much. I do appreciate your help. I feel so bad, but … anyway.' He slipped his hand into his pocket pulled out a US ten dollar note and slid it across to the young lady.

'I can see you're a competent woman. Thank you,' he said with a faint smile developing across his face.

'Thank you, sir, and I'll see to it right away. Have a wonderful evening, sir.'

'Thank you.' He turned looked down at his watch and walked out of the hotel and into the cab. It was twelve-twenty-five in the morning.

Robert woke up with a jolt. His hand flung across at the digital clock fumbling around trying to hit the snooze button. The noise persisted. Within a few seconds it registered that it was in fact the phone that was ringing.

'Hello.'

'Good morning, sir, this is the desk. I have been instructed to advise that your parcel is here for you, and your friend said that he apologises but he couldn't wait. You are to meet him there with the guests. He has left the address here for you. Would you like me to organise a cab, sir?'

'Ah, yes please. Can we make it for one a.m.?'

'Certainly sir. I will organise it now, for a one a.m. pick up. I will see you downstairs soon.'

'Yes, thank you. Also, can you organise a white coffee with two sugars waiting for me at the desk.'

'Of course, sir, that's a white coffee with two sugars.'

'Thank you.'

Simms stood up, moved to the bathroom, splashed some water on his face, tidied his hair, then he walked to his briefcase placed on the floor next to his bed. From its inside sleeve, he retrieved a satellite phone and with the press of one button, he was engaging the central command centre in London within seconds. A cold voice was heard on the other side.

'ID?'

'Tango, zero, four, November, Foxtrot, two zero.' Roberts voice splashed his response against the receiver as a result of the remnant of his bathroom efforts spraying a fine mist into the air near his lips.

'Hello, sir; all is in place ready to activate.'

'Roger that. I'll contact you within an hour. Expect a string of account numbers. This may take some time.'

'Yes, sir, and we have the mini-bus ready to rendezvous with you when we receive the confirmation of location'

'OK, will make contact again soon.'

'Standing by, sir.'

'Okay.'

Robert hung up immediately, bent down and reached under his bed. There he pulled from its concealment, an oversized black leather briefcase filled with half a million US dollars' worth of one hundred dollar bills.

He disarmed all the alarms and walked out the door with his briefcase firmly in grip.

At the desk, he collected his package and the envelope and sat in the foyer with his coffee, waiting for his cab.

CHAPTER FORTY

H e detached the camera from its secure position on the
tripod and placed it in its compact, soft carrying case. Paul
ripped the three slender legs of the apparatus out of the sand and
threw it over his shoulders.

'Hey,' he said softly, 'you coming?' while noting Claire's blank
stare at the two graves directly in front of her.

'Yes.'

Her eyes lifted slowly from the sombre picture of the two
white crosses at her feet to the golden light in the sky.

The sunrise funeral service was brief but moving. Paul offered
a few words of introduction to the camera. Claire was asked to
give a brief word about Jessica, and Paul spoke of the captain.
Both eulogies were fitting in the minds of the presenters. Paul
then shared a short devotion about the comfort that Jesus Christ
offers the living under such circumstances. He closed in prayer,
then proceeded to walk off camera to stand behind the unit and
panned the Sony lens towards the sunrise. Slowly, he zoomed the
picture directly into the face of the rising ball of brilliant light,
waited thirty seconds and stopped the recording.

'OK, that should do it,' he whispered his words reverently. 'I'll
edit it on my laptop later.'

He wondered if it was really worth it. His thoughts went
into a spin.

Would anyone ever see this edited funeral service? Was he just playing a stupid game? He shook himself out of the subtle wave of panic as they began their way back to their broken home.

'That was good ... sad but good.' The young woman gently reached out and held Paul's arm, drawing herself into him. 'It's warm this morning.'

Looking down at her, the doctor smiled and nodded slowly.

'You spoke well. Chip off the old block, ha?' Her eyes searched his face.

Paul shrugged his shoulders in an effort to convey the message that, he didn't know, if he in fact, was like his father, but wasn't prepared to enter into any conversation about the matter. Too much had happened, too much to process. This was their life now, their reality, and he was responsible for their wellbeing. Being a 'chip off the old block' seemed surplus to requirements.

'Do you think the families would appreciate what we did? ... I mean videoing the ceremony?'

'Yeah, I think so.' He broke the silence. He watched their feet sink into the soft white sand as they made their way down to the *Pacific Fair*. Her voice was drawing him back, back to reality. He was expecting Claire to be deeply affected and possibly even emotionally unstable. She displayed quite the opposite mindset.

'It would be good for their closure. Don't you think?'

'Yes. I do. Good for our closure too.' Paul maintained his gaze on their haphazard path to the ship.

'Sure ... true enough,' she replied, maintaining her study of his face. 'You hungry?'

'Not really ... might just indulge in some fruit.'

'OK.'

'Hey, that reminds me.' He broke into a slightly laboured enthusiasm.

'What?' Claire was taken by his change of mood.

'We have to empty that kitchen tidy.' He turned to her, snapping from his melancholy reflections.

'Well, guess who's got that detail?' Claire's face beamed with fun.

'Sounds like ... me, I'm guessing.'

'You guessed correctly.'

'I'll get on to it first thing. Consider it done.' The doctor winked at her. 'A man's got to do what a man's got to do ... What can I say?' He smiled.

'Amen to that brother ... Enjoy!' She laughed, slapped his behind and ran down the rest of the slope that led directly to the back of the ship buried up to its rails in sand and debris.

'Hey, be careful. Remember that cheek bone is still ...' He stopped his warning, realising that she was not listening but was totally focused on her objective of getting to the ship first. The considerable difference in their age was telling at times. To the doctor, Claire appeared to be blessed with a free spirit with much liberty, and she seemed to be naturally at one with their surroundings most of the time.

On his arrival, Paul carried out the garbage and buried it next to the ships' hull that faced the dense foliage, edging part of the small bay. On completion of his domestic duties, Paul wiped copious amounts of sweat from his brow with his forearm. The morning was steaming its way to a hot day. He looked across to the area where the contents of the kitchen tidy had been carelessly disposed previously. There at the base of the ships' hull, small shoots were noted coming from some of the seeds of the fruit consumed on the first day of their arrival. With curiosity on high alert, he moved closer. Watermelon seeds were beginning to root their way into the rich volcanic soil laced with years of rotting vegetation. With the revelation of re-creation permeating its way into his very marrow, he scanned for further signs of germination. A mango and what appeared to be a guava was partly covered by soil as a result of a heavy flow of rainwater carrying the fertile contents in its way. The mango seed was about to unfold its leafy solute to its new world. Paul squatted down to take a closer look.

He scanned all discarded remnant of the fruit.

His personal predicament was stepped aside and joy filled his soul.

There, growing before his very eyes, was a small part of God's future provision for the two castaways.

The remainder of their day was spent on the air-conditioned ship, escaping from the island's uncomfortable tropical atmosphere and being entertained by 'chick-a-dee', their newly adopted member of the family. There wasn't a cloud in the sky for most of the day.

The temperature was the hottest they had experienced since their arrival, and the humidity was more than Claire could bear.

It was practically impossible to walk on the open deck without any form of protection on their feet. Of the two castaways, the man of the atoll was the one able to cope better with the atmospheric conditions.

After dinner, the generator was turned off, and with that, the air-conditioning ceased to function. The tourists transferred to the lounge on the top deck, eager to find any hit of an evening breeze, but the stillness of the breathless atmosphere was all that welcomed them.

'This is a beautiful place but, this heat is unbearable.' She stood up abruptly, removed her shirt and her shorts. She stood before the doctor in her one-piece swimwear.

'Sorry Paul, but ...'

'Get used to it my girl.' He interrupted with a chuckle. 'Welcome to the tropics.'

'Is this normal?'

'Well, yes.' The doctor studied his patient with a new dimension of fascination.

'Why?'

'It's the tropics. The equator is about, maybe three hundred miles that way' He pointed directly out to sea.

'How do you know it's that way?'

'Um, it's called a compass, up on the bridge. Those mongrels didn't take it. Took everything else but left that. One eight zero degrees, that way.' He reinforced his point. 'Due south!'

'How do you know it's three hundred miles away ... that way?' She pointed quickly curiously.

'Well, I don't, but given that we were about four hundred miles away to the north at our last anchorage and given the strength and direction of the wind during that wild night, I guess we could be that close ... Maybe even closer.'

'So, you're guessing.'

'Well ... Yes, but I ...'

'Actually, you know?' Claire interjected, slightly anxious. 'It really doesn't matter. It could be right on top of us for all I care. All I know is that it's so hot.' She threw her external coverings onto the chair next to Paul and walked out of the lounge into the darkness. The deck was still hot but had cooled sufficiently to be able to walk comfortably on its surface.

Claire looked up, tying her hair up behind the back of her head, leaving her naked shoulders to find any relief possible by the night's humid gift. Her slim, well-shaped body posed well, being washed softly by the lights of the five-star lounge.

'Oh, Paul, look! It's like the stars have been polished tonight, just for us.' A sudden change of attitude took control as she raised her hands and spread them across the expanse.

Paul walked out and instantly his visual senses were attacked by a countless mass of glistening twinkles, beckoning him to keep searching for more. He moved behind Claire and nestled into her with his arms around her waist. She rested her head against his chest and drank in the glory on high as a hint of breeze danced around their shoulders, then vanished as quickly as it arrived.

'I want to sleep out here tonight. What do you think Paul? I want to fall asleep under all this.' She tilted her head back and looked up at the doctor, then back to the heavens.

'Give me a hand.' His face beamed.

He walked directly into the lounge and began dragging one of the leather lounge chairs towards Claire.

'Come on!'

She saw his intention and came to his aid. A second three-seater lounge chair was pulled out into the open environment of the ships' deck and placed in parallel position to the other piece of furniture.

'Back in a minute.' Paul walked downstairs and returned within minutes with two sheets and four pillows.

'Here you go.' He handed her a sheet and two of the pillows. 'The sheet might come in handy just in case it gets cool later.'

They both took their positions and lay down together on their respective five-star lounge chairs.

'Hey. Mister Langley, do you think we could be married at night, under the stars?'

She whispered.

Paul looked across at his 'bride to be' and nodded.

'It's like God is watching, and so is all of heaven. It's important to have witnesses, don't you think ... and ... we can video it, can't we?' she said, maintaining her gaze heavenward.

The doctor nodded again with a stronger sense of fascination. His desire for her grew stronger as he studied her face.

'The other day you implied that we might be here for a long time. As I said, something tells me ... you're right,' she said, maintaining her gaze at the expanse above her.

Paul watched as a single tear welled up in her left eye and reluctantly travelled down her face, finding her bare shoulder as its final resting place.

'I know I said this before but, I miss my Mom. I didn't call her before I left Australia.

I said I would, but I didn't. I feel so bad,' she whimpered softly.

The doctor squeezed her hand to which she replied with equal pressure. A meteor streaked its silver-green track across the sky, and hand in hand they fell asleep under the witness of celestial brilliance.

CHAPTER FORTY-ONE

The morning's light kissed the liquid horizon as it heralded the days beginning. Paul lay still on their respective couches, wrapped in the sheet collected by the man of the island the previous evening.

A slither of breeze touched the stubbled Australian face, waking him softly. His eyes opened little by little, taking in the reality of the new day. Ignoring the dawn's beauty, Paul turned his head, expecting to be greeted by his love, but disappointment was his only companion. Sitting up, he pushed his fingers through his hair and looked around. The cloudless day offered a cooler beginning as he scanned the small bay set before him. The outer reef presented no resistance to the still, glassy ocean as the only man on the island continued his scan. A distant splash was heard, and his attention was given to its direction. At the other end of the bay, Claire could be seen swimming.

He made his way to her slowly, not thinking much of her situation, only eager to join her in the morning's perfection. As the doctor drew closer, the morning's light caused the bay to sparkle as the sun rose higher in the sky. A spade could be seen up on the edge of the beach standing upright in the sand with something draped over it. He walked to the edge of the water and looked out into the morning's glare. The sun's first rays were now reflecting off the still water of the lagoon. Paul took off his shirt and began to enter the liquid brilliance.

He placed his hand over his eyes, squinting intensely due to the fierce glare, battling to get a fix on Claire's position.

'Good morning. Lovely morning for it,' he yelled out.

A scream, then a laugh was instantly returned to the searching man.

'Paul. Oh my, I didn't see you,' She called out.

'Where are you? The sun's reflection off this water is unbelievable,' he said, now up to his knees in the salty refreshment.

'No, Paul. Don't come in.'

'What?' He stopped immediately sensing her deeper concern. 'Why?'

'Paul, I have nothing on. I took an early walk with the spade and after, decided to … well, you know the rest. I'm so sorry, Paul. I didn't see you … Really, I didn't.'

'Right, um,' he said temporarily stunned.

'Turn your back, buster. I'm coming out,' Claire said with words mixed with mirth and anxiety.

'Yes ma'am.' Paul laughed as he spun around and walked out of the water. 'You certainly know how to live life to the full, lady. I'll give you that, my dear,' he said, shaking his head.

The doctor reached the beach to the sound of his *wife to be* running out of the water.

She ran up behind him, held his shoulders firmly and kissed the back of his neck.

'Good morning,' she whispered, turning his body to face the lagoon. 'No peeking, doctor!' she said, giggling like a little child.

Claire ran to the spade, making regular turns to ensure he was not looking.

Reaching her covering, with speedy dexterity, she slipped herself back into her one-piece swimsuit, taking care not to deposit any sand from her feet to her swimming attire.

'OK. All clear. You can turn around now' the lady of the island said still giggling.

'Ratbag,' Paul whispered as he shook his head, grinning from ear to ear. 'You know, it might have been easier if I got your swimmers for you.'

'Yeah, right.'

Paul read her thoughts.

'Once in the water, I would have turned around,' he said still shaking his head.

'Mm, maybe ... Anyway, wow, that was close,' Claire said, as she clapped some sand off her hands.

'You are a wild child, Claire Chandler.'

She laughed and placed both hands to his face, holding him gently.

'So, what's on the agenda for today, mister?'

'Well, given that you have obviously got your dressing wet ...'

'Sorry ... forgot. It's not that wet just ... maybe damp?' She looked at her doctor with beckoning eyes, inviting him to see her point.

'No problem. I think ... we might take a serious look at those stitches.'

'You mean their coming out today?'

'Yeah, I think you have been tormented enough.'

'Great and what then ... the hanger?'

'Mm, no, thought we might start preparing for a wedding. What do you think?'

She looked directly into Paul's eyes.

'Are you sure?'

'Yes, … are you OK with that?' he said softly.

She thought quickly, then smiled.

'Yes.'

'OK, well that settles it, but first things first … breakfast.'

Claire flicked her hair back into some order.

'We've been here for quite a few days and not even a sign of any rescue.' She looked up at the doctor. 'You're right; you're so right. We'll be here for a long time …'

Paul interrupted her thoughts.

'Hey, they may be still looking for us.'

'Sure …' Claire looked up at the blue sky. 'Just a thought, wouldn't the company that owned that ship be able to see what happened to us via a satellite or something?'

'Well, that's a good point, but we were in a typhoon … you know covered in cloud.

All a satellite can do, is take pictures from above and all it will see is cloud. Does that make sense?'

'Yes … it does.'

'Anyway, let's not dwell on the negatives; let's look at the positives.'

'And they are?' she intensified her focus on the man.

'Breakfast.'

'Hey, now you're talking.' She watched the doctor's smile lead them to a better mindset.

Hand in hand, they made their way to the ship. Climbing over the rails at the back of the vessel, Claire spun around and looked across at the lagoon.

'It's so beautiful here,' she said softly.

'It certainly is,' he concurred as they both drank in the sight set before them.

'I'll go downstairs, get the generator turned on and get breakfast started. You go and do what you have to do. What do you want for breakfast?'

'You know, I really feel like bacon and eggs, orange juice ... and a cup of coffee.'

'OK, I'm on to it. Meet you in the galley.'

'OK. Actually, I might go for a walk. Give me thirty minutes.'

The doctor studied her.

'Everything OK?'

'Yes, all good. I just want to finish my time with God that ...' She stopped.

'That I interrupted.' He smiled.

'Well, yeah, but it was a good interruption,' she said confidently. She reached up and kissed him. 'Is that OK ... thirty minutes?'

'Sure.'

'And then bacon and eggs, orange juice ... and a cup of coffee.' Claire giggled.

'Done!'

Paul moved down into the darkened corridors, started the ships power plant and began his preparations for the requested meal.

Claire walked around the side of the ship and into the dense part of the island's undergrowth. She meandered around the tropical beauty. There growing in the trees were different varieties of orchids, some in full bloom. She wanted to collect them, but they were too high in the branches. *Another job for Paul,* she thought. Her heart pondered on all the events of the past week. This man she had met, this doctor, he had set her life upside-down.

She called out to her Creator from her heart for confirmation.

'Is this right? Is this really your will for us, Lord? What if we got rescued within a month ... what would people think if they found out that we had married ourselves ... so to speak? Are we being deceived by the enemy, enticing us to be sexually active prematurely?

What if we were rescued, and I was pregnant? Oh, Father, give me wisdom I pray. Show me, Lord.'

She stopped her prayer and stood still, taking in her surroundings. A quiet comfort slowly overflowed her soul. The God of Abraham, Isaac and Jacob was with her. She moved around the trees, focused on her fellowship with her Creator. Claire began to softly speak out her thoughts logically, breaking the silence of the new day.

'Now let's put everything into perspective, girl ...' she whispered. 'Our circumstances are ordered by God. Paul is a Christian man with similar theology. He has come from a good background, a good family. I love Paul dearly, and he loves me. This has all happened in a very short time, I know, but ... well, I know that he is God's man for me, and that is that.'

Claire stopped talking. She looked around and took a deep breath, then continued.

'We are marooned on this island together. We haven't engineered this. God allowed this to happen, and because of that, we, in a sense ... the circumstances, are forcing us closer together, and we are getting closer very fast. It won't be long before we ...' Claire looked up through the canopy of the trees and softly cried out to God.

'Oh, Lord, I want to do your will. I want to please you, my Heavenly Father, but my body aches for him. I have never known this in my life before. I don't know how long I can ... before ...' She dropped her gaze to the tropical ground. More peace flooded her soul.

'Paul is right,' she whispered. 'It is time, time to commit before you, Lord. We need each other, as it is written '*it is better to marry than to burn*'. It doesn't matter what people think. It only matters what you think, Lord.' Claire's mind raced with all the facts. 'Lord Jesus, what do you think? What do you really think, Lord?' There was a profound sense of the surreal at play, like a dream, but it wasn't a dream. In fact, for Claire, the whole thing seemed more like a nightmare. A nightmare however, that offered periodic moments of indiscernible peace in the midst of periodic panic. It was, however, the peace that was memorable, not the panic. It was real peace regarding their situation on the island and real peace regarding this marriage. Again, Claire looked up through the canopy of the trees, revealing the blue sky.

'Lord, I stand before you, your maid servant. I accept this situation here on this island.

You have saved us from the enemy, you have kept us through the tempest and, you have put us here in this place. Have Your way, oh Lord, have Your way. You are the potter; I am the clay. Join Paul and me together in your will that You may be glorified. May I be the wife that You have called me to be. May he be the husband who will glorify Your name all his life. I seal this in the mighty name of my Lord Jesus Christ and what He did for us of the cross of Calvary. There's power in the blood. The power of redemption, the power of righteousness, the power of salvation. May we know Your redemptive, righteous, saving power in our marriage until death do us part. Amen.'

She felt good. The single woman of the island continued her early morning adventure with her Creator in that tropical arena. The temperature drop, due to the thick foliage around her, was a welcome relief. Suddenly the foliage cleared, revealing a tiny beach of brilliant fine white sand. It was the place she had found days previously but had approached it from a different direction.

The small body of water was approximately fifty yards long and thirty yards wide.

This picturesque area led to a tiny inlet. Claire walked to the beach and dug her toes into the squeaky white sand.

'I can't believe this place,' Claire said in a normal voice as she turned a three hundred and sixty–degree circle, taking in all that she was seeing. A sudden surge of emotion flowed as tears welled up in her eyes.

'Oh Lord. Look at this place.' All her life, Claire loved the water, and as long as she could remember, she had always wanted her own private beach. Now, it seemed God had given her the desires of her heart, delivering it through strange circumstances.

The slender female walked straight into the warm still saltwater. Claire slowly released her body weight into the water's warm support. She swam casually around the inlet, dutifully keeping her bandaged head dry. Beneath her feet, small yellow fish darted around the white sandy bottom, welcoming her presence.

'Sorry, Paul, but I'm going to be a little late.'

After breakfast, the promised discussion of wedding plans began. It was decided that they would go through the rooms looking for the right clothing. Paul would look for something formal, Claire would match that theme, and the honeymoon had to be somewhere away from the ship.

'Hey, Paul, what about the cave?'

'The cave?'

'Yeah, why not?'

'But there's nothing there, just a big dark hole in the rock'

'Well, why couldn't we prepare it?'

'How?'

'There's plenty of beds here, we could set up a solar lighting system, you know, we would be building our own honeymoon suite. How cool would that be?' Claire said.

'That's a lot of work.'

'So? It's not like our schedule is that busy at the moment.'

'Why can't we set up one of the rooms here on the ship ... you know make it special.'

He laughed softly.

'Really? Don't you think it would be extra special up there in the mountain ... like we'd be in *the cleft of His rock* ... how neat would that be? And besides it might be good to have somewhere away from the sea ... You know in case of a tsunami or storm surge or something. What do you think?'

'Sure, fair enough.' Paul thoughts were certainly for security, but to achieve such an objective would take more than a few days and a lot of hard work.

'So, why don't we start on that today?'

'You really want to be up there?' he asked frowning slightly.

She nodded expectantly.

'You realise that you're asking me to carry everything way up there?'

'It's only halfway up the big rock, and I'd help you.' Her face was irresistible.

'Well, I sure can't do it on my own ... Exit wedding clothes, enter furniture removalist. OK. If that's what you really want ... then ... the sooner we do this the better, I guess,' Paul said already weighing up all the logistical problems he could see with such a project.

'Happy wife, happy life,' Claire said throwing her arms around her reluctant man.

'So, they say,' he whispered throwing caution to the wind. 'This will take some time.'

'Well, maybe that's a good thing. Keep our minds off stuff ... if you know what I mean?'

The doctor got her point immediately. 'Frankly, a cold shower would be easier.' He smiled subtly.

'Oh, come on, doctor.' She looked at him expectantly.

'OK.'

It was decided, and she was happy.

After Paul had removed the stitches from Claire's wound, the pair began choosing the furniture that needed to be carried up to the igneous outcrop that towered over their island home. A bed was chosen, dismantled, and carried up to the lounge in ready for the journey up the hill. A lounge chair with matching single chairs were earmarked for the honeymoon residence in the cave, and by midmorning, a generous selection of furniture had been deposited in the lounge. However, it was decided that a solar lighting system needed to be installed first in order to support functionality regarding the placement of the furniture into this new abode.

Heavy duty twelve-volt solar lanterns were strategically placed around the deck of the *Pacific Fair*. Detaching a select few was easier than expected. Additional connecting cable was found in the storeroom deep within the depths of the ship. Claire carried the lamps in a cardboard box with the cable slung over her shoulder. Its weight proved uncomfortable, and after a small period of time, she found she needed to swap its position to the other side of her body. Paul carried one solar panel. Their initial climb up the slope to the cave's entrance was a shock, and by the time they had reached their destination, Claire's shirt was wet with sweat.

'So, who's idea was this?' she said, lifting her wet shirt off her chest.

'This is going to take a week I would think … maybe more,' Paul advised, enjoying the reality now obvious to the young woman in front of him.

'Really? Joy.' Claire wiped sweat off her brow.

'Not too late to take up my idea of cold showers.' The doctor raised his eyebrows, waiting for her response.

'Let's keep going. Doesn't matter how long it'll take, or how hard it will be … it will be worth it.'

'OK, let's get this stuff in the cave then, and back down we go for more.' He walked straight to the entrance. 'Come on … haven't got all day.'

'You're messing with me, aren't you,' she said.

'Come on, old girl. Into it.' He laughed.

'Now, who's the ratbag?' She screwed her face up at him.

The small team made their way back down to the ship, where they rested for thirty minutes while drinking large amounts of water. Paul then carried another panel up the slope to the ancient bubble in the rock. Later he carried a cardboard box filled with other equipment such as a forty-five-amp controller and a two thousand five hundred-watt inverter.

By the time their day drew to a close, Paul and Claire had detached four of the fifteen solar panels from the ship's upper deck roof and carried them to their new retreat home on the island's high point. They then carried two, two-hundred amp-hour, deep cycle, twelve-volt batteries with great difficulty.

Their bodies felt the effects of the tropical heat sapping them of energy.

Clear skies proved menacing due to the sun's relentless presence. Finally, with panels placed casually on the north side of the volcanic plug and the battery secured inside the cave, Paul began running the power leads from the solar panels to the controller. By the time the connection was in place and the solar lights operational, the best part of the day had passed.

They stood in the centre of the large primary igneous room, looking around at the glassy walls and watching the reflective effects of with the ship's deck lights on the walls. One light favoured the room with ample illumination.

'Hey, could we put the lounge chairs over here and that small dining room table and chairs in the VIP suite? They could go over there.' Claire pointed with new vigour.

Paul nodded. The doctor ran cable for additional lights into the other rooms. The second, much smaller room was blessed with a substantial amount of the glassy substance on the walls. This amplified the effect of the heavy-duty solar lantern.

'Hey, Paul, look how the light reflects in all directions. Have you ever seen anything like this?'

Paul remained silent as he looked around the room.

'I reckon this is the main bedroom. What do you think?'

'Sure. The bed could go here,' he said.

The third cavern was of similar size with equal amounts of the silicon substance covering the rough, pitted walls. The fourth, a much smaller cavern seemed to possess a matt surface, and it was decided that this area would be suitable for the solar controller, the inverter and batteries. It was big enough to facilitate other storage of items should they have to live there in the volcanic mountain in the future. With all the lights established in each room, the two made their way back down to the *Pacific Fair*.

As they moved down the slope, the sight of the turquoise blue water glistening straight ahead was more than Claire could bear.

'Last one in has to cook dinner.' She pushed him off the make-shift track, and with a sudden burst of new energy, she ran toward her prize.

Paul watched her agile shape wind its way around the various storm debris to be the first one to crash fully clothed into the welcome liquid relief.

CHAPTER FORTY-TWO

A week had passed since their initial trip to their proposed honeymoon venue.

A full complement of furniture had been transferred to their new room with a view.

The pair sat in the ship's lounge, staring out into the tropical blackness. A gentle evening breeze flowed across the island, bringing a welcome relief from days of still, humid conditions.

'Six days of torture going up and down that volcanic plug,' he said maintaining his gaze into the night.

'But we did it, and now we have somewhere safe in case of another hurricane or whatever.' Claire reached across and touched her man's arm, softly caressing that sunburnt area of his body.

He met her hand with his. Exhaustion and strained muscles had been his keeper over the past few days. The evening was intoxicating as the salt air stirred his senses.

'There's one small problem, though.'

The doctor slowly turned to his potential critic.

'What?' he asked softly.

'If it storms … and it will, you know if it blows a gale, the rain will come straight in.

Don't you think?'

A pained expression poured over his face.

'I mean all our hard work will be .... you know, washed out so to speak.'

The doctor studied her face searching for any indication of jest, but there was none.

'Paul, do you think we could, sort of, board it up somehow?'

'Board it up?'

'Yeah, the entrance. It's not that high, is it?'

'How do you propose we ... board it up?'

'I don't know; you're the engineer.' She smiled.

'Aircraft engineer. I have a light aircraft engineer's license, and aircraft engineers don't 'board it up. Doctors don't, either.'

'Well maybe you should ... um, try.' She spoke with sudden hesitant expression on her face.

The doctor began to think.

'Oh honey, I know it's probably hard, but the rain will come in, won't it? I mean, it looks so good up there now with the lights and the furniture and your desk and ... our bed. If it blows a gale ... it makes sense, doesn't it?'

'I guess it does.' Paul thoughts were immediately focused on his aching muscles and sunburnt skin. Their week of labour had been more than arduous for the doctor who wasn't conditioned to such activity. Claire, on the other hand, had coped well, and she seemed to be blessed with amazing recovery abilities.

'Any thoughts?' she said, waiting for his response.

'Thoughts?'

'Yeah ... thoughts ... like how are we going to board it up? With a door, or ...'

'A door ...'

'Well, a door would be good.'

'Do you want me to paint it blue?' he said dryly.

'You're making fun!'

'Really, how could you tell?' A slight smirk grew in the corner of his mouth.

'Please, Paul.'

'OK, board it up we will … Somehow and maybe with a door. We do have a few on this ship, I guess.' He laughed softly.

'Have you noticed a trend is developing?'

Claire looked at Paul with deep curiosity.

'A trend? What trend?' she asked.

'This wedding seems to be getting postponed a lot. Will we ever get married?' He raised his hands slightly and laughed a little louder.

'Well, of course we will. We just have to keep the rain out, and then it'll be just right.'

'OK, I'll go down into the storeroom after breakfast tomorrow and see what materials I can find. There are some planks down there. Anyway, let's see what we can do. This will take another week I would think'

'Really, why so long?'

Paul looked at Claire with searching eyes.

'Well, I'm not exactly a handyman, I'm a doctor.'

'And an aircraft engineer.' She rushed to his defence.

'Well, whatever, but … hardly suitable qualifications for such a construction project.'

'You'll be fine, and I'll help again. It'll be fun, you'll see.'

'I can hardly wait.'

'Oh, come on.' Claire pushed his shoulder in a gesture to prove her fun-loving intentions.

'OK, assuming that we can pull this concept of yours off, what else do we have to do?'

The 'groom to be' could see her need to take charge. She was making preparations for their new home, their new life. The more time they spent in the cave, the more momentum Paul could see developing in his fiancé. She was moving away from the place of past atrocities and going to a place of consolation, confirmation, and peace—with him.

'Well, funny you should be asking that … We need formal clothes.' Her face sparkled with creative intention.

The doctor stared in bewilderment at this gift set before him.

'Actually, I could start that tonight. I'll go shopping.'

Paul couldn't offer any comment, wisdom, or even a physical gesture. He simply looked at her trying to understand.

'In fact, we can shop together. Shop to our hearts content. No credit card needed.'

The need to say something began pounding through his soul.

'Shop.'

'Yeah, shop … through all the rooms.' Her excited face paused with more revelation.

'You know, I bet we'll find what we need in the Stafford's VIP room.' She stopped suddenly noting Paul's pained expression.

'What?'

'You want me to board up the entrance dressed in formal clothes … what?'

Claire threw her head back and gave out a raunchy laugh.

'Oh, da. The wedding. It's got to be right. Like … hello, we'll be on camera … got to look our best for the family and friends.'

'Oh, right. Wasn't sure what you were …' She cut him off, returning to her focus.

'I'm so looking forward to this. The wedding, our new home, you and me together, you know.'

He could see the construction at the opening of the cave was needed. A new sense of conviction shot through his veins. This was so important for Claire, for them as husband and wife. This was clarity—their clarity—for body, mind and soul.

'Yeah, me too. It's important. I see it.'

She froze still listening to his words as they cut to her heart.

'Yes,' she whispered in deep belief.

'Come on, let's get our wedding clothes.' He smiled broadly.

Claire shot to her feet, took his hand and pulled him to her.

'You'd look great in a tux.'

'Oh, joy.'

'Come on, you will look great, trust me.'

They made their way down the spiral stare case that lead to the VIP room and began a systematic search through the large walk-in wardrobe filled with the untouched expensive belongings of the stolen executives.

Little was found to satisfy the need of the groom. It seemed Robert Stafford was more down to earth than initially expected. Nothing that resembled formal wear was discovered.

'That settles it, looks like T-shirt and board shorts for me.'

'Oh, fiddle faddle.'

'Fiddle faddle?' He laughed. 'Where did that come from?'

'Well if you must know, my grandmother. Anyway, we'll find something.'

She moved across to the opposite side of the wardrobe where there was much on offer.

Claire spun around as if she was suddenly caught getting dressed.

'You can't be here.'

'What? Why not?'

'It's not good for the groom to see the dress before the day.'

'Oh, what a load of 'Hooo Ha.'

'Hooo Ha? And where did that come from ... Hooo Ha.' She giggled.

'Don't tell me ... your grandmother?'

'Actually no.' He smiled broadly, suddenly enjoying their banter.

Claire focused on him for the joy of getting even.

'My Dad.'

'Your Dad says ... Hooo Ha?'

'Yes, he does,' he humbly confessed.

Paul's sense of humour began to rise to the occasion. He suddenly saw their absurd conversation in this absurd situation. Both parties took the cue and together laughed hard, so much so that they slowly crumbled to the floor in this desperate fit of humour.

Again, the doctor recognised their emotional outbursts were to be expected given all that they had been through, but this point in time even took him by surprise. Tears rolled down their faces as they lay together gathering their composure. As the heaving of chests subsided and emotional temperament regained normality, the two castaways lay still on the floor, concealed in the five-star wardrobe.

'Hey.' She gasped looking straight up at the ceiling.

'Yes?'

'What about the captain's cabin? ... Wouldn't he have some sort of formal wear?'

'Mm, maybe.'

They lay together, still and silent on the floor looking up at the varnished wood-panelled ceiling. Time seemed irrelevant in that quiet space.

'You know, maybe not.' Paul's voice warmed her heart as it resonated around the walk-in wardrobe.

'Excuse me?' She turned her head to him, noticing for the first time, three day's growth on his face.

'Not sure I'm comfortable wearing the captain's clothing. Maybe ... a bit disrespectful ... possibly?'

'Sure. Yeah ... maybe.' She continued her gaze at this man deep in thought. 'You know something?'

He turned to her and looked deeply into her blue eyes.

'You need a shave. When was that last time you shaved?'

'Um, I don't know three, maybe four days ... You think I should shave every day?'

'Mm, well I think kissing that face like that could be a deterrent ... Maybe.'

'Uncomfortable?'

'Possibly ... experience will tell ... I'm sure.'

'Fair enough ... so growing a beard is out of the question?'

'Mm ... absolutely.'

'You do know the math. given time plus a limited number of razors ... equals a beard ... eventually.'

'Well ... God will just have to rescue us at the last razor. Won't He?'

'Right ... I'm sure the most-high God has copied those instructions.'

He reached over to her and rubbed his face against hers. A scream of delight shot from her mouth as she stood up and fled out of the wardrobe.

'OK, behave, mister... off you go. I'll stay here and choose my surprise for you.'

Paul laughed, and sitting up he looked at the dresses directly in front of him.

'I find it interesting that most of the personal belongings of the guests and staff were taken by the pirates, yet the owner's stuff ... wasn't touched,' Paul said looking around at what was surrounding him.

'There's ours as well. They didn't take any of our stuff.' Claire said softly as she pondered his point. 'And for millionaires, they don't have a lot of clothes with them. Maybe belongings were taken.'

'Yeah, maybe and why didn't they steal everything in the storage room, or the diving gear, or the dingy and the outboard motors.'

'And what about the food?' she said now looking at her man totally won over by his perspective.

'It's like they left in a hurry.'

'Maybe they couldn't fit it all in,' she said.

'Doubt it. That was a big boat that cruised into the bay that afternoon.'

'Do you know what I think?' Claire's face was full of excitement.

'What?'

'I think that God stopped them.'

'Do you know what I think?' he asked with a wink. 'I think that you might be right,' he said, focusing back on the dresses in front of him.

'Yep, me too.' She giggled.

'Um, do you think they'll fit?'

'Excuse me?' She stopped her merriment.

'I mean she was a bit bigger than ….' The doctor pointed to the small selection of female attire. Claire butted in before he could finish his sentence.

'Oh, the dresses. Hey mister, you leave that to me.'

'Really? You can do the necessary alterations?'

Claire looked the doctor straight in the eye and winked.

'Sure can.'

'Well, aren't you the surprise package?' He laughed as he got to his feet.

'Hey, you're not the only one with many talents … Off you go.' A mischievous giggle came again from the young woman.

'OK, but I'll give you thirty minutes and the generator has to be turned off. Will give you a yell before I do it.'

'OK, night … hey,' she said watching him walk out of the room.

He turned to face her.

'Love you.'

Paul smile in full appreciation and nodded.

'You too, beautiful,' he replied watching her face beam. 'You know, you're doing well.'

'How so?'

'You're asking to be left alone. A different woman to what I had a week ago.'

She smiled.

CHAPTER FORTY-THREE

There was a knock on the door.

The lady of the house was quick to satisfy its call and opened it.

'Mrs Langley, good evening, I don't know if you remember me, I'm Constable ...'

The officer's introduction was interrupted abruptly.'

'Love? ... you'd better come,' she yelled out. Her whole body turned from the two police officers as though she couldn't face what news was about to be declared.

'Coming.' The pastor raced to the front of the house in aid of his troubled wife.

Facing her husband, she placed her hand over her mouth amidst perplexed emotions.

He reached the front door fixing his gaze on the two once they came into view.

'Hello, we were here a few weeks ago, sir.' The female officer offered a faint smile.

'Hi, of course, yes ... please come in.' His voice was unusually course as he beckoned their presence into the lounge holding his wife close to his side.

'You have news of our son I take it?'

'No sir, I am sorry, I really don't have much to offer there. We are here to advise that the search for the ship that Doctor Langley was on has been called off.'

A gasp of air was sucked uncontrollably into the lungs of Mrs Langley followed by quiet controlled sobs against her husband.

'The ship, the *Pacific Fair*, is now categorised as lost at sea and ...' The officer's words were once again cut off.

'So, he's dead,' her words splashed their way across the official's sentence.

'Love, we don't know that, do we, officer?' the reverend asked, trying to comfort his wife.

'Yes, that's correct. In fact, we have statements from the passengers all saying that your son was below deck in the ship's clinic, getting things ready to receive a patient from another ship ... That actually turned out to be ... pirates. They all say he wasn't harmed. Many heard a conversation between one of the criminals ... we think he was the leader and his partner in crime ... an officer of the *Pacific Fair* ...'

'What?' Mrs Langley questioned with newfound composure.

'Yes, it was an inside job. Anyway, the other passengers heard the two criminals say that they couldn't find your son. Now it seems that orders were given to forget him and leave him on board.'

'Excuse me, didn't you say the last time you were here that the passengers had all been taken away and held for ransom?'

'Ah, yes, my apologies Reverend Langley, the ransom has been paid and the hostages are all back in safe hands.' He stopped, regretting his last few words. The officer watched the faces of the two adults seated in front of him sink into a deeper reality. Quick to retrieve his insensitive description, he took the liberty to keep command of the conversation.

'Doctor Langley was not harmed, and from a number of accounts neither was Claire.'

'Claire?' The man of the house asked, seeking clarity.

'Yes, Claire, you know, Dad, she's the young lady we talked about ... remember Paul rang on the Sunday and spoke of her?' Lynn said walking into the lounge from the study at the back of the house.

'Lynn.' the female officer broke her silence, stood up and shook the daughter's hand.

'Oh yes, of course.' The pastor replied slowly.

'If you remember, Mr Langley, it was thought she might have been shot? ... but now it's believed that she was probably knocked out or fainted. One passenger swears that the bullet from that gun went into the roof directly above her head, and this eyewitness looked down at Claire and saw that she was definitely breathing. So, we believe that Paul and Claire would have been alive on that ship when it was abandoned by the pirates.'

'So, if they were alive ... why stop the search?' Paul's mother asked.

'Oh Mom.' Lynn sat down close to her mother and comforted her.

'Folks, I can't imagine what you must be going through, but the authorities, the owners of the ship ... they have done all they can. If there had been fair weather conditions, there would have been a good chance of finding them in time, but as we stated last time, there was a category five typhoon with two hundred and fifty knot winds due to hit the area the next day. That's extreme ... and there simply is no trace of the ship ... no debris, no oil slicks ... nothing. A spokesman for the company that owned the ship said it was like the hand of God reached down and just took them. I guess that doesn't help, but that's what he said. I thought you should ... know what he said, given you being ...' He stopped abruptly. His professional posture began to deteriorate rapidly as his female partner looked at him incredulously.

Silence followed. All sat quietly in that large lounge room. All overcome by the gravity of the moment. There was a presence felt, unseen, not heard but known by most in that room.

'Paul's alive, and so is Claire.' Lynn spoke softly.

CHAPTER FORTY-FOUR

The ship's deck was ablaze with light. The early evening was unusually cool as a soft breeze whisked around the broken structure of the ship's form. Two cameras were in place and ready to capture the night's celebration.

Paul walked over to the first unit and positioned his finger on the record button.

'You ready?'

He stared at the spiral staircase, waiting to hear her voice.

'Yes, sir, with all my heart ... are you?' she called out from below deck at the base of the staircase.

'Of course.'

'OK, then let's do it.'

'Roger that, recording camera one.' He walked over to the second unit positioned for a head-and-shoulders frame and adjusted the viewfinder screen to assure himself of the desired outcome.

'Hey, what are you doing up there, bucko. Can I start walking up yet?'

'Hang on.'

Paul reached over and pressed record. Facing the camera, he began to speak.

'I can't tell you what the date is, but I'm sure it's Saturday, and we have been marooned on this island for a month now. Given all things considered here and of course, our feelings for each other, Claire and I believe that God would have us marry. With that in mind we wanted to document this occasion for family and friends ... particularly family. So ... wedding day of Paul Langley and Claire ...' His identification for the production was suddenly interrupted.

'Hey dude, um, I'm still here. Any time now would be good.'

'Just a minute.' He focused his thoughts.

'Now where was I ... oh yes, wedding day of Paul and Claire take one ... and only one.' He smiled.

'OK, we're rolling.'

Claire slowly made her way up the mahogany spiral staircase humming the wedding march. As she came into view, Paul was captured by her beauty. She was wearing a blue silk evening dress that fitted her body perfectly. Across the top of the garment, hundreds of sequins glittered in an explosion of splendour as they came in contact with the lights of the lounge. She walked to the doorway of the lounge area that led out to the deck where Paul stood in awe. Holding a small bouquet of orchids collected from the rainforest, she stopped her journey and her humming of the grand old tune. Staring at her husband to be, Claire burst into laughter.

'Oh, Paul!'

Feeling uncomfortable about wearing the captain's clothing, he finally found a white shirt and dinner jacket that belonged to the head waiter. Its oversized dimensions hung awkwardly over his shoulders. There he stood in a pair of his blue jeans, accompanied by clothing that just didn't fit and a pair of nearly new joggers.

'It's not that bad...is it?'

'Well it's not that good, either.' She put her flowers on the floor at the doorway and walked to her man.

'I'm sure you can fix this up in the edit suite.' She said referring to the cameras.

'Here, take that jacket off. Let me look at that shirt.' She quickly undressed Paul of his jacket and placed it on the deck.

'Why have you folded up the sleeves under the jacket?'

'Well the shirt is too big.'

Claire took a close look at the fit.

'Not that big, here, let's roll them down.' In a flash, she had the cuffs adjusted.

'Now that jacket. Let's have another look.' Claire retraced the jacket back along the arms of the doctor and across his shoulders.

'Yes, that looks better.' She pulled the cuffs out to frame the end of the jacket.

'Let's do this jacket up first and see what we have.' She began pulling the jacket back from behind to draw the slack from the front of the garment.

'Yep, that will do it. Stay right where you are. I'll be right back.' She rushed off down below deck leaving Paul in a state of near stupor. Within minutes, Claire was back busily fidgeting behind the groom's apparel.

'Hey, look at that ... they'll never know.'

Paul looked down at the front of his clothing. All seemed in order and looking a tidy fit.

'So, how did you do that?'

'It's called ... paper clips.'

'Really.'

'Yes, four large ones. Don't move too much, they may come apart. Mm, maybe just one more thing.'

Claire walked to the doorway picked up her flowers and separated one orchid from her collection. Making her way back to her lover to be, she directed the stem of the glorious blossom into the eye of the jacket's lapel. After carefully positioning the flower she took two steps back and viewed her handiwork.

'Wow, what a man.' She smiled.

'So, we right to get this show back on the road?'

'Happy now.'

'OK, so back down the stairs you go, and we'll take it from the top.'

'What! I have to do all that again?'

'Yep.'

'OK.... Hey, remember, stay still they're just paper clips holding you together.' She giggled as she raced back down the stairs.

'Joy,' he said softly as he turned to the viewer to check his position on camera.

'OK, whenever you're ready ... you can start walking up.'

The ceremony began again and under the canopy of billions of heavenly lights, the two shared their vows with each other. In closure, the newlyweds bowed their heads in prayer and committed themselves to the God of Abraham, Isaac and Jacob.

After a light dinner, the marooned couple turned off the *Pacific Fair*'s power plant, and left the ship bathed in darkness.

'Will you look at that?' Paul brought the attention to the clear skies above them.

'Looks like you got your wish, Claire ... under the stars ... magnificent.' A meteor scratched its fiery way across the canvas of night lights.

Flashlights in hand, they slowly made their way up the steep track in the cool tropical air to reach their choice of place for their union.

CHAPTER FORTY-FIVE

T welve months had passed since the wedding and not a sign of any rescue was to be seen in the air or on the horizon.

The couple had developed a rigorous routine each day. Every morning, weather permitting, they would go swimming in either of the two lagoons. Paul would take the speargun that he found on the ship in case a catch was on offer. Claire would search for oysters or lobsters, depending on what could be found. She was an excellent swimmer and had no problems diving down among the coral clumps to search for the ocean's treats. The ship's perishable food supply was dwindling slowly, but the dried and canned food were still holding out, mainly due to careful rationing. This was helped some days due to healthy catches of fish which were added to their supplies and placed in the ship's freezer. There were still ample supplies of diesel fuel on board, but Paul had limited the use of the generator to three hours per day which kept the freezer adequately chilled. In addition to fishing and general swimming, after breakfast a few hours were scheduled in their garden.

This was Claire's passion, and she decided to establish it close to the hanger due to the fertile volcanic soil in the area using permaculture principles. All the seeds from the fruit found in the galley's chiller were planted, and much success was found to be theirs that year.

Watermelons, passionfruit and papayas were the first to bear fruit. In addition to these plants, a number of mango trees, guava trees, avocado trees and tropical citrus trees were well established, though not producing fruit. Vegetables, such as tomatoes, egg plants, zucchinis, cucumbers and beans were growing well. Claire had persevered with her aim to propagate some of the macadamia nuts and almonds and finally succeeded in seeing two of each variety growing into healthy trees. As the fresh pineapples on board were consumed, their tops were cut off and planted, and over twenty of the plants were flourishing.

Once again, no fruit was forthcoming at that stage of their stay. Claire transferred the hydroponics garden from the ship to their cave and transplanted some of the plants into pots.

Their rocky home was strategically decorated with tin cans and pots of basil, chillies, coriander, mint, parsley and other herbaceous plants, often spreading a clean, refreshing sent throughout their home in the mountain. At the garden near the hanger, vanilla beans and healthy clumps of ginger were also on display. The young shoots of the banana trees that the Americans planted years prior at the construction of the hanger were transplanted on the other side of the garden where better light was on offer and generous bunches of the fruit were beginning to bear.

Chicken coups were established by renovating two of the smaller buildings at the back of the hanger. One building was dedicated for the layers, where chicken perches were built from wooden crates placed side by side, and makeshift boxes were set on top, filled with grass, offering a comfortable environment for the hens to lay their eggs. The other was dedicated for breeding the birds to ensure future egg supplies and meat.

During this time, Paul would spend familiarizing himself with the B17 bomber in the large World War II hanger. He laid out all the maintenance documents on a makeshift table, and he would spend hours per day studying and gathering practical experience with engines and systems, eager to learn as much as he could about this bizarre find in their tropical isolated home.

After lunch, the afternoon was set aside for sleep and escaping the tropical heat. By mid-afternoon, the island's inhabitants would go to the *Pacific Fair*, start the generator and begin preparing their main meal. It was decided to continue their use of the galley until the gas that fired the burners on the stove had been depleted.

At times, they would remain on the ship for days on end, sometimes weeks, particularly if the weather was cool, but when the hot sultry nights returned, the couple would opt for their rocky hideaway. During their first year as a married couple, more items of furniture, such as kitchen benches, sinks, a small bar refrigerator, bookshelves and, even the captain's office chair were transferred to their mountain retreat. The small kitchen bench had been taken out of the VIP room, and a large bucket was placed under the sink to catch the water after dishes were dealt with. This was considered a milestone in their quest for independent living from the stranded, leaking vessel. The refrigerator, on the other hand, was not as successful, as more batteries were required to power it adequately, and the engineer felt the batteries were better left on the ship for the time being. Every time it rained, the broken ship would leak in various places, causing mould to be found in certain areas of the vessel. This raised growing concern for health reasons, and Paul continued to monitor it closely. It was therefore becoming obvious that their days of living on the ship were numbered.

It was a cool, overcast morning. The wind had picked up overnight, and the deep blue ocean mercilessly smashed large waves against the outer reef that surrounded their island home, bringing unsettled waters to the lagoon. It was decided that swimming would be taken off the agenda for the morning. After a breakfast of fruit, flapjacks and coffee, they journeyed around the island with a full garbage bag of kitchen scraps for their chickens, following the old road that led to Claire's garden of fruit and vegetables. They wore hooded jackets to protect from the morning's unusual cool conditions, and they chatted about further plans for their garden, while walking barefoot along the lost road built in years gone by. That side of the atoll always seemed more protected from the prevailing winds, and this day was no exception. On arrival, a quick inspection of various plants of interest was made.

'Those bananas will be ready in a week or so. Maybe less. What are we going to do with all that fruit?' He laughed, scratching his head.

'Eat them, I guess,' she said innocently.

'What a novel idea … Hey, we could have banana flap-jacks.' He joked.

'Don't laugh. That's a good idea,' she said with a straight face.

'You're not serious.'

'Absolutely, they're great.'

'You've eaten banana flapjacks?'

'Well, they weren't exactly flapjacks. Your countrymen intro-duced me to them. Went up to Townsville in North Queensland with some work associates on business, and we all went out to dinner. I ordered for dessert this dish that was essentially banana flapjacks with pecan-nut ice cream and some sort of sauce … so yummy.'

'So, you think you can make it?' he asked.

'Don't know. Worth a try. How hard could it be?' Claire said displaying her usual confident outlook. 'Mind you, we'd have to find other ways of using them. I could make banana jam.' Claire saw the doctor's face. 'Don't worry; you'll like it, and there's paw-paw jam. That's nice too.'

'Really? Most intriguing, but as for all the bananas? … well, what we don't eat, the chooks will. You need me here?' The man reached around her shoulders, drawing her to himself and kissed her.

'No, not really, just some weeding, feed the chickens, that's about it. Within an hour or so, I'll be done … if that. I'll come over to the hanger then.' Claire looked deeply into her man's eyes.

'OK, … you alright?'

'Yeah, just a bit tired. Didn't sleep well last night.'

'Oh, OK, well, see you shortly at the plane.'

'Is today the day?'

'Yeah, I think it might be, so ... I might need your help, come to think of it. I'll give you a shout.'

'Sure, this won't take long. Hey, can you let out "chick-a-dee"?'

Paul nodded and walked straight to the original chicken coop built so many years ago.

The dilapidated structure had been haphazardly patched up by the newcomers, and the roof had been replaced with sheets of rusty corrugated roofing iron found in the shed where the gas tanker was housed. The small door of the shanty town shelter was flung open.

'Come on, old girl, out you come.'

The bird stood to attention at the sight of the master of the island.

'Hey, where are the kids?'

As if on cue, the well-fed bird shook her feathers, and out from the security of their mother's wings fell six bright yellow chicks.

'Come on, Chick-a-dee, come on girl!' Claire called craning her neck to see the spectacle. At the sound of her mistress's voice, the bird ran slowly to her favourite person with a train of yellow balls of fluff clumsily following in single file, cheeping fiercely at the thought of losing sight of their security. Once at the garden, mother and chicks began scratching in the fertile loam for rich in tasty morsels.

Ever since their arrival Paul had spent a considerable amount of time at 'The Centre', the name Claire had given the hanger. In the primary storeroom, at the back of the complex, Paul found an arsenal of spare parts for the aircraft which included four brand-new engines in their original crates, completely assembled and covered in light grease, and two sets of tyres for the aircraft in surprisingly good condition. In addition to this, boxes of spare parts smeared in thick grease and covered in a wax-paper material, were discovered, leaving each part in mint condition. Such parts included sparkplug leads, pistons, piston rings, valves, connector rods, nuts and bolts of many sizes.

Paul began preparing the aircraft for its big day. For ten months, the doctor had been working on engine number one. Following the maintenance procedure manual meticulously, he had stripped down the engine. Spark plugs were removed and replaced. Each of the cylinders were checked for tell-tale signs of corrosion and none found. After the 'all clear' the engine was rebuilt in readiness for the remounting to its frame. With Claire's help, number-one engine was successfully secured back to its original position, using a mobile chain and pulley mechanism. He also worked on the 'tug', a small gasoline vehicle designed to move the aircraft around when the 'war bird' wasn't powered.

Soon after their arrival,' Paul had spent weeks freeing the huge hanger doors from the effects of years of weather. Finally, the nineteen forties engineering slid open, revealing the regal winged warrior to the awaiting elements. The new light bathed its form with profound brilliance, and the man walked around the lethal legacy of battle in awe of its potential.

He began to cycle the propeller of engine number one, by pushing each blade in an anticlockwise direction, thereby enabling the oil to be pumped through the engine making it ready for the start-up of this redundant technology.

'Hey, want a hand?'

The voice startled him. He turned to her, and with beads of sweat running down his naked chest, he gestured to her to position herself to take the cycling blade that was circling down. She took its cool metal trailing edge and followed his example by pushing it in her man's direction.

'Why are we doing this?' She strained against the blade's resistance.

'We need to lubricate the cylinders.'

'Well I guess that's important ... for whatever the reason.' She laughed, still none the wiser.

'Oh, it's important all right.' He laughed softly enjoying her character.

'Paul, are you really going to try to start this thing?'

'Yep.'

'In here?'

'No, out there' The doctor pointed to the large area of cracked concrete directly in front of the hanger.

'So how do you intend to get it out there? There's no way we can budge this ugly thing.'

'You would be correct, my dear, that's why we have that.' He tilted his head toward the tug.

'Oh ... that little thing's going to drag this hunk of metal out there?'

'Yep.'

'OK,' Claire said making conversation.

He stopped the cycling of the propeller. Wiping sweat off his forehead with the back of his hand, he walked over to the tug and promptly sat on the cold metal seat. With a push of a button, the small tractor like vehicle fired into action. Claire shook her head in disbelief as she watched her man position the unit with squealing caterpillar treads grinding its steal against the hanger's concrete floor. With hanger doors wide open and tug hooked up to the metal towbar, the doctor began to increase the revs of the engine, releasing the clutch slowly, but no movement was on offer from the massive monolith. Claire watched Paul closely as he carefully rode the clutch of the tug. More revs were asserted. A groan was heard. Claire quickly turned toward the direction of the guttural sound. A screeching noise pre-empted a jolt, and then the large tyres of the B17 bomber began to surrender to the demands of the lead vehicle. For the first time in many decades, the aircraft began to move.

Claire stepped back, clearing herself from the engine coming her way and watched as the wing moved over her head.

The moment was surreal, and she acknowledged its demands by bring her hands over her mouth as she watched the winged fortress being escorted out into the open.

Finally, positioned parallel to the hangers opening, Paul switched off the tug. Claire walked over to her man in awe of his accomplishments to date and both stood in front of the aircraft.

'Wow.' Claire held Paul's arm and drew herself into him.

'Looks bigger out here, doesn't it?'

'Yep.'

'You really think that engine is really going to start?'

'Well, we are about to find out.'

He ran into the hanger, leaving Claire standing on her own and then returned wheeling out a small petrol generator.

After it was placed under the nose of the B17 bomber, he again ran back into the hanger only this time to return with a cable.

'OK, now this goes in here.' He connected one end of the cable into the generator and walked over to the aircraft.

'And this goes here.' Paul connected the other end of the cable into the section of the fuselage beneath the pilot in command's position.

'What's that?'

'Power to systems.'

'The engines don't have batteries?'

'They do but the current units are U.S.'

'U S?'

'Unserviceable,' he said.

'Oh, unserviceable,' she echoed his words thoughtfully.

'Could they be brought back to serviceability?'

'Unlikely; I think their stuffed.'

'Well, that's not so encouraging,' Claire said softly.

'No problems. Anyway, I'll put you to work soon. See that fire extinguisher over there in the hanger?' He pointed to a unit he brought from the ship some weeks previously.

'Yes, I can see it.'

'Can you get it for me and stand it behind and to the side of engine number one. Then I'll meet you in the cockpit.'

'Yes, sir.' She saluted the man in command and smartly walked off to do her duty.

Paul hardly noticed her effort of comic relief. He moved straight to the small generator, started it and then made his way to his favourite place in the flight deck ... the left seat. Claire was soon to join him, and together the team began its journey with this antique specimen of aviation.

'OK, beautiful, there should be a checklist over there.' The doctor pointed to an area next to Claire's seat.

She reached down to the spot, where she found a tarnished metal plate with an engraved list that was still very legible in a pouch.

'Is this what you're looking for?' She lifted it up in front of her face and wiggled it slightly.

'Sure is.'

'So, what do you want me to do?'

'Well, for a start, read it out loud ... one line at a time.'

'OK, Right ... Pilot pre-flight.'

'Don't have to worry about that.'

'Why not?'

'Well, we're not flying.'

'Right. Praise the Lord for that.'

Paul smiled as he watched her reaction closely.

'What's next?'

'Form one A.'

'No ... not relevant. What's next?'

'Why not? Isn't that important?'

He took stock of her curiosity.

'Well there's no doubt about the importance of form one A. It tells you all you want to know about the aircraft, like how much fuel it carries, etcetera, but we just want to start the engine so keep reading.'

'OK, controls and seats?'

'Don't worry about that ... next.'

She looked at him, demanding to know what the checklist was asking.

'Man, this is going to take all day at this rate.'

'Well, I'm interested.' She stared at him, smiling with great expectation.

'OK,' he sighed, expressing a slight amount of frustration.

'Seat belts secured and enough distance between the seat and the peddles to allow your feet to have full play with the peddles. You want to be able to get full rudder.'

'OK, well that sounds good. Thank you.'

'You are welcome. Right, read on.'

'That was seats explained, but you didn't explain controls.'

'Claire!'

'Well, you didn't.'

'Right, we make sure that the controls are unlocked. That's elevators, ailerons, rudders, trim tabs'. He moved the column in front of him.

'Actually, they're locked, so let's leave them that way. Now read on, beautiful.'

Her heart warmed. She sat back in her seat and looked at her man.

'Am I really?'

'Excuse me?'

'Beautiful.'

'Um, that's my professional and, might I say, very personal opinion.' Paul smiled, winked and pointed to the checklist, indicating focus was in order.

'We'll see what you think in the months' ahead ...' she said softly. 'OK, handsome, now where was I ...? Oh yes, ... Fuel transfer valves and switch.'

Paul looked at the back of the wall behind them, totally focused on the task at hand, missing her subtle news.

'OK and off.'

'Next, intercoolers.'

'Cold.'

The team began to work well in sequence, one calling the check and the other calling a satisfactory finding. The fuel shut-off switches were switched to open and all the checks up to engine start-up were satisfactorily catered for.

'OK, now for engine start-up checks. So, we start with Fire guard and call CLEAR left and right.' Claire looked at Paul. She was amazed by his focus. In the past twelve months, she'd been constantly made aware of the provision that God had given her with this man and found herself thanking her Creator often for this gift—her husband.

'OK, now normally they would have a guy down there with the fire extinguisher.

He'd be standing behind the engine ready to put out a fire just in case there's a problem.'

'Paul, we don't have a man down there, right?'

'Right.'

'So, who's going to operate that fire extinguisher down there?'

'You.' The pilot smiled.

'No way.'

'Why not?'

'I wouldn't have a clue how to operate that thing, and where would I point it if there's a fire?'

'Well, to simplify things, why not just aim it at the fire? That should do it, but keep it away from the prop. Don't want to damage the prop.'

'Well, yes, that would be a crying shame.' Her sarcasm was noted.

The man in the flying machine studied his female opponent.

'And how do I operate it?

'Easy, did you see the pin?'

'Yes.'

'Release it and pull the trigger. It's that easy.'

'Very well, I'll try.'

Good girl. Hey, are you OK?'

'I'm fine. Let's keep going.' Her words were a little short, and he felt odd as he looked deeply into her eyes.

'OK, next ... Master and ignition switches.' Claire blurted out the next command.

'OK, now we only want engine number one and ... ON.'

'Batteries and inverters.' She looked up from the checklist and watched his fascination with the task at hand.

'Now we start by turning on our alternate inverter and use it to test our batteries, but we don't have a battery so ...'

'So, we use the generator power, right?' She interrupted his thoughts.

'Well done, you! That's right.'

'What can I say ... you need me.' She smiled.

Paul was shaken out of his procedural trance and reached over and squeezed her hand.

'More than you know.'

'Thank you. I needed to hear that,' she said softly.

'OK ... Claire, are you all right? Have I done something wrong?'

The young woman laughed.

'Actually, no, you've done nothing wrong ... In fact, it's not what you've done wrong; it's what you've done right.' She began to giggle.

He looked at her with a puzzled expression.

'It's OK; we'll talk about it later. Let's keep going.'

The checks continued until it was time to start engine number one.

'OK, down you go and get ready with the extinguisher.'

'Hey, I have a question.'

'Shoot.'

'Wouldn't the fuel on this aircraft be past its expiry date?'

'Good question. I have checked it and there's no white scum to be found in the tanks.

That's a sure giveaway that there's something wrong.'

'So, no white scum, so all good?'

'Well not really. I have taken samples from each tank. There was a lot of water because of temperature changes over the years.'

'Water?'

'It's OK. I drained all that out, so we'll see.'

'OK, Captain. I'll go down and get ready for a fire …. Oh man, I can't believe I'm doing this … the things you do for love … there's a song there somewhere.' Claire muttered to herself as she stood up and quickly sat down again.

'Woo wee, that didn't feel right.' She laughed a little.' Might try that again, girl.'

'Claire, are you OK?'

'Yeah, sure, just got up too quickly.'

'All right, just remember keep clear of the prop.'

'Will do my best.' She walked out of the flight deck and across the bomb bay walkway.

'Man, I have the strangest need for chocolate. Wow … glory … give me chocolate, Lord. My Kingdom for some chocolate.'

'Well, there's plenty of that in the galley. Once we get this done, I think we can treat you to some chocolate,' he yelled his offer from his command seat as she moved away from sight.

'No way! That's cooking chocolate, I want some of that Aussie chocolate … Yum.'

Claire yelled her return.

'Well, that's all we have.' The doctor yelled out. Paul turned and watched his wife walk out of the aircraft. He pondered on her strange behaviour, then quickly returned his attention to the task at hand. Turning to the instruments, he looked around the flight deck. A sudden sense of isolation gripped him. Would this monster be their saving grace? Could he fly it? With no training on such an aircraft type, was he being irresponsible to even consider such an endeavour. His thoughts were racing. His need for guidance had never been so intense since their arrival on the island.

He looked up heavenward.

'Oh, Lord, here we go. Keep us protected'

Claire had moved out of the aircraft and around to where the extinguisher was standing behind engine number one.

'OK, bucko, I'm in place.' The voice carried well from behind the engine.

'Right Oh, here goes. ALL CLEAR.'

'You better believe I am.' Claire yelled out curiously.

The doctor placed his right hand on the throttle and moved it all the way to the forward position and back to closed position. Then he pushed the throttles three quarters of an inch forward. With further adjustments to throttles, he was ready to fire up the first engine.

With one hand, he held the starter switch for fifteen seconds and with the other he set the hand primer for number one engine. He pumped it a few times in order to get any air out of the primer lines. Paul unlocked his mixture control and placed his hand on the mixture control for the engine one.

'Ready?' He called out to Claire.

'As ready as I'll ever be, I guess.'

'OK, don't worry if she blows a bit of smoke. That's normal.'

'OK … smoke means normal. Got it.'

The pilot in command engaged the starter button accompanied by the *mescher* switch.

Immediately the propeller began to turn with a whine, accompanied by a series of metallic clicking sounds, indicating a functional engine turning over. The doctor continued to prime the engine. A loud spluttering sound was followed by a slight explosion indicating some combustion, but no primary ignition was on offer. Paul persistently maintained his focus.

'Come on, girl, you can do it.'

Another explosion spun the huge propeller, then another explosion, followed by a positive ignition and the 1200 horsepower Wright R-1820 engine spluttered into life. Claire stood speechless at the back of the engine being bathed in white smoke. The smoke cleared quickly and with no fire visible, she edged away from the deafening brute, running back into the flight deck to join her husband.

Climbing around and under the apparatus of the top turret, Claire called out to her husband.

'Oh my goodness, you did it, Paul. I can't believe it! You actually did it.'

He turned to acknowledge her words of affirmation only to find her face about to plant a passionate kiss directly onto his vulnerable lips. His smile was as broad as it could be, and it was more than difficult to return her passion while he was smiling from ear to ear.

Reluctantly, he tore himself away from his only fan to maintain his focus on the power plant, swinging its fury through the air.

'It's actually working. Thank you, Lord.' She stood behind him, and leaning over his right shoulder, she gazed at the miracle performing as engineered before their very eyes.

'Yeah, it's working all right.' His attention was back to the instruments and then out the window at the mighty sight set before him.

'Right. Hang on. The temperature is coming up OK, and pressure is looking good. I'm going to bring the revs up. Let's see how she goes. I'll just give it a little more time to warm up.'

'So, the right running temperature is important even if it's not going to fly?' Claire yelled out over the explosive noise of the engine.

'Critically important.' He satisfied her quickly as he watched the temperature and pressure gauges closely. After a little more scanning of his instruments, he was ready.

'OK, the temp is good. Here we go.'

With that, checking that breaks we secured and locked, he gradually moved the throttle for number one forward and the engine thundered in obedience, offering a deafening noise as congratulations to the engineer on board. Paul performed a full operational check on the power plant, including ranging the propeller through its full fine and full course parameters. Engine oil temperature and pressure were within acceptable parameters. All systems regarding engine number one were deemed as satisfactory.

'Well, she checks out 'A OK'. Wow! You little beauty,' Paul screamed out over the thunder of engine number one. 'OK, that's good.'

He brought the throttle back to idle and looked straight at his wife. He was overwhelmed. The doctor had painstakingly followed the maintenance procedures over the last ten months, and his obedience to its demands delivered a positive outcome.

'OK, let's shut her down.' The mixtures were adjusted to idol cut and the engine, being starved of fuel, came to a stop. Paul Langley switched off the masters and sat back in the command seat.

'OK, all off and secured up here, now let's check out the engine.' He beckoned his wife to lead the way out to the place of victory.

'With pleasure. I never thought I'd ever get off on an engine starting ... crazy.' She stood up suddenly. As though suspended in mid-air, her face grew pale, and she sat back down again.

'Wow.' Her hand began to slowly rub the top of her forehead.

'Claire. What's the matter? You're not well, are you?'

'Well that's depends on how you want to look at it.'

'And how do you propose I look at it?'

'Let's check this engine and get this monster back in its hanger. I'm fine!' She stood up again, steadied herself, leant over and kissed her man on his forehead.

'See ... I'm fine.'

'We might go down to the clinic later. Might give you a check-up.' The doctor suggested.

'Oh, I'm sure you will,' Claire said to herself softly.

He stood up, turned and followed her close behind, exhilarated by the day's achievements. A quick investigation found all in order, and the two castaways stood directly in front of the nineteen forties technology in the midday tropical heat.

'I know I said this before, but I can't believe I'm getting excited about an old engine. What's happening to me?' She giggled. 'But wow, that was neat.'

'Really?' Paul questioned her softly.

'Yes, it was ... but do you know what was really neat?' She didn't wait for his answer.

'You.'

'Me?'

'Yes, you.' She poked her brown index finger onto his naked chest.

'You did it, Paul. You pulled that grease bucket apart, rebuilt it, and it works perfectly. You actually pulled it off. I am so proud of you.' She hugged him then suddenly pulled away.

'Wow, dude, you need a shower.' She lightly slapped his chest. 'Come on, let's get this brute inside. How about a swim at the falls?'

'Sure.'

With his sense of worth now lifted high for all to see, he turned off the generator, unplugged its lead from the fuselage and returned the equipment to the hanger. Claire maintained her communication with her man, asking many questions about the engine. Paul happily, answered his curious fan with detailed answers as he made his way to the tug, carefully sat on its sun-scorched seat and went to work returning the aircraft to its original position in the hanger. After the metal monster was returned to its original position, the doors were slid closed, securing the bomber from the tropical elements. Once out of the hanger, the husband and wife team returned chickadee and her chickens to their pen, and the human residents began their leisurely journey around the island to the pool at the base of the seasonal waterfall.

Upon their arrival, they stopped and looked around. A distant roll of thunder announced an oncoming disturbance.

CHAPTER FORTY-SIX

S torm's coming.'

The doctor strained his eyes through the canopy of leafy green branches, searching for the thundery direction of the potential tempest.

'Last one in has to swim with his shirt off.' She quickly stepped forward, then, dived fully clothed, submerging her form into the six-foot depth, rinsing her clothing of the day's sweat. Breaking the surface, she flicked her hair back and laughed.

'Oh, that feels so good. Come on slow poke … what's keeping you?' She raised her hands in the air and watched the water run down her arms. 'How odd. It was cool and breezy this morning, and now it's quite still and hot. Odd weather. Don't you think?' There was a splash. She turned to her husband.

The doctor dove into the liquid delight and arrived next to her side in their fresh water reprieve. He surfaced breathless due to the chill of the water. The two frolicked together like children. Suddenly another blast from the heavens heralded the storms closer proximity.

'Better not stay too long. That storm's coming from the east. We always get a good one when it comes from that direction.'

Claire looked towards the sky.

'Oh, while I think of it,' Paul turned to his wife. 'let's continue that conversation we were having back at the plane. You said it depended how I wanted to look at it ... Well, how am I supposed to look at it, whatever *it* is?' He posed his point whilst fingering his hair off his forehead.

'OK.' She reached up and threw her arms around his neck and nestled into him.

'You could look at it this way. The population of the island is about to significantly increase ... well from a percentage perspective.' She stared directly into his eyes and smiled broadly.

'What?'

'Another person is going to be joining us here on the island.'

He looked at Claire with a perplexed expression.

'What? Really, and how do you figure that?'

'Oh, I just have this feeling deep inside,' she said smiling as she patted her stomach.

He stared at his wife.

'Oh dah! You are going to be a Daddy, dude.'

Paul froze, maintaining his focus into the face of the most important person in his life.

He stood speechless.

Claire moved her nodding face close to his, confirming his disbelief. Her beaming personality overpowered him.

'You're pregnant?'

'Um ... yes, that about sums it up.'

'How did that happen?'

'Well, if you don't know that, then my respect for your professional status medically has just taken a serious blow.'

The stark reality of her news pieced his heart and fear felled his mindset. He had considered the possibility of conception on countless occasions and had taken as many precautions as could be from a natural perspective. He was confident that he had charted her cycle accurately, but there he stood, confounded by the Creator.

'My love, you're not happy about ...' Her delight began to subside as she read his face. The thought of not meeting her joy with his was too much to bear.

'No, no ... I'm just ... gob smacked.'

'Is that good?... I can never tell with you sometimes ... I mean your crazy language ... you Aussies!' A faint smile crept back over her face expecting a favourable return.

'Oh Claire, yes, yes, yes, yes, yes!' He picked her up, and she wrapped her legs around his waist. Acknowledging his heartfelt reaction; she threw her arms around his neck tighter and tucked her face up against his.

'Oh, Paul, I am so happy. I love you so much.'

Suddenly a blinding flash followed instantly by an ear-splitting explosion shook the lovers from their embrace, announcing the arrival of a severe tropical storm. Within seconds torrential rain pounded their secluded home, persecuting the green leafy canopy above them.

Another flash lit up the island as lightening darted around the terrain, webbing its menacing electronic lashes across the sky. With attention to scurrying detail the saturated castaways ran through the dense undergrowth making their way to the broken *Pacific Fair*.

Breaking through the sheltered undergrowth, husband and wife found themselves battling their way through stinging sand being whipped up by the howling wind as they ran to the ship. Finally, on deck, they ran to the lounge and promptly secured its formal décor by closing all the doors and windows.

'Man, this is going to be a bad one.' Paul said as he watched his wife slowly rid herself of her sodden, sandblasted clothing, leaving them in a heap on the floor. The naked castaway then proceeded to walk down the spiral staircase.

'Be careful here ... slippery when wet ... you coming?' she yelled out turning to face him. The wind began to increase its forces against the ship's form, and the doors of the lounge rattled furiously under the control of the elements.

'Sure ... Hey, you're bleeding.'

The lady of the ship turned and looked down to the point in question. On one side of her right leg, tiny red spots began to well up with small drops of blood where the sand had been shot against her exposed skin.

'That explains why it's stinging like crazy,' she said, slightly perplexed.

'Better get down to the clinic. I'll clean it up with an antiseptic wash.'

'Fresh clothes first, mister, and then a shower.' She looked down at her arms and legs. Sand had been deposited all over her. 'Oh man, look at this ... sand.' She began to brush the tiny grains off her arms, then glanced across at her husband. She began to laugh.

'Oh, Paul, look at you. You've got sand all through your hair. In fact, it's everywhere.'

Claire laughed harder as she glanced outside. The wind had quickly settled, and the rain began to thunder down on the roof of the ship's lounge. The two had never seen rain fall so heavily on the island.

The doctor took note and examined himself.

'Oh brother. Can you believe this?' he said shaking his head whilst brushing the sand from his arms.

Claire walked carefully back up the stairs to her man.

'Care to join me for a shower?' Paul said grinning from ear to ear, as he gestured his invitation towards the weather outside, dropping his clothing from his sand blessed form.

'You're on,' she said and promptly ran outside taking the opportunity to slap him on his bear behind as she ran past him.

The task of rinsing was a speedy process due to the heavy downpour and within minutes they were making their way back to shelter.

The door burst open to an explosion of laughter as the couple raced into the ship's lounge.

'Wow. Can you believe this rain? It's so heavy. Oh man, that was so much fun. What do you think, good doctor?' Claire said, excitedly looking down at their feet, as the water pooled its way around the two.

'Um, we have a problem.' The merriment stopped immediately as the man's statement crushed the moment. His wife shot her focus instantly to her husband. 'All our clothes are up in the cave.' He revealed his revelation slowly.

'Oh, my goodness!' Claire said giggling, shacking the rain's remnant from her hands and arms. 'There are towels downstairs,' she continued.

'It'll be rather dark down there,' Paul said, taking stock of their odd situation.

'We could always walk back up to the cave,' Claire said calming her jocularity.

A flash of light and an immediate burst of thunder pealed its way across the island.

'OK. Maybe not. Where's the flashlight?' Claire said, looking around the lounge for a possible answer to their need.

'The closest one would be in our room,' Paul said. They had kept one room ready should they need the air-conditioning to escape the tropical conditions but had not thought to leave clothing in case of an emergency such as this.

'Oh joy,' Claire said, her face filled with fun. 'We'll be right. We'll feel our way.

Our eyes will adjust eventually.'

The plan was settled, and they moved downstairs, leaving their wet clothes on the floor of the lounge. The naked castaways inched their way to their bedroom and finally reached the prize. The door of the room was opened, and the dim tropical light coming through their window gave enough visibility to find the flashlight. Another flash of brilliance followed by a deafening explosion from the heavens frightened Claire as she draped a towel around herself. A violent shudder from the window caused both guests of the island to spin around quickly in the direction of the sealed glass opening.

'Oh man, I hate it when it does that.' She stared outside through the rain-swept window as associated lightning strikes and distant thunder continued to dance its heavenly ritual.

'I'd say that strike was metres away.'

'What would happen if it struck the ship?' she asked now drying still her dripping hair.

'At a guess, it would probably take out all the electrical equipment, or at least make a mess of things.' Paul picked up the flashlight and switched it on, then switched it off.

'Not much charge left in this ... better move quickly before it dies,' he said making his way to the door.

'Hey! Forget something?' Claire threw a towel at him.

'Oops,' he exclaimed, 'See what you're doing to me?'

'Oh, you love it,' she said, her countenance filled with mirth.

Another flash of lightning preceded a thunderous expression in the heavens, shaking the ship.

'You know, sometimes I just feel so much safer in the cave,' she said, walking back to the bathroom. She reached for the spare brush and slowly began to comb her hair whilst deep in thought.

'It's like we're being ... I guess it's like the biblical principle of being hidden in the cleft of the rock. I think I've said that before. But anyway,' she blurted out the thought.

He nodded.

'You might be right.' Paul turned and walked out the door, reflecting on his wife's observations.

With the dim glow from the poorly charged flashlight, they made their way to the engine room and started the generator. Lights burst into life, and the patient's leg was finally attended to, negating any possible infection for the mother to be. A simple dinner of cold left over fish caught the day before and some warmed up leftover rice satisfied the pair.

They stayed in the galley for some time, away from the noise of the tempest outside, drinking iced tea mixed with passion fruit and talking about Claire's news of the new arrival soon to be coming their way.

'Paul?... I've been thinking.' Claire looked up at her husband.

He turned his head slightly to one side and waited for her point to be made.

'Do you think ... um I'd really like ... to. If she's a girl ...' Claire said. She stared at her husband, though her thoughts were miles away, pondering wondrously at the miracle that was happening deep inside her body.

The doctor laughed softly.

'What?' Claire's focus snapped back to her man.

'Nothing, continue.'

'Paul, what?'

'Just a slight technical issue there ... no problem, continue.' His soft smile spread across his face.

'What? ... What technical issue?' she asked softly.

'You said if she's a girl ...'

'And?'

'Well, if the child is a 'she'... then, she's going to be ... a girl.'

'Paul, I'm serious.'

'Of course!'

'I am.' Claire pressed her point sternly.

'Sorry, keep going.' Paul suddenly felt quietly rebuked that he'd given into his odd sense of humour.

'Do you think we could call her ... um ... Jessica? I really ...'

He reached out, held both her hands and kissed them tenderly. She stopped her discourse, captivated by his sudden move.

'Yeah ... sounds good ... Jessica, she was a good kid,' he said reflectively.

Claire threw her arms around her man and held him tight.

'You do know she'll get Jess, don't you? You OK with that?'

'Yeah, I'm OK with that ...' Claire said.

'In fact, actually, I really like that ... Jess.' She kissed her husband deeply.

'And if it's a boy?' he asked breaking away.

'What about ... Jessie?'

'Well ... that needs work.'

'What's wrong with Jessie?'

'Jessie?' He looked at her as though he questioned her point of balance in life.

'Yeah, I like Jessie for a boy's name.'

'He'll turn out to be a criminal.'

'What? ... Why do you say that?' Her face expressed full concern.

'Jessie James? ... You know, the bad guy?'

'What? Oh, come on, that's so bad.'

'Yep, he certainly was.'

'Oh, get out of town,'

'Actually, he did that a lot.'

"What?'

'Jessie James ... he was always getting out of town.' The doctor smiled.

'Paul, stop it ... you know what I mean, dude. Jessie James indeed ... I love Jessie for a boy's name.'

The man of the island squinted at the thought.

'You need to get some sleep, buster!' She reached over and punched him on his shoulder.

Paul released one of his classic heart-filled laughs and proceeded to slap the table.

Claire joined in with his infectious jocularity and after just a few minutes the castaways settled down.

'So, you are OK with Jessie as a boy's name?'

'Um ... no. As I said it needs work, but I'll pray about it.'

'Well that's a 'no' if I ever heard one.' She smiled.

The pair continued to discuss the pregnancy for quite some time before retiring for the evening. They finally made their way to the engine room, turned off the generator and finally walked along the dark hallway leading to the room with the aid of their fully charged flashlight.

'That does it!' Paul broke the silent journey to their room.

'What?'

'It's a girl!'

'Why do you say that?' Claire moved closer to her husband holding his arm waiting for his revelation with great anticipation.

'Well, there's no way I am calling my son Jessie ... He'll be a right ratbag with a name like that ... so it's a girl. Jessica Langley.' He looked at his wife and gave an over-exaggerated grin.

'You're the ratbag dude.' She poked his rigs with her index finger.

Throughout the night the tempest maintained its thunderous attack on the island, whipping up huge seas that pounded the outer reef. By one in the morning, torrential rain and howling wind continued to beat against the stranded vessel with huge waves now thumping their weight of water against the beach and splashing their aftermath across the bow of the beached *Pacific Fair*. Paul woke in fright immediately drawing attention to his sleepless wife.

'Hey, you OK?'

The doctor brought his hands up to his face, rubbing his eyes, and then proceeded to comb his fingers through his untidy hair. He rolled to face Claire.

'Mm, all good. You can't sleep?' he said muttering his reply.

'No, been listening to the wind. Reminds me a little of the sound ... you know, the night we got here.'

'It does. Not sure but, this might be a typhoon.'

'Great,' she said sarcastically. 'There goes our garden. My tomatoes will be toast.'

'Look on the bright side ...'

'Yeah? What's that?'

'We have shelter.'

'True, God has kept us, hasn't He?' Claire rolled over and hugged her man.

There was silence between them as they both listened to the tempest outside. Claire turned her head suddenly towards her husband.

Paul?' she asked urgently.

'Yep.'

'Yesterday. When we left the cave. Did you board it up?'

'Yeah, I did.'

'OK. This will be a test then,' Claire said as she began to reflect on their life there on the island.

The doctor said nothing.

'It's hard living here isn't it?' Claire said softly. 'Are you worried about the baby?'

'Things ... can go wrong. We'll go down to the clinic tomorrow and check things.'

'It'll be fine,' she said. 'The Lord has Jess in His hands.'

'Yeah.' Paul reached over and squeezed her hand. She rolled over to her man. Paul held her close and kissed her on her forehead. The doctor's thoughts were racing.

'So, you seem confident regarding the sex of the child,' he said, eager to distract his wife from his medical concerns.

'I wasn't going to say anything but given that you've asked ... I had a dream.'

'Really ... and?'

'Well, I heard this voice ... it was the Lord.'

'You saw the Lord in a dream?' Claire had her husband's full attention.

'No, I didn't see the Lord in the dream... I heard the Lord ... big difference, dude.'

'Sure, sorry ... keep going.' Paul chuckled under his breath.

'Well anyway, the Lord said ... *daughter look*. I was with him, but couldn't see him but, I saw myself with two children ... one on each side of me ... hand in hand dancing along our beach just out there.' Claire pointed to the beach directly in front of the stranded yacht and, then he said ... do not fear ... I will bless her ... and the little on ... I will bless her with a different measure.' Claire repeated what she heard deep in thought.

"Really ... a different measure?'

'Yes, that's what was said. Do you think I'm strange?'

'Every day.' He laughed.

'I'm serious. Do you?'

'Of course not. What then?'

'Well, I woke up.'

'So, it's twins.' The doctor confessed his fears.

'You know, I don't think so ... one seemed smaller ... younger.'

'Wow, this is all very prophetic ... Mm, time will tell ... I guess,' the doctor confessed, reaching over to hold his wife closer.

The rain belted its presence against the window as though countless demands for attention were being repeated, beckoning a look from the occupants.

'Mm, I love this place.' She snuggled into her man as she listened to the comparative insecurity on display outside, and slowly Claire drifted off to sleep.

The metrological tension increased throughout the early hours of the morning, offering nothing but screaming winds and torrential rain. Paul lay on the bed next to his sleeping wife, keeping watch, whilst listening to the fully developed typhoon mercilessly ravaging their paradise home.

A sudden vicious rattle of their room's balcony window shook him with fright. He sat up quickly, expecting to see their ocean-view vantage point explode open with violent intentions, but blessings prevailed. The reinforced glass along with its structure held true to its design and stood its ground.

Paul looked down at his watch. Its phosphorous markers around the face indicated three in the morning. He heard a faint groan, and then the warm body of Claire rolled over toward her husband. Sweat beaded down the side of her face as she opened her eyes in the stuffy darkness.

'Hey,' her word gurgled its way from her throat as cognitive clarity tried to win the occasion.

'Is that storm still going? What time is it?' She rubbed her eyes desperate for focus.

'It's three a.m., love … think we definitely have a typhoon on our hands.'

No sooner had he offered his understanding to his awaking spouse when a terrifying crash was heard against their window accompanied by a brutal gust of wind that shook the ship. A succession of coconut branches and other assorted debris had smashed against the side of the ship incorporating their five-star balcony.

It seemed within seconds a deeper concussion announced its crescendo of determined destruction as a storm surge commanded the oceans fury to deliver a line of angry waves to pound their force against the hull of the ship. Claire screamed, then, she threw herself around her protector's neck.

'Wow, I think the bridge might be the best place for us tonight.'

'Paul, can we fire up the generator? At least until sunup. I want to be able to see what's going on around us … Please?'

'Sure, generator first, then the bridge.'

With flashlight in hand, he switched it on. A dim glow was its miserable offer.

'Oh man this thing has lost its charge overnight.' He looked at Claire with despondent countenance.

'Where are the others?' she asked.

'Two in the engine room on the chargers, two in the maintenance room on chargers, one in the clinic, one in the galley ... Um I think it might have some charge left and two up in the cave.'

'Looks like the galley wins ... it's the closest. You think this will last?' she gestured to the apparatus in his hand with its yellow light.

'Soon find out.'

'Oh man, why did we have to disconnect the batteries from the system?' Claire asked with slight annoyance.

'Want to safeguard the batteries' longevity. With the generator off, the emergency power would engage. That therefore is powered by the batteries. Not good when the generator is only running for a few hours each day. Pointless to have the emergency lights on practically all the time. Want to keep those batteries ... just in case we are here for a long, long time. They're still connected to the solar panels, therefore keeping their charge but, not to the inverter.' He quickly rose up from the bed.

'Hey, wait for me, dude. There's no way I'm staying here in this tin can on my own.'

'It'll be black down there if this thing dies.'

'Don't care ... Lead on, good doctor. You know what they say?'

'What?'

'Behind every good man, there's an awesome woman.' She suddenly grabbed his ribs and proceeded to tickle him.

'Later, girl.'

'Hey …. You spoil all my fun.' She giggled.

'Do I now?' He turned to face her, patted her abdomen and smiled.

Paul began to laugh softly as he moved out of the room with Claire close behind.

'Well, there are two ways to look at that, bucko.' She said slapping him on his backside.

They both ran down to the galley laughing as the flashlight slowly diminished to a faint glow. Finally, in the blackness of the ship's kitchen with little help from their hand-held technology, they fumbled their way to the last known place of stored brilliance.

'Got it.'

Claire took the dying unit from Paul and held it close to the switch of the replacement.

'Please work, please work, please, please, please,' she fumbled her whisper as though an expected spark was needed to light dry tinder.

With the sound of a 'click', the room lit up as the beam of light danced its circle of effect against everything it came into contact with.

'Yes, thank you, Lord.' Claire burst forth with praise.

The pair moved swiftly down to the engine room listening to occasional pounding against the hull.

'What's that?'

'The ocean?'

'What?'

'I don't know love ... Maybe … storm surge, I'm just guessing. Let's get this generator going … get out of here, up to the bridge, and see what's going on outside. We might be in for a rough day.' Paul's tones were cold and calculated.

With a rattle and a roar of obedience, the generator came to power once again, and the ship was bathed in light ... Inside and outside.

They dragged a mattress from another room to the bridge, threw it down on the bridge's floor, then, suddenly they both stopped. Seized by the sight set before them, they both stared outside.

'Paul?... that's ... not good.'

There was silence.

'Paul?'

'No ... that's not good, love ... not good at all,' he said softly close to her ear as he drew his wife to his side.

Claire turned to him and buried her face into his chest holding on with all her might. She lifted her head and turned back facing the danger for one last look.

There, before their eyes, the external lights of the *Pacific Fair* revealed large waves breaking onto the beach of their lagoon. With the occasional surge overtaking the entire beach, the breaking thunderous mass of water crashed up against the ship's hull and over the ship's deck, causing a curtain of water to be whipped up by the wind, smashing its way across the deck and onto the windows of the bridge.

'Lord ... keep us safe.' Given the roar of the cyclonic winds, his words were not heard by human ears. His words were only heard by an ancient presence.

CHAPTER FORTY-SEVEN

⁓

T he next few days proved to be challenging.

The storm continued to rage for another day and due to the circumstances, we were forced to wear those towels all night until we found some bathroom gowns that the pirates had neglected to take. They had taken practically everything that wasn't fixed to the floor, which included most of the Saturn sheets, pillows, towels, soaps, conditioners and most of the passenger's belongings. Claire rinsed out our clothes that we had worn on arrival the day before, and she hung them up to dry in the lounge.

Up until that time, I had never seen such heavy rain fall from the heavens. Claire and I had gotten into the habit of taking our showers in the rain with the view of not only conserving water (for those first few years, privacy wasn't a problem on our island, of course, given the need for intimate privacy, things had to change as the kids started to grow up), but also from the point of view of sheer convenience.

However, during that week, the heavy rain proved quite uncomfortable if not painful.

The rain drops were the size of golf balls.

We slept in the bridge for the next few days in fear that more storm surges might attack our place of refuge again. I have to confess on one occasion during that first night of the storm, I thought the ship was going to be tipped over by the large waves that crashed against its hull.

The damage to our beach was significant due to tons of fine sand being dumped across the bay's line, leaving a much wider beach area, and I might add that a considerable number of coconut palms on that side of our island were stripped of their fruit and branches.

Frankly it looked like a bomb had been dropped. Our other smaller, more protected bay seemed to escape the pounding experienced in our area. Its beautiful coral also escaped damage, which was a vivid comparison to the coral in our open bay. The Pacific Fair's bow was now practically buried up to its deck in the fine coral grindings.

Since that occasion, more typhoons have struck our place but nothing like that one.

Claire continued to develop with our first child, Jessica. As a doctor, I have seen many pregnant women but none so beautiful as my wife in this state. I am so blessed to have my wife by my side.

Claire experienced very little morning sickness; however, occasionally dinner was out of the question and I was left to my own means. This I didn't mind, as it gave me an opportunity to be a little more creative in the kitchen with a couple of glasses of 'red'. It also offered a chance to reconnect to my passion for the classics, particularly certain operatic pieces. These were found in the form of mp3s on a selection of memory sticks from the captain's cabin. Needless to say, Claire has no interest for the finer things in music but much prefers the more contemporary feel. I find it interesting that Jessica has been given my taste in music, and her voice just begs for classical training, whilst Tiffany is like her mother. I might add Claire can sing well and is quite handy on the guitar as am I, and in those early years we would often be found whiling away rainy days playing guitar and singing. We have three on the ship (why the pirates didn't take them, I have no idea), and the kids love to listen to Claire and I play.

In fact, it was Claire's birthday recently, and our two daughters decided that we should hold a concert as a birthday present for their mother.

Jess and I practiced on the ship while Tiffany practiced an Australian indigenous version of 'I Still Call Australia Home', originally penned by Peter Alan. This was an extended version of a Qantas television commercial. It of course was hardly applicable for Claire, given her American background, but Tiff wanted to sing it for her Mom because Tiff liked it, and that was that. She had discovered this commercial on my laptop. Someone had given me some of their videos of aviation museums that they had shot during their visit to the States, and it was mixed up in the files. I have no idea what it was doing amongst the footage, but there it was, and Tiff discovered it. Another file that took Tiff's fancy was footage of Australian aboriginals doing what our girls call the 'Kangaroo Dance'. They are both fascinated with the kangaroo. The concert was truly wonderful and thrilled Claire's heart beyond expression. Just as the concert was concluding, a small earthquake shook the island.

It lasted for seconds only but was enough to cause us to leave our cave.

There was no noticeable damage anywhere, but the children were a little concerned, and Tiffany asked many questions, which took us well into the evening discussing the subject of geology.

But back to our first year on the island: The rest of the year consisted of maintaining our calling to stay alive and drawing closer to God. In that first year, after an early dinner, our nights consisted of reading, talking and praying together, and sometimes when the moon was full and there was no cloud cover (which is often the case during the winter months here), we would walk the beach hand in hand and often swim in the shallows of our bay. I was amazed at how fast the island recovered from the typhoon's devastation and our vegetable garden bounced back quickly from the storm with bountiful crops. The tomatoes, corn and beans were the stars in the 'veggie' category that year, and the bananas and paw paws topped the charts in the fruit department. This was largely due to the efforts of my wife who without a shadow of a doubt has a gift from God when it comes to the garden.

Every morning I would try to spend at least four hours (sometimes more) in the hanger, working on the B17 bomber (and still do). As Claire's term drew closer, she found it harder to work in the garden and during the last few months, I was given the task of weeding, etc. Needless to say, the garden suffered, and so did the maintenance on the aircraft, short term.

It also became more difficult for Claire to walk up to our mountain home, and we decided to live on the ship during the last three months of Claire's pregnancy.

Appropriate clothing was a big problem for my wife. I might remind the reader that we had packed for a three-week vacation; therefore, we had a limited wardrobe to begin with. It didn't take long before her clothes weren't fitting. After a couple of months, underwear was completely discarded due to its inadequate design for a pregnant woman.

Maternity clothing was a non-entity here on the island, and she was forced to wear a bathrobe. That, however, proved problematic on hot days. When her discomfort was too much, she would walk down to the lagoon and lay in the cool support of water, naked.

During her term, the weather was particularly hot, and she suffered greatly from its effects. At times heat rash was her constant companion. One day, toward the end of her pregnancy, I came home from working on the other side of the island and found her lying upstairs in the lounge on one of the ship's lounge chairs, furiously fanning herself whilst in a state of undress and crying. I might add that we had decided to live on the ship due to its (at that time) functioning conveniences.

I must confess seeing my wife in that state, tipped me over the edge somewhat. From that point, I began to battle fear, knowing that so many things can go wrong, and we had no human support. I felt so frustrated that I couldn't provide what was required. At times, I fought a sense of failure. Those last few months, we kept the generator on at night much longer (sometimes all night), so Claire could sleep due to the ship's air-conditioning system.

It was a stressful time. Will we ever escape from this place? I frankly don't know.

Claire's labour was reasonably short. She claims that it's because of her Sioux Indian ancestry. Apparently, her mother was blessed with the same gift. On the night that our first child came into the world, I remember holding Jess just for a few seconds before laying her on Claire's chest.

Never before had I seen such a thing (and I had delivered a few babies in emergency).

There she was—my daughter—as brown as a berry. She opened her eyes and looked straight at me, took a deep breath and cried. I cried with her.

I looked at Claire, and she started to cry, and there we were, the three of us, just having a merry sob.

Suddenly, there on the spot I began to pray out loud (still crying).

I began giving thanks to God for a healthy child (well she seemed healthy ... I had done no tests, but that cry was a healthy one). I suddenly realised that I couldn't present her to my Mom and Dad ... and panic set in again (something I battle with). I realised in a deeper sense that we were restricted, dangerously separated from many things, one of which was proper medical care. How were we going to feed her, would our food last, would we be able to sustain this castaway lifestyle? The thought continued to pound my panicked heart. I lifted my soul to the Lord in a silent plea, and this is what came into my heart: 'This is just for a time.'

I took great comfort from those words. I looked down at mother and babe. I was totally confounded by the sight set before me. There was my wife feeding Jess. Claire's milk came down immediately, and though a little uncomfortable for mother initially, the child was taking to the first flow with great relish. God was showing me that He had it all under control. I watched my wife and daughter bonding beautifully as tears continued to flow down my face, now with copious measure.

Tiffany came into the world three years later (not planned). She was a breach birth, and this took all my focus. Again, I was hit with the reality that I had no support on the island. Thankfully, I had assisted a paediatrician mate with such an emergency some years prior. Having to perform such a procedure on my own wife and child really tested my metal.

Well, two children later and we are still here. I have been reminding the Lord (respectfully) that it's been a bit of a long time; however, to this date there has been no comment from our Creator. However, over the last ten years, we have seen God provide during this time.

A new addition to the family always brings uncertainties, tensions, etc. Such issues are amplified here on the island. We found ourselves throwing our situation into God's hands every day. He has provided every day. We have never gone hungry, and we have always had clean water to drink.

I am amazed just how adaptable Claire is, and I find her ways speaking to me deeply at times. She is one with the land and it seems (and I know this will sound odd to many) that the land responds to her.

For example, I will plant something ... I do everything that she tells me to do, and the results aren't brilliant, but she plants the same plant type next to my effort, and it sings its praise to God and gives fruit abundantly. She truly has a gift, and she truly is a gift to me.

Now, on the subject of the aircraft, I am pleased to advise, that I have had all four engines, along with the turbo supercharges, serviceable for a number of months. I have been engaging in a number of taxiing trials to gage the functionality of my maintenance on the undercarriage.

In addition to this, I have been doing run ups of the engines, with more than satisfactory results and checking the instruments that I have replaced. These replacements were discovered in a large storage building. I am amazed how well this building has been constructed.

The consequences are that inside this well-preserved structure is well-preserved equipment, such as spare instruments, engine parts, aircraft and vehicle, tools and even some maintenance documents (this stuff is worth a fortune back home and as for the aircraft ... the mind boggles). On the subject of instruments, I haven't dismantled the units to seek their internal integrity for fear of disturbing any of the mechanism. I have little training in this area. The directional gyro (DG), and artificial horizon (AH), now replaced, are performing as expected during taxiing (that's a good start).

I have checked the aircraft's compass .... All seems 'A OK', however I have no way of checking the integrity of these instruments when airborne, especially the compass's accuracy.

I have tried the comparison with the hand-held GPS (this was found in one of the storerooms of the ship. This GPS is a dinky thing, a bit basic). It seems OK, that is the compass, but sometimes I notice unstable variance. The big question is, of course, will this girl fly? And if it does, how long will it stay airborne? The ultimate question is, can I fly it, and of course, more importantly, can I land it?

Claire is less than interested in the possibility of flying in it. Her concern is warranted. You don't just hop in a very old, World War II bomber that's been sitting in a hanger for all these years and fly back home, especially when it's this old and especially when one isn't trained. This is one serious aircraft, but in my heart of hearts I keep looking at the bigger picture, and that is, that God has given this plane (what is this thing doing here for crying out loud?). I am a qualified aircraft engineer (not that experienced, I admit, but I'm all that can be found on this island). I do have some experience regards working on radial engines, and I have a fully equipped workshop (admittedly a little outdated, but nonetheless functional), so maintenance has been possible. The AVGAS is a real concern, but so far, I have only found a few drums with bad fuel (a lot of white scum inside the drum around the edges). Over the past ten years, I have used the aircraft's capacity of fuel (over 2,500 gallons) as a result of my engine run-ups and taxiing practice. I have only refuelled it to the brim a few days ago. If we were to ever fly this beauty and she stayed airborne, we would have a little over eleven hours' endurance (flight time).

When all is said and done, I am amazed that I've been able to achieve so much on this bird. Wow! So much has happened over the last ten years.

Claire and I have been through a lot together, and it all started with the pirates. God has put us through a testing crucible of circumstances. Those ruthless, selfish heartless individuals may have meant it for evil, but with all my heart, I believe that God has meant this for good (somehow). However, I can honestly say that I have forgiven them, but the memory still lingers.

CHAPTER FORTY-EIGHT

P aul sat quietly in his chair, thinking. The memory of past events was drilling into his emotions. Tightness began to seize its grip into his jaw. The pain of all those years resurfaced. A slight tremor developed in his little finger on his right hand.

Soon it spread, and his whole hand along with the pen he was holding began to shake as a tear flowed generously down his face. He recalled that afternoon as clearly as he remembered his last meal, the faces, the confusion, the fear, the hatred, his then hatred— and—there was the blood. As the dawn began to melt away the tropical darkness, his heart turned cold as he relived that day.

'Daddy?'

The familiar sound ripped him from the terror of his past. He swung his head towards the savour of the moment. His daughter, Jessica, stood next to him. She reached out and held his unsteady hand.

'Are you cold?'

'No, baby, just thinking about something sad.'

The little girl climbed up on her father's lap and wrapped her-self around his neck. She remained silent and clung to the only man she has ever known. Her silence was a welcome gift. Words were too cumbersome, too trite. He held the little namesake close to him and cried quietly to himself, thankful that this one was safe, thankful that Claire had been saved from a horrible fate. He had much to be thankful for, and, there holding on to this precious cargo, he poured out his heart to God in thanks.

Finally, Jessica unravelled herself from her father and looked at his face. Ignoring his tears, she placed her hands one on each cheek.

'Dad?'

'Yes, beautiful.'

'Has it stopped raining?'

Paul laughed softly. 'Yes, I believe it has.'

'Can we go swimming this morning?'

'Hey, that sounds like a good idea.' A voice came from behind them. 'Can I come, too?' It was Claire tying her hair back in a bun.

'Yeah,' he said smiling.

'Me too,' a smaller voice accompanied a sleepy face with hair all upset in tangles.

'Hey, of course you can, baby. It's been a few days now since we've had some salt water,' Paul said, looking up at his wife.

'Neat,' Jessica said, hopping off her fathers' lap.

'OK, get your snorkelling gear,' Claire said with great enthusiasm, as she focused on her husband.

The man of the household stood up, walked over to the secured door and with little effort opened it in time to offer his youngest an escape route to freedom. Tiffany raced out in all her natural wonder with snorkelling gear in hand.

'Hey, girls, you wait until we all get there. Don't get in the water, OK?' Claire said.

'OK, but I'm going to be first down there. Come on, Jess,' she said looking at her sister whilst dancing with excitement outside the opening of the cave.

'OK and I'm second, but first I need to pee,' Jessica said running outside as her snorkelling equipment slapped itself against her legs.

'OK, whatever.' Tiffany called out already on the run.

Claire spun around to watch her eldest daughter. Her face was frozen.

'You OK?' Paul said, seeing his wife's face change colour.

'Sure.'

'Claire?'

'Did you hear that?' she said, snapping out of her frozen state of shock.

'What?'

'That's exactly what Jess said on that last day on the ship. Did you hear what our daughter said just then, Paul?'

Paul nodded.

'It was like Jess was here ... like she said it ... the same way,' Claire whispered to her husband then held her hand over her mouth hiding her emotion.

'Yeah, I know what you're saying.' Paul watched his wife. 'That's not the first time I've heard similarities,' Paul softly returned.

'Oh, Paul, will we ever get over it?'

'It's a process, my darling. It's a process,' he said. 'Come on; let's have some fun with the kids.'

The morning greeted them with its brilliance as they all made their way down the haphazard track that meandered its way to the beach, passing through some thick tropical undergrowth. The girls were well ahead of their parents and could be heard yelling with great expectation. This was the early morning ritual where the family would swim together, but more importantly from their father's perspective, it was an opportunity for the group to be cleansed by the saltwater thereby reducing the possibility of infection. Scratches were a common occurrence on the island, and if not treated would often become septic, offering serious consequences. The daily baptism in the ocean would help combat such infections, thereby saving what medication they had left.

'Paul?' Claire looked up to her husband as they nimbly made their way in pursuit of their offspring.

'Yes?'

'You said before you had heard similarities previously ... you know Jess?'

'Yep. A number of times,' he said, managing his snorkelling gear and his spear gun in one hand.

'Why didn't you say something?'

'What was the point? ... and besides, given that you didn't make any comment when I had heard similarities in the past, I just thought it must have been my imagination, perhaps best left unsaid.'

'Well, it's not your imagination. She sounded just like Jess before ... you heard it.

Didn't you? Oh, I miss her... I know that's weird I knew her for only a couple of days, but she was such a beautiful kid. She was like the sister I never had. I always wanted a sister, someone I could share with ... you know, girl stuff and ...' Claire stopped as she looked ahead holding back a potential flood of emotion.

'Well, God's given you a couple of daughters ... you know, to talk girls stuff,' he said lovingly.

'True, and we do, Paul ... already.' Claire looked to him and smiled faintly.

The couple moved down toward the water and edged their way alongside the small hill that overlooked the yacht some fifty feet below. The man looked up at its crest not thirty feet away, where two small white crosses commanded attention.

'I just realised this morning that it's been ten years,' Paul said looking back to his wife.

Claire exhaled deeply. 'Why, Paul ... Why?' She looked straight ahead.

'I was thinking this morning. When God allows one to be found in a ... a crucible of circumstances, we are commanded to give thanks. It's a test ... not easy. In our case, a pretty severe test.'

'A crucible?' She asked, with a slight smile across her face.

'It's a container that can withstand very high temperatures. It's used in all sorts of ways, like it's often used in laboratory processes.'

Really?

'Yes, historically they were usually made from clay, but they can be made from any material, providing that the material can withstand temperatures high enough to melt its contents.'

'OK,' Claire replied doubtfully. 'But how does that apply to ten years ago?' she said curiously.

'Well this morning, I began to think that what we went through was in a way a purging, a melting.'

Claire turned her gazed to him and frowned.

'I mean, think about it. For example, to purify metal, the raw product has to be heated up so as to release its impurities. It gives up the rubbish and that stuff comes to the surface and is discarded. You have to admit after that day we have discovered a whole new set of priorities. We've let go of things that aren't that important. We've grown up a bit, wouldn't you say?'

She nodded her head as they made their way down to the children.

'So therefore, a part of growing involves letting go. So, we are to look for areas where we need to let go, release stuff and from a spiritual perspective: let go of your cares, your pain, forgive your enemies and so on … and put them in God's hands. You were sort of saying that the other night about the kids and being put here, for whatever the reason'. Paul stopped, as he took a deep breath and filled his lungs with the scent of the sea air.

'You know your idea of writing down our history here on this island has been a good one. Rather therapeutic to say the least'.

'Really?' Claire asked, putting her arm around her man. 'Go on, you have my attention.

'What else?' She said, hugging at his side as they continued their trek.

'OK, I asked myself a question.' He paused as though hesitant to be vulnerable.

'What?'

'Well, I asked myself, was I available to trust God, to orchestrate our situation here as He chooses, or am I trying to make things go according to my will?'

'And?' Claire asked.

'I'm not scrubbing up too well on that one.'

'Hey, I love you, and if it's any consolation, I'm not much better,' she said, as she kissed his arm and snuggled into his side as they made their way past the stranded yacht.

'Claire, from my perspective, you are way ahead of me when it comes to the trust thing,' the doctor confessed with a broad smile, 'but I think He's working on me in that department.'

She simply smiled whilst looking down at the track before them.

'I like your point about the melting of the metal concept. That's very good.' She said, looking back up to her man.

'Can't take credit for that one; it's an illustration that my youth leader shared all those years ago.'

Claire was admiring this thought-provoking man.

'A fascinating concept, I never forgot,' he said drifting off in reflection.

'OK ... and?' she asked, prodding his side with her finger, wanting more.

'Oh, sorry, well. The youth leader's father was a metallurgist or something, and the story goes that as a boy, the youth leader was with his father looking over a huge vat of molten metal. The workers were scraping off the slag, or impurities, off the surface, and the young son asked his father what that stuff was that the guys were scraping off. His father told him that it was impurities, and that's why they were melting the substance to make it pure—and to make it even more pure, they had to increase the temperature, and more slag would come to the surface and have to be scraped off.

The young boy then asked his father how did he know when the molten metal was pure, and the father said it was when he looked on the surface of the molten substance and saw his reflection in colour. In many respects, that's love; that's what God is doing with us'.

'My goodness, Paul; that is profound.'

'It certainly spoke to me all those years ago ... never forgot it.'

A splash was heard from the direction of the rocks and then another one, followed by squeals of delight.

'Um, didn't I remember you saying something about waiting for us?' Paul said, with a smile from ear to ear. 'So much for your authority,' he said laughing.

'Oooo, those little toads,' she said, rising to the occasion and ran off in the direction of the disobedience.

Paul watched his beautiful wife sprinting to meet the challenge, leaving him and his sense of humour.

The water was crystal clear, and the two cherubs were duck diving down beneath the surface to the fifteen-foot ocean floor fossicking around for treasure, such as shells and other interesting finds to increase their personal booty.

Claire waited for her daughters to surface.

'Girls! Come over here, please,' Claire announced with soft loving authority.

'What, Mom?' Jessica asked, as she swam immediately to her mother.

'Tiff?'

'Mom! Look what I've found!' Tiffany held up in her hand a perfect Corrie shell that would have only recently lost its owner.

'Tiff, come here please,' Claire said sternly.

The shell suddenly slipped from her hand and submerged quickly to the bottom.

'Oh no,' the youngest exclaimed watching it sink gracefully to the lagoon's floor.

'Forget about the shell. Come here, please.'

'But Mom … I need to …' Tiffany was immediately interrupted.

'Tiff, I said come here'.

The baby of the family made her way to her sister at the edge, holding on to the rocks for support.

'I thought I told you girls to wait for us.' Claire softened her voice.

'Sorry, Mom,' Jessica replied.

Tiffany however just frowned then broke her silence. 'I just couldn't help it. It's so nice, Mom,' she said trying to justify her action.

'Is that so?' Claire replied with a surprised look across her face.

'Ah Ha,' Tiffany said nodding her head, with a bright look assuming victory.

'Well, I am sure that you can enjoy how nice it is by standing on the edge and watching Dad and I have a nice time together in this beautiful water,' Claire commanded, reaching out to both girls to help them disembark from their liquid pleasure.

'But Mom!' Jessica spoke whilst Tiffany offered no opposition.

'Out ... and stand there until we tell you can come in.'

The defeated two made a clumsy effort and slowly climbed out only to stand by to watch their mother disrobe and dive into the tropical splendour.

Paul slowed his pace as he watched the event, laughing heartily under his breath.

After enough composure was mustered, he made his entrance into the tropical fern-blessed area.

'Good morning, my darlings. Lovely day for it,' he said and with that he dove straight into the water fully clothed.

No response was on offer from his children other than a pair of forlorn faces watching the spectacle of their parents enjoying this beautiful morning in paradise.

The two children walked back and forth at the edge of the rocks in hopeful anticipation of a pardon.

'Dad?'

'Yes, Jessica, my love,' Paul said enjoying it all.

'Dad, we're really sorry, aren't we Tiff?'

Tiffany simply agreed by nodding her head ... again.

'Really? And Tiff what about you? Are you really, really sorry?'

Their youngest daughter's face stood firm, then finally shrivelled up in final surrender.

Tears began to flow.

'Daddy? Can I swim with you? ... Please?' she said, with a soft surrendered voice.

Paul turned to his wife quickly, then back to his daughter.

'Well, I think that might be up to your mother to decide.' He turned back to Claire and maintained his back to his children, trying not to laugh.

'Mom?' Jessica asked.

'No!' Claire replied and immediately ducked dived into the world beneath.

'Ooo, nasty,' Paul whispered, hiding a laugh and hoping the girls didn't hear his response.

Claire returned to the surface with Tiffany's lost shell.

'Look what I found.' Their mother burst to the surface with manipulative enthusiasm.

'I found it first.' Tiffany said. Her face, now defeated, looked down at the ground.

Their mother noted Tiffany's posture, then turned to her husband.

'Paul, your clothes. The saltwater?'

'Um, these clothes are stinking a bit, but I think we have a very forlorn daughter up there on the bank. You might have been a little blunt.' He cocked his head in Tiffany's direction.

'Is that so?' she huffed and with that proceeded to dive back down under the water.

The doctor maintained his back to his children whilst slowly losing his battle not to laugh.

Claire's head suddenly surfaced with a rush.

'Well, are we sorry, young lady?' Claire said breathless.

'Yes, Mom ... Sorry.' A humble confession slowly entered the conversation.

'Well, I guess you both have had enough time to see the error of your ways ... OK, in you come.'

A second invitation wasn't required. Hardly had the words left her mouth than the girls were by their side in this liquid miracle. Their father surrendered to his need to laugh and did so with great gusto.

'Paul,' Claire protested.

'You're priceless, girl.'

'Stop it,' she demanded skimming water into his face while a smile graced her face.

An hour went by, some fish were speared and, some oysters were gathered. The sun was well above the horizon, and the heat of its' rays was beginning to concern Paul.

'OK, I think it's time to get back home and have some breakfast.' He said, holding up the catch of the day.

'Can I help you gut them?' Tiffany asked.

Their youngest would often be involved with the task, though more for reasons of curiosity about such things as the functionality of the intestines and would express delight when allowed to do a dissection on the entrails.

'Sure can,' Paul said, throwing the fish up on the rocky edge of the shore.

The adults were first standing on the volcanic rock whilst the children swam slowly to the edge. Paul attempted to shake the water from his weather-worn clothing by stumping on the ground and shaking his arms by his side, then proceeded to be followed closely in turn by his wife. She spun around to check on her offspring.

'Come on, you two, out you get,' Claire said warmly, as she reached out to gather her babies one by one from the morning's bath.

Paul squatted down to gather his equipment along with the morning's breakfast. As he stood up, he threw his arms up in the air to stretch. A small flash caught his eye right on the edge of the horizon. He blinked to clear his eyes from the morning's saltwater and saw it again.

'Claire?'

'Yes?' The mother of the island said, as she gave the children instructions to make their way back to their cave by simply pointing with her hand.

'The horizon. See it?' he said pointing.

'No. What am I looking at?' she asked, searching out to sea.

'Look. See that?' he asked, as the tiny flash broadcast its position in the morning's stillness.

'Yes ... Yes, I did.' she said looking at Paul for opinion.

Concern entered their heart at the same time.

'A boat?' Claire said.

'Maybe.' Paul stood still looking out to sea, hoping for another indication. He saw it again.

'I think so'. Another flash appeared. 'Let's get up to the cave,' he demanded

'I'll grab the binoculars.'

'Oh Paul, what if it's ...?' She stopped and looked for the girls, who by now were some fifty yards ahead of them. Her concern spread fast.

'The kids, Paul.'

'Love, we don't know who it is yet. Let's get back up home, we'll keep out of sight, feed the kids and afterwards I'll check with the binoculars. It will be a while before they get here, if indeed they are coming in this direction.' Paul said keeping watch on his own emotions.

'This might be our rescue,' he said brightening the conversation.

'But what if it's not ... what if it is?' Claire showed the strain already flowing from her face. 'I couldn't bear it. Not the kids', she begged, clinging to her clothes now bundled up against her chest.

'Steady, old girl. Let's get some more information before we jump to any conclusions, and let's not forget, the Lord is with us. ... Besides it might be a tourist ship,' he suggested, trying to keep the perceived panic from taking control.

'And it might be something else,' she said insistently. 'They'll find us ... It's a small island. What then, Paul, what then?' Her voice began to run with panic as she focused on her protector, insisting on an answer.

'Enough!' he raised his voice. Claire realised her downward emotional slide. Paul saw his error.

Jessica and Tiffany spun around to look directly at their father.

'We have ENOUGH fish here for breakfast and dinner. What would you like?

Fish or fruit?' he yelled out, disarming the surprise on the children's face.

'Fish, Daddy, we're hungry.' Jessica called out.

'OK, fish it is. Now, when you get home, don't forget to wash that salt off,' Claire said coming to her senses.

'OK.' The girls turned around and began to run up the hill in quest of a competitive victory.

'Sorry,' Paul said softly.

'Me too.' She flung herself into Paul's arms.

'We'd better move,' he said searching out to sea.

Claire nodded, released herself from her physical security, picked up her tattered clothes and together, husband and wife began their trek back up the path that led to their home. Suddenly Claire stopped, gripped by her nakedness. She quickly began to dress, as exposed vulnerability met her soul for the first time in ten years.

Paul stopped with her. He watched her dress. Reality was crashing in on them. Their life was about to change. Evil was coming, and he knew it.

'Look love, if it is ... them, well ... you're right; they will find us eventually. It's obvious somebody's living here.' Paul took a deep breath.

'What are we going to do?'

He looked at his wife. 'There is always ...'

Paul waited for Claire's reaction, knowing she was immediately on his wavelength.

'Paul, no way ...' Her panic began to build to greater heights.

'What other option do we have?'

'No.'

'If it is them, and we don't know ... but if it is, what else do we have ... Mm? What?'

'Oh, Lord ... not the eagle, Paul. You don't know if ...' Her words were cut off.

'Look, I think we're being a little presumptuous. So, we'll get back home, we'll keep stock of the developments and we'll make intelligent decisions as further clarity is forthcoming,' he said forcefully.

Claire's mind was wandering as they walked on the vague track that lead to their rocky hideout.

They passed the ship, stranded high on the beachhead, and the small weathered white crosses and swiftly made their way back home.

The girls were still playing with the fresh water from the forty-four-gallon drums after their rinse off. The parents quickly joined their children in silence in the morning's ritual of freshwater washing.

Claire walked over to the clearing high up on their vantage point followed by her husband and looked out to sea.

'What are you doing, Mom?' Jessica asked.

'Oh, just having a look at our beautiful view. You guys go inside and get dressed,' she called out.

'Jess, can you bring me the binoculars?' her father asked.

'Why?' Her inquisitive mind took over.

'Oh, just want to have a look around.'

Claire maintained her gaze seaward.

Jessica ran out with the requested equipment.

'Thank you, Jess. Now in you go and get dressed. We'll be in shortly,' he advised, to which she promptly obeyed.

Paul placed the ship's binoculars to his face and studied the horizon.

'Oh my, Paul, they look … like they're coming closer.'

Paul agreed.

'It's them. I know it is. I'm so scared … so scared,' she cried softly throwing herself into her mans' arms. 'I can't go through that again.'

Paul held her as she turned her back to the potential intruders, burying her face into his well-formed chest. With his wife in embrace, he placed the glasses to his face again and fine-tuned the focus with one hand. The powerful magnification revealed the picture. The shape of the ship looked similar to the one on that dreaded day, but it was still too far away to be sure.

'After breakfast, let's pack four backpacks. One with some food and water, I'll carry that ... one with our clothing, you carry that.

Make sure we have those wind jackets packed, all four, and the girl's clothes and whatever you reckon in the other two. They'll have to carry theirs. Oh, and grab our passports, the Aussie dollars, the bundle of US cash and that old hand-held GPS. We should get the two laptops, the video cameras as well. Wack that stuff in our bag.'

'Paul, they hardly work.'

'Sure, but we'll take them anyway. After breakfast, I'll race down to the ship and get the charts.'

Claire looked up at her husband.

'It is them, isn't it?' she said with a whimper.

'Well if it's not, there's another boat mighty similar, which is possible of course,' he said endeavouring to inject a positive note again.

'Let's cook all those fish and pack plenty of fruit, nuts and, plenty of water.'

'OK,' she replied, rising to the occasion. She turned to undertake his wishes, only to spin around to face him.

'How long?' she asked sadly.

'Four hours, maybe five, but I think by the time they anchor, assuming they are headed our way ... Yes, probably five and they'll be ashore,' he estimated.

Paul watched as his wife walked towards their home.

She turned to face him.

'So, we're really going to do it?' she asked.

He nodded, 'If it's really them ... no other option.'

She looked out to sea then back to her man and simply nodded in reply, surrendering her fate to faith in an uncertain option.

Paul's heart was pounding in his chest. The day had arrived.

CHAPTER FORTY-NINE

Adrenalin pounded throughout his system as copious amounts of sweat poured from Paul's body. He sprinted up the hill from the *Pacific Fair*. Time was of the essence.

A small backpack was stuffed with maps and some medical supplies, and he strapped it to his shoulders. The doctor reached the top of the track that led to their igneous dwelling. He had collected everything he could carry from the ship's navigation chart room, which included some very outdated aviation Jefferson approach charts that he found in a top cupboard in that room some years previously as a result of a thorough search of the vessel.

What the charts were doing in that environment, he had no idea, but he was certainly thankful they were there. Time would tell if he had a need to use them. He turned for one last look at the potential intruders, and to his dismay the glassy seas had offered little resistance to the sleek vessel. The clearly identifiable intruders were much closer than expected and making a direct course for the castaway's island.

'Paul?'

The doctor spun around. Claire had the children in toe with bags packed.

'Dad? Are we going camping in the plane again?'

'Yeah, kind of, Tiff.'

'But it's not raining, Dad. That's only when it's wet season we do that.'

'But only sometimes Tiff,' Jessica said correcting her sibling.

'Or sometimes when there's a typhoon coming, Tiff' The eldest daughter offered further detail to close the case.

'Oh yeah, there's no typhoon coming, and there's no rain. It's not raining, Dad.'

Tiffany added.

'Don't worry about it, Tiff.' Claire looked out to sea.

'Well, I'm just telling ya, Mom ... It's not raining.'

'It's OK, peanuts. Today will be a little different,' Paul said softly.

'Will it be exciting, Dad?'

Paul's sense of humour took over, forgetting the danger coming. He focused on his youngest with a laugh.

'I would say the most exciting thing you have ever done in your entire lives blossom.' He looked at both his children with expectant eyes.

'Are we going to start the engines again, Dad?' Jessica asked.

'Yes ma'am.'

'Oh boy! Are you going to rev them up loud today, Daddy?' Tiffany asked with expectation building.

'Like never before, peanuts.' Her father replied with exaggerated joy across his face.

'Paul?' Claire's question was directed at the impending doom now close to their island home.

His tone changed.

'Yeah, I see it.'

'How long?'

'Two hours, three max.'

'Two hours for what, Dad, the exciting thing?'

'Ah ha.' Paul glanced across at his wife.

'I can't wait.' Jessica blurted it out.

'OK, girls, well let's get to the eagle quickly. The sooner we can get there, the sooner we can …'

Tiffany spun around and took over the moment.

'The sooner we can kick them tyres and light them fires. Come, Jess, I'll race ya.'

No sooner had those words left the minor's mouth, the two were racing with their backpacks bouncing haphazardly across their backs.

'Paul, I can't believe you taught her that. It sounds gross.'

'Come on, it's from that movie with Tom Cruise? He and his buddy were …'

'I don't care for it, given the circumstances. I just hope those tyres last the trip down the end of the runway. Forget kicking them … And I don't want to go near the lighting the fires bit …' Claire's emotions were swinging wildly.

Her two greatest fears were accosting her normally solid faith.

'Tiff likes it.'

'Oh, Paul, for goodness sake. Let's go.' With a hint of terror now spreading over her face, Claire was speeding away with reckless abandon before the doctor had time to react.

'Claire, keep it together, girl,' he whispered to himself as he watched his wife running away from him.

The adults moved swiftly down the path to meet their children at the side of the hanger. Paul had taught the two girls never to enter the hanger without their father, and so, obediently yet impatiently, they waited.

'Mom, why is Dad always so slow?' Tiffany went straight to point.

'He's getting old.' Claire stood by waiting for her husband who approached quickly.

On arrival, the island's captain opened the hanger side entrance with a shove due to a buckling of the metal from the last typhoon. The doctor's shirt was wet through with sweat.

He wiped more liquid offerings from his brow to his sleeve as they walked into the Eagle's dwelling place. The bomber stood silent in the dim light.

'Dad, what really is … old?' Tiffany, their curious youngster, begged the question.

'Um, your mother.' Paul said as he walked over to the hanger and unlatched the huge sliding doors and began to push them to the side one last time.

'Dad, is that bad?' Tiffany asked a little concerned as she helped her father introduce the aircraft to the tropical atmosphere.

'Is, what bad, peanuts?' The island's pilot continued the task at hand, hardly appreciating his youngest daughters need for information.

'Being old.'

'I don't know; ask your mother. She seems to have all the answers.'

'I heard that.' Claire made her way to a spot under the front of the aircraft. Directly above was the pilot in command's seat.

'Mom?' Tiffany turned to her mother expecting satisfaction.

'Let's get our gear into the plane, and then I'll explain.' Claire beckoned the children to the front entrance. The small door was already opened, and their mother lifted the girls up into the aircraft's nose and followed quickly.

There, sitting in the bombardier's seat, she explained to the girls this foreign concept of age as she stowed away their belongings. Jessica and Tiffany were captivated.

'So, Grandma and Grandad Langley have wrinkles?' Jessica asked.

'Well, you know, I really don't know, but I suspect so.'

'And the other ones, do they have wrinkles?' Jessica asked referring to Claire's parents.

Silence was next on the agenda. Claire suddenly remembered the last time she saw her parents. Her heart sank. She thought of the grief they must be carrying.

'Mom?'

'Last time I saw them, um, no they didn't, but they probably do now … Maybe little ones. They aren't as old as Grandma and Grandad Langley.' Her words were slow and reflective.

Claire watched intently at her prodigy processing this new dimension in their life.

'Do they hurt?'

'Does what hurt, Jess?'

'Wrinkles.'

Claire smiled.

'No, Jess.'

'What do they look like, Mom?' Tiffany's face filled with curiosity.

'Well, you know when you stay in the water too long?'

'Yes.' Jess replied quickly.

'What happens to your skin?'

'It gets wavy.' Jessica maintained her command of the moment.

'Mine gets squishy,' Tiffany interjected insistently.

'Well, maybe not squishy, but wavy … that effect is sort of what wrinkles look like.'

Claire sat back feeling slightly pleased with herself.

'Can they swim?' Tiffany was deep in thought.

'Excuse me? Can what swim, Tiff? The wrinkles?' Claire smiled, looking straight into her daughter's face.

'No, Grandma and Grandad Langley.' Tiffany exploded into a cackle of laughter followed by the other two females.

'I'm sure they can, Tiff.'

'I'd like to swim with them.' Jessica said softly as though sadly reflecting on a sudden revelation of something missing in her life.

Mom?'

'Yes, Tiff.'

'Why can't we see them? They could live here with us.'

'Well, we'll see, Tiff, we'll see.'

Silence followed as all in the aircraft pondered on the subject. The mother on board was suddenly struck with the reality that she didn't know Paul's family, and Paul didn't know her family. A spin of thoughts attacked her head. She began to reflect on family and friends at home, when a jolt echoed through the metal monster. Paul had hooked the aircraft to the tug, and the B17 flying fortress moved forward with a lunge and a squeal.

The day's bright morning sunlight bathed the machine of war with brilliance as it was towed to the front of the hanger with its fuselage parallel to the building's doors. Its stance offered nothing but menace to any enemy that dared touch this precious cargo on board.

'Claire?' The pilot yelled from a point underneath the nose of the bomber.

'Coming! Stay here, girls. Dad and I have to rotate the props.'

Paul had detached the tug and driven it back into the hanger one last time.

Approaching the first of the three bladed monsters, Paul took hold of one of the blades and pushed it anticlockwise, while his wife caught the next blade rotating down toward her and followed suit. This was done a few times, and then they moved on to the next engine and repeated the procedure. They had performed this ritual many times over the years; however, this time, a profound sense of purpose was now in place.

'Paul, I am so scared. I can't believe it has come to this.'

'We have no option, love,' his breathless reply was matter of fact and hardly reflected any sentiment at all as he continued to lead the way with the aircraft's propellers.

'Paul, I know we have no option. I'm just saying that I'm scared … I mean really scared. How do we know this thing will fly?' she whispered to her man, hoping the children weren't listening, as was often their habit. Claire began to cry softly.

Paul stopped and spun around to face his love.

'Claire. think of it this way … Imagine those cut throats coming over that hill, or around by the old road. Can you see them? I mean, imagine that they are coming. Can you see them?' He pointed sternly to the base of the ancient volcanic plug and then to the vintage coral-based road that meandered its way along the water's edge to the island's only airport.

'Paul, stop it!' she cried.

'No, can you see them?' His voice demanded her obedience.

'Yes!'

'Good, now imagine those mongrels coming this way, and this aircraft isn't here.'

She slowly stopped crying and thought. Paul waited for her composure.

'The facts are, that we have an aircraft. Possibly more than we need ... I don't know, but nonetheless, here it is, a plane, for goodness sake. Now, how do you feel? ... this little beauty is a gift from God.' He patted the blade, turned around and went back to work.

Paul returned to what he was doing. Claire said nothing but simply followed his lead as she wiped her tears on her shirt sleeve.

The props were cycled through a number of times so as to lubricate the cylinders with oil.

At each propeller, Paul prayed for each engine. He prayed for normal engine temperatures and fuel flow. He prayed against icing problems, for the tyres to keep inflated, undercarriage functional during take-off and landing. He prayed for wisdom, good judgment, despite whatever the weather, and he finally prayed that they would be guided home by an angel of God.

Claire returned to the children on board while the doctor did his ground checks by systematically performing his circle tour of the aircraft at a run. He began at the right hand main undercarriage, checking that the tyre was inflated and the rubber hadn't slipped on the rim. He checked the outboard break line on the hub for any signs of oil leakage, as he did also with the other side of the wheel hub.

'An inch and a half of olio cylinder showing, yep, that's what we want.' The pilot whispered to himself breathlessly. The doctor was very fit as a result of years of healthy living; however, the day's rigorous exercise was proving taxing on the muscles in his legs.

He glanced up at the hill, then looked around. Urgency gripped him, and he moved faster.

'Pitot tube all clear.' The pilot reached down and checked the tip of the whip antenna situated directly under the nose of the aircraft.

'Yep that's good ... the radio is an unknown at present, probably won't work, but at least the antenna is there,' he whispered. The doctor reached up and locked the front hatch found to the side and slightly under the nose.

'Locked and secure,' he said softly.

The doctor checked the other wheel then proceeded to check all the engines and the surface integrity of the turbo chargers, looking for cracks in the welded joints, their wheels were free to move and balanced. He looked for chips in the propeller blades.

'OK, old girl, I'll make you a deal, I know you like to fly high, but given your age and the passengers, what's say I keep you under ten thousand and if—when—you get us home, I'll get you looking and feeling like new,' he whispered.

Paul questioned the functionality of the ice boots on the blades. In fact, all the de-icing equipment hadn't been serviced nor the aircraft's pressurization equipment. During his time on the island, the engines, undercarriage and flight controls were his primary focus.

With all this in mind, the pilot had decided to fly visual and below ten thousand feet, if not only for the comfort of the family. He checked that all access doors and inspection doors were secured. The integrity of both the aileron's fabric was checked along with any obstructions that might cause serviceably to cease. The rudder and elevator along with the trim tabs were also checked. The doctor quickly walked around the machine, looking for any anomalies that may hamper performance. All appeared satisfactory to the one in command.

With all ground checks done, the man of the moment ran into the hanger, found the portable petrol generator, wheeled it out, placed it under the fuselage adjacent to the engines aft of the forward entrance door and proceeded to connect the large three-pin plug into the input socket. Once secured, he started the unit. This power plant brought current to the systems of the aircraft, saving the makeshift battery system salvaged from the large spare petrol generator of the *Pacific Fair*. Paul then ran to the rear door and recklessly threw himself through its opening. As he past the aircraft's radio room, he switched the interphone jack-box to 'Command', thereby allowing him to transmit and receive from the pilot's command seat.

He switched all the communication units on, ready to be powered, then swiftly made his way to the flight deck of this grand old war bird of the nineteen forties. Claire sat in the co-pilot's seat, waiting for her husband with their two daughters standing behind each of the pilot's metal seats. The doctor sat down hard in his seat.

'Dad, you are all wet.' Jessica said, frowning slightly. His eldest had never seen her father this tense.

'And smelly,' Tiffany whispered softly to her sister.

'Crap, I forgot to tell you to get the pillows. These seats will be murder for the time we'll be up there'.

The two children looked at each other.

'I'll get them, Dad.' Tiffany made her way down to the nose of the aircraft where a mattress and pillows were found as a result of the family's camping trips during typhoons.

'Paul?'

'What?' His tone seemed threatened as he looked to his wife for clarification.

'Language.' Claire gestured toward their minor passengers.

'Sorry.' He looked around the flight deck to all on board.

Tiffany was back quickly, mission accomplished.

'Thanks, Tiff. Hey, I love you guys.' He scanned his family as though for the last time. The tension began pounding throughout his body. Claire reached over and squeezed his hand.

'And we love you too, hey kids?'

'Yeah.' Jessica was again first to acknowledge.

'Yep, even if you are smelly,' Tiffany tailed in with a broad smile.

'Tiff?' Claire's reaction was quite involuntary.

'Well, I'm just telling him, Mom.'

'Thanks, Tiff ... OK, we have power to the belly. Let's bring this little lady to life.'

Paul nodded toward the checklist.

Claire took the metal document in hand and paused.

'Oh, Lord, keep us safe.' She began to read.

'Before starting, you should have done the pilot's pre-flight, was that completed?'

'Yes.'

'Form 1 A–checked.'

'Forget that.'

'Why?'

'Claire, it's paperwork. Remember? Don't worry about it; what's next?'

'Of course, sorry.'

'Next?' Paul said almost impatiently.

'Controls and seats checked.'

Paul adjusted his seat so he could achieve full movement of the rudder pedals with his feet, then he moved the flight control column, checking the full movement of the ailerons, elevators and rudder.

'Check, hey, Jess, can you go down to the nose and get me some water?'

'Sure, Dad.' His eldest moved swiftly to comply.

'Fuel Transfer Valves and Switch Off.' Claire watched her daughter nimbly navigate her way below to the bombardier's place.

Paul turned behind them to identify the switch.

'Off,' he said turning back around and looked up at the hill and scanned around its base for any sight of potential trouble. Nothing could be seen.

'What's our time?' Claire followed his scan.

'Since we last saw them? Um, that would have been an hour and a half, I guess. It's times like these, you miss a watch. Let's keep going.'

Jessica arrived with the water. Paul swallowed a modest helping and returned to his duties.

'I need to pee.' Their youngest daughter made her declaration to all on board with pride.

'Oh, for crying out loud.' Her father swung around. He was at breaking point.

'Paul!' Claire quickly retrieved the moment.

'OK, baby, go outside next to the plane's back door. Jess, what about you?' Claire's voice was suddenly tender offering a slight amount of judgment upon her husband's attitude.

'I can wait, Mom.'

'No, go now with your sister, sweetheart.'

'OK.' Jessica obediently accompanied her sister.

'You better go with them, just in case … you know.' He looked outside and back to his wife.

Claire instantly saw his point. They had no idea where the intruders were. For all they knew they were harboured in the bay, lured in by the sight of the shipwrecked yacht. She moved quickly, climbing over the co-pilot's seat to catch up with their precious girls. By the time their mother had reached the aircraft's side entrance, the children were attending to their need. Claire stepped out of the metal menace that she had feared for years and looked around.

There was a strange feeling in the air. She listened intently but only the sound of the gasoline generator could be heard. Minutes went by as Claire watched intently for any danger. The girls climbed back into the plane, leaving behind their mark on the concrete.

Tiffany turned to face her mother who was still standing outside the plane.

'Mom, when's it going to get exciting ... can we go for another swim?' Tiffany looked up at her mother, studying her intense face.

'No baby, back in the plane with Dad.' Claire didn't look at her daughter, but continued to look, scanning the area.

'What are you looking at, Mom?' Jessica asked.

'Just looking at the beautiful morning God has given us, sweetheart. In you go with Tiff. I'll be there shortly'.

Claire suddenly realised that a critical piece of equipment was missing, the fire extinguisher. She ran over to the hanger, snatched the unit from one of the makeshift tables that the island's engineer had set up in the aircraft's place of abode and returned to the bomber. Standing it at the side door on the hot deteriorating World War II concrete, she continued to watch. Suddenly the gasoline generator began to run rough. Claire spun to its demand for attention. It finally spluttered, then revved up only to come to a dead stop.

'Paul?' She called from the side of the aircraft.

The man in command heard the problem and came to a swift conclusion.

'No, no, no!' he whispered softly, as his face screamed his panic.

'Paul?' Claire persisted as she walked quickly to the small lifeless unit.

He stood up from his command seat and, with one step, was across to the co-pilots area with his head, out the window.

'It's run dry of fuel. There's a jerry-can can just inside the hanger... to the left.'

'OK. On to it.' She ran following his directions, found the container and promptly filled the generator.

All was strangely still, except for the sound of the contents on the fuel can finding its way into the belly of the antique machine.

Tiffany, now curious, made her way to the opening at the rear of the aircraft to watch the events unfolding. The familiar sound of the family pet was heard at the corner of the hanger.

'Chickadee,' Tiffany whispered, beckoning her feathered friend to her. With that, the old hen pranced to one of her favourite humans, displaying her characteristic walk whenever excited. The youngest on the island scooped her bird up in her arms and promptly settled it in the nose of the bomber on the mattress, placed there for future comfort.

Once this important member of Tiffany's family was made to feel at home, the young carer made her way back by the side of her sister in the cockpit.

Claire filled the generator's tank and was about to restart it when something took her attention. A faint sound was heard. She listened intently. A sudden breeze whistled through the trees making a judgment difficult. There it was again ... a faint whirring sound. Her mind went overtime, processing. *What is that?* She thought. It seemed to be a little louder. Fear struck her soul. She was listening to the sound of an outboard motor of a small boat. She quickly restarted the small unit and raced into their God given escape and straight to her man.

'Hey, sorry about that before.' He looked at Claire and winked.

'They're here!'

Paul saw her face. There was no need asking for any interpretation. He saw it.

'A boat, I heard a boat. At first, I wasn't sure, but yeah, sounds like a dingy is coming ashore. It may be more than one.' She glanced at the metal surface of the checklist in her now, slightly trembling hands and began to read with urgency.

Both girls were sitting on the cramped space behind their parents playing *'Scissors, Paper, Rock'*, a game they always surrendered to when things were downright boring. Their laughter compared vividly to the tension displayed in the command and co-pilot's seat in front.

'OK, where were we, Fuel Transfer Valves ... oh we did that, it's back there ... Ah, here we are, Intercoolers—cold.'

'That's on your side, love.'

Claire looked down to her right.

'Yes, there it is, OK. Check and cold.'

'I have no idea what this all means ... Oh now this is a little hard to read ...' She held it toward the window to take advantage of the better light.' Ah yes, Gyros—uncaged?'

'Yep, uncaged and free.' He turned its knob to prove its freedom. 'And so is the artificial horizon.'

'Fuel shut off switches—opened.'

He placed his four fingers on the four switches.

'Checked and opened.'

'Landing gear switch?'

'Neutral.'

The couple continued their partnership as their children innocently maintained their serious competition. All the pre-start checks were now completed.

'OK, love, let's get this girl fired up.' Paul looked at his wife.

'The Lord's with us. I know it. We're going home, Claire.'

'Master switch on.' Claire called out.

'Masters on ... indeed.' He looked at her and smiled. 'It's all good love.'

Claire ignored his assurance. She continued her focus.

'Battery switches and inverters, ON and checked.'

'Yep, ON and checked.'

'Parking brakes and hydraulic?'

'Yep, they're on and checked.' He leant over to Claire. 'That's on your side, and pressure about eight hundred ... that'll do me.'

'You really understand this, don't you?'

'Hope so.'

'You hope so?'

'Keep reading, Claire.'

'Booster pumps—pressure ON.'

'Carburettor filters—ON?'

'Yep on ... keeps muck out of the engine and checked.'

'Fuel quantity.'

'OK, let's check.' The doctor reached over to the instrument panel. 'Tanks, one, two, three, four, right and left all full.' He said checking each setting at a click of the rotating switch.

'Right, let's start engine number one and hope the thing doesn't catch fire. It should be fine ... I hope.'

'Shouldn't I be there with the fire extinguisher? It's down there.'

'Yep, but no time.'

'Paul?'

The doctor adjusted the throttles.

'OK, love, let's swap places. I need to get on your side to start this, girl.'

'Paul, and what if there's a fire?'

The doctor froze. His panic was spreading. He was taking shortcuts, dangerous shortcuts. He saw her point.

'Keep your eyes peeled, love. Any sight of them and you get back in here, OK?'

Claire nodded her head. 'I love you.'

He winked at his wife and returned to the task at hand. Paul moved to the right where the relevant switches were situated.

'I'll give you thirty seconds, then I'm firing them up.' He called back to his wife as she disappeared across the narrow bomb bay walkway.

Claire raced outside, took the necessary equipment in hand and stood to the side of the number one engine with its nine radial cylinders ready for action. She aimed the fire extinguisher at the cowl flaps poised to discourage any hint of engine fire. Her senses were brought to extreme.

The sound of the outboard motors couldn't be heard over the generator. There was a different noise. It stopped. She listened intently as she scanned the area. There it was again.

She wasn't sure. Were human voices now yelling there in the distance, or was this her panicked imagination?

The pilot placed his finger on the starter switch for fifteen seconds and set the primer for number one engine with his right hand. He pumped it to get any air out of the primer lines. After this, the doctor unlocked the mixture control.

With starter switch on and the mesh switch engaged the B17's twelve hundred horse power Wright/Cyclone R1820 engine began to turn until it burst into life.

This was successfully repeated with the other three. Finally, with all four engines engaged and no fires, Paul checked that the brakes were secure while Claire moved under the fuselage to disengage the portable generator.

With a quick flick of the switch, the generator stopped running. Rather than returning the unit back into the hanger, to save valuable time, the co-pilot wound up the cable and dragged the unit to the side door of the aircraft. With one quick movement, she had the generator and jerry-can in the aircraft, followed by the fire extinguisher. She looked across inside the hanger and saw all the maintenance documents laid out on the makeshift table.

Claire dashed across and scooped them up in her arms.

'Something tells me these are important,' she breathlessly whispered out the words.

The woman of the island spun on her feet, lifted her eyes to her husband. At that point, their eyes met. The pilot gave his wife the thumbs up.

'Good move, Claire,' he said as he watched Claire awkwardly ran back to the aircraft.

She threw them into the back of the aircraft with reckless abandon. Once inside and side door secured, the island's co-pilot moved quickly to the cockpit.

'OK, kids, now the exciting bit is about to begin.' The pilot winked at his children.

'Right, love, let's swap again.'

Paul stepped across to the command seat, and Claire quickly moved back to her place.

'Now, kids, I want you both to stand behind our seats. Tiff, you stand behind mine, and Jess you stand behind Moms'.'

'Why?' Jessica's intuition was coming of age.

'Because, I don't want you to miss a thing. It's about to get to the exciting bit.' He yelled out across the noise of the four thundering engines ready for battle. He reached down and picked up his headset.

Paul turned the Interphone switch to ON.

'Put those on.' He pointed to the war surplus communication apparatus.

'Put the strap around your neck. When you want to talk, squeeze the strap against your neck'.

'Yeah, I know what to do ... Paul?' she called out as she fitted her hearing aids over her ears.

'Can you hear me?' he called.

'Loud and clear.'

'OK, let's get this old girl over to the threshold.'

With an adjustment of the throttles, the obsolete warhorse of the sky moved with a squeal from the undercarriage, and the aircraft was taxied slowly to the threshold of the runway some five hundred yards away from its initial point of start-up, and the engine run-ups were about to be performed.

'OK, let's put our seatbelts on love. How are you doing, girls?' He looked to his wife and then to their children. Jessica and Tiffany both smiled, nodding their heads with faces filled with expectation.

On Eagles Wings taxied its way to the threshold with the man in command constantly scanning its path. Finally, at the initial destination, the pilot lined the bomber up with the centre of the World War II runway.

'Paul?' Claire yelled, forgetting to squeeze the microphone strapped around her neck.

'Right, let's get these run ups done. These engine temps are coming up quickly.' Paul knew the runup checklist well and completely ignored Claire.

'Paul, they're coming!' This time her hand was pressing the neck microphone against her throat.

His head swung directly to his wife.

'Where?'

'On the other side … there.' She pointed. 'I definitely see them. They're coming!'

'Where?' He strained his eyes to see her reference.

'The road.' Claire pointed out of the window, back towards the old road that made its way along the water's edge that led to the hanger.

'Yep. Got them,' he said coldly.

'There's three and they've got guns … Paul it looks like they're firing at us.'

'They're too far away to hit us.'

The man in command maintained his composure, meticulously checking each engine, watching all engine temperatures and pressures at the various engine revolutions.

Propellers were also checked in their 'full fine' and 'full coarse' mode of operation.

'OK, engine run ups done and dusted … all good there. Turbos OK, Props OK and now we lock the Tail wheel.'

Paul looked to his wife. 'Lock tail wheel, love. Time to say goodbye.'

Claire reached down and delivered, locking it, then looked back to the pirates and back to her husband.

'Gyros set and generators on,' he called out, looking around at the weather.

Cumulous clouds were beginning to develop as the day's temperature increased.

'Would be nice to have a weather report,' the doctor said. He studied the clouds a moment longer, then looked over for one last update as to the position of the oncoming threat.

'Lord, into your hands we commit this plane and this family. Keep us safe, Father.'

Claire duplicated her husband's glance at the sky. The blue sky offered a vivid comparison against the white puffs of cloud that day, and the sun beamed a fresh reminder of God's new mercies on offer. She also looked to the pending menace but kept her silence.

'Guide your Eagle home, Lord. Guide your Eagle home.' Paul look to his wife and then to his children.

'Hang on tight, kids. Today you are going to see the clouds from a whole new perspective.'

Tiffany looked to her sister for clarification, but nothing came. Jessica slowly looked across to her mother.

'Hang on, guys.' Claire yelled out her comfort to her two girls.

With that, the pilot gradually increased the throttle with Claire's help, and the mighty fortress took its cue and lunged forward as the brakes were released.

CHAPTER FIFTY

B eads of sweat ran down the back of the man's neck, soaking the collar of his weather-worn Polo shirt. The weapon of war lunged forward to the command of the charge and after years of solitude, freedom was given to the purpose for which it was designed.

More power was slowly introduced until forty-six inches of manifold pressure and twenty-five hundred RPM was indicating on the instruments in the cockpit. At fifty knots, the rudder was active due to adequate airflow now flowing over its surface and given the slight crosswind, throttle for number one engine was increased to aid the rudder to keep directional integrity as it thundered its way down the crushed coral runway ready to take flight.

'Fifty knots. T's and P's looking good,' Paul called out referring to the temperature and pressure gauges, faithfully relaying their message to God's man struggling at the controls.

All passengers on board looked straight ahead as speed increased and so too the associated vibration due to the journey across the weathered runway. The opposite threshold proved an obvious point for concern, as its position beckoned them.

Tiffany reached over and tapped her mother on the shoulder. Claire spun around ready to attend to the need.

'Mom, what's Daddy doing?' the youngest yelled over the roar of the four brutes of war on the wings, declaring their attack on the relative airflow, hungrily producing thrust as their by-product.

Jessica heard her sister's question and eagerly followed her mother's mouth for an answer.

'He's going to fly the airplane, baby. We're going home, Tiff. Hold on tight, girls,' Claire yelled as loud as she could.

The children looked at each other and braced themselves at the news, not understanding what to expect.

'One hundred knots, rotate,' Paul yelled out. The pilot was about to apply a small amount of back pressure on the control column but, the Boeing B17 flying fortress left the ground with little input from the pilot in command. Within what seemed seconds, all sight of the opposite threshold disappeared as the monster of the island thrust its way to greater heights.

Claire sat in the co-pilot's seat stunned. They were airborne, and she was flying again after a ten-year break, but this time with a pilot in command who had never flown such a machine and in an aircraft that probably had never flown. For the first time in her life, she appreciated airline travel.

'Gear up,' he called to Claire, but her focus was certainly not directed toward her husband.

'Claire! Gear up,' he yelled out, needing to reduce the drag caused by the aircrafts undercarriage.

'Sorry.' She reached over, quickly indicating the lever that had to be activated with a questioned look over her face.

'Yes, that's it.' He winked.

'OK, gear up.' Claire activated the system with a trembling hand. The retraction proved satisfactory as the undercarriage obeyed the demands of the hydraulics and moved up into the safety of its housing for the duration of the flight.

She saw his confidence. *He is actually flying this brute*, she thought. She soaked in their situation. They had left the impending danger on *The Wings Of Eagles*. Her heart suddenly thrilled with explosive revelation.

'Paul, we're flying.'

'Yes ma'am,' he forced out the words, fully focused on the task at hand.

'Check right undercarriage. Is it up?' he asked as par for course for the procedure required.

Claire looked back and there under the inboard engine the wheel of the right undercarriage could be seen securely up and locked.

'Yes, it's up. It really worked, Paul. It's up. Oh my goodness.' Her excited eyes flashed from the source of the commotion to her husband.

Paul looked at her strangely then he checked his side.

'And left undercarriage is up. Good. Now the tail wheel to neutral ... and looking good,' he called out even louder as the target was locked.

Paul scanned the instruments.

'T's and P's Looking good. Airspeed, let's see ... one thirty knots ... let's bring her back a bit.' He decreased the power slowly by adjusting the manifold pressure first, then the RPM and to the required climb speed.

'Now, we'll close cowl flaps.'

'What's that?'

'See those things that are sticking up around the engines?' He pointed to the ring of air vents that circled each engine.

Claire acknowledged positively.

'What's their function?' she asked.

'They allow more air to flow around the power plants when it's operating at full power. Keeps it cool. Don't want it to overheat. Now the engines aren't working as hard, we need to insure that they don't get too cool. Not a good thing, and it gets cooler as we get higher.'

'Oh, OK. Mr Langley, I'm impressed.'

'Now I'm closing the cowl flaps. See what happens? Look!' He ignored her complement. 'Took me a bit to get those functional. Works like a dream now,' he continued.

He closed the leavers on all four engines, and Claire watched with fascination.

'Very neat,' the co-pilot confessed.

Tiffany reached over and held her sister's hand as both looked at each other with mouths wide open. Jessica was the first to look out of the window, then look down.

'Tiff, look!' she yelled out whilst pointing to her sister's side window and indicated that Tiffany should do the same. Not wanting to be left out of something new, the youngster followed the instructions to the letter but, once focused, maintained her gaze at the beautiful sight below. A sudden wisp of cloud washed its presence in front of her, blotting out all sight of the tropical blue ocean. Her head shot back in shock as to escape the white intrusion, only to see the whitest cloud appear in front of her very eyes. A broad smile lit up her face as she made eye contact with her sister.

Another tap on her mother's shoulder from Tiffany drew the same attention as before but, this time a broad smile declared the victory.

'Mom, look. That's a cloud. Are we going to see God today?'

'Well, probably not today, baby. Are you OK, Jess?'

Her eldest nodded with an equalled expression of delight.

Paul settled the B17 down to a climb speed of one hundred and thirty-five knots, with a power setting of thirty-five inches of manifold pressure and twenty-three hundred RPM.

They were on a climb to an altitude of nine thousand five hundred feet. After resetting his directional gyro to his compass heading, he set the aircraft on a bank angle of fifteen degrees bringing it around to due south.

The bank angle took Claire by surprise.

'What are you doing?'

'Bringing her on to track, one eight zero degrees.'

'Why?'

'Well, Australia is that way.' He pointed to the spot on the directional gyro as the *Eagle* came around to the required heading. The aircraft settled on its heading, taking its flight path directly over the island. All on board watched as their island home disappeared directly under the nose of the bomber. Claire simply nodded realizing the gravity of what they were doing. They were leaving their happy home of ten years, escaping those murderers again and, embarking on a very uncertain future.

Jessica broke her silence.

'Dad, where are we going?'

Her father looked across at his eldest daughter.

'We are headed for Australia, Jess.'

Jessica said nothing but looked at her father, processing his every word.

'Mom, when are we going to go back home?' Tiffany's question cut into Claire's heart.

'We aren't, Tiff.'

Tiffany went silent.

'But Mom, what about Chickadee?' Jessica interjected.

In the panic to escape their paradise home, Claire had neglected to consider the ramifications of leaving their faithful old hen behind. Paul had called her the *Methuselah chook* due to her age and other than finding it hard to journey up the hill to their cave, the hen continued to show no signs of deteriorating health.

'Chickadee will be fine with all the other chickens on the island.'

'But Mom, she will miss us, and Tiff and I will miss her. She will be looking for us everywhere and won't be able to find us … ever. Where will she sleep at night? She's old and you said we have to look after old people, and we have to look after Chickadee. Can we go back and get her?' Jessica's heart was breaking and, tears began to flow.

'No sweetheart. Chickadee will be fine.' Claire was surprised at her eldest daughter's reaction, particularly when it was Tiffany who had attached herself to the bird. Claire watched her youngest daughter closely.

'I don't want to go to Australia without Chickadee,' Jessica demanded, looking straight at her father.

Tiffany reached over and tugged on Jessica's sleeve.

'Please, Dad, can we go back and get her … please?' Jessica asked.

Paul looked at Claire. He was visibly shaken by the reaction of his daughter.

'Jess, your Mom's right,' Paul said, slightly short, feeling the stress of the flight now being added to. He forced his focus back to the challenge at hand: flying a multi-engine aircraft that he wasn't familiar with.

'Jess?' Tiffany called.

'Compass to DG, one eight zero degrees, Check. T's and P's … check looking good, airspeed one hundred and thirty-five knots, check. Passing through four thousand feet on climb to nine thousand five hundred feet,' he said, with voice slightly quivering with emotion.

Tiffany tugged on Jessica's sleeve again.

'Jess?' This time the eldest took the cue and looked at her sister. Claire watched as Tiffany stepped over to her sister and said something into her ear.

Jessica looked at Tiffany in bewilderment.

'Really?'

Tiffany nodded.

Both girls looked straight ahead. Claire noticed Jessica's sudden calm countenance.

'Hey, Mom, we're cold. Can we go down and get our jackets?' Tiffany yelled over the loud drone of the four engines mounted on the wings on the aircraft. This made perfect sense, and their mother agreed but, continued to think on what had just happened.

'Hey good idea. Can you bring all the coats up?' The man in command looked around and yelled his request as the two girls moved down to the bombardier's section in the nose of the vintage relic.

'Come on, Jess.'

Paul looked across to his wife.

'Well, Tiff comes to the rescue. Would have thought that Tiff would have been the one to have reacted regards the chook, not Jess. There you go.'

'Not buying it.' Claire looked at her husband.

'What?

'You OK if I go downstairs and see what's going on?'

'Sure. Don't be too long, though.'

Claire unlatched her seatbelts, jumped out of the uncomfortable seat and quickly moved down towards the nose of the aircraft. There arm in arm, the two girls stood laughing facing towards the Perspex nose. Claire craned her neck to see what they were laughing at.

'Oh, my goodness,' Claire said to herself brimming with joy.

Sitting on the bombardier's seat, looking directly ahead was Chickadee, with wings spread out and flapping slowly.

'You, silly old bird.' Claire placed her hand over her mouth and laughed. The girls spun around.

Jessica came to her mother.

'Mom, Tiff brought Chickadee. Look she pretending she's flying.'

Hey, Mom, did Chickadee ever fly when she was young?' A curious Tiffany asked.

'No, Tiff, I don't think so.'

'Maybe she thinks she's an aeroplane.' Tiffany burst out laughing, to which the others in the nose of the aircraft joined the merriment.

CHAPTER FIFTY-ONE

Thirty minutes had past, and their objective of an altitude of nine thousand five hundred feet had been achieved, which positioned them above the clouds. At this level smooth flying was theirs for the asking, and all on board were settling into their new reality.

The children were lying down in the nose of the bomber on the old mattress, wrapped in their oversized jackets and two blankets. At their assigned altitude, the girls complained of the cold, and the cockpits heating mechanism proved inadequate for the chilled atmosphere surrounding the aircraft. The family hen was tucked in between the two girls under the blankets fast asleep.

'Let's see if we can get something out of these radios,' Paul said nervously, as he turned on the VHF unit.

'Do they work?' Claire asked.

'A good question.' Paul looked across at his wife and shrugged his shoulders.

'You never worked on them?'

'Pulled out the HF and cleaned the contacts but that's about all I could do ... Same with the VHF radio. Antennas all good but, couldn't check their signal with anyone because ...'

'No one around ... yeah, I get it.' She studied his face again. 'So, these radios could both be .... what do you call it ... U. S.? What does that mean again?' Her face was washed with concern.

Paul nodded.

'Yep that's it: U. S. ... unserviceable. They may work; I have a feeling the VHF unit might be OK.'

'Really? Why so?' Claire asked with faint hope.

'I heard what I thought was a signal one night when we camped in the plane during that big wet a couple of years ago. I'm sure it was a transmission, but the HF radio ... I should have heard something but not even a crackle ... not a good sign.' He shook his head as he scanned the horizon.

Claire's hope vaporized.

'But the VHF radio is the good one to have, right?' Eager to hear some positive news, she watched her partner for his response.

Paul released his gazed from the horizon outside, looked Claire in her blue eyes and shook his head again.

'No, it's the HF we really need now ... the HF reaches a long way, not this one.' He reached over and tapped the face of the unit in question.

'Oh, that's not good,' she sighed.

'But, we'll give it a go now. I've set the desired HF frequency before take-off.' He pointed back to the radio room.

'At this altitude ... you never know. Higher would be better.' He concluded and began broadcasting using the HF radio.

'But better than being on the ground?'

'Yes, indeed.' Paul set his attention to the task and pressed the button to broadcast the aircraft's first message. 'Pan, Pan, Pan, this is Boeing B17 flying fortress, *On Eagles Wings* ...' The pilot in command continued his push for communication with the outside world.

There was no response. He persisted for a short period of time.

A sudden jolt hit their new home, then another, as turbulence harassed their set track.

Paul checked the altimeter. The flying fortress was climbing through ten thousand feet, with a climb rate of five hundred feet per minute.

'Paul?' she questioned.

'It's OK; we're in a thermal. We'll pop out of it soon with another jolt, wait for it. A lot of hot air being forced up, and we're going up with it. Don't want that to happen.'

'Not good?' she asked with deep conviction.

'Well, Ma'am, we'd all fall asleep; the higher you go, the fewer air molecules. Any higher than this, and we'll need oxygen.'

'And we don't have any, right?'

'Correct. The compressor back on the island's airbase is not real flash, and the old tanks are as questionable on this aircraft. You don't want one of those things exploding in flight.'

'So, the oxygen tanks we have on board could explode?' Claire was looking back in the direction of the large bottles.

'No, they're empty. Don't think they had ever been used. Didn't want to try to use them given their age.'

'Mm, OK. You really *do* know your stuff, don't you?'

'Had plenty of time to sit in the hanger and read the aircraft's manuals.'

Paul adjusted the angle of attack of the aircraft, and the climb was arrested. Another jolt was felt. Then, smooth flying was their rite of passage again.

'OK, I'd say we're out of the thermal; she's settling down.'

'Could I be doing the radio calling while you fly?'

'You bet. You're getting into this co-pilot business, hey? You know what to say?'

'Just say the Pan thing and ...'

'Pan three times, aircraft type, name of aircraft, where we're headed and where we've come from. That should do it. Here's the 'lat' and 'long' of the island.' He handed her the coordinates written on a grease-smudged page torn out of a note pad.

'How do you know this? The 'lat' and 'long' thingy?' She asked holding the page up to him.

'GPS. It's not working well but seems to be able to give us our position ... mind you, it takes its time. I am assuming it's reasonably accurate.' He pulled it out of the compartment at the side of his seat and wiggled it in front of his face, grinning from ear to ear.

'OK, thank you, Lord. Anyway, I'll give this talking on the radio a shot, and you fly the plane. Never thought I'd ever be doing this. Amazing, you hate flying and you end up a co-pilot. Something not right about that.' She rolled her eyes.

Claire had just begun broadcasting when a hard tap on her shoulder released her from her newfound responsibility.

'Mom, Dad, there was an earthquake, just like the one we felt when we finished the concert for Mom's birthday. Do you remember that? Well it was just like that, but longer.' Jessica gushed out the message with Tiffany quick behind her with Chickadee tucked awkwardly under her arm.

'No, there were two. Didn't you feel two, Jess? I felt two, and we went up in the air a little bit and bumped back down on the bed ... boom ... and Chickadee went crazy around the front down there. She flapped her wings and went Brark, brark, brark, and she hit the roof, Mom, and she lost some feathers. Look!' Tiffany showed the feather she brought to prove her point, then, twirled it between her fingers. The youngest placed further theatre into her presentation by using one arm to flap, mimicking her feathered friend. She stopped, realizing her actions must have looked funny and began to laugh.

'No, Sweetheart, that was some rough air, not an earthquake.' Claire looked across at Paul, and both adults smiled broadly.

'Get used to the rough air, Tiff, before we get to Darwin, there'll be a lot more of those bumpy bits.' Her father replied.

'Well, I don't like those air-quakes.'

'Not much I can do about that, kiddo'. Her father smiled and turned back to the controls.

'Well, I'm just telling ya, Dad.'

'OK, Baby, thank you. I'll do my best to miss them, but I can't promise though.' His head half turned to his daughter, keeping his eye on the systems.

At that point, a burst of white noise was heard from the radio. Both adults heard it and looked at each other, ignoring the most important people in their lives.

'Did you hear that?'

'Yes.' Paul turned up the receiver's volume and waited. No sooner had he completed his last action, when another sound was transmitted. This time a faint trace of garbled human syllables were heard in their headsets.

Paul immediately went into action and transmitted his call.

'Dad, can you see those air-quakes? Cause it frightens Chickadee. Oh and Mom, Chickadee pooped on the bed.'

Another crackle was heard over the radio, but still a voice wasn't decipherable.

'Mom?' Tiffany said.

'Oh man, this is crap!' The B17's frustrated pilot yelled out, straining his ears, hoping for better results.

'Yep, that's right, Dad. Chickadee jumped up when the air-quake came and plopped right on the bed, next to Jessica. So close,

Dad. Hey, Jess.' Tiffany declared, delighting in the detail, whilst looking to her sister for confirmation.

'Hey, it could be worse; at least the old thing seems to be up and running,' Claire yelled out as she reached over and touched Paul's arm.

'No, Mom, not running, she was flying, whoosh, up she went and hit the ceiling, feathers came down and poop came down, right next to Jess. Do you want to come down to clean it up, Mom?'

'Mom?' Tiffany now insisting on her mother's attention.

Claire, spun around at the sound of her title finally registering.

'Sorry, Tiff?'

'The poop.'

'What poop?' Claire focused on her daughter now confused.

'The poop on the bed.'

'You pooped on the mattress? Oh Tiff! You're not feeling well?'

'No, not me, Mom. It was her.' Tiffany lifted her shoulder that covered the family pet.

Claire not noticing the subtle cue, directed her investigation to her eldest daughter.

'Jess, you're not well. Oh baby, you should have said something'.

'Mom, no ...' Jessica was interrupted.

The radio broke its silence again with more white noise, but this time ... some words could be clearly heard.

'Claire, that was English. I think someone is trying to respond.'

Claire spun around, soaking in the potential communication with the outside world and leaving the needs of her protégée behind her.

'Aircraft responding to the distress call of Boeing B17 *On Eagles Wings*; please say again.' Paul leant over to the section of the instrument in question, making another adjustment to the radio.

'Jess, who is Dad talking to?' Tiffany yelled to her sister.

'That little box there,' she said, pointing to the only obvious answer centrally mounted in the flight deck. Due to the use of headsets, the children couldn't hear the broadcast.

'Boeing B17 *On Eag* ...' A response was heard promptly, but as soon as it commenced, it was drowned by copious amounts of static.

'Yes.' Paul's face lit up as he confirmed with his wife. 'Did you hear that, love. Oh how sweet the sound.'

The children looked at each other.

'He looks like he really likes that little box. See Tiff?' She pointed to her father's excitement as he reached over and gave his wife a high five.

'Aircraft calling ON EAGLES WINGS, please say again, I repeat, PLEASE SAY AGAIN.'

'Say what again, Jess?' Tiffany asked her sister, whilst studying her father's strange behaviour.

'Mom, why is Dad saying PLEASE, SAY, AGAIN to that box, Mom?' Jessica asked mimicking her father's vocal intensity.

Claire spun around again to her daughter.

'Sorry, baby. Now, do you need to change?'

The two girls looked at each other again, maintaining their total bewilderment.

'Oh, Jess, I know this must be embarrassing for you at your age, but you could have told me. I understand. These things happen. Thank you, Tiff, for helping your sister break the news.'

She spun around back to her husband.

'Hey, Paul, got a problem back here. Will you be OK without me for a bit?'

'Yep sure. I really think we got something here, which means this HF radio is working or to some degree at least. Don't be too long. What's up, anyway?'

'Jess has had a little accident.'

Their two children stood watching their parents.

Paul quickly glanced back to his daughter.

'Hey, sweetheart, you not well? Bit of motion sickness?' he said, taking off the headset speaker from his right ear to hear his daughter.

Jessica shook her head.

'I'm fine, Dad.'

'OK, feeling better hey? That's good. Where did you throw up, love?'

Claire corrected him immediately.

'No, poop.'

'Oh, dear me.' A sudden painful expression came across his face.

'And it was on the bed down there in the nose.' Claire clarified.

'Mom?' Jessica yelled in complete frustration.

'It's OK, baby. Let's get you changed. Come on; I'll give you a hand. I packed your yellow shorts. They'll do for now.'

'Mom? It's not Jess's poop, it's Chickadee's poop.' Tiffany cut into the confusion bringing immediate clarity to all in the cockpit of the flying fortress.

Jessica nodded emphatically and pointed to the guilty party tucked under the young child's arm.

Claire stopped, Paul looked at Tiffany, Jessica, his wife and back to the daughter with all the information.

'Chickadee, not Jess,' Paul confirmed.

Tiffany nodded, lifting up her hen just for a moment and returning it back under her arm.

'Oh, well that's a relief ...' The man on board was cut off.

The radio burst into life again. Static was its constant, but through its transmission, a message could be heard.

'Wow, here we go Claire.'

'Oh, Baby, I'm so sorry. Can you go down and clean it up? There's an old rag in my bag. Sorry, girls, I have to help Dad. We're very busy trying to contact help.' Their mother spun around and focused on the radio.

'OK, Mom.' Tiffany replied, trying to make sense of her parent's strange behaviour.

The girls made their way back down to the nose of the aircraft.

'Dad never talked to that box at home on the island,' Jessica said.

'Nope, he never did.' Tiffany walked behind her sister shaking her head.

'Aircraft in distress, this is Qantas Q ...' The message was abruptly blocked by a swirling sound then returned.'... confirm your call sign, souls on board, the nature of your distress and your intentions ... Qantas Q21 ... 'Further static played havoc with any possible interpretation.

'Yes.' Claire's face beamed with excitement.

'Qantas aircraft calling Boeing B17 flying fortress. There is no call sign. Name of aircraft is *On Eagles Wings*. Souls on board, four. Dr. Paul Langley, Australian citizen, my wife Claire, maiden name, Chandler, American citizen, and daughters Jessica and Tiffany. We were holidaying on the *Pacific Fair* in the Palau region. We were attacked by pirates and left for dead on the eve of a massive typhoon and ended up shipwrecked ... ten years on an uncharted remote island. Well, I'm assuming that it's uncharted.

Unfamiliar with aircraft type. Maintaining altitude nine thousand five hundred feet, heading one eight zero degrees, intended destination Darwin, Request assistance, need to be vectored to Darwin.

How do you read me?' Paul looked at Claire.

'Well that was a bit more than they asked for ... Got carried away ... oops. It feels odd talking to another man.'

Claire studied her husband. She had never considered his point. *How will we cope with other adults in our lives*? she asked herself.

The radio crackled back to life.

CHAPTER FIFTY-TWO

⎯⎯⎯ ∾ ⎯⎯⎯

'C opy that, standby. Qantas Q212.'

'*On Eagles Wings*, standing by.'

The two pilots looked at each other while seated in the cockpit of the Boeing 747 aircraft.

'Just when you thought it was safe to come out and play. This has got to be BS Pete, hasn't it?' The first officer glanced across at the man in command.

The captain shrugged his shoulders.

'Interesting.' The captain studied the notes taken, now placed on his lap.

'Did you copy that Dougy?' the first officer turned, addressing the second officer seated directly behind the command seat.

'Yeah, sounds like someone's been smoking their socks.'

Both men in the front laughed.

'There might be something to it, though. I do recall sometime back, there was a company executive ship that was attacked south of the Philippines somewhere. People killed, some missing and a bunch of hostages held for ransom. Made big news in Manila, it might have gotten some coverage in Australia, not sure. I remember we were laid over in Manila for a couple of days due to a mongrel of a typhoon that hit parts of the Philippines on the eastern side. Saw the full story on TV while we were sitting in the bar at the hotel. Made a bit of a mess of things, including the plans for the wedding anniversary.'

'Ooo, hard to know what's worse, typhoon or ...' The first officer said slowly.

'Mm, lead balloon material that one. Anyway, get back to him. Let's get some more information. We're going to have to verify this story. He's obviously Australian, wouldn't you say? the captain asked.

'Hard to tell. He certainly sounds educated. He could be a Kiwi.' The first Officer reached for the control Colum and pressed the *talk button*.

'Ah, On Eagles Wings.' The man in the right seat looked at the captain and rolled his eyes.

'Qantas Q212 heavy, read you three's. Um, mate, your nationality, would that be New Zealand?'

Immediately a heavy white noise filtered the reply returned.

'Qantas Q212, Ah, steady on ... Nationality Australian. On Eagles Wings.' A faint sound of a female laughing could be heard over the broadcast.

'Thought so, but you are right, John, certainly educated,' the captain confirmed.

'Maybe he's a doctor after all.' The first officer concluded, as he pressed the *talk button* to broadcast again.

'On Eagles Wings, Qantas Q212, Ah, apologies regarding the Kiwi thing. Interesting story, you say you were on an uncharted island for ten years? Are we to assume that you found a World War II B17 on the island and after ten years you're now flying it home?'

'Qantas Q212, On Eagles Wings, that about sums it up. I'm a medical doctor and specialized in emergency medicine, but always had a love for aviation. Had gotten my CPL out of the way by the time I started Uni. Sometime later, got my engineers licence done thanks to a friend who owned an aircraft maintenance workshop. With that, was able to get this old girl running, but it took ten years. On Eagles Wings.'

The crew on the Boeing 747 looked at each other.

'On Eagles Wings, did you get your IFR rating? Qantas Q212.'

'Qantas Q212, did the IREX with Bob Tait at Archerfield in Brisbane and the flying at Maroochydore, Sunshine Coast. Saw no point in A.T.P.L.'s. On Eagles Wings.'

'On Eagles Wings, standby, Qantas Q212.'

'Qantas Q212, On Eagles Wings standing by.'

'Well, Pete, he's got me sold,' the first officer confirmed with the captain.

'Flying home to Australia, not endorsed on aircraft type, expired medical, CPL not current for nine years and probably not licenced to sign off on the maintenance release for a B17 bomber? Man, CASA's going to love him.' A voice behind the captain's seat found an audience.

'Let's see if he has any idea of his position, then we'll report to control, and they can do some checks to verify. If this really is connected with that abduction case ten years ago, I think we'll be in for an interesting flight.' The captain looked at the first officer.

'Hope they don't send us on a wild goose chase looking for him.' The first officer pressed the broadcast button. 'On Eagles Wings, do you have any idea of your current position? 'Qantas Q212.'

Paul broadcast the position found on the small hand-held GPS. More questions were asked of Paul, such as, where he lived, where he worked and other incidentals that might help the confirm his identity. The doctor also advised their reason for leaving their island home.

'In fact, the pirates would still be there. I would think they would stay in harbour for a few days. It's a beautiful spot. On Eagles Wings.'

'On Eagles Wings, Qantas Q212 copy that, given you've got a GPS, why don't you get a fix on Darwin and use it as your Nav. aid? ... over.'

'Qantas Q212, On Eagles Wings, ah, it's not cooperating. I would not be surprised if current position I gave you isn't accurate. On Eagles Wings.'

'On Eagles Wings, Qantas Q212, um, stand by.'

'Qantas Q212, On Eagles Wings, standing by.'

The first officer checked the reported coordinates using their flight navigational systems.

'Given his alleged position, we'll be crossing their track pretty soon.' The first officer sat back after leaning over while studying their navigational screen.

'How long?' The Captain broke his silence.

The first officer's calculation was speedy.

'Twenty minutes.'

'With this current cloud structure, should be easy to make visual with this fellow.'

The man in command pondered audibly.

'On Eagles Wings, Qantas Q212, given your reported position, you're a few degrees left of track for Darwin.'

That captain looked straight at the first officer, showing slight concern.

'Remain on this HF frequency and report in every five-minutes. Qantas Q212.'

'Qantas Q212, On Eagles Wings, will report in every five-minutes. On Eagles Wings.'

The first officer looked to the man in command.

'Might not have been a good move to have confirmed his track for Darwin. He could be anyone, with all sorts of motives,' the captain declared.

'Mm, good point, Pete. My bad.'

'Something to keep in mind for future reference, John, but let's radio ahead to control and brief them about this bloke. I do have a feeling that this is legitimate.'

'And if it is ... this is one hell of a story,' the second officer offered.

The captain chuckled.

'Indeed, it will be, Doug, indeed it will.'

CHAPTER FIFTY-THREE

T he flying fortress gently banked to the right for a few seconds and then returned to wings level.

'What are you doing?' Claire asked.

'Bringing her around to one eight three degrees.' Paul answered.

'Why?'

'Well, the Qantas boys said that we were a few degrees left of track. I am assuming that he was referring to 'at the point of reference' I gave him. If so, I adjust the heading to One eight three degrees, and that will give me track to Darwin.'

'So, you're guessing.'

'I suppose so, but I'll confirm my heading with them at our next scheduled reporting time.'

'OK, I know I should be concerned, but I'm not. Actually, I feel great. Must be the knowledge that we are free from those cutthroats, and we are going home.' Claire said, looking out of the cockpit to the view outside. Her last point struck her. *Home, where was home?* She thought deeply, trying to make sense of everything. Claire scanned the horizon. A familiar peace overcame her. *I am at home with my husband, and I am at home with my God, the Lord Jesus ... Home is where He wants me*. She thought. 'Yes, we are going home,' she repeated her new point of clarity with great satisfaction.

Paul scanned his instruments.

'All systems are as they should be. So far so good, as they say,' he said, looking at the nineteen forties technology in front of him.

'Awesome. Hey, I might dash down to the nose to check on the kids.' Claire released herself from her harness and stood immediately, turned and walked out of the flight deck.

Paul watched her as she left. She looked confident and at peace, a far cry from the person to whom he conversed with on the ground in front of the aircraft not two hours previously.

The clouds maintained their tops at an altitude of seven thousand feet, but the doctor could see ahead, just on the horizon, what appeared to be cumulous clouds growing in height.

The aircraft was trimmed well and sitting steady at their assigned altitude of nine thousand, five hundred feet. He observed the timepiece that featured as part of the equipment on display in the cockpit. He was overdue for his scheduled report with the Qantas aircraft, but concern was not his companion at that point. After one last look at the system instruments, checking that everything was performing satisfactorily, he made his call.

'Qantas Q212, On Eagles Wings?'

He waited for the presumed reply, but there was nothing.

'Qantas Q212, On Eagles Wings?'

'Paul, you should see the view from the nose.' Claire had returned filled with enthusiasm. 'Amazing! Oh man, I sat in the bombardier's seat. Wow it's a long way down there. Can you believe it, the girls are fast asleep, all wrapped up in their blankets? They look so cute.' Claire returned with an uncustomary careless entry to her seat, almost kicking the throttles as she navigated her way back to the co-pilot's place and having difficulties putting on her headsets and throat microphone.

'Qantas Q212, On Eagles Wings?'

He increased the volume to his headset.

'Qantas Q212, On Eagles Wings?'

'They're not answering?' Claire asked.

'Not yet.'

'Well they're probably having dinner.'

'I hardly think dinner would be appropriate at this time in the morning,' he said, gazing at his wife intently. Paul had not seen her as casual as this, and her pleasure expressed during a flight seemed out of character.

'Well breakfast then. What time is it, anyway?' she asked scanning the scenery outside.' It's beautiful isn't?' she declared.

'Yes, it is. Um, the time? Actually, I have no idea but given that I estimate that we saw that ship coming in our direction at around six thirty this morning, I think we would have been airborne around eight thirty. So, time now is about ten thirty, maybe eleven?'

'Oh, really? Still early.'

He returned his attention to his task at hand.

'Qantas Q212, On Eagles Wings?'

Claire began to laugh.

'Oh dear, sorry ... Oh that's funny,' she said laughing even louder.

'Are you OK?' He stared at Claire, concern beginning to grow.

'Oh, sorry, Paul, but when you were doing your call thing on the radio, I thought of the scene in that movie. Oh, what was its name? It had Harrison Ford and that blond gal in it.

Oh, come on, what was the name of that movie ... I'm sure we've talked about it before, haven't we?'

'Absolutely no idea.'

'Yes, you do.'

'No, I don't.' His attention became more focused on his wife, momentarily leaving his primary duties.

'Oh, don't you hate that? ... Right on the tip of my tongue ...' She threw her head back and laughed. 'Got it! ... *Six Nights Seven Days*.' She started to laugh again.

'Oh, that one.'

'See, you did know. I was right.'

'And what's the connection with our situation and that movie?' he asked.

'Oh, come on, don't you remember? They're in that little plane in a storm.' She paused. The doctor continued his observation.

'Paul, aren't you glad we're not in a storm and we're in this big thing? This is so big.

Isn't it? Anyway, Harrison Ford is giving a mayday call, and she has taken all these anti-depressants because she's freaking out. I think she hates flying, and she gets on the mic and says ATTENTION KMART SHOPPERS and then she starts singing MAYDAY MAYDAY MAYDAY. So funny. I mean she was right out of it.' Claire began to laugh harder.

The pilot on command continued to study his wife.

'Oh, I just love it. We are so blessed, aren't we?' She looked around at the view outside and yawned deeply.

'Oh my, I think I might go down and squeeze in next to the kids and Chickadee ... get some shut eye. Oh Chickadee ... our Methuselah chook.' Claire laughed again. 'Oh, Paul you come up with some funny things at times. I'm so glad God has given you to me. So, blessed.'

The doctor watched in disbelief at his wife's strange behaviour. He studied her face then suddenly saw around the edge of her lips ... a slight tinge of blue. Within a flash he realised the problem.

'Claire, show me your fingernails.'

'Excuse me?' A cheeky look came over her face.

'Show me your fingernails,' her husband said, a little more insistently.

'Oooooo, you want to see my fingernails. Are we getting a little frisky, mister?'

'Claire, do as you're told. Fingernails!' He now lovingly commanded.

'What's in it for me, handsome?' she asked.

'Claire!' he demanded.

'Yes sir, fingernail inspection ... attention!' She lifted both hands in front of her face then out towards her man.

The cuticles were blue.

'OK, there it is. Classic case.'

'Oooooo you bet your blue buttoned board shorts I am CLASSIC ... Classic Claire'.

She said wriggling her fingers towards her husband with mischievous intent, then suddenly giggled.

'We had better get you down to a lower altitude.' Paul drew his attention back to the aircraft.

'Why.'

'You have the onset of hypoxia, my darling. I suspect that's why the girls are asleep.

Not enough oxygen.'

'No, I like it up here, sooo beautiful.'

'Well of course it is,' he said smiling from ear to ear.

'Yes, it is,' she echoed with euphoric demur.

'Qantas Q212, On Eagles Wings, on descent to eight thousand five hundred leaving nine thousand five hundred, due to family feeling the hypoxic effects of altitude. On Eagles Wings'

'But I like it up here,' Claire burst out her opinion.

The doctor reduced power to all four engines, and an immediate response was his.

The nose of the bomber gently dipped down and altitude was the victim, delivering five hundred feet per minute rate of descent.

'On Eagles Wings, Qantas Q212. Do you read? Qantas Q212.'

Paul rushed to respond.

'Qantas Q212, On Eagles Wings. Read you two's. On Eagles wings.'

'On Eagles Wings, do you have a serviceable VHF radio? We suspect your HF radio is experiencing problems receiving. We've been acknowledging your calls. Qantas Q212.'

'Qantas Q212, have a VHF radio on board. Not sure of serviceability. It operates on any one of four pre-set crystal-controlled frequency channels, within the range of one hundred to one fifty-six MHz. On Eagles Wings.'

'On Eagles Wings, copy that, standby, Qantas Q212.'

An acceptable broadcast frequency was given in the man in command of the antique warrior. The VHF radio was tuned to the suggested frequency, and Paul broadcast immediately.

'Qantas Q212, On Eagles Wings?'

'On Eagles Wings, how do you read us? Qantas Q212.'

While the broadcasts were in progress, Paul had brought the aircraft to its new altitude of eight thousand five hundred feet and turned off the cabin heat in a desperate attempt to achieve more molecules of oxygen in a given parcel of air due to cooler temperature, thereby offering a more suitable environment for the inbound refugees. This proved a success as Claire had calmed down considerably and was intently listening to the Australian on the radio.

'On Eagles Wings, We have passed on your details to the authorities and have received back confirmation of your story.

Been asked to confirm your aircraft type visually and are cleared to descend to fifteen thousand feet. Request your coordinates and indicated airspeed? Qantas Q212.' The broadcast crackled its message to the airborne fugitives.

'Qantas Q212, experiencing problems with this GPS. Will give you the last reading I got ...' The doctor read back his last known longitude and latitude and indicated airspeed. Claire continued to listen.

'Does that mean that we'll see their aircraft?' Claire broke her silence.

'I suspect it will, although they'll be over six thousand feet above us.'

'I can't believe this is happening, Paul. Are they going to guide us in?'

'Doubt it.'

'On Eagles Wings, we have your coordinates plotted. Our ETA is an estimated fifteen minutes. Adjust heading to one eight five degrees. Qantas Q212.'

'Qantas Q212. Adjusting heading to one eight five degrees. On Eagles Wings.'

CHAPTER FIFTY-FOUR

Grandad, guess what?'

'What my boy?'

'Next weekend we are going camping.'

'Yes, I know and guess what?' Reverend Langley said, sitting back in his office chair.

'What?'

The older man's face lit up with joy as he spoke to one of the treasures of his life, his grandson.

'Your grandmother and I are coming with you,' he said looking across at his son in-law and winked.

'Wow, Dad, is Grandad really coming with us?' The excited youngster looked up at his father.

'Yes, he is. Pretty cool, ha?'

The zestful five-year-old ran off to find his mother.

'Mom, Mom, guess what? Grandad is coming camping with us next weekend,' he yelled, as he ran through the house. Finally finding his mother Lynn in the kitchen with his grandmother, he repeated his news. 'Grandad is coming camping with us.'

'Is that so,' Lynn replied, enjoying the reaction to his revelation revealed.

'Can I come, too?'

'Yeah, Grandma, you can come, can't she Mom?' The boy's face exploded with greater joy.

'Well, I don't see a problem with that,' Lynn said, looking at her mother and smiling.

'Hey, I've got an idea!' Both women drew their attention closer to this new development about to unfold.

'Have you now.' Lynn watched as her boy prepared himself to unfold his master plan.

'Yep. We can all sleep in our tent ... together. Won't that be fun?'

'Oh yeah, that'll be a real hoot but, I think Grandad would prefer to sleep in his own tent with Grandma. ... might be better, sweetheart,' Lynn said looking over at her mother and winked.

He stopped and pondered, then looked directly into his mother's face.

'Why?'

'Well, have a think about it, mate. Why do you think that might be a better idea?' The young mother challenged her son.

His gaze sank to the floor and thought further. The two adoring adults watched the process, eager to see the fruit of this very inquiring young mind.

'Oh yeah.' His face slowly lifted in disappointment to connect with his mother once again, and then across to his grandmother. 'Dad snores.'

The senior adult's countenance suddenly changed, ready to explode with laughter.

'Um, yeah, well that's a fair point.' His mother caught his grandmother's expression.

'Oh, you are precious, but it might also have something to do with the size of that tent. All of us just wouldn't fit together in your tent, my darling.' His grandmother began laughing. The years of grieving for her son, had not been kind to her and it's gripping effects had aged her more than one would expect.

'But thank you so much for that idea of yours. I think you might grow up to be an ideas man.'

'Yeah, I like ideas, Grandma,' he said with pride.

A loud knock was heard on the front door.

'I'll get it.' The reverend Langley yelled out.

He walked swiftly to the stained timber front door, cleared his throat and opened the door.

'Yes?'

There at the threshold stood two well-dressed men.

'Good morning. Is this the residence of the reverend and Mrs Langley?'

'Yes, and you are?'

'Apologies, this is Peter Price and I'm Robert Lawson. We are from the Australian Federal Police.'

The pastor's heart skipped a beat.

Is this about Paul?

'Yes, it is.'

'Please, please come in. We'll sit in the lounge. I'll get my wife' He ushered them into the room where a private conversation would be possible.

The man of the house walked to the kitchen.

'Who is it, love?'

'Federal Police. They're in the lounge. It's about Paul.'

His wife's face went pale. She stood up immediately.

'Who's Paul?' the inquisitive child asked his mother.

'Never mind, sweetheart. Where's your father?'

'In Grandad's office.'

'OK mate, let's find Dad.' She led her little boy to his father, explained the situation and promptly moved straight to the lounge-room.

'Gentlemen, this is my daughter Lynn. I'm sorry, I've forgotten your names.'

'Peter Price and I'm Robert Lawson.' They both stood quickly to their feet.

'Hello.' Lynn sat next to her parents as she had done ten years ago when the news of the tragedy was first announced.

'Folk, we are actually here with interesting news. Australian Air Services has been contacted via Qantas who advise that one of their inbound international flights from Asia picked up a distress signal this morning from an aircraft, also inbound.'

The three adults sitting opposite were drinking in every word uttered by the officer.

Hope sparked as he continued with the detail.

'The flight crew of that aircraft claims that the person who gave the distress call is a doctor ... namely, Doctor Paul Langley and he's given this address as his place of abode when he was last in Australia. He claims that he was on the tourist ship ...' The officer looked down at his notes.

'Um, the *Pacific Fair*, and they were attacked by pirates. It seems that he and his wife, were left for dead on the ship. He claimed that a typhoon came through that very night and within a couple of days, he and his wife were shipwrecked on an island and that's where they have been living with their two children for ten years. He says he fixed up a B17 bomber that was on the island, and that's what he's flying home. I have to admit, it all sounds a bit far-fetched, but so far, it has checked out. We are however, treating this with a great deal of concern, given where the aircraft seems to be coming from. Now, what we need to do is ...' He was cut off by the lady of the house.

'That's not our son.'

Pastor Langley and Lynn looked at the source of the statement with concern.

'Excuse me, Mrs Langley, I didn't mean to sound emphatic, but what I was leading to was that we need your help to ...' The officer was cut off again.

'He is *not* our son.'

'Why do you say that, Mrs Langley?' the other officer softly asked.

'Well, first, Paul wasn't married, and second, he certainly didn't have any children.'

'Sure, we understand, but as I was trying to say, we need to get clarity, so we'll need your help and with that in mind, we have an interesting proposal coming from a certain media ...' The officer was stopped again.

'Excuse me. Can I ask a question?'

'Yes, Lynn.' Frustration began to show across the federal officer's face.

'What's the name of his wife?' Lynn sat on the edge of her seat and directed her question with curious concern, whilst holding back unwarranted hope.

He glanced down at his notes again.

'Um, let's see ... 'he said, rustling through loose pages in the file on his lap.

'Ah, here we go. Claire; Her full name is Claire Chandler ... daughters Jessica, eight years old and ... Tiffany, um, five years old.'

Lynn's mother began to cry softly. Her husband placed his arm around her shoulder.

'Mom, her name was Claire. Dad, you know that Sunday morning when Paul rang me? Don't you remember?'

'Yes, yes I do. I remember you saying that. You told us her name was Claire.' His spirits lifted immediately.

'But, love, Paul can't fly a bomber, for goodness sake, he wasn't married and we don't have two granddaughters.' Tears continued to fall down her face.

'Mom, ten years on a tropical island.' Lynn looked at her mother, then laughed. 'I mean, hello.' She made eye contact with all in the room, beckoning a response. 'Like, wow!'

She continued, now with hands over her mouth, giggling softly.

'Your point is more than reasonable, Lynn.' The pastor laughed softly, fuelled by the new hope of Paul's being alive.

'Well, I'm sorry, but it's all too much to believe,' Mrs Langley said quietly.

'Well, Mrs Langley, be that as it may, but the person who says that he is your son, with his wife and two daughters, is in fact flying a B17 bomber right now. That has been confirmed. The aircraft type that is. There were four people seen on the aircraft. Apparently two of the people on board were definitely children. All this was confirmed a few hours or so ago by the Qantas crew. Folks, as crazy as this sounds, we have to take it seriously as I said, and frankly you need to as well.'

Lynn sat back in the lounge in total awe.

'God is bringing him home on eagle's wings,' she said softly.

The two officers looked quickly at each other.

'Excuse me, Lynn?'

'Nothing, just talking to myself,' she said, deep in thought.

'Um, sorry Lynn, what did you just say then … the eagles wings?'

'Oh, it was something I said … actually it was one of the last things I said to Paul … a prayer really, based on a biblical text, Isaiah 40 verse 31 in fact. "But they that wait upon the LORD shall renew their strength; they shall mount up with wings as eagles; they shall run, and not be weary; and they shall walk, and not faint." I've taken liberty with it … hence rising up on eagle's wings … that's all. You say he's flying back, so it's like God is bringing him home on eagle's wings, assuming it's really Paul, of course. That's all it was.'

'Oh, I see.' Robert turned to his partner.

'An interesting coincidence, hey?' he said in a softer tone. His partner raised his eyebrows.

'Coincidence?' Lynn's mother interacted sharply.

'Well, yes, Mrs Langley, um, you see the B17 aircraft that this guy's flying, is actually called *On Eagle's Wings*, so it's rather interesting what you said, Lynn. Maybe the universe is listening.' He laughed, somewhat amazed at what he had just heard.

'Well, rewind on that universe thing, it's the one who made the universe, He's the one who's listening, or in this case, answering,' Lynn corrected gently.

'You said something about a proposal?' the pastor asked calmly, endeavouring to soften the moment.

'Oh yes. Folks, as painful as this is for you, we will need you to come with us.'

'To do what?' Lynn snuck a question before his next word.

'We are going to try and make contact with this fellow via the radio. It seems he has, though limited, radio communication equipment operational on board that aircraft. You need to speak to him. Everything he has said to the Qantas crew has checked out to the letter… *to the letter*. The family will seal it. Obviously, that's where you come in.'

They all sat silent and looked at each other.

'Where do we do the radioing, in your car?' The senior lady of the house sat upright, drying her eyes with her husband's handkerchief presented just at the right time.

'No Mom, probably at the police station?' Lynn looked at the officers for confirmation.

'Darwin,' the officer replied, then stopped, waiting for their response.

'Darwin?' Lynn asked.

The officer nodded. 'Yes, that's where he's flying to ... Darwin.'

'And the proposal?' the reverend added.

'Ah yes, the Channel Seven Network has offered to fly you up to Darwin in their corporate jet. I'd say they want to break the story. It's one way we can get you there fast and of course, at no cost to the government department. That's if you agree,' Robert Lawson said.

'Hey, look on the bright side, free flight in a corporate jet. It'll be fun.' The younger officer stopped realizing what he said could have been taken offensively. He quickly cleared his throat.

'You know, this could actually be your son, guys,' the second in charge added.

'How would the television station know about this, so quickly?'

'They have their ways, Lynn.'

'Channel Seven corporate jet ... I take it you mean sometime today?' the reverend Langley asked in shock.

'No, I mean now! You've got thirty minutes to pack something light. It's pretty hot up there. We're authorised to take you to the Brisbane airport, where the aircraft is waiting for you. Once we get there, there'll be someone else from the Australian Federal Police to meet you, and he'll go with you to Darwin.'

'Mom, Dad, you have to go.' Lynn's husband stood at the entrance of the lounge room, with his son standing next to him.

'Yes, I agree, you must. Mom, I'll help you pack.' Lynn placed her hand on her mother's shoulder.

'Ah, Lynn, I'm afraid that given your association, you would need to come too. To be absolutely sure, you know? Would be advantageous to get your input and confirmation, either way,' Robert advised.

Lynn looked across at her husband.

'Go, love; we'll be fine,' he said, winking at his wife of six years.

Sudden movement exploded in their lounge-room as women shot to attention and walked quickly to the bedroom.

'Is mommy going camping with GranDad and Grandma without us, Dad?'

'No mate, mommy has to go somewhere first, and then we are going camping. It's going to be so much fun, hey?'

'Yeah!' The young boy hugged his Dad.

'Come on, mate, let's go back to Granddad's office, and I'll show you a neat game on his computer.'

The two walked quickly out of the room. Within thirty minutes, bags were packed, calls were made to appropriate people advising of the situation and asking for prayer, doors were locked, goodbyes were said and the three were crammed in the back of the government car, hastily making their way to the airport.

'Oh, this is so rushed. I hate being rushed, and Lynn, you've got no fresh clothes, nothing other than one of our hand luggage carry-on bags … and that's empty. What do you suppose you're going to do when we get there?'

'I'll get some. Mom, I have a friend.'

'In Darwin? I didn't know that.'

Lynn opened her handbag and found her purse.

'Visa—it's a real friend just when you need it,' she said waving it in front of her face as one would a fan.

'Mm, what will you do if you don't have time, or the shops aren't open?'

'Well, I'll just have to get the hotel to wash what I'm wearing and run around in my room all day wrapped in a towel.'

'Oh, you are incorrigible sometimes, girl.'

'Yes, I know, but don't you just love me?' She laughed and snuggled up to her mother.

'Yes, I do.' Her mother reached across and lightly grabbed her daughter's ribs. 'Yes, I do, girl.' A sudden light-heartedness poured into Lynn's mother.

'I can't believe it.'

'What me running around in a towel.' The two laughed.

'Oh, I can believe that.' Her outburst was something not heard for a long time.

The two offices looked at each other. The younger raised his right eyebrow slightly as they laboured their way through mid-morning traffic.

'No, I mean Paul.' She softened her voice.

The two-way radio in the vehicle burst into life. The junior officer acknowledged the message. After which he advised the passengers of a change of plan.

'OK. Folks, it's going to get a little exciting. We are not making good time due to this traffic. We're going to get a police escort. Motor bike escort, that is, should be waiting for us up the road a bit.'

Within minutes, blue lights were flashing, and quick time was made to the Brisbane airport. At the general aviation section, a sleek aircraft was waiting with a large red *Seven* painted on its tail.

No sooner had they stepped out of the car when a Federal Police Officer exited the media aircraft and introduced himself. This was followed by a female journalist as a camera man who was positioned, at the nose of the aircraft, filming everything. After introductions were made, all were swiftly on board, engines started, clearances received and the business jet was taxiing ready for departure on runway 01 with flight plan logged for Darwin.

CHAPTER FIFTY-FIVE

~

The antique radio burst into life.

'On Eagles Wings, we have you in sight. Your four o'clock high. Let's change to a talk frequency. Will make things easier.'

The new frequency was transmitted to which application was taken.

Claire scanned the sky from left to right. Finally frustrated, she looked to her husband and raised her hands in defeat.

'Think of a clock. If you were sitting in the middle of the clock, where would four o'clock be to your position?'

Claire pointed to the direction then immediately looked to the direction in question.'

'Can't see anything.' She demanded.

'Now look up,' he added.

'Got them, Paul.' Claire swung around facing her husband, then quickly turned back to retrieve the sight coming to them.

'It's a jet airliner. I can see them as clear as day. Oh, my goodness, it's big.' She turned back to her husband, demanding his attention. Then once again, she spun back around to confirm her last visual of the descending Qantas aircraft.

'Ah, looks like my wife has you visual,' Paul casually broadcast, dispensing with standard broadcast protocol given the chat frequency offered by the international flight crew moving into position.

'Copy that, mate. We'll be with you shortly.'

The vintage aircraft climbed steadily to an altitude of fifteen thousand feet to clear the rising cumulous clouds.

'Mom, we're getting cold again, and chickadee is shivering.' The children were standing behind their parents once more with their forlorn pet tucked under Tiffany's arm.

'We had to climb higher again, Tiff, to clear the clouds. We will go down again soon.

Hey guys, guess what? We have another airplane coming down to see us,' Claire warmly comforted her children, pointing to their visitor's position.

The children rushed to the Perspex window behind their mother. They stood in awe as they watched the metal monster descending, claiming its position, next to the vintage spectacle.

'Mom, that's like the plane in that song on Dad's laptop. You know the one with the kangaroo.' Jessica spoke up. Her eyes filled with excitement.

'Yes, baby, it is, isn't it?'

Within minutes, the two aircraft were flying in a close formation. The flight-crew could be clearly seen by the family. Claire began waving to the airliner flying in formation with them. Passengers could be seen responding, waving back to the adventurers.

The Boeing 747 flew with its flaps extended to lower the stall speed, thereby maintaining its slower airspeed to keep in formation with the World War II relic.

'Paul, how long can we fly this high?' Claire asked.

'Not too long,' he said, wiggling his toes as the effects of the chill of altitude made its presence known on his bare feet.

'Give me a look at your fingernails. Kids, you too Claire,' he said, turning to the girls whose gaze was fixed on the Australian icon.

All on the flight deck of the B17 obeyed the man in command and placed their hands in front of their faces. There was no trace of any hypoxic signs.

'OK, looks clear so far, but it won't take long at this altitude. Fifteen minutes, maybe twenty at the max, and then we will have to descend back to a lower altitude, cloud permitting.'

The bomber reached its new assigned height.

The Qantas crew watched as the unique sight in the air joined them at the same altitude.

'John, let's get this formation a little tighter ... want to get a better look, but keep a close watch on this bloke ... He may drift in on us.'

'Sure thing.'

'On Eagles Wings, mate, we're going to tighten up the formation. Hold your heading and altitude.'

'Yep, OK holding heading and altitude. We'd go two very excited kids here.' The broadcast was clear of any static.

The Jumbo 747 flew in closer to its ancestor.

'Man, wouldn't this make the formation shot of the century. Where's that video production team when you need them?' The first Officer joked.

'Reckon it would give Boeing some real serious *warm fuzzies*,' the second officer added.

The captain laughed to himself. 'Yeah, two legends of the skies, and both freaks of aeroplanes.'

'Stagger me, will you look at that,' the second officer said. 'Bloody amazing.'

All three on the flight deck studied the sight set before them. The team could clearly see the bomber in all its glory ... every detail. Suddenly attention was drawn to the family in the flight deck of vintage war horse of the nineteen forties.

'Hey, Pete. That little lady is waving to you ... I think she fancies you, boss.' The first officer laughed.

'What are you doing up here, sweetheart?' The captain said softly, as he waved back in bewildered disbelief.

'Yep, there it is, look ... written on the nose ... *On Eagles Wings*. Nice bit of nose art there.' The second officer added, referring to the striking eagle with its talents extended in an attack pose, painted on the nose of the aircraft.

'Looks like it just popped out of the past,' the captain said absentmindedly as he watched intently.

'Um, Pete? I think that things have just deteriorated a bit,' the first officer said expressionless.

The captain swung around in response to his first officer's announcement.

'Look ... they've got a chook on board, Pete, and it's now waving at you as well,' the first officer said. The children had placed their hen up against the Perspex and waved its claw at the onlookers.

'You devil you Pete. What can I say, Doug? The chicks just love our boss, don't they?'

John continued, looking back at his point of reference outside.

The captain returned his gaze to the old war bird, noted the children and their playful antics. He laughed softly to himself.

'Hey kids, what's your story up here with your Mom and Dad?' he said, as he happily returned the gesture of a wave.

Captain Peter Thompson shook his head and turned to his right-hand man.

'I hardly think there's any threat here. Contact control, John, confirm we have visual, give them his position and current track to station. Doug, might be an idea to give this bloke an amended heading for Darwin, I think he might be slightly off track. Can you look after that, mate?'

'Yep, sure thing.' The second officer jumped into action joining the new focus, eager to do something constructive.

'I think we've done our bit. Let's get back to business. Mission accomplished, gentlemen,' the captain said, looking back at the vivid comparison flying beside them.

'Yes indeed, mission accomplished,' he echoed his own words softly as he stared at the wonder set before him.

'Roger that. Who'd have thought, who'd have thought, flipping amazing,' the first officer said, getting to the task of resuming their original flight plan.

'Would like to be a fly on the wall at Darwin tower and watch him land this thing. Hasn't flown for ten years and no endorsement on aircraft type. It'll be tricky,' the second officer spoke up.

'Yep. God help him,' Peter Thompson replied shaking his head. 'God help him.'

The new coordinates were radioed to Paul. Within seconds of farewells being made, the jet airliner climbed swiftly to its assigned flight plan, leaving the sojourns to face the elements—alone.

CHAPTER FIFTY-SIX

The phone rang.

An astute middle- aged man quickly answered.

'Yes, Jules?'

'Alan, your visitors are here.'

'Right, will be out in a couple of minutes.'

Alan Renton returned the phone's hand piece back on its mount. He had held the position of CEO of the Darwin airport for ten years and was known for his *no-nonsense* approach to management. Tidying up his desk, his thoughts raced ahead in preparation for what could be coming. The federal police meant either of two things: A drug-related issue or another terrorist threat. His posture demanded the right impression. This man was highly organized and claimed competency as one of his primary attributes.

He entered his office's reception area.

'Alan Renton,' he softly said, as he extended his hand to the obvious man to target.

'Derek Brown, Federal Police.'

'Derek.' The CEO reached out and shook the officer's hand. 'And these are?' Alan referenced the three accompanying the Federal Officer.

'Ah, apologies. This is Reverend John and Jenene Langley, also their daughter Lynn.'

'Hi folks, pleasure to meet you. You've had a rushed trip as I understand it. Would you like some coffee, tea, water, something to eat?' He looked at the two inquisitively.

Before anyone had a chance to answer, the CEO turned to his personal assistant.

'Jules, why don't we get these folk some sandwiches, coffee, tea, you know?'

'Of course. Now, does anyone need to use the bathroom?' she said, looking straight at the women in the group.

'Oh yes, thank you so much. Come on, Mom.' Lynn took charge, and the females were directed to a washroom that led off from the reception foyer.

'OK, gentlemen, follow me.' He stopped and turned back to the other males in the room.

'Ah, sorry, guys; there's bathroom attached to my office if you need. Mr Langley? Derek?'

Both men declined the offer, and the three moved to the CEO's office.

'Jules, just bring the ladies into the office when they're ready,' Alan yelled out to his personal assistant.

The two visitors were offered a chair placed around a small boardroom table, tightly placed in the corner of the CEO's office.

'Am I to assume that you were briefed on the situation?' Derek asked, as he haphazardly dumped his heavy frame on the seat offered.

'Not really, other than a quick phone call from Canberra saying that you were coming and passing on your clearance via email. Said you would share all the joy, but he would also confirm the brief by another email. However, that hasn't arrived. Mind you, only got the phone call twenty or thirty minutes ago.'

'No, really? This was registered about six hours ago'.

'I'm sure it'll arrive. The internet's been rather slow ... Well, actually the email is the problem, not the internet,' he said, looking up at the door to see the two female visitors being ushered into the office.

'We've had an upgrade of our email system. Will take time to get it working properly. Anyway, that's not your problem.' The CEO continued his gaze at the entrance of his office.

'Please, come in. Take a seat.' Alan stood up and offered the senior of the two ladies a chair first.'

Moving back around to his chair he looked at the officer and changed the mood.

'Now, to what do I owe this pleasure?'

'OK, you have an incoming aircraft, coming from the Philippine Micronesian area.

We have positive ID of the aircraft type and have done a full check of the people on board. Well, two of them, anyway. The other two are kids and are not known in this country or the USA for that matter. Can only assume that they were born outside either of the countries. The adult male, early forties, Australian citizen. He's the pilot ... been missing and presumed dead for ten years and the female adult, early thirties, American citizen, also been missing, presumed dead for ten years. Aircraft believed to be flying low altitude, maybe ten, fifteen thousand feet. Pilot not familiar with the aircraft.'

'What? ... OK and aircraft type?' The CEO slowly asked his question still processing.

'Um ... hang on to your shorts' The officer screwed up his face slightly as though still in disbelief. 'It's ... a B17.'

There was silence in the room. All the faces were glued to the man being briefed. It seemed the CEO froze, as though time had taken him to a dimension between truth and fabrication.

'As in a World War II flying fortress?' the CEO questioned intently.

'One and the same ... Believe it or not.'

'Really ... you're ... you're serious?'

The federal police office simply nodded and raised his eyebrows at the same time.'

'You said the pilot isn't familiar with the aircraft.'

'Yep.'

'So how did he take off if he's not endorsed?'

'No idea.'

'How did he come by this unit?'

'Absolutely no idea ... Well, actually, that's not quite true. He, the pilot, claims that ... he found it.'

'Found it?'

'Yep.'

'Really?'

'Yep, that's his story ... not verified of course.'

'Mm, found it, how convenient.' The CEO pondered on the point.

'Found it where?' Alan said, scratching the top portion of his receding hairline on his right side.

'Found it on a deserted island.'

'Really.'

'Yep. He claims that he was shipwrecked there for ten years.'

'Where?'

'Well, interestingly enough, he passed on the coordinates via radio communication to a Qantas crew a few hours ago. We checked the lat and long that he gave them, and ... You wouldn't believe it, mate; there is an island there all right.'

'Seriously?', the CEO said, completely absorbed.

'Yep.'

'Airstrip?'

'Yep, looks like an old abandoned World War II strip, with hangar, you know the works.'

'Mm and this B17 is heading our way?'

Derek raised his eyebrows again at his enquirer.

Alan sat back in his seat deep in thought

'Now, whether this aircraft really came from this vicinity remains to be seen.' Derek said slowly, as he studied the face of the CEO.

'ETA?'

'Maybe three hours.'

'And what do these fine-folk have to do with this situation?' The CEO carefully placed his question.

'According to the pilot, these are his family.'

The federal officer went on to explain the story. Alan Renton sat and listened intently, making eye contact with the visitors, watching their reaction to the presentation of this slightly unkempt federal officer.

'So, they're here to try and help us get a positive I.D. We hope to set up a radio link and let them talk to the pilot. The Qantas aircrew conveyed a frequency that flight control nominated for their inbound communications. If anyone can give us a positive ID, the family can.'

Alan looked across at the Langley family.

'Thank you so much for your availability. This must be very difficult for you. So, your son's name?'

'Paul, that's our boy. He has been missing for ten years.' The Reverend spoke calmly.

The CEO shook his head in disbelief.

'You must have given up hope after all these years?'

The family were quiet. Tears began to well up in the eyes of the incoming pilot's mother, which caused the CEO to abruptly change the mood.

'I think the tower will be the best place, Derek. Standby.' Alan picked up the phone and organised the necessary clearances and appropriate transport for the short ride to the control tower.

'OK, all set. There's someone from operations coming to take you to the tower.' He said, redirecting his gaze back to the phone. All in the room watched as he put the receiver down slowly. There was concern written all over his face.

'Has the Defence Department been advised?'

'Yeah, all clued up. The Air Force guys up in the tower have already got the brief.'

Alan's personal assistant suddenly appeared at the door.

'Excuse me, refreshments have arrived and, all set out on the coffee table in reception.'

'Great. Thanks, Jules. Folk you go with Julie. Derek and I have a couple of things to tidy up, and we'll be out in a flash.'

Julie was quick to usher the visitors out, leaving the two men alone.

'So, am I to assume that you are rating this incoming as a threat?'

'OK, we've been monitoring intel for some time that strongly suggests a terrorist attack coming to Darwin from his area. Though sources suggest boat, not a plane, but hey, crazier things have happened. Just go and talk to the boys in New York.'

'New York?'

'Twin Towers?'

'Oh, yes of course … but a B17 bomber, shit Derek, these Muslim extremists … are they really that bloody creative? And a B17 bomber is a bit lame, in my book. This has got to be bull shit.' Alan stopped abruptly.

'Bull shit? … Maybe, but we have to take this very seriously. It's a bomber, Alan. For all we know, it could be carrying a dirty bomb. Who knows?' The officer threw back devastating logic.

The CEO began shaking his head whilst deep in thought.

'Problems?' Derek asked suddenly, pressing a frown across his forehead.

Alan Renton took a deep breath.

'What about flicking him off to an alternate?'

'Namely?'

'The Katherine/Tindal Airport, not much further really.' Alan said, eager to offload, not only the responsibility of such an intruder, but the mountain of paperwork that would accompany this type of clearance, be it only for a standard emergency entry. The thought of terrorist activity was more than he wanted to contemplate at that point in time.

'Ah that's a big negative, Alan, because of the military's use of the runway. The last thing the Australian Defence Authority would want to see is a potential terrorist attack on an Australian defence installation. This bird is landing here, mate … Well, if it's really a friendly.'

'And if it's deemed otherwise?'

'We'll take it out before it gets into Australian Airspace …'

Both men swung their heads to the open door of the CEO's office. Lynn stood there.

'I forgot my hand bag.' She walked in, picked it up, walked back out then, turned and faced the men.

'That's my brother. He's not a terrorist.'

'Sorry Lynn, national security. Be assured though if we can get him on the radio, I'm sure it won't take long before you'll be able to give us the clarity we're looking for. That's why you're here.' Derek's tones were laced with apology.

'If this guy's your brother, the boys in the tower will guide him home. We'll be out in a minute.' Alan added confirmation of their needed solitude.

They watched as she left. Both men stared at the empty space now at the entrance of the CEO's office. Derek stood up and closed the door.

'Shit, that wasn't good. Anyway, I was hoping we could do a deal with the Indonesians. Might have been expensive, but could have been better though, if it's a threat. That would keep it away from the media. At this stage, that's not likely given everything and of course, it's not my call,' Derek said quickly regaining his mindset while taking his seat.

'Didn't you come in the Channel Seven business jet, Derek?' Alan asked with a humours expression on his face.

'Sorry?'

'Your point about the media? You came on the TV networks business jet.' Alan half laughed as he looked at the only person opposite him.

'Oh, yes. Sorry, that didn't come out really well ... long day. Yes, we did, but we don't want the others knowing ... *Seven* will toe the line, but I don't want them up with us in the tower, Alan. We feed them ... the info. If this incoming is classified as *confirmed threat*, then it's out of bounds for the media—all media. Put them somewhere safe. Look after them.

We'll give them something to chew on later.' His face by this time was beetroot red with embarrassment. His day was indeed long due to his assigned case of Paul and Claire's incoming path to Darwin International airport.

'How's our relationship with Indonesia these days?' Alan asked eager to help Derek regain his credibility.

'Mm, well, shall we say that we're not exactly the flavour of the month of late with the Indos.'

'Frankly, I like the idea of Indonesia,' Alan said hoping this might be a positive point to reinforce as his final desperate argument for diverting the B17 from his realm of responsibility.

'Anyway, have a bite to eat, get a coffee into you while we wait for *Ops* to arrive.'

'Sounds good.' Derek once again abruptly stood and marched straight out of the office, leaving his host slightly bewildered.

'That plane needs to land here. That's my brother.' Lynn spoke up with calm authority, directing her concerns to the two officials coming from the inner office.

Her parents swung their heads to face their daughter.

'Lynn, we don't know if it's Paul. We really don't. Let's take this one step at a time, love.'

'Dad, it's Paul. I know it. It's him, Dad,' she said determining not to reveal to her parents the information she had just heard previously at the door of Alan's office.

'Lynn, your father's right. We don't know yet. Your brother's identification could have been stolen, and they could be using it as a sort of *Trojan Horse*, if you know what I mean. One step at a time,' Alan said, turning back to Derek.

'Mind you,' the CEO continued, 'If he's not familiar with the aircraft type he could be at risk of running out of fuel. I've heard those birds can be thirsty at low altitude ... leaning out those engines is critical, I'm told. Too rich a mixture and those spark plugs will foul up as quick as look at you ... tricky I would think.'

'Yeah? I wouldn't know about that, mate, but what I do know is that he's coming straight at you, and he'll be here in a couple of hours ... three max.' The officer dumped it bluntly at the CEO as he tucked into a ham, cheese and tomato sandwich.

'Actually, Paul was acquainted with those types of engines.' The man of the family spoke out.

'Really?' Derek frowned.

'He used to help work on the engine of his friend's plane. It was a World War II single engine aircraft. I think Paul called the engine a radial engine. He was well qualified to do so. He really enjoyed working on it when he could'. The reverend sparked up with enthusiastic defence.

The federal officer was taken back with this sudden revelation.

'Mm, very curious. My information has him as a doctor who specialized in emergency medicine. That's a far cry from a grease monkey,' Derek questioned with slight suspicion.

'Yes, he was, but he was also a pilot with a commercial licence, and he had just finished his aircraft engineer's licence maybe a year or so before he ... disappeared,' Mrs Langley said with new-found confidence.

Derek looked at her husband for some measure of confirmation.

'Yes, that's correct. Paul used aviation as an escape from the high pressures of his medical specialisation.'

'Interesting, but, be that as it may, frankly, I don't care what he can do, I need to know who he is, so anyway, what's say we get this show on the road, yeah? Where's this operations guy, Alan? Time is ticking.' The Federal Police officer began to show signs of intolerance. Lynn matched his slight impatience with a stand-off posture. She watched him closely, and her heart began to pray.

At that point, a young man walked into the reception area.

'Ah, here we are. Operations will take you to the tower. Folks, it's a pleasure meeting you. All the best.' The CEO calmly announced as he switched his gaze to Lynn.

'Hang in there.'

She nodded. 'Thank you for all your help.'

'You good Derek?' Alan said with a smile.

'Absolutely! OK, let's go. Thanks mate.' He reached out and shook the CEO's hand.

'Keep me posted.'

'Sure.' He said, shaking the CEO's hand firmly.

Derek turned to the family.

'OK, guys, time to get you talking on the radio and hopefully … it'll be your boy.' He looked straight into Reverend Langley's eyes.

Quiet tension began to mount as expectations replaced doubt.

'Mom, Dad? Paul's coming home!' Lynn whispered to her parents.

CHAPTER FIFTY-SEVEN

I don't like the look of this.'

Both seated in the flight deck looked straight ahead as though in a trance.

'Paul, what will we do?' Claire quickly broke the silence.

'We're going to have to descend'

'Can't we fly over this?'

'If we had a functional oxygen system … maybe we could, but we don't. The tops of these clouds would be twenty-five, possibly even thirty-five thousand feet. No, we have to descend, love.'

Paul took the throttles in hand and gently reduced the RPM. Instantly the vintage aircraft obeyed the wishes of its master and dipped its nose towards the watery mass below, endeavouring escape from the blackness ahead.

'I've never seen anything like this.' Claire scanned east to west. A flash of lightning streaked its way across the tops of the building cloud formation.

'Welcome to the tropics. This is a classic squall line. What this is, is a long line of thunderstorm cells.'

'But this looks like it's a hundred miles wide.'

'Actually, probably more. They have been reported to be several hundred miles wide.

Anyway, this could get a little rough.' Paul studied the instruments, as the aircraft descended smoothly through nine thousand feet on its way down to the base of the cloud below.

'How low will we go?'

'That depends on the ceiling of this squall. It does look rather low, though.' He looked ahead at the weather waiting to welcome them. Some fifty miles away heavy rain was falling under the dark mass of thermal mischief.

The altimeter wound its way down through the numbers as Paul adjusted the fuel mixture at various stages of the descent. Five thousand feet and still the air mass offered smooth flying. At three thousand feet, a strong jolt belted the B17. Distracted by the potential dangers on offer ahead of them, the adults had neglected to consider the children on board.

'Might be an idea to get the kids tucked in on the mattress downstairs. Use the blankets and tie them in, just in case it gets really rough. I'm going to start a gentle descending turn. We're getting too close to this cloud. If we keep going at this pace, we'll be in the soup. So, I'll be just circling down gently,' he said. 'You all right?'

Claire nodded and moved out of her chair, directing her children as she climbed out of her position of importance. They moved quickly down to the nose of the aircraft amidst a series of turbulent jolts that unsteadied all.

'OK, guys, now I want you two to stay here with Chickadee, and I'll wrap you in these blankets so you won't fall out. It might get a little bumpy.' Their mother competently manoeuvred the blankets around and under the mattress, securing her prodigy to the innerspring base. Using the last of their supply of warm coverings, she threaded the woollen cloth under the mattress and secured it with a knot in front of the children. She placed a pillow under the head of each child.

'There we are, all snug and secure,' she said, making light of an uncertainty that secretly troubled her.

'Are we going to go in the water?'

'No, Jess. We have to fly under the cloud for a little while. That's why Dad is flying the plane lower.'

'Mom?'

'Yes, Tiff'

'Dad is really clever, isn't he?'

'Yes, he is baby.' Claire took a strand of sun-bleached blond hair that had fallen across Tiffany's face and tucked it behind the child's left ear.

'Dad is just like God, isn't he?' Jessica said, simply as a matter of fact.

Claire smiled. 'I'll tell him you said that, Jess. Now you two sit back and enjoy the flight.'

'Mom, when I grow up, I'm going to be just like Dad and fly aeroplanes.' Jessica interrupted her mother.

Claire was seized by the comments of her daughter.

'Not me, I'm going to learn to be a doctor, so I can dig out all the people's splinters.'

'Really, Tiff.' Claire held back the laughter.

'Yep. I'm going to be a professional splinter puller.' Tiffany exploded with a huge voice.

'Wow, a splinter specialist, that would be … very special.' Losing control, her mother laughed.

'Well, I definitely have much to tell Dad, don't I?'

'Yes, you do,' Tiffany replied, now more focused on patting her pet chicken that was also securely tucked into the blankets.

'OK, now if it gets bumpy stay here, OK? You can hold on to each other but stay in this mattress.'

'OK.'

Claire made her way to the flight deck only to be greeted by blackness close by.

'Wow, this is not looking good,' she said, as she strapped herself back into the co-pilot's seat.

Before Paul could reply, another flash of lightening darted its tongue of white light toward their flying vessel.

'Kids all secure?'

'Yes, all good. Hey, I think you need to know what Jess said about you ... oh and Tiffany ... Oh Paul, I had troubles containing myself. That kid just cracks me up sometimes. You know, these kids of ours, they really ...' Claire's train of thought was cut off by a crackling of the HF radio. Both adults looked straight at the radio. The children's antics were no longer a point of priority. A faint communication was heard but not at all distinguishable.

Paul turned his attention to the radio, turning up the volume waiting for a repeat performance, but nothing was heard.

'Oh well, at least it's nice to know it still works.'

'True, but let's see for how long. Man, this is a low ceiling. Look, one thousand feet!'

Paul pointed to the altimeter as he levelled out the four-engine, noisy monster, settling it back to its heading.

'Hey, kind of warm down here.'

'Yeah, it is and it's not just the cabin that's warming up,' he said. Paul reached over and pointed to engine number one's temperature gauge.

'Been watching its temp climbing slowing as we've been coming down.'

Claire's face lost colour. She studied all the gauges, compared their indication and looked back at her husband.

'Is it going to die on us ... catch fire?' she asked in a calm manner.

'No, love. I'll shut it down before that happens.'

'But, there weren't any problems up higher ... why now?'

'Cooler up there maybe ... could be a number of things.'

Lightning slithered its way across the sky in a glorious display of power. Large drops of water suddenly hit the windscreen making the pilot and his co-pilot jump. A bright flash of sheer, white light shot directly in front of them followed instantly by a thunderous explosion.

The B17 shuddered in the air.

'Here we go,' Paul said, as he tightened his seat belts. He looked across at his wife and suggested that she do the same.

The aircraft flew under the darkness. Heavy rain and severe turbulence hammered the war bird as Paul struggled to keep their ark of the sky flying.

The radio burst into life again, and this time certain English words were heard, but the pilot couldn't give any attention to its demand due to his need to keep control of their flying fortress as the weather buffeted them incessantly.

'Mom, it's too bumpy down here,' Tiffany yelled.

The parents swung around only to be confronted by two small anxious faces. Another jolt hit the plane sending its small passengers to their knees. Tears began to well up in the eyes of their youngest daughter.

'Daddy I don't like this. I'm scared. Make it stop,' Tiffany cried out to her father.

Claire reached around and dragged her daughter over to her lap.

'It's OK, baby. Just some bumpy air,' she said, as another massive wave of turbulence crashed its presence over their plane. Claire quickly adjusted the length of her seat belts, then opened them and strapped them securely over Tiffany who was now seated and firmly pinned against her mother.

'Daddy?' their eldest cried out to her father.

'OK kiddo, over you come.' To which Jessica promptly jumped on to her father's lap.

The pilot promptly secured his daughter just before another jolt from disturbed air mass attacked the vintage war bird.

'Good call Claire.'

Before any response was possible, the aircraft suddenly pitched its nose up and sharply banked to the left. Savage yawing, then a downward pitching of the nose followed.

Paul instinctively added power and exercised the full right rudder, noting a five-hundred-foot loss in altitude. The aircraft had fallen out of the sky. At five hundred feet above the water, their bomber was flying again.

'Paul. What happened?'

'The bird stalled. We experienced a huge thermal updraft. Nose went up, lost airspeed quickly, and the wing stalled. At least I think that's what happened,' he yelled out over the four power plants thundering on the wings. Fresh sweat poured its way down the side on his pale face. He was visibly shaken.

No sooner had the man in command gotten the aircraft trimmed and flying straight and level, the nose of the plane pitched up again but then seemed to right itself as the altimeter began reading an increase in altitude. Paul exercised some forward pressure on the yoke and reduced RPM to bring his B17 to the assigned altitude, but as much as he tried, he couldn't arrest the climb. They quickly entered the cloud and all reference to the horizon was lost. He was forced to rely on his instruments.

'Um, care to advise what's happening now?' Claire asked as discretely as possible using her throat mic.

'Well, we are in one almighty thermal, and there's not much I can do about this. It's a free ride up I'm afraid.' His voice was strained as he regained control of the aircraft using instruments only.

Two thousand, three thousand, four thousand feet, the numbers were growing as the massive storm cell thermal maintained its grip on the aircraft, sucking the metal warrior into its heart. Lightning flashed all around them now with claps of thunder clearly heard over the raw of the four radial engines. Heavy rain pounded the aluminium frame of their flying marvel. Paul concentrated on the instruments. It had been a long time since he had performed any instrument flying. His feelings were conquering his belief in the instruments. Panic set in.

Paul was losing his composure. Disorientation was claiming the seat of authority. Seven thousand, eight thousand feet and rising. Engine number one was indicating cooler temperatures, but the turbulence continued its thumping force. Then, the voice of one of his flight instructors came into his head. '*If you experience disorientation in cloud, just focus on the Artificial Horizon and pretend that it's a peep hole to the outside. You have visual.*' He followed the voice in his head. Instantly his senses returned.

Panic vaporized as he concentrated on that sole instrument. The hellish conditions had also suddenly disappeared, as though a tap of wrath had been turned off by a higher authority. The lightning was still around, though certainly it seemed that the worst was behind them.

Nine thousand feet and the pilot was in control.

'Hey, I'm praying,' the voice in his World War II headsets warmed his heart. He looked across at his wife. She smiled.

'You OK?' Her tones were sweet to his ears.

'Yeah, all good. That was hard work.'

'I could see that. I'm not a pilot, but I think you did well.'

The darkness had given way to white light as the cloud thinned. Another jolt of turbulence brought Paul's attention to detail back in place. He continued his focused on the Artificial Horizon, keeping the bomber's wings level.

'Why did you bring us back to nine thousand feet?' She pointed to the altimeter.

'I didn't. As I said, that was a huge thermal we were in. We were climbing at five hundred feet per minute with a low power setting.'

'How do you know that?'

'The VSI.' He pointed to the Vertical Speed Indicator now indicating level flight.

'That was unbelievable. I've heard about this sort of thing happening in the tropics but never thought I'd ever experience it. Man, amazing.'

At that point, the aircraft broke out of the cloud. The pilot and passengers were overwhelmed with what was set before them.

An hour had passed since their arrival to the control tower. After introductions were made to the Australia Air force controllers in the tower, the work began.

'Inbound B17 On Eagles Wings, Darwin Approach.' The young woman looked at Derek.

'Are you sure they were given this HF frequency?' she asked.

'Yep, that's the one I was told. Keep trying.'

'Have you notified the Indonesian authorities? If he's flying as low as you are suggesting, he will be violating their airspace,' the young female controller asked.

'Yes, we have notified them. It seems that, from their point of view, our mystery man and his aeroplane is nowhere to be seen,' Derek replied. 'Not sure what to make of that.'

The Reverend Langley turned to the federal police officer.

'So, we have a working relationship with the Indonesians regarding aviation?'

Before Derek could answer, the young controller released all the information she knew on the subject with profound enthusiasm.

'Oh yeah, for some time now. We had to overcome deficiencies in airspace coordination that sometimes result in violation of controlled airspace events or even worse. 590For example, back in the late nineteen hundreds ... ninety four, or was it ninety five, anyway, there was nearly sixty incidents as a result of inadequate communication between ATC operators. An ongoing process aims to familiarize controllers with the ATS procedures applying in each other's nation. Our ATS also links with Japan, Philippines, Fiji and other national airspace controllers.'

'Mm, well anyway, let's keep this broadcast going,' Derek said, somewhat taken back by her eagerness to express her wealth of information and, from his perspective, quite unnecessary details.

She nodded and quickly returned to her duties.

'Inbound B17 On Eagles Wings, Darwin Approach.'

They listened, but there was still no response.

'Why isn't Brisbane Centre looking after this?' the young woman asked.

Impatience began to show across the Federal Police officer's face, but for the sake of the family next to him, he answered her question.

'The big boys want to keep it ... shall we say ... local. Not too much attention, if you know what I mean?'

'Mm, is that why it's classified as VFR?'

'I would think so! Not as much ... paperwork.'

'And no major responsibility from Air Transport Services.'

The Federal Police Officer didn't respond to her point, but looked across at the family, monitoring the conversation and their reactions.

'So, we could have contacted Paul's plane from Brisbane?' Lynn broke her silence with concern written across her face.

Derek felt suddenly uncomfortable. He was beginning to feel that he was losing control of his little environment set up in a quiet corner of the control tower.

Again, the young woman rushed in.

'Well under normal circumstances, yes indeed. Brisbane Centre is responsible for the airspace from forty-five nautical miles north of Sydney, up to the airspace boundaries with Indonesia, Papua New Guinea, and east to the airspace boundaries with New Zealand and Fiji. Brisbane Centre also manages the upper level airspace for the Pacific Island nations of the Solomon Islands and Nauru ...' She was cut off mercilessly.

'However, under the circumstances, the authorities have deemed this case a ... local priority,' Derek quickly interjected regaining his authority as he looked at the young woman, ready to metaphorically hit her.

'I see. Thank you,' Lynn replied. She watched the look on the face of the man in charge and began to see a number of reasons why a good belly laugh might be appropriate.

'OK, good, now that's all cleared up, let's keep this broadcast going, shall we ... please?' he said, short and sharp.

The young officer got the message.

'Inbound B17 On Eagles Wings, Darwin Approach.'

CHAPTER FIFTY-EIGHT

'Oh my,' Claire gasped her words as they broke through the cloud.

Blue sky above and an assortment of vivid white fluffy clouds littered their track below. Further in the distance, dark green shapes were distinguishable on the horizon. Paul's emotions placed him in a spin again. The shock of visual flying after spending the better part of an hour in cloud was concussive.

'Look, land!' She pointed ahead. 'Can you see it?'

'Yep, sure can.' He was exhausted, and his wife noticed a slight tremor in his left leg.

'What island is that?'

'No idea, other than one of the many islands in the Indonesian group, one would assume.'

'Look over there, more land. Hey, that's much bigger, I think. Could that be Australia?' She pointed to the edge of the horizon where a large portion of land caked with hazy mist and storm clouds could be faintly seen. The pilot in command studied her reference left of their track.

'Doubt it; they look like big mountains over there on that horizon. Hard to tell from here, but at a guess, I'd say we are looking at the tip of West Papua.'

'Couldn't we go look for an airstrip to land on?'

'We'd waste a lot of fuel, not knowing where we are going. The boys back there gave us a track to Darwin. Let's stick to the known way,' he said, moving his neck as though it was bothering him.

'But, you don't know. There might be a strip over there, much closer.'

'That's precisely it; we don't know ... that way,' he pointed to her suggested track. 'But this way, we do know,' he pointed to their current heading, 'Darwin ... we were given a track from someone, who came down from a higher authority. Namely ... Qantas. Let's keep going.' He winced as a dull pain mounted at the base of his neck. He moved his head to the left and to the right.

'You OK?'

'Yeah, a bit tired. Can you take the controls? I need a break,' he asked, continuing his movement of his neck and shoulders. He winced again.

'Paul, are you OK?'

'Yeah, all good, all good. That stretch back there was a little challenging without an autopilot, really challenging to say the least.' He laughed softly, now lifting his shoulders up and down looking for relief. 'Can you take the controls, love?'

'Paul?' Fear shot across her face.

'Please?' the pilot asked in pain.

Claire nodded and held the yoke with her youngest still seated on her lap.

'I think it's smooth enough,' he said, indicating the children's current position.

The two minors happily disengaged from their parents, making their way behind the command seat.

'That was fun Dad,' his eldest yelled over the thunder of the engines. 'Bumpy is fun.'

'Not me. I don't like bumpy.' Tiffany declared.

'I'm going to be a pilot, just like you Dad.'

'Not me. I'm going to be a Doctor so I can pull out people's splinters.'

Their father laughed looking at his wife.

'OK, pick a point on the horizon, right in front of you. Now, can you see a mark on the windscreen that lines up with the mark on the horizon that you've chosen?

Claire studied the Perspex in front of her.

'Yep, got it. It's like a small chip or something like that.'

'Great, so keep that mark on your chosen point on the horizon. Won't be easy, given the cloud, but better than nothing.'

'Really? OK. I'll give it my best shot.' She hesitantly surveyed the area in question.

'OK, I see a point, and ... I am flying to it.'

Her efforts were well received by her husband. A slight thermal shuddered the aircraft to which Claire wildly responded using the controls. Paul had his hands back on the yoke in an instant.

'Wow, small corrections. This aircraft is nicely trimmed. She's a very forgiving aeroplane, so small movements,' he calmly replied.

'OK ... You know, I'm not sure this is such a good idea, Paul,' Claire placed her concerns squarely at the feet of her man in command.

'You'll be fine. I'm not going anywhere. Just taking a break, but still watching.'

'OK, but make sure you do.'

'Yes ma'am!' Paul sat back and began to rub his shoulders and his neck feeling relief almost instantly.

A few minutes past Paul looked around. He noticed cloud build-up ahead, but nothing to be concerned about.

'How's it feeling so far?'

'Mm, well I've really just started, but yeah, OK, I guess. I'm worried about these instruments, and this direction thing, whatever it's called.

'The Directional Gyro ... don't worry about that, I'll keep an eye on the instruments.'

'Good, I have no idea how to fly with those things.'

'Just keep that mark on the windscreen on your point on the horizon.'

Within a fifteen-minute period Claire was satisfactorily keeping their metal monster straight, level and on course.

She glanced across at her man. A smile came across his face as he looked straight ahead at the big picture.

'What?'

'Nothing.' He began to laugh.

'Paul, what.'

'Well, your biggest fear is flying, right? ... and what are you doing? You are flying in a B17 bomber ... but you're not just flying in a B 17 bomber, oh no, you are actually flying the thing.' Paul laughed. 'Hey, works for me.'

'Oh, ha ha.'

'Man, when God deals with your fears, girl, He really brings out the big guns. No pun intended.' The pilot in command released another one of his characteristic belly laughs.

'So not funny, buddy.'

'Oh yes, it is. God is good ... in a B17.'

'Ha, ha,' she huffed her reply.

'And ... He is with us. Remember our scripture? *They will have no fear of bad news; their hearts are steadfast, trusting in the Lord*. Psalm 112, verse 7……. Remember? … Even in a B17 bomber … for crying out loud.'

The HF radio spluttered an utterance. Both instantly pushed aside the possible concept of divine dealings of fear and listened.

'Inbo B…….On…… Eag… Darwin……..'

The two looked at each other

'That said Darwin. I heard the word Darwin. You heard it right? … didn't you?'

Claire burst forth with her news.

'Certainly did.'

CHAPTER FIFTY-NINE

'Inbound B17 On Eagles Wings, Darwin Approach.' The Australian Air Force controller methodically repeated her line every thirty seconds with intervals for monitoring possible response.

The duty officer in charge of the tower approached Derek. They spoke quietly to each other then, moved to another corner and continued their conversation for some time, exchanging pages of information. Derek wrote down notes on the pages given to him. They finally shook hands, and the Federal Police officer returned to the private cluster of people eager to hear any form of encouragement.

'OK, well, it would appear the Indonesians have picked up an unidentified aircraft flying through their airspace. It seems, however, that it's been difficult to maintain any consistent monitoring from their side.'

The Langley family listened intently eager to find anything that could paint a positive picture.

'It could be because the aircraft has been forced to fly low due to weather, or it may be due to equipment breakdown. The Indonesians have been experiencing some down time. Frankly, I wouldn't get your hopes up, folks; this could be any aircraft that just so happens to be coming in our direction ... Seriously, who knows.'

Reverent Langley nodded. He cleared his throat to ask a question but was stopped due to a surprised look on Dereck's face.

'Oh, and here's something interesting, the guy flying that B17 gave the coordinates of his point of departure. The authorities checked it out, and sure enough ... there was an island, but there was also a ship in the small lagoon. The pilot said that this is the reason why they left the island ... that these were the pirates who attacked the *Pacific Fair* all those years ago. To cut the long story short, there was an American navy ship in the area that just so happened to have some Navy Seals on board and ... bingo ... we got them ... confirmed. It seems they have been after them for other things. Your son ... I mean the guy flying that inbound bomber did us all a big favour,' Dereck said, his face was beaming.

'That's wonderful news,' Janene Langley spoke with an air of confidence

'Yes, indeed ... so do they know where Paul is?' The Reverend Langley spoke softly.

'Firstly, we don't know if this is your son, but the last known position was fifty nautical miles southeast of a town called Ambon on the island of Ceram.'

'Where's that?' Lynn asked.

Derek swung around and yelled out to the duty officer in command. 'Got any maps of Indonesia?'

One officer began to sort through a collection of aeronautical charts. He searched methodically, but before success was his, a voice yelled out.

'No need, I got it.' Lynn held her cell phone up for all to see. 'So, where is this place?'

Derek took the phone and in seconds pointed to the last known position fix of the incoming aircraft in question.

'There!' he said, passing it around for all the family to see.

'He's close, isn't he?' Lynn asked, with a face that revealed strained desperation.

'Inbound B17 On Eagles Wings, Darwin Approach,' the controller maintained her stance. She looked up at Derek.

'Can I see?' She increased the volume setting of the transceiver, listening for the faintest response. The cell phone was offered to her.

'What's their heading?'

Derek looked at his notes.

'Last known is One eight three degrees.'

She scrolled the map on the screen down, then back up, then back down, then found the spot that said '*Darwin*'.

'Looks like he's headed in the vicinity for one of the VFR inbound approach lane of entry, or close enough to it, at least. If he continues tracking his current heading, he'll go past the lighthouse off the western tip of North West Vernon Island. He'll then get to the VFR waypoint of Jacko's Junction. He's bang on track.'

Derek listened intently. He turned to the only other male in the secluded corner of the control tower.

'Just out of interest, has your son done any flying in this area?'

'Yes, he has. He and a group of friends chartered a small plane and flew up to Darwin from Brisbane.' The Reverend responded immediately.

'Why would he do that?' Derek asked coldly.

'They were getting their hours up to qualify for their commercial training, but that was a long time ago.'

'Really? Who was in command when they came into Darwin?'

'I have no idea.' The Reverend answered looking at the rest of his family for clarity.

'I do! … Paul … It was Paul. He landed the plane in Darwin. I remember him telling me all about it. He was so excited,' Lynn interjected promptly.

A faint intrusion of white noise spat its presence from the small speaker mounted above the transceiver. All heads were aimed at the sudden source of interest. All listened.

Silence was their reward.

'Inbound B17 On Eagles Wings, Darwin Approach,' a hasty reply to the possible inbound broadcast was offered.

More static was an immediate gift to the onlookers who were hungry for any response. No one said a word. Silence continued to rule. A violent explosion of garbled audio attacked the speaker to which the controller reduced the volume. More static mounted but now a human voice was heard though its presence was very faint.

'Inbound… B17… On… Eagles… Wings … Darwin…. Approach.' This time the controller communicated labouring each word slowly.

A reply was immediate.

'Darwin Approach, B … On Eagles W….' The faint broadcast was cut off.

'Inbound B17 On Eagles Wings, Darwin Approach, go ahead, I read you two's.

Darwin approach.'

Jenene Langley gasped and instantly placed her hand over her mouth. Her daughter came to her side and held her arm.

'Darwin approach, B17 On Eagles Wings. Tracking one eight four degrees, current position not known. Estimate three hundred and fifty nautical miles north of station given flight time, nine thousand five hundred, inbound, request airways clearance, On Eagles Wings.' A full yet very faint return welcomed the small group.

'Oh Lord.' The pilot's mother whispered a prayer to the throne of God.

'Mom?' Lynn moved closer and held her mother.

'Oh Lynn, that sounded like Paul. Oh Lord, please.'

Derek looked at the Reverend.

'Sorry,' he said, shaking his head. He looked across at his daughter.

'I need to hear more, Dad.'

'Inbound B17 On Eagles Wings, Darwin Approach. Are you equipped with a transponder? Darwin Approach.'

More static was heard, then gave way to a portion of solid audio.

'... approach, On Eagles Wings, negative, but I have an old hand-held GPS with que ... serv ... On Eagles Wings'

'Inbound B17 On Eagles Wings, confirm status of hand-held GPS, Darwin Approach.'

More static and another faint broadcast but, this time, readable.

'Darwin approach, On Eagles Wings, negative, have an old hand-held GPS with unreliable serviceability. On Eagles Wings.'

The young controller turned and yelled across to the other side of the tower.

'No transponder and a hand-held GPS. Thoughts anyone, given this incoming's status?'

The head controller took the lead and directed his initial command to the young female air-force officer.

'Stay with him. Let's get the low down on that GPS. I doubt if it's got ADS-B.

Dereck, can you step over here for a moment please?'

The young controller followed orders immediately while the two went to the other side of the tower, their every move being watched by the Langley family.

'Problem?' The Federal Officer came straight to the point.

'Well, technically, yes. He can't come in here without a transponder, and he can't be using a hand-held GPS.'

'Why not?' the federal officer asked.

'It's a CASSA regulation, Dereck, and the aircraft needs to be equipped with ADS-B.'

'What the hell is ADS-B?'

'Automatic Dependent Surveillance — Broadcast.'

'What's that?'

'It's a system in which aircraft broadcast their position, velocity, identity and other information at a high rate. It's broadcast so that anyone can receive and display the information. Ground stations receive aircraft ADS-B transmissions and forward them for display on Air Traffic Control or ATC consoles. Typically, ATC can use ADS-B information in the same way as radar.'

'OK, well, just use radar.'

'Yes, we can use radar, but …'

The federal officer cut in abruptly.

'Look, who cares, mate? We have a potential terrorist attack coming in our direction, and if it's proven that this guy's not a terrorist then, we have an emergency on our hands. OK? So, don't give me ADBs or whatever the hell it's called. I want to know who this bugger is, and that's your job for the moment. If he's a terrorist, then you Air Force guys will go up and blow him out of the skies over international waters. That's why we're here in Darwin … all out of sight out of mind up here in at the top end and away from the eyes of the rest of the country. OK? Let's confirm who he is first and not get ahead of ourselves. OK?

'Excuse me, sir, radar has picked an unidentified aircraft inbound tracking one eight four degrees,' a controller yelled across from the other side of the tower. Heads turned to the person.

'This is got to be him. Everything else in the sky is identified. Suggest a heading change of one eight zero degrees to confirm aircraft,' the controller added.

The senior controller looked over to the young woman in contact with the bomber.

'Have we still got him?'

'Yes sir, but his broadcast is poor.'

'OK. Get him to change his heading to one eight zero degrees.'

'Roger that.' She pressed the broadcast button. 'Inbound B17 On Eagles Wings, Darwin approach, change heading to one eight zero degrees, Darwin Approach.'

The reply was prompt.

'Darwin approach, Inbound B17 ... Eagles Wings, cha... hea... to one eight zero degrees, Darwin Approach.' The immediate reply was menaced with static and an eerie phasing effect over the broadcast.

All waited.

'Anything happening?' the senior controller asked, eager to break the silence.

'No sir, aircraft maintaining one eight ... um, standby sir ... yes sir, aircraft changing heading, standby.' There was silence as the controller waited for confirmation. 'Yes, we have inbound aircraft heading now one eight zero degrees.' An excited air exploded in the environment of the control tower.

'Inbound B17 On Eagles Wings, Darwin Approach, we have you confirmed on radar.

Standby, Darwin Approach.'

'Darwin approach, B17 On Eagles Wings, standing by, B17 On Eagles Wings.' The broadcast was clear.

More silence.

'This could be difficult. The equipment is likely in poor shape.' Derek walked over from the other side of the tower and spoke discretely to the pilot's father.

'And the engines?' The reverend honoured Derek's discretion by dropping his tone of voice.

'Who really knows; this is an old aircraft. In fact, it's frankly all a bit sketchy. Many questions, but one thing we do know and that is this: someone who says he's your son is flying a flaming B17 to Darwin. God only knows how he's going to get this damn thing down safely if he gets here.'

A pained look came across the senior man's face.

'Well, I'm glad that God does know and I'm looking forward to seeing how he's going to do it.' The pastor replied quietly.

The controller yelled out from the other side of the tower.

'Distance from station?' the senior controller asked.

'He's three hundred and ten miles from station, sir. His track to station ... still maintaining one eight zero degrees.'

The young female officer looked up at Derek.

'OK, let's find out who he is first and check to see if systems are OK.' Derek looked around at the family.

'Ready to do some talking?' he said. The family confirmed positively.

'Inbound B17 On Eagles Wings, Darwin Approach. Are you declaring an emergency?

Darwin approach.'

'Darwin approach, B17 On Eagles Wings, the only emergency we have on board is two small ratbags who need a toilet. I speak of our daughters, five and eight years old …' The pilot released a laugh and signed off his broadcast. 'B17 On Eagles Wings.'

Three adults flashed their eyes to each other, begging confirmation of what they had just heard.

'Ratbags. He would also say that. I never liked it,' the senior female was first to speak.

'If that isn't Paul, then someone is taking him off perfectly,' the pastor offered.

'Can I talk to him?' Lynn beckoned the man in charge.

Derek nodded at the controller.

'Tell him that there is someone here that he might know, but don't tell him who it is'.

He said to the young controller, who went straight to work.

'Inbound B17 On Eagles Wings, Darwin Approach, copy that. Got someone here you might know. She'd like to say G'day. Standby, Darwin Approach.'

'Darwin approach, B17 On Eagles Wings, standing by, On Eagles Wings.'

Lynn slowly took the microphone.

'Press that button to talk and release it to listen.' The controller suggested.

'Thank you. What's your name?'

'Robyn.'

'Thank you so much, Robyn. I can't do it the way you do it, the talking thing that is.

Can I just talk to him?' Lynn asked hesitantly.

'Absolutely.' Derek barged in. His impatience was showing again.

She pressed the button.

'Hey, Big Fella, how you going? Can you hear me?'

There was nothing but periodic amounts of static.

'Hello, Paul? Do you catch me?'

'Copy, the word is copy, as in, do you copy me.' Robyn quickly corrected with a broad smile across her face.

'Who gives a shit. Just let her talk.' The federal officer barked his impatience directly at the Air Force controller.

'It's OK,' Lynn raised her eyebrows, acknowledging her teacher's correction, then pressed the button on the microphone.

'Um, Oh, sorry, I believe that should be ... do you copy me? Hey, it's great to hear your voice, big fella.'

'Darwin approach ... B17 On Eagles Wings ... um ... is that you ... Lynn?'

Robyn looked straight at Derek who turned his gaze at the one being questioned.

'Sure is.'

'Hey squirt, what on earth are you doing there in Darwin?' His voice came back filled with emotion.

Lynn swung around addressing all before her. Her face was wildly animated.

'It's Paul!' Lynn screamed with pure delight, forgetting any need to reply to her long-lost brother. 'It's Paul, Mom. Dad, it's Paul ... He's alive. Oh Lord, thank you! He's alive! Derek, it's my brother. He always called me Squirt. No one else would have known that, no one Derek ... no one.'

The Federal Police officer looked at her father. The pastor's face was beaming and eyes were welling up with tears of joy.

'I have to concur. That's definitely our Paul, no doubt ... no doubt about it. Squirt ...' He laughed and took his wife in his arms who, at this stage was sobbing joyfully.

The officer in charge of the tower walked over with a box of tissues.

'I take it we have a positive ID on this one?' The officer asked Derek, whilst handing the goods to the people in need.

'Yep, I'd say that's an affirmative, mate.'

'OK, Robyn, better hand him over to us. If he's three hundred clicks away, he'll be here in an hour and a bit.' The officer in charge calmly instructed.

'Darwin approach, B17 On Eagles Wings, hey Squirt, you still there?'

'Inbound B17 On Eagles Wings, Darwin Approach, we have some excited people here. To answer your question; yes, she's still here. We also have your parents here, but back to business; I'll hand you over to the boys on the front desk. Stay on frequency. Time to guide you home, Big Fella. Darwin Approach.' Robyn looked up at Lynn and winked.

'Why don't we have a word of prayer. Let's thank the Lord and pray for Paul ... and we have three new members of our family and for their safety?' The reverend spoke discretely to his family.

'Derek, we're just going to pray. Is it OK if we stand over there?' He pointed to an out of the way area, next to a large filing cabinet.

The Federal Police officer was taken back by the request.

The Reverend Langley noted the odd look on Derek's face.

'Would that be a problem?'

'Well I guess not. You're not going to sing ... hymns or anything like that ... are you?'

'No, we'll behave ... unless you'd like a tune. I'm sure we could belt out *'Onward Christian Soldiers'* if you like, or what about *'Amazing Grace'* that one really identifies with the crowd. We could all sing along. It would be a real hoot,' Lynn said, making fun of Derek's naïve concerns.

Derek's face changed. He saw her point, and for the first time since his association with these Queenslanders, he laughed hard. The rest of the Air Force personal took the cue and joined in.

'Right, no, probably not a good idea,' he said still settling down.

CHAPTER SIXTY

———— ∾ ————

The atmosphere on the flight deck of the inbound vintage aircraft was electrified.

'Oh Paul, That, was your sister?

The pilot nodded.

'I can't believe your family are all there in Darwin. How's that possible?' Claire asked in pure astonishment.

The pilot in command, who was back at the controls, shrugged his shoulders, but said nothing. He was struggling with checking instruments, looking for confirmation that all was 'A OK'. However, all wasn't, 'A OK'. He wasn't OK at all. His face was strained. Now, joyous emotions were getting the better of him and causing him to lose focus. He had just heard the voice of his sister. It was all too surreal. Memories were returning, such as recollections of family, his medical past, his favourite food. He was coming home. A tear slid down the side of his face. A quick wipe from his right shoulder dealt with the complaint before his wife saw it. His thoughts began to race through his head. He felt suddenly overwhelmed. An unexpected bolt of panic attacked his joy. What was he thinking putting his family in such danger? How irresponsible can a man be? Then again what other option did they really have? Will they make it? Can he land this monster? He shook himself from these deadly doubts. The Bible verse, *I can do all things through Christ who strengthens me*, shot through his heart, attacking these heady doubts from hell.

'Yes, I can,' he spoke it out, forgetting his company.

'Excuse me?' Claire spun around and stared at her man at the controls.

'Sorry.'

'Battles?'

'Yeah. Philippians four thirteen.'

'Oh yeah, good one … yes you can indeed, my love. We all can.'

'Mom?' Tiffany tapped her mother on the shoulder.

Claire turned to her daughter.

'Mom, why is there a long cloud coming out of that engine?' She pointed to the power plant closest to the pilot. Tiffany was now standing behind her father pointing to the engine.

As he looked back. He suddenly saw it. A faint wisp of white smoke was streaming its way from the underside of the engine. Panic returned, commanding its place back in his heart.

His gaze shot straight to the engine's temperature gauge. Temperatures were slightly higher, and oil pressure had dropped a little on number two engine.

'No, no, no,' he said softly.

'Paul, is it on fire?'

'No.'

'Well, why the smoke?'

'We might have an oil leak, not sure.'

'What are we going to do?'

'Shut it down and try to restart it when it's time to land. I'm thinking it will be more useful then. It'll be tricky enough landing this thing with four engines, not sure I want to consider doing it with fewer.' His grim face set the new tone. He looked over at Claire and shrugged his shoulders again.

'Really? How will you restart?' The thought of turning off an engine was more than Claire wanted to consider, but not being able to restart it added to her concern.

'Will use the force of the airflow to turn the prop. Same principle as a windmill.'

'Oh, OK. We can fly with three engines?'

'Yes, but not as well, of course. We might initially loose altitude. OK, so, hold on, this might get interesting. Before I shut it down, I'm going to bring the power back on that engine, and we'll see how she responds. I suspect we might see some yawing and rolling come into the picture.'

'Joy.' Claire braced herself. 'Hold on kids.' The children held on tight to the back of their parent's seats.

'OK, old girl. Let's see what you'll do with this.' Paul took hold of the throttle of engine number two and began to retard it back slowly to idle setting. He was focused again.

A noticeable difference was heard when the engine was commanded to reduce its workload.

'Wow,' he breathed out aloud. The flying fortress responded immediately.

'Why is it doing that?' Claire instinctively spoke out expressing her need to know whilst holding on firmly to the dash.

'Hang on.' His hands were full. Unable to continue the lesson on 'Operations and Effects of controls', the man in command immediately exercised rudder and aileron initially to correct the yawing and the rolling movement that greeted the new power settings.

Resetting his rudder trim, Paul sat back, carefully gauging the aircraft's stability.

'Right, that was interesting. Now, to answer your question; We've just reduced the amount of thrust off the left wing; therefore, we have more thrust being generated off the right wing, so that wing will be sucked, so to speak around to the left due to that imbalance of thrust. That's called yawing and the secondary effect of yaw is roll. That's why you saw the wings banked to the left. With all that in mind, I had to exercise right rudder to correct the left yawing response and right aileron to correct the left bank. Interesting stuff, hey?'

'Right ... '

Paul quickly studied his wife's face.

'That was as clear as mud, wasn't it?'

'Yep ... but I see that you are happy with how it went. You happy, me happy.'

'Would be happier if this engine was happier,' Paul said.

The pilot in command brought the power of the troubled engine back up to one thousand RPM; then he disengaged the turbo charger. After which the specific mixture control was used to cut fuel flow and the ailing power plant spluttered to silence. Once the propeller was feathered, reducing the drag, additional power was applied to number one engine, thereby aiding power required for balance.

'Inbound B17 On Eagles Wings, Darwin Approach'

Paul focused on the task at hand. His aircraft had settled well, given the new power equation. He continued to fine-tune his trim settings and monitoring his remaining engine temperatures and pressures. He particularly watched engine number one's gauges, given the higher power setting now in place.

'Paul, are you going to answer them?'

'First things first, love. Flying this aeroplane is more important than talking to the tower.'

'Oh really?'

'Absolutely.'

'Aren't you supposed to jump to their commands, you know, like they are the boss, yes?'

'Not exactly, we have a rule in the aviation industry; Aviate, Navigate, Communicate and in that order. The tower won't be much use to us if I can't maintain control of our plane … Make sense?' he asked, focusing on the task at hand, ignoring any effort to make eye contact with his wife.

'Inbound B17 On Eagles Wings, Darwin Approach'.

He continued to scan his instruments, checking the aircrafts new trim setting as part of the process until he was satisfied that all systems were functioning well.

'Darwin approach, On Eagles Wings, Go ahead,' he said, now totally in command of their situation. Claire watched her husband. She had seen him deal with many difficult situations during their ten years of marriage, from securing their mountain home during an intense typhoon, to the breach birth of their youngest daughter, but never had she seen her man, with such strain written on his face.

'Inbound B17 On Eagles Wings, Darwin Approach adjust heading to one eight five degrees, Darwin Approach.'

There was no response.

'Inbound B17 On Eagles Wings, do you read, Darwin Approach?'

More silence was their companion again.

'Inbound B17 On Eagles Wings, Darwin Approach' The controller looked across at the officer in charge as he tapped the B17's flight progress strip directly in front of him.

'Darwin approach, On Eagle's Wings, apologies got my hands full up here with an engine problem. Adjusting heading to one eight five degrees. Have three engines operational maintaining seven thousand five hundred. On Eagle's Wings.'

All heads turned and eyes shot to the family. Their prayer stopped.

'Derek, did I hear Paul say that he has engine problems?' Lynn spoke up.

'Ah, yeah.'

'Oh Lord.' Lynn hushed her prayer heavenward.

The retired pastor took out his cell phone and immediately rang the senior Pastor of the church that he and his wife attended in Brisbane.

A prayer chain had begun. Lynn contacted her friends on Facebook, using her cell phone.

She shared the story and asked for prayer. Those friends contacted their network also asking for this heavenly supernatural support. A network of prayer began to grow steadily within minutes. The news spread rapidly. Emails, texts, Facebook, Twitter, phone calls, Skype messages, all mounting a massive prayer vigil globally.

'Inbound B17 On Eagles Wings, Darwin Approach, do wish to declare a state of emergency? Darwin Approach.'

'Darwin Approach, On Eagle's Wings, affirm, On Eagles Wings.'

'Inbound B17 On Eagles Wings, Darwin Approach, confirm again that you have the aircraft under control. Darwin Approach.'

The atmosphere in the tower was tense.

'Darwin Approach, On Eagle's Wings, confirming aircraft is under control, flying straight and level, seven thousand five hundred, all systems satisfactorily operational, except for engine number two. Have been losing oil pressure, due to possible oil leak, I intend to try a restart on long final. We'll see how we go. On Eagles Wings.'

'Inbound B17 On Eagles Wings, Darwin Approach, copy that, Darwin Approach'.

A young woman entered the control environment and walked directly to the officer in charge.

'Excuse me, sir, it seems that we have a group of journalists downstairs asking questions about the inbound World War II aircraft.' She looked across at Derek and quickly looked back to her superior.

'Really, Corporal? They got clearance?'

She shook her head and looked across at the Federal Officer again.

'Derek, I've just been advised that we've got the media wanting a statement. They know what's going on it seems.' The officer in charge distracted Derek's focus and stood ready to do the bidding of the Federal Police officer.

'What? I told them to wait.'

'They're downstairs,' he added.

'How the heck did they get downstairs? Derick's face was strained.

'Absolutely no idea,' the officer replied.

'I told Channel Seven to wait. I'd give them the story. They got us up here, and they'd break the story. That was the deal. They know exactly what's going on. We spent four flipping hours together in their dam aircraft. Stagger me!' Derek rubbed the back of his neck in frustration.

'Excuse me, sir, it's not the Seven network.' The young Air Force corporal offered some clarity.

'Oh OK, thank you, Corporal.' Derek offered a quiet response. With that she promptly made her way back downstairs after being dismissed by the officer in charge.

'How would the TV station know what's happening with Paul's plane?' Lynn was listening.

'They monitor our broadcast.' The Air Force officer replied. The tension was mounting further, and Derek was beginning to lose his composure. He didn't want this aircraft to go down, and he certainly didn't want to face the media.

'They listen to your communication?' Lynn asked.

'Oh yeah,' the officer in charge answered her while looking straight at Derek.

'Bloody hell! OK, let's go down. Mate can you get someone to get the seven boys up here? A deal's a deal. Ring the CEO. He's got them caged somewhere.' A frenzy of phone calls were made.

In minutes the Seven crew were on their way. Derek stepped through the control room's exit, ignoring the family and made his way down to the ground floor.

Outside the entrance of the control tower, the camera men swung their units around to the officials coming their way.

'Hi guys. I can't give you too much time, a lot going on upstairs, so let me confirm that we have an inbound aircraft that is facing some challenges at the moment. I ...' His statement was cut by a reporter.

'We have heard that this aircraft has been classified as a threat. Can you confirm this?' The journalist asked with great passion.

'No, that is incorrect.'

'There is a rumour that the pilot on board has been missing presumed dead for seventy years, and he is flying a missing World War II B17 bomber. Can you substantiate this?' Another journalist hastily grabbed his opportunity.

'This person was on our missing list for some time, but not seventy years, and we have no information on the aircraft, other than it is a World War II aircraft.'

'Some are saying that he was abducted by aliens and could be returning on an abducted aircraft. We believe that he has others on board with him. Could these people be other World War II crew members who have come back with him from a different dimension?'

'What?' Derek jerked his head back and frowned. 'Firstly, the person in question is not of World War II vintage and secondly, if you mean *little green men* type abduction.

Absolutely not.' His tolerance was running low again.

'So, who's accompanying him?'

'Just his family. Anyway, I'd better get back upstairs. I don't know how you got here, but I'll organise someone to escort you back to the terminal.' Derek turned and started to walk away as abruptly as he arrived.

'What time will the aircraft arrive?'

He turned slightly as he continued his way to the entrance of the tower.

'See ya, guys. Sorry I can't stay longer,' he said, turning away from the eager media team whilst waving goodbye.

'Alien abduction, what have these guys been smoking?' He looked at the officer in charge of the tower and shook his head. 'I'd like to find out who's their source of information. Alien abduction, strike.' Derek said in total disbelief. 'Mate, the Seven TV crew will be here in a minute. Can you organise someone to make sure that those *nut cases* don't come in with the Channel Seven guys? I wouldn't put it past them. Alien abduction. That really tops it.' He began to laugh softly.

Back in the control tower, Derek walked straight past the family and stood with the senior controller who began to talk with another Air Force officer. An influx of incoming aircraft was creating a busy time for the military on duty. Derek waited until the senior controller had finished with his subordinate.

'OK, mate, I'll get you to take this incoming mystery bird. He's your baby.'

'Approach and ground sir?' The officer questioned.

'Yes, bring him in and park him.'

'GA sir?'

'Yeah, General Aviation will do for the time being.'

'Yes, sir, we can chuck him right over in the corner. There's plenty of room today. So what's the deal with this war bird?'

'Get him down and in one piece. That's the deal.' Derek interjected.

'We'll guide him home, but he has to get it down ... in one piece.' The answer was equally as abrupt as Derek's demands.

'Have we got the fire boys on standby?' Derek asked ignoring the controller's terse reply.

'Ready to go.' The senior controller answered noting the tension mounting between the two men. Derek turned away and moved to the family.

'ETA circuit?' Derek asked with his back to the one answering.

The reply was delayed. All eyes were fixed on the source of information.

'Strike, he'll be in circuit in forty-five minutes.'

Derek spun around. 'What?'

'He's picked up a tailwind.' The man in charge looked to Derek. 'How's his track to station?'

'Five degrees left of track.'

'OK, get him back on track. We'll bring him through the northern inbound VFR lane of entry.' He took the binoculars placed on the centre consul in the top deck of the tower and aimed the apparatus at the general vicinity of the inbounds expected position. His search was thorough, but futile.

'Inbound B17 On Eagles Wings, Darwin Approach, adjust your heading to one eight eight degrees. Expect runway one, one, QNH one zero one two, please reconfirm that you have the aircraft under control and flying assigned altitude of seven thousand five hundred feet. Darwin Approach.'

There was no answer.

'Nothing?' Derek stood next to man with the authority.

'If he's forty-five minutes away, should be able to see a dot at least.' He adjusted his focus on the binoculars.

'Those things powerful enough? He's a fare way away.'

'Oh yeah. Can see a flea on a dingo's bum a mile away. Matter of time. He's probably out a bit too far to get visual yet.'

'Can I have a look?' Derek asked with hand out ready to receive.

'Sure.'

The Federal Police officer haphazardly took the unit, flicked its strap over his head and placed the high-powered binoculars to his face.

'Darwin approach, on Eagles Wings, adjust heading to one eight eight degrees. Expect runway one, one, QNH one zero one two, confirming that we have the aircraft under control and flying assigned altitude of seven thousand five hundred feet.' The broadcast cut through stronger than before. The Langley family stood calmly in the corner, watching every movement and listening to every sound. Their faces lit up as the broadcast continued to confirm their hope.

'Excuse me, sir, the television crew is here.' The young female corporal entered the restricted area once again and spoke to her superior.

'No strays with them?'

'No sir.'

'OK, bring them in.' Derek took over, with the technology still against his eyes, eagerly searching for the dot.

With a simple nod, permission was granted and the two well-dressed media employees entered with equipment at the ready. Derek quickly looked across at the emerging media presence and then returned to his surveillance.

'Hey fellas, stay out of the way, no talking to anyone on duty OK? Oh, by the way the only reason you're here is because we owe your boss big time, and your competition has got wind of this. Anyway, get your camera rolling; he's coming from that way.' Derek pointed to the general direction still with the Air Force assets fixed around his neck.

'So, I'll leave you with the family. Oh, and by the way, ... there's no little green men, OK?' He placed the binoculars back up to his face and continued his search.

The attractive blond female journalist looked at her partner in astonishment, both having no idea what he was talking about. She went straight to work getting permission to interview the Langley family whilst the camera man began shooting various footage useful for the exclusive in the making. Within ten minutes the family were busy answering questions, whilst the camera hungrily recorded every response.

'You've all been through an horrendous journey where for ten years you were mourning the believed death of your son and now an amazing revelation ... your son's alive. How do you feel?' The journalist asked with emotions running higher than the ones being questioned.

'Got him,' Derek yelled out. All heads spun around to the one declaring his find.

Derek took the binoculars from his face, and he pointed exactly to the flying fortress's position. 'Here, have a look, mate.' He gave back the unit to the man in charge standing next to him. 'At least, it might be him. It's just a dot.'

The officer quickly retrieved the visual aid and focused towards the suggested direction. After a few seconds, victory was his.

'Yep, I'd say you might be right, Derek. He's still a way off, but I'd say that's him.

Well done.' He dropped the binoculars down in front of his face, gaining perspective with the known landscape. 'OK, what other inbounds do we have left to process.'

'Three heavies ... Um, all due in twenty minutes and two outbound ... heavies. Do you want the incoming to enter a holding pattern?'

'No, get them in. Expedite them, hey? And the others? ... when are they due to depart?'

'Both thirty minutes.'

'Mm, very tight ... Let's go with it, business as usual. We may have to vector the fortress in for a straight-in approach. Keep him headed for the lane of entry for the time being.'

The controllers moved with a new sense of purpose. Communication with the incoming aircraft was stepped up, advising them to increase speed ensuring an earlier arrival at circuit for the respective domestic carriers. Each aircraft was assigned different altitudes maintaining constant separation.

The three cell phones owned by the respective family members were increasing their activity, interrupting their interview with the television crew. The incoming callers were asking for clarity, regarding the news just received or further information required for prayer. Social media was running hot as the compounding effect of the news grew.

Commercial radio networks began to ring, somehow obtaining the private numbers of the family members.

Within twenty minutes, the three incoming airliners were in circuit of the Darwin airport. The first, a Qantas flight, was on short final. The second, a Jet Star flight was positioned on long final and the last incoming, a Virgin Atlantic flight, was turning on the base leg of Darwin's circuit area. All aircraft were targeting runway one one. The two outbound flights had just been given permission to taxi to the entry point and advised to hold.

'Nice piece of work, mate. They should all be out of our hair by the time our long *lost-boy* and his family arrive. You blokes really know how to move metal, don't ya?'

'All in a day's work,' the officer in command replied softly as he stared at the incoming fortress through the high-powered binoculars.

'Here, take a look at this.' The visual aid was given to Derek.

'Where am I looking now?'

'That way.' The officer in command pointed in a northeast direction. 'Don't see that every day.'

Derek snapped the unit to his face and searched.

'Got him?'

'Hang on ... Ah, there you are. Wow! Will ya have a look at that? Holy ...'

The sight of the mysterious vintage aircraft took Derek by surprise. Its presence came with an unusual aura of authority. A cluster of cloud parted, as though on cue, revealing the sun's golden rays bursting its glory directly onto the surface of the aircraft, spotlighting its maiden flight into the twenty-first century.

'Hey, Pastor! You might like to have a look at this.' He swung the binoculars towards the oldest man in the room whilst pointing in the direction he wanted him to search.

Quickly, the reverend was at his side, adjusting the focus searching for the reward, closely followed by the cameraman hungry for the right angle.

'Oh my, that is one big aircraft. Wow! Frankly, it's hard to believe that Paul is ... actually flying that thing.'

'Well, given all the reports and your confirmation, that's our understanding.' Derek hinted a slight amount of sarcasm.

'It certainly looks like it's not to be messed with, doesn't it? … Powerful! What a picture. What an amazing sight … Wow! … He's coming home.'

'Yeah … sure looks that way, Pastor, and … Uncle Sam is bringing them home … On Eagles Wings … go figure … go figure,' Derek said softly, as he gazed out at the speck now growing by the minute.

'Well, yes, I guess you could say that Uncle Sam is certainly doing that, for which I am thankful but, the question needs to be asked, who was underpinning America throughout that time when this aircraft was made? Who was ensuring their success?'

Derek snapped out of his daze and looked straight at the one responsible for his wake-up call. 'Um, don't know … the Rockefellers? … you tell me.' A slight smirk travelled across his face.

The reverend laughed softly. 'You OK if I quote the Bible?'

'Sure thing. Fire away,' he said softly, moving in closer, suddenly oblivious to what was happening around him. His curiosity was ignited. The Man of God continued to watch his son's vehicle of deliverance through the binoculars, yet very conscious that God was speaking.

'Well, in Daniel two, verse two it says, '*He changes times and seasons; he deposes kings and raises up others. He gives wisdom to the wise and knowledge to the discerning.*'

'OK. So, you reckon God's the one who gave them a kick along.'

'Yes, I do, Derek! So, looking at the big picture in this context? … I would say the God of Abraham, Isaac and Jacob is bringing them home … Using the *gift* He gave Uncle Sam …

This B17 bomber and now, somehow, He's given it to Paul to fly home … On Eagles Wings.'

'Yeah? Ya reckon?'

'Mm, I reckon!'

'Right, OK.'

'That's just my opinion, but right now we are seeing God in action, Derek, and as I said, He's using one of the gifts He gave America that helped win the war a long time ago, and now it's winning this war on our behalf.' Reverend Langley continued his surveillance of his son's transport. Derek looked around. By this stage, the camera was pointed directly at the pastor's face.

'Mate, can you buzz off?' The Federal Officer spat his request with his usual lack of finesse. The cameraman left immediately returning to the women of the family.

'Looks like it's being used to win a different war.' Derek looked back at the incoming deliverer deep in thought.

'Yes, indeed, set aside for a time such as this, so to speak.'

'Maybe eh? ... but why do think God was on the Yank's side and .... say, not Hitler's side or .... you know, why our American cousins?' Derek hushed his words, as he moved in respectively closer to the man who knew God.

'Interesting question, Derek' The reverend released his visual aid from his face.

'Yeah, I thought so.' The Federal Officer said with a cheeky grin across his face now turning to his teacher.

'Firstly, I think they chose to be on God's side, and Hitler didn't. In those days, America wasn't afraid to spell it out to the world.'

'Yeah? How so?'

'Well, first you need to understand the country's foundation. In the beginning, the country was dedicated to God.'

'Bull shit! No way!'

'No bull about it. It's a fact. Just read the history books. It's all there. Read America's constitution and so on. It's brilliant doc-umentation. The country was set up by their forefathers for real freedom and authentic liberty.'

'Dedicated to God, hey? Didn't know that.'

'Yep! It's true! The only other country that was dedicated to God as I understand it was Israel.

'OK, but how did they spell it out'

'Just a tick.' The father of the pilot put down the visual aid. Using his cell phone, the Reverend Langley searched the internet. Derek watched this man with new interest.

The pastor suddenly looked up at the federal officer.

'Here we are. It started back with President Thomas Jefferson. This is what he said Derek: *'The God who gave us life gave us liberty at the same time'* and he asked *"Can the liberties of a nation be secure when we have removed a conviction that these liberties are of God?"'*

'Wow, that's, um ... pretty deep.'

'Yes, it is.'

Yeah, but ... how was that spelt out to the world?' Derek insistently posed his question.

'Well, eventually, they printed it on their money for one thing. I think the coins first.'

'Ah yeah! That's the *IN GOD WE TRUST* thing.'

'Exactly and after World War II, the US dollar became the international reserve currency, and to this day the one-dollar note declares it all over the world that America trusts in God.'

'Stagger me ... makes you think. Mind you ... wouldn't know it today, would you?'

'Yes, it seems that Uncle Sam is not as eager to make that declaration these days.

Mind you, we'll see what this current presidency will do in that area.'

'Darwin Approach, On Eagles Wings?' The radio speaker suddenly demanded attention.

CHAPTER SIXTY-ONE

Over the previous period of three hours, the inbound pilgrims had tracked their way over many islands, around high mountains with considerable cloud hanging over or covering the mischievous terrane. Some were too high to climb over, given the lack of oxygen on board. Many altitude changes, heading changes and the corresponding adjustment to power settings proved a taxing responsibility of the man flying this nineteen-forties technology. Finally, a broad expanse of land came slowly and vaguely into view on the horizon, from east to west.

'Paul? Look.' Claire pointed to the horizon. 'Can you see that?'

'Yep. Been watching it for the last five minutes or so.'

'Is that land?'

'Yep, sure is.'

'Australia?'

'I think it might be, love.'

Claire swung around to their children.

'Girls, see that faint line on the horizon?' She slowly swung her pointed finger from east to west.

'Mom, what's horizon?' Tiffany, the curious one of the family asked the most important question of the moment.

'Where the sky meets the ground, baby.'

Both girls acknowledged the reference referred to by their mother.

'That's Australia.'

'Will we see kangaroos, Mom?' Jessica yelled out over the roar of the engines.

Claire nodded, and the children expressed their delight to each other and began to dance their version of the Australian indigenous, *Kangaroo Dance,* in the cramped space behind their pilot's seats.

Another hour's flying and the man at the controls showed further signs of strain.

Claire studied her husband. His face was pale. She asked their children to get the water and the remainder of the fish that was cooked for breakfast earlier the morning. In an instant Jessica and Tiffany brought what the doctor's wife had ordered. Jessica passed the bottle to her father, to which he received the gift happily and took large gulps of its contents eagerly, almost greedily. The subtlety of dehydration had its hold on the man in command.

'Thank you,' he said, wiping its surplus from his stubbled face in readiness to consume a small piece of fish.

'Drink more. You don't look good, my boy,' Claire instructed the doctor on board.

'Here, let me take the controls again. You take a break. Keep drinking that water,' she firmly instructed. He needed no convincing. Fully confident that his wife could handle what was required to keep their flight on course and at altitude, he handed over God's gift to her control, if only for ten minutes or so. Quickly Claire settled into the work required. Her husband sat back, drinking more water and snacking of the reef fish caught that day. Within minutes a sudden need to relieve his bladder arrested his attention.

'Hey, I got to go take a wee walk.'

'What? You are so not leaving me here on my own buster.'

'I so am. Look, I'll just be there.' He pointed to the area a few feet away from their seats.

'Paul?'

'She's trimmed up nicely, and it's as smooth as silk. Just remember, small corrections if there's any turbulence. I'll just be there. Back in a jiffy.' He released his seat belt, stood up and made his way to the edge of the bomb bay well. Paul had only recently taken the antiquated infamous B17 toilet from the aircraft.

His intentions of toilet modifications weren't realised due to their sudden departure from their island home, and the consequences were that they were forced to use the bomb bay well which proved a little difficult for the females. Upon his return, he noted Claire's attention to detail.

She was handling the aircraft well, checking instruments by pointing to the ones in question whilst maintaining her reference to the horizon. In fact, Claire had refused to use the only option for a bathroom on the aircraft.

'How's it going, Captain?' he said still watching her mastering her newfound responsibilities. 'You're doing well,' he added.

'I hope you are going to clean out that bomb bay because I'm certainly not going to do it.'

'Listen to you, girl.' He laughed. 'Give you a few minutes in command, and you're throwing your weight around.'

'It's pretty disgusting.'

'Good enough for the girls, good enough for me. When I take back to the controls in a bit, maybe you should go ... you know, before we land. Come on; it'll be fun ... you'll see.'

He laughed.

'Paul, what would people think.'

'I do remember many years ago that you labelled me as a prude ... now who's the prude?' The pilot snickered to himself 'and what would people think? … well I think that they would think better go there than in your shorts … and besides, by the time we land, it will all be dried out. No problems. If you don't tell … I won't tell.' He laughed again.

His face was showing better colour. He sat back after strapping himself into his command seat and sipped on more water. 'Are you right to keep flying? Will try to restart the engine soon, and I'll advise approach of our intentions.

Claire agreed, keeping her focus on the task at hand as her husband readied himself to make the broadcast.

'Darwin Approach, On Eagles Wings.' He sat back looking around admiring the topography coming toward them from over the horizon.

It had been ten long, difficult years. Questions began to mount again. Will the children cope with the new home awaiting them? Would they be able to cope with other people, and for that matter, would he and his wife ever be able to deal with crowds again?

He felt strangely unsettled. Paul looked down at his faded pants. The edges were rotting, and a cluster of small holes revealed a section of his well-tanned right hip. Under his jacket, his shirt was falling apart at its collar and its base. His clothing may have been in tatters, but physically he was returning home a different man. He was tanned, trimmed and muscularly toned. The doctor looked closely at his wife and studied her in this new light. Her clothes were equally as tattered, but her body was in good shape. Paul noted that their girls under their jackets, they were still dressed in their pyjamas, which amounted to oversize T-shirts and no underwear. Given the sudden departure, not one of the family had combed their hair.

Reality hit him hard. They all looked like healthy, well-tanned vagabonds with no shoes. He imagined their entry into Australian immigration and then customs. He began to laugh. *One look at us and customs might put us all into quarantine*, he thought. Then, there was their pet hen. Out of all the family, she was the one who would present in public the best. *Now that will really raise eyebrows*, he considered further. *What a sight this is going to be*, he thought.

Dr Paul Langley is returning to Australia with his vagabond family, accompanied by their stowaway hen, Chickadee, who is not *to be considered as an optional extra.* His sense of humour rose to the occasion.

He began to laugh uncontrollably.

'Inbound B17 On Eagles Wings, Darwin Approach, go ahead.'

Claire looked to her man, somewhat puzzled at his outburst.

'Darwin Approach, On Eagles Wings, will be attempting a restart of engine number two. On Eagles Wings,' he said, desperately trying to control himself.

'Inbound B17 On Eagles Wings, copy that. When ready, descend to two thousand, five hundred feet; you are cleared to track direct for a straight-in approach runway one one, wind one one two degrees, ten knots. Report ten mile long final. Darwin Approach.'

Paul took a deep breath, seeking more composure.

'Darwin Approach, On Eagles Wings, when ready descend to two thousand five hundred feet cleared to track direct for a straight in approach runway one one, wind one one two degrees, ten knots. Will report ten-mile long final. On Eagles Wings.'

'Care to share the joke?' Claire asked, maintaining her position at the controls, with curiosity getting the better of her.

'Look at us.' He gestured, looking down at his pants and then at her rotting attire.

'Oh my.' She saw his point and began looking more closely at the family.

'Anyway, let's get this engine started,' he said wiping the joy off his face, and he began procedures to restart his ailing engine.

'OK, taking back the controls.' He took the yoke and reached to the master and ignition switches. 'Turning on engine number two, mixture full rich. OK, all is set.'

'Oh, my goodness, Paul. You're right. Look at us.' Claire surveyed her family. 'What will your family think?' she said beginning to laugh. She placed her hand over her mouth in quiet shock. A new reality was finding its roost.

'Actually, you know, we could be naked and, something tells me it wouldn't worry them. It's all going to be fine. They'll be overjoyed to see us, whatever our state.' He winked at her.

With systems ready for combustion to begin, the pilot in command engaged the pitch lever, reversing the propeller's feathered configuration.

'Well, under the circumstances, I'm so glad the Lord didn't wait for another year to bring those cutthroats to our island,' Claire said, her face exploding with wonder. 'Then, we might have been in that state.' She chuckled.

The propeller of engine number two began to turn as a result of the two hundred nautical mile per hour airflow, finding favour with the leading edge of each blade of the propeller.

'What do you mean?' the pilot said while they all watched as the power plant claimed centre stage. One, two, three, four, five, six cycles of the propeller, but no ignition.

'Well, within another twelve months, we probably would have been at that stage. Can you imagine? Oh, my goodness, Paul, what a sight we would have been then.' Claire laughed.

'We probably would have been arrested for indecent exposure.' She paused. 'Actually, come to think of it, we might get arrested for that when we get off the plane today,' Claire continued. 'Look at the side of your pants. You can see your hip, and I only noticed this morning after our swim that my back pocket in these shorts is coming apart and just starting to reveal a little too much. Oh, my goodness. I'll have to strap a pillow to my butt.'

The man in command was tuning out of the conversation. Something was wrong. The engine wasn't starting. He double-checked his systems for number two engine. Everything looked in order. Panic began to surface.

'We've got a problem,' he called out.

Claire snapped out of her dichotomy and gave her husband her total attention. Paul threw out a quick prayer before the throne of the most-high God.

Then, he suddenly saw it.

'Primer! Oh, come on, man. Primer!' he said, realising that he neglected to prime the engine and corrected the oversight immediately, as the propeller was still windmilling.

Smoke spewed from the engine as it coughed into life. The aircraft yawed to the right, with a roll quickly following. The pilot took the controls and addressed the new settings required.

At one thousand revs per minute, the super charger was engaged. Temperature and pressure gauges were monitored for the engine. He waited for engine temperature to increase before returning it to practical service. Within minutes, required readings were reached. Number two was brought back to service and joined the battle again.

'Well done.' Claire declared with much enthusiasm.

'Let's pray it stays with us until we land.' Reality was offered quickly.

The pilot in command radioed for vectoring to intercept the runway heading. After satisfactory communication with Darwin Approach, Paul reduced power, and the mighty World War II warrior began descending at a five hundred feet per minute rate of descent.

Turbulence welcomed the incoming family.

'Hang on, girls. This will get bumpy again.' Claire called to the children who were all eyes, eagerly watching everything their father was doing. Tiffany held on to the same chair as her sister with her pet chicken tightly tucked under her arm. Claire came to the rescue of the seemingly uncomfortable bird.

'Baby, put Chickadee downstairs.'

'Mom, she likes being with us,' the youngest of the family insisted.

'Tiff, put her in the turret,' Jessica quickly suggested. The girls knew that if the hen was put downstairs in the nose of the aircraft their faithful pet would only make her way back to the family.

'I'll do it, Tiff. I can reach it.' With that, the taller of the two children took the bird from Tiffany's armpit and carefully perched the hen in the gun turret set on top of the fuselage behind the flight deck. The old bird fluffed her feathers, faced the flight path and then remained perfectly still as though mesmerised by the expanse set before her.

'Hey. Look, Tiff. She likes it.'

Both girls stood under the glass dome and watched the family pet. The aging hen flapped her wings gently, then, lifted them as if in flight herself.

'Mom, Chickadee thinks she's flying again, just like she did downstairs.' Tiffany came to her mother with the exciting news.

'Is she now? She's a funny old thing. OK, now we'll be landing within a half an hour, so you guys better stand behind these seats and hold on, OK? Jess, you stand behind Dad and, Tiff, you stand behind me.'

'Mom, when are we going to get there?' Tiffany's question took her father by surprise. He looked to his wife.

'Strike! The "*are we there yet*" gene has just kicked in,' Paul yelled out.

'Now, didn't I just say that we would be there in half an hour or so? That's around thirty minutes, baby.' The children just stared at their mother. Time had never been an issue for the children, nor had much specific reference been made to it other than sunrise, morning, midday, afternoon, sunset and night-time. Paul smiled at his co-pilot.

'What's a minute, Claire?'

She saw his point. They had re-entered their old *time-hungry* world, taking on its perspectives immediately, but their children didn't come from this great southern land. The table was about to be turned for them, and soon they would be controlled to some degree by a timetable, day in and day out. Claire thought deeply on the subject.

'Baby, imagine that we are walking down to the yacht from our cave and then we come back the long way via the swimming hole and back up to the cave. That's how long it will take before we land the plane in Australia.'

'Oh, OK. That's not long,' Tiffany said totally satisfied, now looking back to see if her pet was still trying to fly behind the Perspex of the gun turret.

'Darwin Approach, On Eagles Wings, Two thousand five hundred, On Eagles Wings.' The pilot in command broadcast.

'Inbound B17 On Eagles Wings, copy that. Do you have the runway in sight? Darwin Approach.'

'Darwin Approach, On Eagles Wings, affirmative, runway in sight. On Eagles Wings.'

'Inbound B17 On Eagles Wings, cleared to land runway one one, winds one one five degrees, ten knots, QNH 1108, report ten-mile final. Darwin Approach.'

Paul followed procedures by reading back the instructions to the tower. The pilot set the aircraft up on base in preparation for a long final approach and aimed the aircraft at the threshold of the runway.

'OK, checklist, love.' He pointed to the document on his wife's side situated in a side pocket. She acted promptly to his command and began to read it.

'Um, Radio call. Yes, you've done that, Altimeter set.'

'Set with QNH of one one zero eight.'

'Crew positions.' She looked around at the children and answered for him, 'All good.'

'Autopilot off?'

'Was never on ... because she's not serviceable.'

'Booster pumps on?'

'Yep, on.'

'Mixture controls, auto rich ... I still have no idea what I'm saying here.'

'You're doing well ... Auto rich ... set,' he said smiling, obeying every command the Claire was calling out.

'Intercooler set?'

'Yep, set it is.'

'Carburettor filters ... open?'

'Yes, indeed ... open.'

'Landing gear.'

'OK, love, gear down.' The doctor pointer to the undercarriage lever, and Claire dutifully engaged it by pulling it down. A frenzied whirring sound could be heard immediately, followed by some grinding noises and finally a loud thud heralded the fact that the landing gear was down and locked.

'I have visual left and down.' He said, identifying the landing gear on his side.

'And I have right gear down and looking good.'

'Looking good hey?'

'It's down, Paul, and that's good ... no, very good. Do you have three greens?' she said making reference to the lights indicating that the undercarriage was down and locked.

'Yes, three greens. Hey, you're really getting into this flying thing, aren't you?'

'Should really get my commercial ... you know, get serious. I think I have a gift,' she said, mocking him.

'Qantas, here you come.'

'What can I say ... They need me.' She broke into a somewhat stressed chuckle, then continued her checklist readout as matter of fact.

'Tailwheel down, antenna in, ball turret checked ... Um, hydraulic pressure OK, Valve closed.'

'Yep all good ... and valve closed.'

'And flaps?' She looked across at her man.

'OK, one notch of flap,' Paul said softly as he engaged the appropriate lever.

All in the tower watched the distant incoming miracle in silence.

A phone rang. The head controller picked up.

'Hello. Yes, he is. Just a minute.' He turned to Dereck.

'Dereck, it's for you.'

The federal officer took the call. 'Yes,' he spat, still watching the incoming aircraft.

'Yes, Sir, just got positive ID. Doctor Paul Langley and his partner Claire Chandler and two children ... no confirmation of names so far regarding the kids,' he smartly relayed back to his authority. More questions came to the Federal Police's representation in the tower.

'That's right, two girls. Ages eight and five, I believe,' he advised as he began to write down more instructions. 'Oh really? Jessica and Tiffany. Yes, certainly, Sir. I will pass that on to the party in question,' Dereck said as he wrote further instructions. He scribbled down some notes and looked back at the incoming bomber.

'Well, Sir, assuming he can land this thing, he'll be down safely in about ten minutes,' he answered. More notes were jotted down. 'Yes, Sir, I'll relay that to them. Thank you, Sir and thank you for the call and the commendation, Sir. It means a lot. Goodbye, Sir. Yes of course. Thank you; goodbye, Sir.' The Federal Officer placed the receiver on its mount.

Dereck walked over to the family.

'Just got news from high up in Canberra. It looks like they want you all to stay in Darwin for a few days. This has just hit the media, and we'll keep you out of all the fuss. In addition to this, Claire's parents in the States have been notified, and they will be on a plane to Darwin tonight ... should get here by tomorrow afternoon.

You have all been booked into a hotel here in Darwin, complements of Channel Seven, and they have also contacted some clothing store here for everyone who needs stuff. Whatever you need, they will foot the bill. It seems they have already broken the story, and it's gone viral. Your son's a national hero over here. It looks like it's making big news in the States as well with that line ... Uncle Sam is bringing them home ... So probably better you guys are all up here for a while.'

'My goodness, thank you,' Reverend Langley said humbly.

'Oh yeah, and there was some nut case who rang Channel Seven after she saw the news of your son and said that she had had a dream the night before that a little girl flying into the country on an eagle must be given a pink dress. Anyway, the TV station interviewed this wacko, and after the interview was made public, they had children's clothing shops donating clothes, and of course a pink dress. Can you believe this? Anyway, thought you better know.' Dereck looked at the stunned faces standing in front of him.

Janene Langley hugged Dereck then kissed him on the cheek, followed by Lynn.

'Wow,' he gasped with a face as red as a beetroot.

'Thank you so much, Dereck,' Janene whispered to him. 'What a blessing.'

'I'm just the messenger, love ... that's the mob who's doing the blessing.' He pointed to the television crew. Both women turned, walked over to the journalist and threw their arms around her. The cameraman initially focused on the incoming aircraft, saw the commotion and immediately took the shot of the three women.

'Right, this might be all warm and fuzzy, but we've got an aircraft to get down safely,' he said wiping the remains of kisses from the side of his face.

The B17 Flying Fortress gracefully made its way through the thick tropical air of Darwin airspace.

'Come on, mate, bring her around easy like,' the head controller whispered, breaking his silence, as he watched the long-lost pilot gently turn the metal monster on to its first, final approach. He brought the binoculars from his face and looked over at Dereck who still had the pilot's father standing next to him.

'So, he's never really flown anything like this before?' The officer in command asked, with a deep frown now forming over his face.

Dereck shook his head slowly as the pastor watched on, equalling the concern, but for different reasons.

'Well, he seems to have her nicely under control, given everything. Let's hope that engine hangs in there for him ... poor bugger. Man, he'd have his hands full up there,' he continued, as he brought the binoculars back to his face, eager to regain his visual on the incoming.

A greater battle was raging. A visual of which would bring any human heart to failure. Leaving Dereck's side, Reverend Langley walked to his family and whispered to them.

'Pray. There is something evil at play here. I was just reminded that our fight is against principalities, against powers, against the rulers of the darkness of this world, against spiritual wickedness.' He looked deeply into the faces of his loved ones. Both women nodded in agreement, excused themselves from the journalist, bowed their heads together and began to pray quietly between themselves.

With the runway's threshold as its aim point, *On Eagles Wings* thundered its way down to its divinely appointed destination.

'Darwin Approach, On Eagles Wings, ten-mile, long final, runway one one. On Eagles Wings.' The radio burst into life.

'Oh Lord, bring them home safely ... Please,' Reverend Langley said quietly.

'Inbound B17 On Eagles Wings Darwin Approach, copy that, on landing take exit left B2 for GA parking. At exit B2, stay on this frequency for assistance to General Aviation.

Darwin Approach,' the controller broadcast. 'Come on, mate, you can do this,' he said off mic.

CHAPTER SIXTY-TWO

———— ❧ ————

Stress possessed Paul's face.

'Darwin Approach, On Eagles Wings, take exit left B2 for GA parking. Stay on frequency for assistance to GA parking. On Eagles Wings.' Paul read back the tower's commands.

Claire watched her man at the controls. His face grew pale again. The strain was eating its way into him again. The weight of the unknown pounded insistently into his very soul. Again, panic birthed its horror into his imagination. She saw his demeanour. He was under attack. Claire reached over and touched her husband's shoulder.

'But they that wait upon the LORD shall renew their strength; they shall mount up with wings as eagles; they shall run, and not be weary; and they shall walk, and not faint.'

She smiled.

With those words, an outpouring of peace suddenly filled the flight deck and light-heartedness was instantly known by all. The look on Paul's face changed.

'Thank you. ... Do you feel that?'

'Yes, I do.' Claire said, looking around her face wildly animated.

'Something tells me the Lord is with us, love,' the pilot spoke, with new vigour.

'Mom, look, look,' Tiffany yelled with great excitement. 'There's a big yellow M down there ... look, Tiffany,' beckoned her sister. 'Look, Jess, a big yellow M.'

'Oh yeah, Hey Dad ... Look, Dad. A big M ... M is for Mom.' Jessica yelled out.

'Can you see it, Mom. It's a big M.'

'Yes, Jess, I certainly can see it. It looks good enough to eat.' Claire laughed shaking her head.

The two children looked at each other slightly confused.

'Oh, my goodness, Paul, look at that. Can you believe it? We haven't even put foot to ground, and the kids have spotted McDonalds.'

'Inbound B17 On Eagles Wings, Darwin Approach, you have smoke coming from your number two engine. Darwin Approach.'

Paul swung around to confirm the report just received. There at the base of the cowling a fine stream of blue smoke was flowing freely again.

'Darwin Approach, On Eagles Wings, copy that. On Eagles Wings.'

'Here we go again ... hang in there, old girl, not long to go now.' The pilot got to work. Despite the circumstance, a new hope had entered the chosen man at the controls.

There was real peace in their flight deck that day, a peace that truly transcended all understanding, and a new confidence was birthed. Paul's right hand went straight to the throttle. The RPM on the engine in question was retarded a little, and engine number One was given to make up the loss in power again.

'Are you going to shut it down again?' Claire asked calmly. She looked straight ahead. *There's the runway. There we have safety. If only we can make it*, she thought.

'No, I'm sure it's an oil leak … I'm sure. I'm taking a chance, but I don't want to try to land this thing with three engines. The temps are still OK, but the oil pressure is dropping slowly, so I'll just drop its workload a little … we're almost there.' Tension was mounting in his neck, indicated by a prominent vein now jutting out.

Engine mixtures were checked to ensure that they were set to 'full rich'. The aircraft slid down the glide slope with graceful ease. Turbulence suddenly buffeted their final track to station, making all on board uncomfortable. Paul's workload increased. Two hundred and fifty feet and the fortress continued her track directly to the large white numbers, *one one* at the threshold of the runway. One hundred feet and the pilot, with hands on the throttles, adjusted power requirements when necessary to ensure rate of descent was constant. His bare feet were hurting due to rough rudder pedals. He wished he had shoes. At fifty feet, the aircraft was at the threshold of the runway.

The power was eased slowly, allowing their metal deliverer to glide just above the runway. It floated longer than he expected.

He realized in a flash that he had forgotten to engage full flap therefore his speed was faster than what was recommended at the point of flare.

He had two choices, add full power and go around and try another approach or get it down now.

Given number two engine, he had no choice. In one swift movement he brought her down, hitting the concrete runway with a thump that caused its frame to shake violently. It then bounced back up into the air some six feet. The aircraft quickly returned a second time, only to bounce again and again until it settled to an eighty-knot journey down the runway of the Darwin international airport. Once the tail wheel touched the ground, the pilot applied the brakes, which squealed loudly as in protest to their use. Their vintage ark of the air slowed down to taxi speed just in time to take the exit B2 off the runway. The two inboard engines were shut down, and they made their way to the designated parking zone.

'On Eagles Wings, take the next taxiway 'Z' then turn right onto taxiway 'V1', taxi direct to General Aviation parking. Contact us before you shut down for further instructions.

Your family are making their way over to General Aviation. By the way, nice recovery with that landing, mate. Welcome home … Big Fella.' A burst of cheering could be heard in the background at the tower over the broadcast. Paul looked across at his wife. Her tears were flowing.

'You did it, Paul. You did it! I am so proud of you. Lord, thank you so much … thank you, Father.' She turned around to the children. Their eyes were as wide as plates, looking to the left and right. Whatever direction they turned to, information overload was on offer. Both girls were now standing between the two pilot seats to ensure a better view.

'Wow. Dad, can we do that again?' Jessica asked as she reached over her father's seat to give him a hug.

'Not today, baby,' Claire quickly replied, smiling broadly.

'Not me. I don't like it when Dad makes earthquakes.' Tiffany shook her head insistently.

Paul began to laugh.

'Hey kids, let's go and find some kangaroos, hey?' He slid open the pilot's window allowing the tropical late afternoon air to pour into the cockpit.

'Dad, can I sit on your lap … please?' Jessica was ready to move.

'Come on, then.' No further invitation was necessary. In a flash, the girls picked the closest seat. Jessica sat with her Dad, and Tiffany perched herself again on her mother's lap.

The pilot exited the runway and taxied *On Eagles Wings* to the General Aviation parking area. Looking ahead to their final destination, two ground handlers could be seen in the distance waving them on, directing them to the place chosen for *On Eagles Wings* to safely shut down and wait for its next assignment.

'Are they there for us?' Claire asked, focused on these two brown-skinned men. One was darker than the other, and he had pure white curly hair.

'Yeah, I'd say so. A bit odd though.'

'Why? That's so nice.'

'Sure.'

'But ...?'

'This is the General Aviation section. We get no priority over here. They don't give a hoot. You get this attention over at domestic or international, but not here ... a bit odd.

Anyway, we'll take all the help we can get,' he said with a chuckle.'

'On Eagle's Wings, Ground, we'll leave you be now. Taxi right to end in the corner of GA, there's plenty of room there for the fortress. Park her where ever you like. Customs will arrive with your family shortly and collect you to process your papers. They'll want to do a full inspection of the aircraft and so forth. OK, once again welcome back and given that you're not type rated, nice job on that landing, mate.' Cheering could still be heard in the background of the broadcast.

Paul looked across to his wife who also heard the raucous of jubilant celebration over the airways.

'Ground, On Eagles Wings, copy that. We have a visual on the guys on the tarmac, will follow their directions. Thanks for all your help. So, what's been happening to the world since we've been away for ten years?

'On Eagles Wings, Ground. Um, not sure what you're referring to regards the guys on the tarmac, but we can see that you are heading to the right spot. As far as your question is concerned: don't know where you've been ... what's been happening to the world? ... well, what's left of it ... it's a mess, mate. Seems you've got a fare bit of catch-up to do. All the best. Ground.'

The two adults looked at each other puzzled.

The pilot in command continued their journey, following the cue of their ground handlers. As they approached the point of entry, one of the men stepped out and walked fifty paces in front of the older man and indicated the bright white line to follow. Paul applied the right break and increased the power on engine number one. Immediately the aircraft obeyed the commands of its pilot, and *On Eagles Wings* turned onto its new direction, headed straight for the older handler with the younger one walking beside the aircraft looking straight up at Claire.

Claire smiled at him. 'Hello.' She mouthed the words, then waved. He nodded then smiled back. There was immediate connection. Her heart thrilled.

'Oh, what a lovely man,' she whispered.

The aircraft taxied slowly toward the older handler who, just by looking at him, one could see that he commanded authority. He moved to the side and indicated to Paul it was time to stop by crossing his arms in front of his chest, then he raised his crossed arms in the air. Paul applied the brakes, their aircraft came to a screeching stop, and their journey was complete. The pilot applied master brakes and cut the mixture, starving the engines of fuel.

Their menace was brought to silence in seconds.

The engine's thunderous roar was now replaced with the sound of constant clicking as the engines hot metal cooled quickly in the afternoon sea breeze.

From a distance, three official cars could be seen driving toward them.

'OK, love, I'll tidy up here and put the old girl to bed. I'll meet you and the girls under the wing.' He indicated the left wing.

Claire moved with new vigour, eager to walk on solid ground again after many hours of vintage air travel. Paul shut down all systems, checking and double checking that all was in order for him to vacate his position of command.

He stood up, slowly realizing the strain their travels had had on him. With weakened legs as a result of hours of rudder work, he made his way to the nose of their aircraft, opened the hatch and swung himself down to the ground where both handlers were waiting for him.

Misjudging the technique required for disembarking from the front hatch, he lost his footing and his weakened legs couldn't hold him for the correction needed. Suddenly he acknowledged his weakness, and he fell towards the ground. Without the pilot seeing it, a dark hand caught him before he hit the cement surface of the General Aviation parking area.

A shocking strength shook him to his feet. He looked directly into the face of his assistant.

Not a word came from the strangely familiar victorious indigenous face, but his eyes were fill with a quiet wisdom.

'Wow, thank you. Not sure what happened there, but so glad you were quick off the mark. Man, that was lightning fast. That could have been nasty.' He looked over at Claire.

She turned to him, and their eyes met. 'OK, thanks again, fellas ...'

They both nodded their heads and smiled. Paul was struck by their character. Jessica ran over to her father. He turned to her, picked her up and hugged her tight.

'Hey there, kiddo.' Jessica returned his embrace. He was home. They were home. He began walking towards the rest of his family. His emotions were swinging wildly.

He turned to the two with their blue uniform and iridescent green safety jackets.

'Hey, I just want to thank you again for your help ... Really appreciated it ... We've been away for ten years shipwrecked ... believe it or not ... we were really on our own for all that time and just to get your help ... you don't know what it means .... I'm not making sense I know, but thank you ... and thank you for catching me,' he said, with quivering voice, enjoying his one-way conversation with the first man he had seen in ten years. The reality hit him hard, and he wanted to burst out into tears ... tears ... of joy.

Jessica watched the two intently.

'Dad, that nice man has white hair,' she said shyly to her father.

Paul nodded his head and kissed his daughter. He joined his wife and other daughter under the wing.

'Are you OK?' Claire asked after watching his presentation.

'Yeah. Did you see what that guy did? I came out of that hatch, and ... I don't know ... like I fell, yeah ... I fell out of the plane I think ... did you see what he did? Just one hand ... caught me. In fact, if I didn't know better, I'd say that I've met him somewhere before ... It's like we knew each other ... you know?'

'No, I didn't see anything other than him holding your arm. He seems a lovely man, though. They both do. The other guy? Did you see his face ... seriously? ... he could have come from an American Indian reservation. So, so similar.' She looked across at the two men standing there and waved. Her gesture was welcomed by the two watching them. They smiled at her, raised their right hand and hinted a slight bow of their head.

'Chickadee!' Tiffany interrupted her absorbed parents.

Snatched from their focus, the child's parents watched as their youngest ran to the front of aircraft only to be met by the Aboriginal man. He walked under the nose of the bomber. Looking up at the hatch positioned at the bombardier's compartment, he called out in an unknown language. In no time, the ageing hen flew down into the arms of the elder.

'Oh my,' Claire hushed her words.

The indigenous elder turned to Tiffany, knelt down and presented her with the family's pet. Tiffany's parents watched as their daughter accepted the bird, turned and began to walk away. She stopped, turned, placed Chickadee on the ground and swiftly ran back to the good Samaritan. With bold intent, she threw herself into his arms said thank you and ran back to her bird, then smartly proceeded to walk back to her parents.

'Mom, that nice man ... he's like an angel.' Tiffany declared, matter of fact, as she attended to her pet's comfort.

Paul and Claire looked at each other bewildered.

The three official cars pulled up clear from the aircraft, and the doors flung open. Paul watched as familiar people stepped out of one of the vehicles, followed closely by a cameraman and journalist from one of the other cars. His heart thrilled and emotions were getting the better of him as tears began to grace his eyes.

Claire slowly turned to her previous focus for one last look. There was something about those two men. She looked back. Her world stopped.

'Paul!'

He quickly turned in reaction to her urgent tone.

She pointed back to their previous reference.

'The two guys,' she declared the obvious.

He gasped.

They were gone!

JOHN 14:1-3

"Let not your hearts be troubled. Believe in God; believe also in me. ²In my Father's house are many rooms. If it were not so, would I have told you that I go to prepare a place for you? ³And if I go and prepare a place for you, I will come again and will take you to myself, that where I am you may be also.

CPSIA information can be obtained
at www.ICGtesting.com
Printed in the USA
BVHW042032300920
589949BV00009BA/73